THE Immortal Detective

D. B. WOODLING

THE Immortal Detective

THE IMMORTAL DETECTIVE SERIES

CamCat
Books

CamCat Publishing, LLC
Fort Collins, Colorado 80524
camcatpublishing.com

Hardcover ISBN 9780744308013
Paperback ISBN 9780744308020
Large-Print Paperback ISBN 9780744308037
eBook ISBN 9780744308068
Audiobook ISBN 9780744308082

Library of Congress Control Number: 2022945183

Book and cover design by Maryann Appel

5   3   1   2   4

For Linda and Sharon

"UNABLE ARE THE LOVED TO DIE;

FOR LOVE IS IMMORTALITY."

—EMILY DICKINSON

CHAPTER ONE

T he only thing worse than never waking up is waking up dead. My eyes blinked open, and I expected to see the last thing I remembered. But the bright specks that identified the magnetic fields within the sun's barren and crusty surface were gone. As, at first sight, were Tristan, Bianca, and Raina, and I saw only a grim concreted catacomb. I listened for the music I'd heard before, the melodic lilt of Beethoven's *Moonlight Sonata,* of Vivaldi's *L'estate,* of the underlying bells pealing a sanguine yet haunting melody from the Unity Village Tower. But I heard only a cryptic silence. I ran my fingers over the wound Yesenia had inflicted, the once gaping tissue now fused and like silk beneath my translucent fingers, and there was no denying what I had become. Nor could I any longer deny Yesenia's insalubrious obsession toward Tristan, a fixation that had endured centuries of bloody battles, ecstasy and agony, angels and demons. Convinced I was to blame for his waning interest, she wanted me dead. But when all the dust had settled over her severed head, I was the one to claim victory. Rather than kill me, separate me from Tristan forever, she had granted me the means to remain with him for all eternity.

I winced when a mouse skittered across the cement floor, the sound oppressively loud, like a plow raking hard ground. Tristan stepped aside, revealing the harsh glow from a naked bulb, and I squeezed my eyes closed and cursed him under my breath. Every sense augmented, the stimulus was overwhelming, the sound of my heart thumping against my breast reminiscent of froth-mouthed competitors galloping around the track at Downton Abbey.

The toe-curling pain took on a life of its own. I released a scream from the depths of my soul, and I shuddered and squirmed, like a caterpillar attempting to escape its cocoon with no other recourse but to digest itself. Memories of Nick's horrifying screams during the early hours of his transition came to mind, as neurons awakened, firing chaotically and resulting in a near paralyzing level of agony. If only Bianca and Tristan had left my body to rot in the sun, allowed nature to take its course after Yesenia's attack. Surely, they understood I would never have chosen their form of immortality.

Their reckless selfishness guaranteed my damnation, and, blinded by rage, I lunged toward the unyielding bars as Tristan drifted toward the cage, his approach maddeningly slow and not the least bit reassuring. He whispered words from a sonnet that had never failed to move me, words he'd first introduced as we made love on the cliffs above the Missouri River. His tone was as comforting as a savior's embrace. And I wanted nothing more than to claw out his eyes and cram them down my mother's throat. I snarled past emergent canine teeth, barbed and sharp, and I flew in his direction and smacked face-first into the metal bars. The anchor bolts, securing the cage to the concrete, loosened and squealed as the cage continued to rock.

"Celeste," Tristan pleaded, and he gripped the bars while his dark eyes screamed in silence.

A hostile blade of twilight trespassed a tear in the velvety black draperies and instantly blistered my skin. A hiss escaped my cracked and bloodied lips as I scampered toward the darkest recess of the cage. Overhead, a large spider—a black mustache supported by eyelashes—scuttled across a gauzy tightrope and, in a homicidal frenzy, injected its tangled prey.

Landing inside the cage with a *whoosh*, Tristan whispered the words again, beckoning me from the world I now inhabited, a place neither suitable for the living nor the undead. I tilted my head and widened my eyes, in that way he'd never been able to resist, while I plotted an escape.

"The time is upon us, my love. Do not be afraid." He gathered me to him with hands that had both driven me to unimaginable ecstasy and consoled me over the past year, then we floated through the metal bars of the cage as if they were themselves an apparition. His eyes penetrated mine with an intense stare that promised a perilous course with an auspicious outcome.

The pain increased, drowning erotic memories of our lovemaking, memories now murky like priceless treasures awaiting rediscovery beneath stagnant waters. Tristan, whom I had loved more than my twin brother Nick, more than my biological or my adoptive parents, suddenly meant nothing to me. He was a freak, an abomination, a repulsive reflection of what I'd become.

I blinked past the gauzy glaze disrupting my vision and attempted to bring him into focus. Was the pain corrupting my eyesight or did my supernatural abilities now enable me to see him for what he really was? An unholy entity. Should the latter be true, what a deceptive but effective façade he and the others presented to the world! But my eyes were open now, and I thought his nose, which I had once considered Romanesque, now more beaklike and misshapen, as if plastered haphazardly above lips no longer sensual or inviting but rather two deflated folds, somehow grayer than the slack and mottled skin that surrounded them. His gaze held mine and I fought to look away from his reptilian-like eyes, set too far apart, vacant yet penetrating, and hooded as if long-suffering guilt and the promise of eternal tedium were far too much weight to bear.

"Dear God, what have I done?" I heard Bianca sobbing from somewhere beyond.

I craned my neck in an effort to see my mother and prepared myself for her true form. But her long auburn hair shone in the moonlight, her dark eyes reflecting the love she held for me just as they always had. High cheekbones dominated her breathtaking oval face; a straight-edged nose with a slightly upturned tip provided little shelter for the plump cupid-bow lips beneath. I stole another glimpse of Tristan, expecting the ghoulish shell I'd discovered just moments before. Instead, I saw only the man I'd loved for as long as I could remember, his eyes like the Mediterranean Sea—alternately gentle and turbulent, intense; his lips soft and inviting, daring me to discover how they moved in a kiss.

Bianca reached out, long artistic fingers skimming my forearm, and I gasped. The pain had lessened. The sensation of molten lead sizzling every organ, every vein, dissipated—a forest fire reduced to glowing embers, then a transient spark, and finally a smoldering haze. She withdrew immediately, as if that miniscule shred of familiarity augmented a sense of betrayal from which she might never recover, and my pain reignited, neurons firing up and down my spine, and I dug my fingernails into my flesh, while my scream rattled the windows.

"Oh, my darling," she sputtered, her hand quaking as she attempted to conceal her trembling lips. "Please do not despair, I beg you! One of the Elders shall perform the Adaption, after which you will remain in the Hollow Earth for as long as they deem necessary. Consider this but a pathway to unimaginable reward."

The Adaption! What a benign term for something so godless, something so incredibly fucked up. In my current state, I was no longer human, yet I wasn't a full-fledged vampire. The Adaption transcended immortality—particularly if performed by one of the Elders. Consuming the blood of an ancient not only secured eternal time on earth but also fortified the fledging with unimaginable supernatural capabilities. And should they deny me, should I refuse, an agonizing demise awaited, not so unlike the end of Yesenia, whose writhing body had deflated before my eyes and disappeared entirely amid a mound of smoldering ash.

If what they were offering, if the Adaption were the only alternative to death, I didn't want any part of it. I was ready to throw myself at God's feet and beg for mercy.

"Why didn't you give me the potion?" I demanded past frothing incisors, my mother's image blurred by blinding rage. "How could you do this to me? I will *never* forgive you!" I fell to my knees, fists hammering the pavement, and my bloody tears blemished the cement floor.

She clutched her heart and murmured my name. "Someday, it is my hope you shall understand."

Once again, my fingers flew to my throat. The wounds pulsated and throbbed as if something living lay beneath, an unholy entity biding its time, scheming, reveling in the calamity it intended to release upon the world.

I searched for Nick, looking over every dismal recess of the basement. Over shelves mortals reserved for half-empty paint cans, assorted chemicals, discarded toys, and glistening Christmas ornaments and assorted holiday fare, shelves that stood abandoned and vacant within the Torok household save for the skeletal remains of small rodents, decaying moths and beetles, and layers of dust, shimmering beneath a blanket of mold.

I hiccupped a sob when I couldn't find him, then threw back my head and laughed. What possible help could my brother offer me? *I* was the one who had always rescued *him*. Sharing a womb was the solitary thing we had in common: Nick collected admirers. I collected neuroses. Nick defied danger. I avoided everything remotely resembling it. In the end, his blatant disregard for his own welfare sealed his fate. Nick in the pool. Lightning streaking across an ominous sky. My brother floating lifelessly. I chased away the memory, choking on my hypocrisy. Did he resent me for insisting Tristan grant him immortality? Did he lie awake, as I did, wondering why I hadn't insisted he take the potion in the months that followed? Did he hate me as I now hated Tristan and Bianca?

I told Tristan as much as I hammered his chest with my fists. He loosened his grip when I jabbed a finger in his eye, and I tumbled from his arms, legs pumping madly as I ran toward the door leading to my mother's rose garden, beyond it the Olympic-sized swimming pool. Tristan soared overhead and blocked my path. Snarling, I lunged for him, canine daggers pricking his jugular.

"Enough!" Bianca yelled. She flicked her wrist, and my feet left the ground. The rafters brushed the top of my head, and I was unable to move. "You must embrace this transition, Celeste. Can you not see that this is an opportunity most rare? Seldom do the Elders set aside precious time to teach a fledgling the secrets of the Ancients."

I didn't recognize my own laugh. Hollow. Evil. "I would rather be dead than join your circus of freaks."

Bianca buried her face in her hands and began to weep, and I plummeted to the floor. On only one other occasion had I seen her cry, her sensibilities eaten away over the years and steeled by centuries filled with loss, regret, and betrayal. To say it didn't affect me, if only for a moment, would be a lie.

But I quickly rallied.

"Go ahead! Cry! Because this is *your* fault. Look at me! Look what I've become! Why didn't you give me the goddamn potion?"

Tristan and Bianca shared a helpless expression. I had never seen either of them display such vulnerability, and their weakness fueled my anger.

"I have never asked you for anything! If you genuinely love me, you'll spare me an existence that isn't of my own choosing and put an end to this horrific pain!" Bianca's pleading eyes wandered to Tristan. "Don't look at him! This has nothing to do with him. It's what *I* want." She shook her head and mouthed the words *I cannot*. "For God's sake, Mom," I screamed. "Give it to me!"

"Is that really what you want?" Bianca stammered. "To never set eyes on your brother again?"

Tristan glided across the room. Beneath his blank expression, I knew a formidable adversary lay in wait, and I tempered my rage, bided my time. "Don't be a fool, Celeste. Should you consume the potion, you will be returned to the point of death."

I swallowed past a lump; I understood the implications. The potion's main ingredient was the herb vernicadis, which counteracted immortality. Tristan had discovered its antidotal properties centuries ago and had recently divulged his long-kept secret to my father. As a result, the potion proved an effective weapon in the Realm's battle against renegade vampires known as the Harvesters.

"Get your hands off of me, Tristan," I said, tracking his face with sharp fingernails. "Are you even listening to me? Are you both so narcissistic that you actually believe I would trade my soul to stay here with you? I'm ready to leave this life. Give me the potion!"

Bianca shot across the room and gripped Tristan's forearm so tightly a welt appeared and smoldered beneath her fingertips. She whispered, "Perhaps you should summon Nick."

"Leave Nick out of this!" I screamed. "I want my brother to remember me the way I was."

They ignored me, and I balled my hands into fists and spit words in a language unfamiliar. A murder of crows suddenly appeared and blanketed the rafters. I repeated the phrase, and the birds swarmed them both, pecking flesh and eyeballs.

"Ad infernum," Bianca shrieked, and the flock fell, lifeless, and splatted onto the concrete.

My father emerged suddenly from within a thick caustic fog. He and Bianca shared a quizzical expression, and I got the impression my summoning of the crows was something extraordinary. He pulled me to him and held me there, despite the dagger-like fingernails I sank into his putrid flesh.

"Dispel all fear, Celestine, for in this, too, you shall prevail. You have me at my word."

Gripping my shoulders, he took a step back, his gaze riveted on apparitions flocked together in a macabre sort of huddle. Had they been there all along? The creatures, with their hawkish noses turned up in a show of defiance, swarmed me and formed a winged blockade. Velvety feathers, resembling more military weaponry than anything seraphic, muffled my screams for Tristan.

"Give me a goddamn minute with her!" Nick shouted. "For shit's sake, it's not like you don't have all the time in the fucking world." The creatures parted and Nick tugged me close, held me as I trembled. "I know you're scared, Celeste, but you're the one who has always kept the faith, no matter what." He raised my chin, compelling me to look him in the eye. "Hasn't it ever occurred to you it was no accident that both our parents were at the courthouse *and* killed that day? That the Toroks taking us in was our divine destiny or some such shit?"

I didn't respond. I'd always thought dumb luck responsible for our biological father's whereabouts that day. Although it wasn't that unusual for a prosecuting attorney to request my dad's testimony—he was a cop, after all—the timing was unfortunate, nothing more, nothing less. As far as our mother's presence that day, she was a court reporter; in all likelihood, she would have been in the courthouse regardless of the day of the week or the time of day. But leave it to Nick—the animated, reckless one, the one who literally didn't have sense enough to come in out of the rain and had the lightning strike scars to prove it—to turn the tragedy into some preordained melodrama.

"I think we both were destined for something far greater," he insisted as I gritted my teeth. "So, be brave, Celeste. If you ever needed to keep your shit together, now's the time."

He drilled his lips into my forehead, then stepped aside. I cringed when my captors once again encircled me, and I cried out for my mother. When she didn't intervene, I steeled myself for what lay ahead.

Within the mansion one minute, hurtling through a menacing sky the next, I felt the air turn cold. Colder still with each mile we traversed, eventually becoming so thin I couldn't catch my breath. Nearing exhaustion, I continued to kick and scream, battling both the creatures and the darkness—a black abyss suffocating me within its unrelenting glassy grip. One of my abductors tapped the tip of its wing against my forehead, and I welcomed the warm sensation that always precedes sleep and surrendered to unconsciousness.

I woke when the hypnotizing *chuff-chuff-chuff* sound of wings suddenly ebbed to a clatter. Ice began to form on the tips of their wings first, then migrate toward the scapulae. No longer able to fly and losing the battle with gravity, my abductors and I pitched headlong toward earth. My mouth froze in a scream as we tumbled through miles of inhospitable darkness. Just as the wide swaths of farmland below no longer resembled a mossy ill-conceived quilt, a ring of fire erupted, encircling my captors as if they were participants in a shamanic ritual. Able to hover until the ice completely dissipated, they soon continued on, billowy smoke emanating from wings now sounding an impotent *whip-crack, whip-crack.*

Nearing the South Pole, a Symmes Hole twinkled ahead in the vast darkness, like a haphazardly adorned ornamental orb. Propelling me through the sprawling opening, my captors zigged then zagged around gargantuan trees, the tops too high to study despite my preternatural vision. Several apes of gigantic proportions swung from the tree limbs and chorused to one another, the lush forest deadening the creatures' fierce grunts and alarm-barks.

Years ago, I'd listened to Nick's description of the Hollow Earth and assumed, like everything else that came out of his mouth, that he had made it all up or, at the very least, exaggerated. For once, everything he had said was true. A cavity in the earth did exist, as did an entirely separate galaxy, the mountain of coal sparkling with diamonds, prehistoric and current lifeforms of gigantic proportions, as well as the lakes, rivers, and tropical-like vegetation. It was like the Garden of Eden but on steroids.

The ground shook and, in its wake, a stegosaurus loped by. A common cow heron the size of a Rottweiler bounced precariously on its back. The prehistoric reptile graced us with a simple nod, one reptilian eye winking as if a coconspirator in an enigmatic plot. I was stunned and wary. With all the crazy phenomenal shit I had witnessed in the past year (vampires shapeshifting into griffins, chimeras, or gargoyles, even three-headed winged dragons), I thought I was prepared for anything.

The atmosphere oozed humidity and covered everything with a punishing dew. Off to my right, fronds swayed. From within the vegetation, a Camarasaurus appeared. With truck-sized feet, the dinosaur stood stockstill and studied me, keen eyes suggesting an advanced intellect and the means to protect itself. Up ahead, a snake measuring thirty feet slithered along, five-hundred-fifty pounds crushing any vegetation beneath it.

Nearly colliding with a prehistoric bird, my captors soared higher, and my feet dangled over the smaller treetops. The bird continued its descent, enormous talons landing with a reverberating thud, a massive beak drilling the snake with hatchet-like jabs. My stomach lurched as bloody geysers spewed from the wounds and colored the path red. The anaconda whipped its tail side to side, contacting the bird with an echoing *thwack*. Feathers and fibrous membranes peppered the surrounding foliage, and the serpent continued on its way.

The pain had become intolerable, every cell proliferating at breakneck speed. Burning calcification attacked every bone and joint and elongated every nerve ending, and my deafening screams pierced the euphonious sounds of calling birds, hooting monkeys, and cascading waterfalls. To think I often fantasized my parents not actually dead but instead vampires like Razvan and Bianca, simply called away to assist the Realm, counting the minutes until they might return to Nick and me. And now, suffering this ungodly pain, this soul-gripping emptiness, I thanked God my parents had never experienced this, that it was only a fantasy.

"Goddamn it, destroy me! I'm begging you!" I managed before everything went dark.

CHAPTER TWO

"Poor little wretch," someone afflicted with a heavy British accent and a sense of entitlement said, and I opened my eyes. Effortlessly slipping from Greek to Italian to French and finally reverting to the English language, the woman, dressed in an emerald floor-length velvet gown—her face oily and starkly white—smoothed her golden-red hair beneath a crown drowning in rubies, emeralds, and sapphires. Clucking her tongue, she said, "Oh, how I remember the agonizing pain. It was not so unlike finding oneself on the Duke of Exeter's rack within the Tower of London, would you not agree, Socrates?"

Socrates sniffed long, crinkling his nose. "Unarguably, a most barbaric device, Elizabeth." He puffed his chest, muscular in appearance beneath a plain floor-length ivory garment, and narrowed his eyes. "But leave it to indolent Englishmen to resort to medieval torture, not content until the enemy is torn in two. Because, God knows, a philosophical approach requires far too much commitment."

Elizabeth stomped the frigid floor. "For heaven's sake. Now is not the time to quibble over our ancestral shortcomings. There's much to be done."

Looking down his nose, Socrates scrutinized me from head to toe. "I believe I have stated my opinion on the matter at hand. Granting a mortal immortality is one thing; equipping a fledgling with our extraordinary powers is quite another."

Elizabeth tipped her head toward a shoulder and sneered. "Hypocrite! Am I mistaken, or did you not insist on accompanying us to collect the girl? We have made our decision, so I suggest you either take your leave or, from this moment forward, keep your self-indulgent opinions to yourself." She loomed over me, her alabaster skin a sharp contrast to cheeks caked with rouge. She brushed my cheek with her hand, leaving behind a feathery layer of dust. And just as when Bianca had touched me, most of my pain subsided.

"Is this true that you are in agreement, Leonardo?" asked Socrates when another vampire approached, tugging multicolored hosiery toward his thighs.

Leonardo da Vinci's exaggerated gaze swept the room. "As I do not see Bianca or Razvan present, the task falls to one of us." A prolonged smirk stretched his lips. "We have discussed this in tedious detail. But perhaps the passing centuries have rendered you absentminded. The deed done, do allow us to carry on."

"My dear sir, was it not you who voiced the loudest objection when Bianca and Razvan chose to adopt Celestine and Nicholas?"

Hands stationed at his hips, Leonardo smirked. "Ah, *that* you remember. It would appear your forgetfulness is most selective, Socrates. Do make your point."

"As I recall, it *was* you who said, 'It is only a matter of time before the Toroks petition their children's immortality.' And, if I'm not mistaken, you flew into a rage, the likes of which scattered every enchanted creature deep into the forest."

Leonardo sighed and rolled his eyes. "Circumstances change. As I see it, in a world brimming with calamity, we can use all the help we can get."

"Agreed," Socrates replied, "but why should we contribute our remarkable abilities? Let us appoint Bianca as Celestine's Maker and be done with it."

Elizabeth puffed her cheeks and sliced the air with a bejeweled hand. "You know very well that even though it was Yesenia who performed Bianca's Adaption, she refused to bequeath every one of our extraordinary powers. Besides, I think it best those closest to Celestine keep their distance for the time being. As Leonardo said, Socrates, the deed is done. Our predecessors have given the ceremony their blessing because, apparently, the Omniscients comprehend the benefits in granting a decorated detective such exceptional powers. Who are *we* to argue?" She cleared her throat and rattled off something that sounded French, directing the remark to a curiously sedate man huddled over quill pen and paper in a far corner. "Michel de Nostredame." When he didn't respond, she crossed the room with a whoosh, creating a transitory and unwelcome draft. "The time is at hand. Do set aside your propensity to prophesize every little thing for a time more fitting."

Queen Elizabeth I, Socrates, Nostradamus, Leonardo da Vinci! Is it possible? My head felt as if it might explode, growing anxiety making it nearly impossible to catch a breath. Homicidal and suicidal urges competed with equal fierceness, the bone-gnawing pain tempting me to rip sections from my hair and gouge out my eyes. Those moments of unadulterated insanity passed nearly as quickly as they began, only to return minutes later with increased severity and without warning.

Taking the infamous prophet by the hand, Elizabeth whizzed him across the room with a dramatic flourish. Puffing an objection to the layers of petticoats flying about his face, Nostradamus wiggled free, trailing indigo ink.

Elizabeth straightened her skirts and wig with chalk-like hands. "After much debate, Celestine, we have chosen Nostradamus as your benefactor. Despite my disagreement, it seems Leonardo finds favor with the good physician's ability to foresee future events in a timelier manner. Pfft. In my day, soothsayers were a shilling a dozen, most motivated not by God's whisper, but rather a pint or two of ale or a flask of canary wine. Nevertheless, let the Adaption commence!"

"If I may have a word," Nostradamus said and pulled the others aside. As they huddled inches below the vaulted ceiling, my eyes scanned the palatial room constructed entirely of crystalline ice. A large spaceship-inspired chandelier dominated the ceiling; jagged, reflective icicles served as pendant lights. Smaller creatures of various species inhabited each dangling ornament suspended from the glacier's center, as if imprisoned in a ghastly terrarium. The lush grass—more a dense, velvety green carpet—transiently recorded anything that contacted its surface. Dusk had long ago claimed its grip and a brilliant but counterfeit constellation revealed itself—that of Orion, which emerged through a sluggish progression of twinkling lights, nearly blinding its observers as it reflected off the iced enclosure in a sporadic sequence. Fragrant scents of mint, mimosa, cinnamon, rose, violet, and jasmine assaulted my nostrils—my sense of smell now was heightened, but the combination failed to mask the underlying and unpleasant odor of something strikingly similar to decay.

The majority of the palace was nearly identical to images I'd seen of Hampton Court, the great hall higher than it was wide. Above it, a minstrel's gallery spanned the entire back section and a large stone fireplace sat idle against an exterior wall. Weighty, blood-red drapes dressed floor-to-ceiling mullioned windows. Snarling impish gargoyles, stationed on either side, clasped the ends of braided golden ropes between jagged teeth and secured the draperies in a partially open position.

The furnishings were sparse, a testament to the Elders' pragmatic disposition. Other than a meticulously carved conference table and cathedral chairs, and a high-backed chair—so large it dominated the room—the hall lay empty. The palace was about as welcoming as a mausoleum. God, I wanted to go home.

For this to be a nightmare from which I would soon awaken, grateful for my mundane life catching criminals, my biggest fear drawing my weapon, my greatest fear squeezing the trigger.

Elizabeth raised her voice. "How you drone on, dearest Nostredame. But, yes, I suppose we should have told you. If you're unwilling, do speak your piece or allow us to proceed."

I got the impression Nostradamus was previously unaware the others had chosen him to perform my Adaption.

"Prior notification would have proved most courteous; however, I have no objection," Nostradamus replied with a wave of his hand.

The Elders floated from the ceiling, Elizabeth's satin slippers kissing the glacial floor with a soft rustle.

"We have decided against your destruction, as you most certainly are aware, Celestine. Consider this a gift, one we can reclaim at a moment's notice, should you fail to cooperate." She gripped my wrist and brought her nose within an inch of mine. "Need I elaborate?"

I swallowed past the lump in my throat and shook my head as I thought of Nick. Neither Razvan nor Bianca was present for his Adaption. They'd locked themselves behind my father's study door, my mother's quiet sobbing and their hushed angst-filled words often seeping into the marbled hallway. Common sense convinced me that they weren't nearly as worried about the process itself as they were Nick's ability to obey the Realm's strict code afterward. Nick had never been able to control his urges. We all worried he'd slip out and exsanguinate every mortal he could lay his hands on. Because Tristan had granted Nick immortality, he was the one most agitated. He paced the hall outside my father's study, with his head in his hands, as he mumbled incoherently; if Nick failed to obey the code, it meant the end of them both. Surely, if Nick could resist temptation, so could I.

I felt a tickle inside my head, like a feather swish-swish-swishing over the nerve endings, and from my experiences living with Bianca, I knew one of the Elders was either intruding on my thoughts or instilling a few of their own.

Unable to resist the intrusion, I surrendered to memories of Nick and me, hand-in-hand, as we roamed the Torok mansion. I closed my eyes, cherishing Nick's crooked smile beneath sapphire eyes glowing giddy with anticipation as he sought mischief around every eerie corner, undaunted by the ill-tempered vampires we'd often encounter—piss-yellow eyes gliding over us coolly as if our very existence were a scourge requiring decimation. Nor was Nick afraid of the ghoulish apparitions, whose long spidery fingers snagged our ankles and wrists and tested our courage. My brother was part of me, despite the occasional denouncement or our disparate convictions that often bubbled to the surface and somehow fortified our connection. I often wondered what it would be like, my growing older, Nick never aging. As much as I resisted my current circumstance, a smile tugged my lips when I realized, maybe for the first time, that now he and I would always be young, and together forever.

"Celestine," Elizabeth bellowed, yanking me back to the present. "We may as well tell her before we continue," she said to the others. "Because should she not consent, I see no reason to proceed. Which will most certainly break Bianca's heart," she added under her breath.

My eyebrows twitched as they knitted together. *What else could they possibly have in store?* I cringed when considering the possibilities. My heart was already in my throat. Up until Yesenia's attack, I had thought I had nerves of steel. No more.

I was on the brink of a nervous breakdown.

She blew out a long breath. "While it is true that the Omniscients agreed to your Adaption, that agreement comes with a few strings attached."

"I don't understand."

Her lips strained against a tight smile. "Oh, I think you do. You're a very astute young woman. But while you will not be permitted to grant immortality willy-nilly, due to the growing number of our enemy, it is imperative we fortify our ranks. Which means if and when the occasion presents itself—"

"Wait. You're saying you expect me—"

"You know precisely what we expect. You are to grant those dying and deserving the gift of rebirth."

I pitched forward, shaking my head and failing to rein in a snarl.

Just when I nearly had my head wrapped around accepting their idea of immortality, she had changed the rules. "I can't agree to that," I said, choking on the words. "I won't."

Leonardo materialized directly before me. "I pray you reconsider. Either that or prepare to carry your severed head into the afterlife . . . should one even exist for our kind."

CHAPTER THREE

I was weighing Leonardo's threat and everything Nick had said when Elizabeth interrupted my train of thought.

"Yes, Celestine. This is indeed your destiny. I strongly recommend that you take your brother's suggestion to heart."

I was tired of them hijacking my thoughts, tired of feeling like a rat in a cage, disregarded until it was time for experimentation. I turned my back to her, then crossed to the other side of the room, despite knowing any distance between us would have no effect on her abilities. My thoughts jumbled, I attempted to resurrect the pros and cons regarding my decision—maybe my salvation existed in the lives I would save, the evil I could destroy. But I remained obsessed over Nick's struggles, how a few of the Realm's warriors had devoted every hour of every day to watch over him for months following his Adaption. Would I, too, have an irresistible urge to exsanguinate mortals? Particularly given my occupation—car accidents, shooting victims, natural disasters. All that blood! Could I even entertain the risk of harming those I pledged to protect? How could I possibly resist those compulsions upon my return to law enforcement? And even should I manage to contain my impulsive bloodlust, I still struggled with the matter of granting immortality, the epitome of blasphemy, in my opinion. I dropped my head in my hands, no more certain of my decision, and bit my lip so hard it bled. I heard the others refrain a torturous sigh as droplets of blood pitter-pattered, stark against the glacial floor.

"Let's give her some time alone with her thoughts," I heard Leonardo say, and I watched Socrates rocket toward the ceiling, where he retired upon an ivory throne. Elizabeth ascended soon after, content to perch on the edge of a gilded swing supported by enormous downy wings that seemed to flutter for no other reason than to entertain her.

Various scenarios continued to torment me, streaming through my head like a terrifying slideshow. Among them the exsanguination of innocents, including children. As much as I wanted to exist, never say a final goodbye to Tristan, or Nick, or my parents, I refused to put the innocent at risk.

I knew what I had to do. The Elders gasped simultaneously, and I assumed they were aware of my thoughts.

"I, for one, am prepared to wash my hands of the entire endeavor," Socrates boomed and the creepy chandelier beneath him shook then swayed side to side, the creatures within either scurrying for cover or squashing bulging eyeballs against the glass.

"Why the change of heart, Socrates?" Elizabeth asked past a squint.

"Have you not interpreted her thoughts as I have? The girl does not believe she can resist unsanctioned urges. Nor is she committed to granting rebirth to those who warrant such a generous offer. One must honor another's limitations, Elizabeth."

She waved her hand in his face. "Tsk. Who among us did not have our doubts in the beginning?" Abandoning her roost, she accomplished a Mary Poppins-like descent. "All Celestine needs is an effective demonstration. I'm sure of it."

"You are making a dire mistake should you persist, Elizabeth. Mark my words," Socrates called after her, shaking both fists.

Elizabeth wrapped her arms around me, and I was on my feet one second and sucked into another dimension the next. My head spun and I balanced precariously on wobbly legs when we arrived, the air acrid from spilled blood and gunpowder, the stench augmented by fear of death. "What is this place?" I stammered. "Where are we?"

"Near the ruins of Nicopolis within Egypt," she replied, like we'd just arrived at a shopping mall.

I studied the horde of soldiers whose number blanketed the ground like unpretentious leaves. The British Army of fifteen thousand hardly seemed an intimidation to the French Army's regimen of thirty thousand soldiers. England's involvement in Elizabeth's revelation came as little surprise. From nearby Aboukir Castle, the Blockhouse, and several surrounding sand hills, the French opened musketry fire on British Lieutenant General Sir Ralph Abercromby and his troops arriving at Aboukir Bay.

I shrank back as artillery shells blasted the beachfront. Abercromby's somber men robotically trudged through the wet sand and attempted to access the slickened shore while dodging gunfire. A collective, bloodcurdling scream competed with the deafening volleys fired by the cannons. Within minutes, the waters lapping the shore resembled a chunky tomato soup, and my heart felt like it was in my stomach.

Despite the casualties, Abercromby, flanked by his officers, ordered the surviving fourteen thousand soldiers to scale a sand hill and drive the French into the plains. The French intensified their assault and the English soldiers dropped to the ground, one after the other.

Thunder shook the hillside, and intermittent bolts of squiggly lightning danced around two shadowy figures as they exited the angry clouds and descended upon the beach, the hilts of their swords blazing orange beneath glistening angry blades. I recognized an even more stoic Elizabeth but not the woman at her side.

Transforming herself into a gargantuan prehistoric bird armed with needlelike teeth, Elizabeth led the attack, swinging her mammoth broadsword as if a sickle and the French mere tender blades of grass. Her accomplice morphed into something part-octopus and part-Medusa, then took up position alongside. From each tentacle dangled the equivalent of an agricultural stone rake. Swooping over the retreating French soldiers, she mowed down one after the other, razor-sharp tines mutilating tissue and bone with an earth-shaking *thwack*. Blood, guts, and wormy membranes spattered in every direction, showering Elizabeth and me with a repulsive slime.

"Now do you see?" she voiced beside me. "Had it not been for my intervention, the English would not have prevailed."

"What about the French?" I asked. "Why should they fail, and the English succeed?"

A sinister smile perverted her lips. "As a Frenchman, Nostradamus held a grudge for quite some time. It certainly worked to my advantage that, on that particular day, he found himself otherwise engaged."

"But what if he *had* come to aid the French? What then?"

"I fear you are missing the point, Celestine. I saved lives, lives that I considered consequential. And it is my hope that someday soon you will do the same. We should return." She grasped my hands and searched my eyes. "I beg you. Weigh your decision very, very carefully. We are offering an opportunity that, in time, can change the world."

CHAPTER FOUR

I was surprised to find I had actually drifted off to sleep, having spent the first thirty minutes within the coffin never quite adjusting to the suffocating sensation brought on by my exaggerated fear of confined spaces. Once I realized pounding on the lid and demanding my release was futile, I lay awake for another hour contemplating the battle and all that Elizabeth had revealed.

When Nostradamus pried open my coffin lid the following evening, I squinted as the sunset's vibrant rose, blue, and purplish hues quickly surrendered to a dark, opaque, and suffocating horizon.

I fought a wave of depression. I missed the sun, the calls to morning carried on the fluttering wings of colorful songbirds amid the sounds of zooming automobiles and chugging morning buses shuttling passengers mindful of time constraints. I missed the way a morning breeze greeted the trees, whose leaves responded with a demure wave, smaller branches bowing as if acknowledging a higher power, while honeybees furiously flitted bloom-to-bloom, alert to a rigid schedule not so unlike the people bound for work.

Elizabeth waited nearby and observed me, a worried expression creasing her forehead. "I trust you slept well, Celestine. Regretfully, we found it necessary to secure your coffer. Please understand that this is only a temporary measure."

Who could blame them? One minute I felt calm and self-assured, the next deranged and homicidal. Besides, I'd taken advantage of the time to myself, weighing the justification for taking a life, the conviction Elizabeth expressed prior to our retreat from the Battle of Alexandria. The lives she'd saved. The lives she'd felt worth forfeiting. Those deserving life and those deserving death. Unlike what I'd witnessed in Egypt, in my line of work the distinction between the criminals and those upon whom they preyed couldn't be clearer. The Elders presented an unimaginable opportunity, one that would allow the defenseless unparalleled protection from those mortals committed to heinous acts. But was I ready to commit?

"Come. Join us." She rocketed across the frozen tundra, just as quickly returning with a chalice, ruby-colored droplets spilling over. Pressing it my way, she said, "Take a seat at the table. As I am not accustomed to the ghastly assignments of servitude, you shall, from this point forward, handle your own affairs in this regard."

Socrates puffed his cheeks. "Need I remind you she has yet to make her decision, Elizabeth? Therefore, she may well consider your instruction moot."

Elizabeth stayed quiet but glowered. "Few develop an appetite for traditional food," she said to me. "Socrates has always been the exception, in this and many matters I simply haven't the desire to discuss."

Leonardo glanced in my direction and, unassisted, my glass slid toward me and thumped my knuckles. "Drink."

I raised the chalice, and the distinct smell of fresh blood bathed my nostrils. My eyes penetrated the metal exterior, revealing the rich red syrupy liquid within. Salivating, I parted my lips to accommodate eager incisors and gulped the entire contents. When I set the glass down, I discovered them leering, nostrils winged, dark eyes fixed and easily communicating their disgust. Defiantly, I swiped a hand across my mouth, then gripped the table edge when the teeth-chattering tremors began, a powerful surge awakening every cartilage, every muscle, and every bone. My hair follicles tingled, and I resisted the urge to rip the skin from my scalp. Leonardo grinned, his expression suddenly stoic when his eyes met Socrates. They all seemed so far away, and I strained to make sense of their garbled conversation.

Elizabeth suddenly zipped alongside, startling me. Her face seemed magnified, her nose inches from mine. "Have you made up your mind?"

I shook my head, which only exacerbated the dizziness. "I need more time."

"Look there," she said, gesturing beyond me before taking to the air and standing alongside a murky mirage.

I twisted around and saw Nick stooping alongside a coffin, fingers entwined around the corpse's long blond hair, his forehead pressed against the cool surface. Tears ran down his cheeks and created a puddle while his body shuddered amid violent inhalations. It was bad enough the Elders pilfered my every thought, but to pervert those thoughts, to graft such grievous suggestions of what might be was nothing short of monstrous. And I hated them for it.

I faced her, aware that protruding canine teeth engulfed my lower lip. Was she actually smirking at me? I lunged for her with plans to rip off that smirk and every inch of her caulk-like makeup. Flying through the air, I smacked into an invisible shield. She laughed outright, collected my dislodged teeth from the floor, opened my hand and slapped them against my palm.

"The Code prevented the Realm from saving your parents. Surely, you've considered that," she said without missing a beat. "Have you also considered that Nicholas lost his parents that day, as well? Would you have him lose his sister, too, particularly when it is within your power to prevent it? Bianca's inability to grant your parents the gift of immortality haunts her to this very day. Of that, you can be sure. Imagine if the decision had been solely hers, Celestine. Your parents would be here, beside you, today."

Suddenly, Nick's apparition vanished, the only sound my rapid heartbeat, my hair fluttering behind me the lone sensation. An orb of light beckoned in the distance, the sound of an explosion sending shockwaves beyond dimensions. Elizabeth had once again taken me inside the Circle, the vampires' innocuous term for time travel. The year: 1997. Bodies lay scattered within the courthouse, the Harvesters' preternatural screeches filling the air as they scavenged the demolished building searching for victims. Exsanguinating those they found, grotesque fangs punctured throbbing veins, my biological parents among the attacked. Bianca, Razvan, and the Realms' warriors appeared soon after, shapeshifting into various creatures: glistening gargoyles, three-headed dragons, salivating chimeras, and the most frightening, a Manananggal—a vampire-like creature capable of severing its upper torso, sprouting prodigious wings, and presenting a face more human than monstrous. Overpowering the Harvesters, the Realm flung them one by one through the vast opening created by the explosion, where they writhed, their bodies instantly igniting beneath the scorching sun. The Realm then turned its attention to those with gaping wounds inflicted by the Harvesters.

"Stop it!" I cried. "I remember the rest." The Realm pitched the bodies of my biological parents to the ground below, atop what little remained of the Harvesters—odiferous mounds of smoldering ash.

"Am I to assume that at some point Bianca chose to reveal this event?"

"Yes," I said, staring daggers. "And once was enough."

"I am aware, Celestine, you consider what you have become an abhorrence, that you are thankful your parents never found themselves in the same predicament. I can tell you—with near certainty—that they wish we had granted them such a glorious opportunity. I venture your father—Russ, if memory serves—would have given anything in exchange for the exceptional powers we are offering. He would have understood that such extraordinary abilities could only enhance his success as a law enforcement officer and his contributions to public safety. Had the Realm arrived only moments before, your parents would not have suffered an attack by the Harvesters."

I started to interject but discovered Elizabeth must have cast some kind of spell because I couldn't move my lips or tongue.

Socrates materialized beside us. "Enough of this coddling. What say you, young woman?" Elizabeth laid a luminous hand on my shoulder and searched my eyes. "I sense the pull between good and evil is intensifying, Celestine. You must make your decision as we are only allotted so much time."

Bianca had always been very evasive, either dismissing my questions regarding the rogue vampires she called soulless demons—relegated to hunting and destroying mortals—or offering only vague explanations. Now it all made sense. The Harvesters either never received the Adaption or they didn't receive it in time. The exception, Yesenia. Because her powers surpassed both Bianca's and Razvan's, I suspected one of the Elders had performed her Adaption and because Socrates opposed my transition, I felt sure he was responsible.

"Well," Elizabeth said, tap-tap-tapping a satin slipper, "do you wish to accept our offer?"

I tamped down my expansive emotions, which ranged from fear to self-pity to unresolved anger. I had two choices—accept annihilation and God's probable wrath or embrace the Elders' version of immortality.

"Yes, I accept," I said, feeling every bit a defector and finding it impossible to look her in the eye.

Elizabeth arched a brow and pursed her lips. I sensed her skepticism. She squirmed while readjusting her corset, then faced the others. "In that case, gentlemen, let us begin." She pressed her palm to my forehead and a violent gasp escaped my lips when the pain returned.

The others leaned toward me in perfect unison and performed a simultaneous and impassioned nod, their skin shimmery and colorless, save startling bloodstained lips, their posture reminiscent of the creatures from the movie *Alien*. Nostradamus tugged his linen shirt—partially hidden by a leather jerkin—toward his shoulder and exposed his throat.

"Why do you suppose she hesitates?" Elizabeth whispered.

"Perhaps the dear girl requires encouragement," Leonardo said, a sly grin testing his lips as his eyes glowed, the pupils bathed with an amber hue. Elizabeth flicked her wrist and sneered. "The honor is yours, good sir. Godspeed."

Waiving any semblance of fanfare, da Vinci sank dagger-like teeth into Nostradamus's neck, infusing the air with a metallic, sweet aroma. Outside the ice palace, the gorillas thumped their massive chests, chorusing a deafening round of discordant shrill screams. Beasts of prey joined in, their maniacal vocalizations competing one with the other, resulting in a frenzied staccato symphony from hell.

My lips furled in response to razor-sharp fangs, sparkling icepicks oozing a milky, blood-tinged froth. I lunged for Nostradamus and clamped his head between my palms, as if it were a ripe melon, while I staved off an overwhelming urge to break his neck. I sank in my fangs, withdrawing a fraction when they scraped bone.

Instantly, hundreds of thousands of synapses fired off in a rippling wave, producing both brilliant color and deafening sound while revealing all the horrific occurrences humankind had withstood to include Christ's crucifixion, the Holocaust, and 9/11. Everything Nostradamus knew, I now knew. He had not only imparted his ancient powers but also his knowledge of every cataclysmic event known to mankind. Desperate to distance myself from the horrific images, I withdrew my bloodied canine teeth instantly, ripping a wide swath of Nostradamus's throat in the process. Bitter cold enveloped me, an arctic chill so severe it conjured memories of the Ice Age he had just revealed to me. My entire body shook and every muscle responded to newly discovered power with a grotesque and sustained twitch.

Elizabeth approached with guarded posture, inching toward me like a ballerina unsure of her mark. Sweeping my long blond hair behind my shoulders, she said to the others, "Now that we have created the beast, it falls to us to tame it. We shall familiarize her with her powers, tout de suite."

CHAPTER FIVE

⎯ ⎯

The adrenaline rush I'd experienced following the Adaption hadn't subsided. My thoughts continued to swirl, a slurry of competing doubt and certainty. Memories seemed almost tangible, haunting remembrances at my fingertips, so implausibly vivid it felt as though they flashed across a cinematic screen, and I could reach out and touch them. And now the Elders intended to familiarize me with my *powers*? How could I possibly focus on anything in particular with all those random, chaotic thoughts driving me toward absolute insanity?

I closed my eyes and attempted a deep calming breath. *Come on, Celeste. You can do this.* After all, hadn't I survived a myriad of preposterous experiences throughout the years? The fact that Nick and I remotely resembled normal young adults was a miracle.

We were four years old when we arrived at the Torok Mansion following the death of our parents. Because Bianca avoided the sun, and we were so young we required supervision, playtime outdoors began long after sunset. During the winter months, the nightly temperature would often hover around twenty degrees, and Bianca would bundle Nick and me in so many polyester layers we resembled the Michelin Man. We couldn't walk, let alone play.

Because vampires slept during the day and four-year-old mortals didn't, Bianca soon realized she needed help and hired an au pair. Between Nick's shenanigans and the unsettling occurrences in the household (vampires floating down hallways, vaporizing from one room before appearing in another, shapeshifting into terrifying creatures—usually to entertain Nick), we went through a dozen in one year alone. The ensuing gossip unsustainable, my father instructed a few of the Realm's warriors, Trandafira and Yesenia, to watch over us, Tristan often charged with keeping Nick in line as he grew older. I smiled, thinking of the time Trandafira foiled Yesenia's plan to harm Nick and me, and the two of them began to argue as to which of them played the larger role in the fourteenth-century Battle of Bannockburn. I'd always thought they were sisters, but even Bianca could never say for certain.

Dinnertime at the Torok Mansion wasn't a family gathering around a table. If our parents did make an appearance, they disappeared soon after. The menu consisted of one, maybe two, wine glasses filled with blood for them, and duck, geese, or thick slices of pork—roasted on a spit within a stone structure—for Nick and me. Smoke habitually plumed from a stack in the roof, seeping into every crevice of the drafty mansion. As a result, Nick and I went to school smelling like either bacon or a barbeque restaurant.

Elizabeth snapped her fingers, and I followed obediently behind the others.

"The notion that a fledgling can pervert any one of our thoughts is positively absurd," I heard Nostradamus rant, after which the others gathered shoulder to shoulder, their combined arguments a cacophonous and impassioned whisper.

The chatter from the others ebbed when Elizabeth said, "Ah. It would appear we have a visitor."

I followed her gaze, and I choked on a gasp. My knees buckled, and a flush ignited my entire body.

Elizabeth zoomed in Tristan's direction. "I thought I'd made it clear that your absence during this time is in Celestine's best interest."

Leonardo drifted in her direction. "Perhaps you have forgotten that love knows no bounds, dearest Queen. Do afford the young lovers a few moments together," he said, clasping her elbow.

"Young, you say?" she said, jerking free. "Surely, you scoff. Need I remind you that Tristan of Tomisovara arrived on this earth twenty centuries before either one of us?"

A pinkish-orange ring encircled the pupils of his eyes, and Leonardo coaxed Elizabeth not nearly far enough to suit me.

"Fine. We shall grant them a few moments," I heard her growl. "But only a *few*. Perhaps, we can task Tristan with instruction on matters of teleportation."

"I should think not," Nostradamus said. "That would be akin to enlisting a flight attendant to pilot a plane. Only the Ancients have perfected the technique."

Elizabeth flapped her hand, dismissively. "In that you are correct, sir. Our warrior's limitations briefly slipped my mind," she twittered. "Might I then propose he instruct her on her ability to simply navigate through the air?"

The Elders nodded in agreement, directed a stern look at Tristan, then evaporated. He seemed to wait for me to approach, apprehension evident in his eyes. I didn't know what to say to him, how to undo the damage I'd caused between us. Suddenly self-conscious, my eyes darted over our surroundings, settling on a nearby fruit orchard whose enormous trees bore fruit the size of bowling balls.

The moon and the stars hung low in the sky, more a Disneyland-like simulation than the real thing. The stars randomly and sequentially pulsated as if sending out Morse code, the Venus flytraps beneath opening and closing with an identical rhythm.

"I didn't mean the things I said . . ." I eventually managed, toeing the ground and unhousing a neon crab with a human face.

"You never have to apologize to me, Celeste," he replied and crossed the distance between us in a blink. He took me in his arms, and a multicolored plume emanated from his body and mine. "Forgive me," he began, "but I'm *not* sorry things turned out as they have. The thought I might lose you forever awakened so much I wish I could forget."

Was he seriously thinking about his dead wife? At a time like this? The question poised on my tongue, I decided I'd rather not know. I had enough emotional shit to deal with. Regardless, I pushed him away. "How long will they keep me here?"

"Until they're convinced you are no longer a threat."

I wanted to go home, to sleep in my own bed within the Victorian house I'd put my stamp on, orchestrating every detail from paint colors to period-correct wallcoverings to antique furnishings. "What do I have to do to convince them?"

He pulled me into his arms again, closer this time, and I couldn't catch my breath. "Accept the hand you've been dealt, my love, and spend your time here learning everything you can from them."

I thought of the beautiful five-year-old girl—taken by the Harvesters when they seized the ship, *Grace*, off the coast of Australia in the 1800s—left in my care following the most recent battle with the Harvesters. "How is Raina?"

"She misses you, but, much like the rest of us, she understands that your absence is necessary."

"What about school? Who's taking care of her when you're not around?"

He looked away, and I sensed there was something he wasn't telling me. His finger was hot against my lips. "Relax. Bianca has everything under control." He pulled me closer, his hipbones digging into my ribs, and whispered through my hair, "Aren't you happy to see *me*?"

I was happy to see him! I'd been desperately, sickeningly, in love with him since puberty. For as long as I could remember, I'd linger long past my bedtime, in the hope I might catch a glimpse of him within my father's study or elsewhere within the mansion.

"Of course," I said, finding it hard to temper the passion he always inflamed.

"I don't believe you. You may have to prove it," he teased, long fingers flirting with the buttons on my blouse, a fevered kiss blistering my lips.

"Not here," I said, turning a cheek to a second kiss. I could smell his hypnotic scent—musky and feral with an undernote of myrrh and sandalwood. When he persisted, I pushed him away and he sailed against a tree, landing with a thud.

"She is quite right. Now is not the time nor the place," Nostradamus interrupted, materializing within a burgundy mist. "Come," he said to me. "You are most welcome to observe, Tristan, though I must warn you that suggestions or criticism are decidedly unwelcome."

Nostradamus took my hand. "Where are we going?" I asked, sensing Tristan just a few steps behind. He pointed to a mountaintop and transported me there, where he bent to retrieve a large rock. He threw it, his forearm radiating light. Rather than fall, the rock hung in the air. Then it began to spin, increasing its momentum as it traveled in our direction. He zoomed toward it, catching it in midair. As phenomenal as I thought that entire spectacle was, what was I supposed to learn from it?

"Gravity, Celestine, is merely one's perception," he said.

Beside me, Tristan grew tense, a sound catching in his throat a split-second before Nostradamus shoved me off the cliff. Sailing headfirst toward a jagged outcropping, my fingers clawed the air. My hair streamed behind me, snagging on spindly branches. The ravine drew closer, closer, so close I could see fish feeding on the bottom.

"Up, up!" they shouted.

I harnessed a scream and rocketed skyward. Dazzling stars surrounded me, the galaxy laid out like an astronomical quilt, and I climbed higher and higher, a smile reaching my ears as I set my sights on the Big Dipper.

Tristan caught up to me, flanking one side, Nostradamus the other. Sailing past brilliant flickering stars, I felt inebriated and giddy, uninhibited, perhaps for the first time in my life. I no longer had to accept the reality that someday I would have to leave Tristan, Nick, Raina, and the Toroks behind and slip through the thin veil separating life from death, whether abruptly or following a debilitating illness, whether whole or crippled or infirmed. I was free! Free of death, the paralyzing apprehension that haunts mortals nearly all the days of their lives.

My eyes met Tristan's, and I wished Nostradamus would return to the others, leave us to celebrate my awakening, to christen my immortality, to finally make licentious love, unafraid and with total abandonment.

Nostradamus shared a look with Tristan, and I sighed through a whimper, realizing the time had come to return to the palace. Tristan laced his fingers through mine, and soon after our feet touched the ground simultaneously.

"The time has come for you to depart, Tristan," Nostradamus said, sandaled feet contacting the earth with a swish. "I'll leave you to your goodbyes."

Tristan nodded somberly, then stood motionless while he scanned the area beyond, seemingly unconvinced of Nostradamus's departure. With one last look around, he tugged me close, our bodies melding into one. Then he kissed me, long and hard, tiny explosions arcing from his fingertips as he cupped my face. When I opened my eyes, he was gone, and Leonardo stood before me.

CHAPTER SIX
Leonardo

With each passing century, I find myself growing more restless, craving wars or disasters or some heinous turmoil that will require my intervention. I am not proud of this, but I attribute this minor infraction to escalating boredom.

How long has it been since I picked up paint and brush or settled in my chair, this invention or that demanding escape from the recesses of my mind, a ream of paper spread just so on the tabletop before me? In the beginning, I grew annoyed when called away from the canvas, content to while away the night, immortalizing the creatures of the Hollow Earth in precise detail and blazing color. This is something I miss, yet the motivation eludes me, perhaps because I can no longer share it with the world.

I am aware that Socrates suspects that it is I responsible for his recent bouts of forgetfulness. I am not. Perhaps a compromised bottle of blood from Torok Laboratories is to blame. Indeed, a miniscule droplet from a donor vaccinated with the herb vernicadis might very well explain the dear boy's malady. But would it be a significant enough quantity to alter Socrates's immortal state? Uncertain, I decided the ramifications might still prove disastrous and, under a preponderance of caution, I disposed of every bottle allocated the same lot number, straight away, and clandestinely alerted Torok Labs so as not to alarm the others.

Seldom do we have visitors here, and I find it difficult to distance myself from the girl, the scent of the living still emanating from her porcelain skin and her long, lustrous hair, evoking memories of maidens, their cheeks aglow with passion and the night's promise. She is looking at me now, her eyes betraying curiosity and a willingness to succeed. I hope I don't disappoint.

"Do not be intimidated," I begin. "Teleportation, at its essence, is merely emitting one's psychic field while commanding the molecules to separate, thus allowing movement through solid objects."

I don't find her blank expression the least bit encouraging. I tell her as much and her modulating pupils enlarge, all the while sporadically flashing a brilliant orange. She is expressing her anger, which is understandable, and I don't take it to heart. Some emotion is better than no emotion at all, I always say.

"Dear girl, think of yourself as nothing but imperceptible molecules and breach that tree behind us." I ignore her slack-jaw expression, but I am already losing my patience.

"You can't be serious," she says, stuffing a strand of fragrant hair behind one ear.

"You will try. You will fail. And then you shall try again. Now, give it a go."

I watch from behind as her hands ball into fists, her shoulders shake, and I can only imagine her constipated expression. Then she smacks face-first into the unyielding oak. A sweet, metallic scent fills the air and I know she has broken her nose, but I resist the urge to lap the blood spilling from her nostrils.

I spin in circles, debating a more forgiving object but find none. "Given your valiant attempt, we shall set this aside for a future date and return to the palace."

She shakes her head, and I know she is thinking that the sooner she masters that which we expect of her, the sooner she can leave us behind and return home. The silly imp. We shall always remain nearby, whispers beyond the mist. "I'll try again," she says.

I flick my hand and tell her to have at it.

Her body trembles, a purple haze radiating all around her. A loud *whack* echoes throughout the forest on her second attempt. This time the impact propels her backward, and the deep laceration across her forehead resembles pulverized meat. I watch her blood congeal over the wound, and I think it is only upon canvas that one can truly appreciate a blood red.

"Do you understand the concept of quantum frequency?" I ask, following an exaggerated sigh. Judging from her knitted brows, I think she does not. "Consider it merely mind over matter." Again, I receive the type of acknowledgement one might expect from the most simplistic of species. "Perhaps permeating the mighty oak was a bit unrealistic," I say, instead of the disparaging remark on the tip of my tongue. I clasp her hand and zoom the two of us inches above the ground for one hundred yards. We come to rest just outside the wooden structure I constructed centuries before, a serene place I would often visit in the past, whether to paint, draw, or further my inventions.

"The objective is to materialize on the other side," I say with a nod toward the building. "Simply free your mind and focus on what lies beyond the structure."

Her thoughts, though easily transcribed, lack the proper direction. I implant a suggestion and I watch, with great pride, mind you, as she concentrates on a rotted section near the foundation. She believes her bones are nothing more than pliable putty—her method, not mine—and moments after she presses both palms against the oak planks, she vanishes and then reappears on the opposite side. I deny an urge to dance a jig amid the wildflowers embracing my feet. And I so want to play the rogue—to take her in my arms and kiss her, but I bow before her instead.

CHAPTER SEVEN
Socrates

⌐◄━━━►¬

A h, the ability to pause time. Not so long ago, I would employ this exquisite skill at every opportunity. My brows become one, as I revisit an earlier suspicion, long unruly hairs tickling the flaccid skin beneath. My wariness has not abated; why had the others appointed me the task? Particularly given my mishaps of late. Undoubtedly, they expect I will fail, and they are nearby, scrubbing their palms in feverish anticipation, waiting to share a robust laugh at my expense.

I arrive on the shoreline, the girl in tow, and discover that this, most certainly, is not the destination I intended. The seagulls dive and zigzag overhead, and I associate their squawks and squeals with vicious reticule. How could I have possibly misremembered the location? My shoulders sag, until it occurs to me—not for the first time, if I am remembering correctly—that one of my devilish brethren (Leonardo comes to mind) has played a cruel trick, perhaps slipped a mind-altering herb into my blood-filled chalice. Should that not be the case, what *is* happening to me?

Remembering Cicero's accolades, I disguise a sorrowful chuckle. I wonder if my peers might still consider me the True Father of Western Thought.

My eyes dart in my young protégée's direction to see if she is aware, but she remains lost in her own thoughts.

"I thought you might enjoy a moment of repose by the sea before we proceed with your lesson," I say, repulsed by the ease at which I vocalize this falsehood. The look in her eyes suggests peace an impossibility, that she has conceded tranquility to all her yesterdays.

I shake my head, the corners of my mouth inching upward, amused by my own idiocy; such attempts have long had little effect on the rest of us, to include Leonardo. I sense he is becoming self-destructive, and I fear he longs to seduce reckless abandonment, to petition the wrath of the Omniscients.

The girl's eyes meet mine, a question, or perhaps a confession, waits timidly behind her soft virtuous lips. I yearn to convince her that by agreeing to the Adaption she has made an irreparable mistake. But it is a bit late to lay claim to romanticized chivalry. My mood brightens some when reminded that, unlike the rest of us, her existence shan't be regulated to the Enchanted Earth, venturing beyond it only when called upon to assist our many factions throughout the world.

After which my mind wanders to Yesenia, more specifically her betrayal, and a thick oppressive fog envelops me when I fail to contain explosive rage. I have long obsessed over her unexplained disappearance all those years ago. Where had she gone? Why did she return? And what sinister plot had sent her into hiding?

Dear God, I think as I wring my hands, I alone unleashed that demonic plague onto the world. Oh, how I have openly applauded Bianca's decision to rid mankind of the evil wretch. But was I now aiding in the creation of another? I study Celestine, perhaps for too long and much too intently. How easy it would be—the two of us alone—to terminate her, here and now, and put an end to my apprehension.

She seems to understand that I am deliberating her very existence. Her eyes grow large and luminous, and I am reminded of a frightened woodlander. She takes a step back. My heart twists when I acknowledge her vulnerability, and I decide what's done is done, that Yesenia was but a demonic fluke, that I must resist the urge to destroy Celestine and, instead, commit to ensuring her success.

"It has been a grueling turn of events, wouldn't you agree?" I offer, to calm her nerves (afterward berating myself for such an impotent attempt to assuage her fear).

Ferocious waves suddenly slap the shore before she can respond, and I cringe, knowing the unsettling mirage will soon appear. I press my lips together tightly—before an ungentlemanly obscenity manages an escape—as the bow of the damnable Viking ship rises from the water. I have endured this phantom vision countless times, the spectacle quite entertaining in the beginning, but persistently a most unwelcome irritation, particularly at this moment. A large flag bearing crossbones and the inscription *Draken Harald Hårfagre* flaps in the wind. From the bow, water spews from an elaborately carved dragon's head while the ship's ghostly crew choruses an ancient (but annoying, nonetheless) Nordic maritime tune. I roll my eyes when the muscled men heave defiant coils of thick rope, biceps and triceps pumping resolutely until every rope is secure. Toasting their accomplishment, the crew passes one bottle then another, either substituting laughter for the proper lyrics or a flurry of energetic kicks performed in a Polska three-quarter rhythm.

"Drat," I say, and trust it will serve as a forewarning to my young fledgling, when a second ship of much greater proportion rises from the ocean and capsizes, then sinks the smaller vessel. She looks at me, her eyes so wide they reflect the cruise ship *Titanic*. I try to muster a little empathy, but I fail. Her mouth lies open, revealing pallid tonsils, and all I can do is wait patiently for the infuriating ship to return to its own dimension. I drum my fingers on my forehead as passengers leisurely stroll the ship's deck, oblivious to the preordained cataclysm, well-dressed and comely women twirling parasols, content to saunter arm-in-arm with their cigar-smoking and debonair companions. Barreling full throttle ahead, the ship collides with the inevitable iceberg and the collision perpetuates a tsunami wave. "Yes, yes! Sink already!" I yell amid mounting impatience and look away when the girl's eyes dart in my direction. I assume she perceives me some form of callous scoundrel. "Please don't make me explain," I say. The girl remains transfixed, just as the others and I had been when we first discovered this disturbing phenomenon. "A most distressing event," I manage. But she remains mute, content to gape at the sea as if the crashing waves might offer the explanation she craves.

Without warning, I spirit her in the direction of the waterfall. The water breaking against the cliff has served as an audible guide, and I smile to myself when I see we have arrived at the correct destination.

"Mora Temporis, or rather the Pausing of Events, may certainly prove a challenge," I sputter. Her response is that of one intellectually compromised, but I press on. Oh, if only I could pause *this* event! I have already determined our course (you can be sure that I have perceived the disastrous outcome). "Shall we begin?"

She tips her head by way of acknowledgement and waits patiently beside me, oozing a noxious melding of apprehension and resolve, while the soothing refrain of the waterfall, as the current claps the rocks below, fails in its effort to calm either of us.

"Your task," I say, "shall be to pause the torrent."

"How?" she asks.

How indeed. "Surely, you've witnessed this occurrence before," I encourage. She nods with robotic enthusiasm, and I think of a chicken pecking hard ground. I am inside her head now, in awe of her hyperactive brain activity, the alpha waves firing frequently and often surpassing thirteen hertz. She is thinking of Bianca, and I see them both in a crowded restaurant, Bianca employing Mora Temporis before relating a salacious account of Tristan tumbling from a bed inhabited by Julius Caesar's mistress *and* her ladies-in-waiting. Waiters are stationary, patrons sit statue-like—silverware suspended in midair. The girl's thoughts shift as she recollects a recent battle with the Harvesters. Her chest rises and falls when she recalls the first responders— the law enforcement officers obeying Bianca's silent commands—mute in midspeech, frozen in midstep.

I stimulate the essential parts of her brain and say, "Close your eyes, dear woman, and envision a water spigot. Then simply shut it off."

I feel a grin tug the corners of my mouth. She is obedient and eager to learn, a prized pupil to be sure. She is thinking of a pump house within the large garden on the Toroks' property, the baroque pump handle specifically. Her temples throb as agitated brainwaves skitter across her thalamus. She focuses on the pump handle, thrust in an erect position, and she grimaces as she attempts to shut it off, telepathically. Her eyes pop open when she hears the eerie silence that suddenly surrounds us. Suspended in the preternatural time warp, the waterfall is no longer a cascading wave of water but mere droplets, dangling motionlessly, like sparkling translucent jewels attached to a necklace.

CHAPTER EIGHT
Elizabeth

I am most aware Celestine finds my appearance daunting. As, too, am I of the ridiculous speculations regarding my cause of death. Lead poisoning, indeed. As if something as innocuous as applying multiple layers of lead and vinegar over unsightly smallpox scars could bring down a queen. "As unconventional as the pasty concoction may very well be," I once told Lady Bess of Hardwick, "one who rules England must always put her best foot forward."

How I envy our young fledgling. How rich my life might have been had I a lover the likes of Tristan of Tomisovara or the devotion of a sibling such as Nicholas. Oh, to be sure, I allowed (and encouraged) the amorous attention of Robert Dudley—more so prior to the death of his inconvenient wife—and it is true I was often enamored with Sir Francis Drake, but, in the end, I knew I could only entertain one true love: England's throne.

It is her relationship with Nicholas that I admire most. Oh, the years I longed for the companionship of my half-sister Mary and my half-brother Edward, despite our only commonality our father, King Henry VIII, and our absent mothers (mine beheaded, Edward's dead from childbirth-related complications, Mary's exiled to Kimbolton Castle). I study the girl as she returns with Socrates. Is that relief I see on both their faces? I find myself up-lifted by the philosopher's unusually peaceful countenance. How many days did I lie awake within my coffer, tormented by that which seems to plague both Leonardo and Socrates? You can be sure that I did not hold my tongue when the Omniscients decreed the Code obsolete. Quite the contrary. I re-joiced—and loudly! I remain convinced our factions require reinforcements, equally convinced that Socrates and Leonardo, all of us, really, shall benefit from the frequent interactions with those newly reborn as they undergo fas-tidious training. Yes, new blood. That is precisely what we need around here.

I only have to think the command and she turns to look my way, then follows me and we float over well-worn pathways, soaring higher when we encounter dense forestry. I lead her beneath a tree, one so tall it extends into the clouds racing across a globular moon. A magnificent gorilla squats on a resilient tree limb, while it attempts—and fails—to conceal itself behind a generous spray of slippery green leaves.

I lace my fingers and nestle my hands against my skirt, never tiring of the feel of the smooth satin. "We shall now address the Power of Persua-sion." I return her disinterested stare as she gnaws the inside of one cheek. I don't know what I expected, but most assuredly it was some modicum of acknowledgement. "Look there," I tell her, gesturing toward the ape. "Per-suade the beast to climb down and dive into yonder lake."

She blinks (annoyingly and repetitively), first at the gorilla and then at me as if I have lost my mind. "You have the power, Celestine," I say and grasp her hands, after which I force her to look into my eyes.

I feel a surge of energy leave my body and enter hers. Her eyes glow a brilliant yellow and she struggles to break free, but I hold her there and re-peat my instruction. The gorilla grunts, pounds its chest, and then scrambles from the tree. Appendages slap the forest floor, the sound like thunderclaps, and the ape dives into the water.

"I did that?" she asks, as we watch the primate expertly navigate the lake, and I pretend I don't see that her entire body trembles.

Her self-doubt grows, takes on an entity all its own, and I try but can't muster even the semblance of a smile. I have always found it difficult to place my faith in those who cannot find it within themselves.

She shakes her head. "I still don't see how you expect me—"

I thump the top of her head with a fan given me by the Earl of Leicester. "Oh, for heaven's sake. Think of it as a switch, your resolve the conduit that completes the circuit. This is merely an introduction to the powers you now possess, Celestine. Practice makes perfect, my dear. Your command of these capabilities will take time, and we shall always be little more than an invitation away."

CHAPTER NINE
Nostradamus

I confess that for the first time in quite a long while, I feel a purpose for my existence. The girl has given me that. My revered ability to predict future events aside, I am convinced it is possible—no, a near certainty—that Celestine can alter the mortals' inexorable path toward destruction, and I rejoice in the fact that I played perhaps the most important role. However, I also foresee an illicit event that may very well destroy her before she can even truly begin.

I pace a circle as I reconsider this vision. I pray God it is among the handful of inaccuracies I have misforecast in centuries past. But I have called upon Him before, have I not? *Called upon* is a rather unimpassioned description; I pleaded until blue in the face as days became nights and nights became sleepless expeditions in time.

Oh! Will He hear me now?

The loathing toward my own immortality I owe to the brutal realization that many of my premonitions (the French Revolution, the rise of Hitler, and the assassination of America's beloved John Fitzgerald Kennedy) *did* come to fruition. I had always assumed I would be dust beneath the ground long before the atrocities occurred—my soul safeguarded from all things grievous and heartbreaking—and blissfully unaware of the cataclysms.

I push these harrowing remembrances aside as she floats in my direction. Her face is still aglow and her eyes, too, retain the shimmer of unrequited passion, and I curse Tristan for his unsolicited visit. Now is not the time for distraction. But I sense her overwhelming gratitude, and I exhale a sigh, relieved that she has finally embraced her destiny.

"Because I am your Maker, I cannot teach you the ability to read another's thoughts," I say. She nods, which comes as no surprise. Perhaps she has acquired this fact from time spent with the Toroks, but I suspect this is purely intuition. From the start, I was aware of her intelligence, but more than that, her advanced instinct that will only serve to enhance all that I have given her. I clear my throat, and I am most grateful she will always be unaware of my thoughts and I of hers—shrouding my latest vision from the others has proven quite arduous. I am convinced that one (undoubtedly Socrates) would seek the Omniscients' counsel should they discover my secret. Moreover, it is my belief that upon hearing this confession—premonition or not—the Omniscients might very well call for Celestine's destruction. I shudder at this possibility. In truth, I have become quite fond of the girl.

"Therefore," I continue, "I propose I introduce you to the ability to transform oneself into something decidedly different."

"Shapeshifting?" she offers and cocks her head toward a shoulder.

"A most rudimentary term for something that is anything but simple, though accurate, I suppose." My eyes meet hers and I hold her complete attention. "Prepare yourself for disappointment, Celestine. Not a one of us accomplished this feat straightaway. Simply put, envision that which you wish to become, and it shall be. I have given you the power."

The glow has left her face, and in her eyes I see not the remnants of rapture but presumed defeat. I needn't the power of telepathy to know she hasn't the slightest idea how best to achieve this objective. Leave it to the others to task me with the impossible, as I am unable to guide her telepathically.

"Let us begin with something familiar, with someone you know as well as yourself. Perhaps your brother, Nicholas. Close your eyes and see him there, feel his presence, then merely replicate what is in your mind's eye."

Judging from her clenched jaw and pinched eyelids, she is most determined to succeed. I wait patiently, with words of encouragement and consolation at the ready. Wait! I lurch closer still so that I might observe her more closely. Is that a hair blemishing her sculpted chin? Now two? Now three? My breath catches when a goatee sprouts and her breasts flatten beneath her blouse. My hands fly to my mouth, and I smother exaltation when her long golden hair shrinks before my eyes, and she readjusts her trousers to accommodate newly acquired manhood.

"You have done it, mademoiselle!" I say as she swaggers into my open arms.

CHAPTER TEN

The following evening, I found Nostradamus, deep in thought, looking out over the ornamental pond just outside the palace. "Where are the others?"

"Ah, you have arisen," he said, turning to greet me with a smile that seemed forced. "The others have gone to greet Empress Matilda." A crimson aura ebbed and flowed across his retinae. "She much prefers the woodlands to the palace."

"Who's Matilda?" I asked, while crossing the room to grab a chalice.

"An Omniscient," he said, "and Elizabeth's Maker."

I nearly dropped the goblet, and a few drops spilled over the rim. "Will I get to meet her?"

"Of course. She is here to celebrate your Adaption."

I sensed there was something he wasn't telling me. "Is that the only reason she's here?" I asked, my eyes locking on his over the top of the glass.

"Before your commencement celebration, we must evaluate your ability to deny temptation. Traditionally, one of the Omniscients presides over the event."

"Maybe you can explain something I've never understood. Bianca once told me that the Code allows for the destruction of all unworthy mortals. Isn't that a contradiction?"

Nostradamus bowed his head, his hands clasped tightly together. "I suppose it does seem somewhat hypocritical, although exercised more frequently prior to the Omniscients' addendum, in the late-sixteenth century. We shall assess not only your ability to make the distinction between those deserving life and those deserving death but also your self-restraint. So much can go awry in the heat of the moment." He tinkled a laugh, transient and strained. "Oh, the grief I caused my Maker. I remain astonished she did not call for my destruction."

"Who performed your Adaption?"

He blew out a long breath and looked away. "Sainte Jeanne d'Arc."

"As in *Joan of Arc*?"

"Oui."

"Will I get to meet her?" I asked, failing to temper my enthusiasm.

He shook his head as blood-tingled tears swelled his eyes. "She was beheaded in the Great Battle of Domrémy-la-Pucelle while defending her fellow countrymen. Alas, though I did not arrive in time to assist her, I did return her head to the Hollow Earth, where it has resided ever since."

I immediately regretted my inquiry and decided to change the subject. "What about the others? Who performed Socrates's Adaption?"

"He holds a most illustrious position. For, it is said, he was the only one Thales of Miletus chose to lend immortality."

I shook my head. "I don't know who that is."

"Surely, you jest."

"I honestly have no idea."

"Thales holds an illustrious title. He is one of seven legendary wisemen."

"So he was a philosopher?"

Nostradamus puffed his cheeks. "You say *philosopher* as if the definition of the word were a conventional man. Had it not been for his brilliant mind, we may never have realized, as thoroughly unpretentious as it is, that in simple water exists the essence of matter."

"Impressive," I said and hoped it rang sincere. "Tell me more about Elizabeth's Maker."

"So much can be said of Matilda," he said, tapping an index finger against his chin. I got the impression he was debating just how candid he should be. "I am not the only one who wonders if Matilda not only gifted Elizabeth immortality but also her frequent ill-temperament," he followed with a chuckle. "Matilda was mother to England's Henry II. And, to this day, she declares herself the rightful heir to the throne."

"Was she?"

"That remains a vigorous debate. One her cousin, Stephen of Blois, was only too happy to contest at the time."

"Did he take the throne?"

"Oui, though he did pay the price. For you see, Matilda persisted her challenge throughout his reign. A most exasperating anarchy."

It was somehow comforting to know that family drama had existed throughout the ages. "What about Leonardo?"

"Giovanni Bellini, a Venetian painter, came to his rescue as King Francis the First held Leonardo's head in his hands, or so it is rumored."

"Why haven't I met any of them?"

"The Omniscients were called away before your arrival. Perhaps you shall have the opportunity to meet them before you take your leave." He yawned, a kaleidoscope of primary colors escaping his lungs. "Shall we?" he asked, offering his arm. "The others await."

I heard voices long before we glided toward the riverbank. Nostradamus pulled me into a thicket and pressed a finger to his lips.

"Did you think I intended to deny her whatever she needs?" an unfamiliar voice asked. "Assumption, all too often, nearly led to your downfall,

Elizabeth. Had it not been for me setting your course straight, you would have assuredly surrendered England to the Earl of Desmond or lost the War against the Spaniards. Had you managed triumph without benefit from me, you would have done so most certainly by God's good grace alone."

Nostradamus tipped his head toward the river. "*That* is Empress Matilda."

Matilda drove the tip of her sword into the ground, I assumed for emphasis, and showered the muddy bank with shimmery silver particles. "Furthermore, I remain convinced England would have fallen to that lubberwort, Hugh O'Neill during the Tyrone Rebellion without my intervention."

Elizabeth awkwardly curtsied, one foot catching the hem of her gown. "I intended no affront. I beg your forgiveness."

Matilda threw back her shoulders and readjusted her chainmail tunic. "Which of you has been relegated instruction?" Her intense gaze swept over each Elder before coming to rest on Leonardo. "If memory serves, da Vinci schooled a most promising pupil in the art of the Grand Illusion a century or two past, after which the unfortunate young man went mad, thinking himself from that day forward little more than a nettlesome mynah bird. As I do so adore Bianca, I certainly hope you have not tasked her beloved daughter's tutelage to one so entirely incompetent."

Da Vinci popped a finger toward the clouds waltzing overhead but seemed to reconsider a response. Socrates cleared his throat, and I sensed his desire to vocalize something he shouldn't. Elizabeth busied herself with various hair accessories, plucking out this or that jeweled comb only to return it to its previous position.

"We all played a part," Elizabeth eventually volunteered.

"A most appropriate decision. Where is the fledgling? We need to begin. I have more important matters to attend to."

"Here," Nostradamus said, leading me from the thicket.

Matilda's eyes rolled over me, then met my stare with a vulturine glare. "I am not convinced of her devotion. At this very moment, she ruminates over her ability to grant a mortal life eternal." In a flash, she dashed across the expanse that separated us, her misshapen nose within inches of mine. "Your pious contemplation is both frivolous and detrimental. If God was so opposed to our ability to grant immortality, why did he grant us the power?"

I shrugged. "Regardless, I believe that my friends, my colleagues, should have a choice in the matter."

"These *friends* will come to think of themselves as angels, saviors, just as you shall one day. I find your indecision most concerning. Now is the time to dispel all doubt. Shall we or shall we not proceed? Speak now!"

My eyes flew to the Elders, to Elizabeth in particular, whose pupils pulsated from black to blinding yellow, then to scarlet red.

"Well, what say you?" Matilda screeched, the hilt of her sword suddenly aglow.

"All right! Yes, I'm ready," I said and witnessed Nostradamus exhale his relief.

Matilda gave the order to begin, then sprawled across a garish gondola and pitched live pheasants to the crocodiles that towed her Venetian rowboat in a monotonous circle. All I could think about was rescuing the pheasants; just when I thought I couldn't dislike Matilda any more, she proved me wrong.

"Unlike your experiences within the Circle, Celestine, this time you shall make the journey alone, with no one to provide counsel," Elizabeth said.

"But rest assured," Matilda added, "we will be aware of any misstep . . . to which I shall take prompt action."

Just as before, I experienced the sensation of weightlessness. Pulled backward through a tunnel of dizzying strobing lights at incredible speed, gravity promptly reintroduced itself and everything came to a brutal and sudden halt. The blood within my veins no longer a dormant slurry, my heart began to thwack against my chest, every organ celebrating the return of vital nutrients.

The humid air hung heavy over the rolling hills adorning the Pennsylvanian landscape, augmenting the stench of gunpowder and decaying bodies.

A hasty glance in all directions revealed a colony of men and boys, dripping sweat beneath dark blue cloaks of wool. By contrast, the hodgepodge but far less cumbersome wardrobe of their Confederate soldier counterparts provided a welcomed but feckless agility. A lethargic breeze blew from the south, prompting men young and old to turn faces etched with fear, fatigue, and dehydration into it as they halted their march and awaited orders.

General Robert E. Lee cantered his eager stallion across an infinite row of twitchy troops arranged in tactical formation and shouted words of encouragement. Lee's gray-blue coattail fluttered behind him, steely eyes penetrating and determined beneath a crown of silver ruffled hair. His lieutenants gave the command and thousands of Confederate soldiers began to march across one mile of open ground under heavy fire. The Union Army lobbed jerry-rigged explosives, one after the other. The Confederates, adept at intercepting the undetonated artillery, hurled them back across the field where they exploded, showering the grassland with dirt, blood, and body parts. The deadly hiss of minié balls and booming cannons rocked the hillside. Wails of the dying and shouts of the living created a disharmonious blend. Bodies crashed, one on top of another, mortal wounds infusing the heavy air with the metallic but intoxicating scent of fresh blood.

A primordial hiss escaped my lips. A feverish glow augmented my diaphanous shell. My jaw ratcheted open to accommodate deadly spiked fangs. Fiery blood surged through my arteries, my veins bulging like cherry-black ropes, while glowing embers spewed from my eyes as I searched for my first victim.

The body count rising, a few baby-faced deserters fled the battle. Eyes wide with the caliber of fear only men of war lay claim to, they sprinted across the field made slick by blood and guts, dodging musket and howitzer fire as they raced in my direction.

I soared toward the enemy's stronghold and, midway to the scrimmage line, ambushed the pair of defectors. Swooping toward the ground, I blocked their path. Paralyzed with fear, their mouths hung open in glorious surrender. I gripped them by their collars and the cloth began to disintegrate between my fingers. One broke free and ran. Latching on to the other, I sniffed the sulfurous odor emanating from his body, the intoxicating fear pheromone every bit as appetizing to me as the aroma of freshly baked bread is to a mortal. He continued to struggle. I jerked him off the ground and suspended him overhead. Helpless, he scissored his dangling feet and tried to scream for help but produced only an impotent yelp. Giddy with anticipation, I drew my head back and prepared to sink in my teeth.

Nick appeared from within a fluorescent smog. "Let him go, Celeste." When I didn't, he said, "You kill this guy and you're screwed. They'll take you down. Let him go!"

Nick pried my fingers loose, and the soldier wiggled free and dashed away from the battle.

Then Nick grabbed me by both shoulders and shook me until my teeth rattled. "Snap out of it, Celeste! Look at me."

My head swam, and I tried to bring my thoughts into focus while I fought an onslaught of nausea. When everything became clear, I realized what I'd nearly done. "Oh, God! Nick, if you hadn't come, I would've killed him! What if it happens again? What if I can't—"

Nick jerked me into his arms, and I burrowed my face into his chest. "Then I'll be there to stop you. Relax, Celeste. It's over." He held me until I stopped trembling. "We'd better get back."

I grabbed his arm, afraid to return. "Nick, they'll know you were here! What will they—"

"Do to me?" He shrugged. "It's like this, Celeste. They only pretend they've always had their shit together. That they never fucked up. I know for a fact that's a load of crap. Every one of them had a babysitter in the beginning. Mine was Tristan. And if I have my way, I will be yours."

CHAPTER ELEVEN

Matilda and the Elders were gone when Nick transported me back to the river. "Where are they?" I said, my eyes darting in every direction.

Nick trumpeted his lips. "Damn, take it easy, will you? They never expected you to succeed. That old broad—Matilda—just gets off on intimidating people. She pulled that same shit on me when I was here. If I hadn't been there to stop you, one of the others would have stepped up."

"I'm proud of you, Celeste," Tristan said, his shape slowly materializing through sparkling beads of water as he hovered above the river.

My breath caught when I saw him, my body aching at the sight of him, goosebumps forming despite pores oozing sweat. A sidelong glance at Nick confirmed his irritating grin and deflated my lust like a spent balloon.

I pushed past Nick just as a swath of darkness obliterated the sun, black ribbons in frenzied motion, descending upon us rapidly. Matilda was the first to transform into flesh and touch down, the Elders swooping behind her.

"Tristan of Tomisovara, I presume," she bellowed. Her eyes pulsated from red to ebony as she glared at Nick with an intensity so terrifying I feared she might disintegrate him. "I shall forgive your recent rant, Nicholas, and attribute it to your inexhaustible idiocy. However, I suggest that both you and Tristan take your leave and take it now." She waited until they vaporized within a sputtering fog, then took one look at me and smirked. "A kingdom, the crown jewels, the stars above endure, Celestine. But lovers?" She shook her head, erecting an index finger for emphasis. "Lovers come and go, no matter the vehemence with which they profess undying love and all that falls blissfully upon our ears. I suggest you take my words to heart and rid your mind of such trivial matters. For a treacherous road lies ahead for you, for all of us really, should the mortals discover your vampiric state. Perhaps Nostradamus has told you the story of Adelina?"

Nostradamus cleared his throat, and I noticed him duck sideways, seeking cover behind Socrates.

"I shall assume from your reluctance to answer the question that he has not!" She inhaled so deeply that her chain tunic expanded and clinked its objection. "Her extraordinary beauty often rendered men both motionless and speechless, mere hapless hounds frothing about the mouth. Despite Adelina's determination to fend off the Romanian Warrior Stefan's various attempts at seduction, she eventually failed, and Stefan's infatuation grew, exponentially. The two were inseparable until the day Adelina grew tired of him, and, enraged, Stefan sought his revenge, sharing the secret to her powers with Emperor Leopold I. The emperor amassed his army, which ambushed her and took her prisoner as she slumbered within her coffer. Following days of ruthless interrogation, Leopold called for her head, afterward demanding his army burn her at the stake. Supplied with the names of her immortal comrades, the bloodthirsty army systematically hunted most down and destroyed them. So you see, Celestine, our secret shall never be safe with those outside the Realm. To compromise yourself is to endanger us all."

Elizabeth timidly stepped forward and slipped an arm around my waist. "I am quite certain Celestine understands the consequences, Your Empress."

Matilda soared our direction, creating a dust-filled and transitory whirl-wind. "Are you now? Has my story of Adelina rendered the girl mute, thus incapable of vocalizing her own agreement?"

"I understand," I said past a hollow laugh. "Haven't I kept my parents' secret for over twenty years?"

"Very well. See that you continue. Now, with all the unpleasantries out of the way, might I suggest we return to the palace and enjoy your celebra-tion?"

Inside the palace, I first saw Bianca, the only mother I had ever really known. How could I possibly make up for all those horrible things I had said to her? She had sacrificed so much for Nick and me. Until we'd come along, she and Razvan had traveled the world unencumbered for centuries, most often while leading the Realm as they conquered packs of werewolves daring to hunt outside designated perimeters, or clans of rebellious vampires preying on mortals. But, sometimes, they roamed the earth simply for pleasure.

They'd met American presidents dating as far back as John Quincy Ad-ams, physicist Albert Einstein, inventor Nikola Tesla, humanitarians Mahat-ma Gandhi and Mother Teresa, artist Frida Kahlo, author John Steinbeck, movie stars Marilyn Monroe and Humphrey Bogart, and entertainer Elvis Presley. Autographed private photographs documenting those extraordi-nary adventures graced an entire wall in my father's study. My favorite re-mained the one of Ernst Hemingway with a death grip on a bottle of rum, red-nosed and revealing all his teeth as he fished from an austere boat off the coast of Cuba.

Her eyes met mine and she landed beside Nick and me with a *whish* and a delicate scent that always made me think of puppy breath, sun-warmed sand, and freshly blossomed lilac. Brilliant green one second and milky white the next, her eyes exposed her torment. She studied me for some time and then asked, "Do I have your forgiveness, Celestine?"

I stared at my hands, kneaded my knuckles, and culled the tears forming with long sequential blinks. "I'm the one who should ask forgiveness."

"Nonsense. We shall have no such talk," she said and opened her arms.

I went to her without hesitation and crumpled when she pulled me close.

"If you two are going to start all that gushy crap, I'm outta here," Nick said, and I watched until I could no longer see his shirttail flapping behind him, the words *Send help! My Family is Nuts* screen-printed across the back.

Bianca rolled her eyes in Nick's direction but laughed. "Oh, Celeste. The thought of losing you forever was far too much to bear," she sputtered, kissing every inch of my face, now sandwiched between her palms.

"You did the right thing, Mom," I whispered. "I see that now."

She plucked a heart-shaped note from her bone-whaled corset. "I nearly forgot. Raina sends her love. She penned this delightful little memo with strict instructions I give this to her *mummy* straight away."

I opened the letter carefully so as not to destroy the delicate handtied ribbons and bows littering the outside. "Who's looking after her?" I asked, smiling as I read Raina's clumsily crafted poem.

She shifted her weight, seemed hesitant. "You must realize our options were severely limited. What with an au pair totally out of the question and every available member of the Realm engaged in the destruction of those dreadful Harvesters, in one part of the world or another, I am afraid we had little recourse but to charge Fane with the task."

I laughed . . . until my eyes met hers, and I realized she was deadly serious. "You're joking."

"In the beginning, he was quite resistant. To say that he threw a tantrum worthy of an overindulged child would be an understatement. One would think I had petitioned him to rake the oceans free of filth or slay a mutinous horde of foes. He can be quite theatrical, you know." She covered a giggle with a hand resembling polished porcelain. "I must admit, I do find his expressive demeanor rather amusing at times."

Thinking of Fane's many transgressions, particularly the time he suddenly appeared in a moving elevator with an unsuspecting elderly neighbor of mine, I felt a scowl form.

Fane was unicorns and rainbows, tornadoes and Armageddon, all wrapped up in one disturbing package.

Bianca suddenly chirped a laugh. "Darling, do you recall the times you discovered him in your bedroom, miming sexual instructions to that ineffectual ex-husband of yours?"

"I *recall* that I never told you about that."

She cleared her throat, shifty eyes landing on everything but me. "We seem to have deviated from the subject of Raina."

"How is she?" I heard the trepidation in my voice. "Please tell me that you *do* check in as often as possible."

"Most certainly. And not only because Fane insists on some *me-time*, as he calls it. I have grown quite fond of the child, though I must confess I can sympathize with his need for retreat. I, too, have grown weary of daily interactions with the preschool's dreadful headmistress." She began to imitate the headmistress. "'Raina refuses to account for the class's missing toad but has apparently replaced the specimen with a creature we've yet to identify. Raina maintains she can fly and that she was born in a region no longer on any map. Raina insists she's personally met Queen Victoria and'—with dramatic inflection, mind you—'she continues to correct her instructor on matters of all things, including the young woman's personal attire.' I could go on. It is positively exhausting, Celeste. For the life of me, I do not know how you manage."

I shook my head, hoping to clear it of so many frightening possibilities. "Seriously? You thought it would be a good idea to put Fane in charge?"

"Let it go, Celeste. You shall return home soon, and we can then put this all behind us. Perhaps we should join the others. I am told this evening's entertainment was placed in Leonardo's charge, and I must admit I am positively giddy at the prospect."

The operetta sounds of *Orpheus in the Underworld* commanded our attention, and we gathered before a gilded stage. Aligned in a colorful row, high-kicking stilettoed ostriches segued seamlessly into a familiar musical number I remembered from *Moulin Rouge*. Rousing applause followed the chorus line through chartreuse curtains, from which appeared a massive tuxedoed bullfrog clutching an antiquated shotgun microphone as it belted out a tune in the style of Frank Sinatra. I managed to tear my eyes from the stage and discovered da Vinci sweating laser-focused concentration and Matilda rolling her eyes.

Tristan covered my hand with his. "Tearing myself away from you the other night wasn't easy," he whispered in my ear, his breath blowing warm and soft across my cheek. "But eternity is now ours, and I have not been this happy for centuries."

Before I could respond, da Vinci's orchestra, comprised of bawdy, animated orangutans, then began a heavy-handed rendition of "Night Train," more commonly known as "The Stripper Song." The draperies parted, revealing a set reminiscent of vaudevillian days, and a feathered-fan-wielding elephant gradually rose from a vampire trap beneath the stage. The whining sound of the gears straining against the weight disrupted the conductor's concentration, and the gargantuan owl maestro puffed its downy cheeks, afterward stomping its mammoth batons in two with a crescendo-like flourish.

The African bush elephant appeared undaunted and proceeded to balance tremulously on one rear foot, afterward performing an impressive pirouette, while teasing the audience in grand burlesque style and occasionally offering an ingenious peek of what lay beyond her fans.

When the show was over, Elizabeth stared daggers at da Vinci and hissed, "Utterly disgraceful."

"I, for one, find it most delightful," Socrates said. "It so reminds me of the grand time had by all at this or that symposium. Memories most dear, I assure you."

Razvan attempted to camouflage a grin. Bianca revealed a tight smile and pitter-pattered applause. Nick pitched coins of various denominations onto the stage floor and called for an encore. I just wanted to go home.

Matilda cut loose with a high-pitched whistle. Once all eyes were upon her, she said, "Quite vulgar but most impressive nonetheless, Leonardo. I tip my hat to you, sir. The Elders and I have pressing matters to discuss, dear Toroks. Therefore, we must bid you au revoir."

"Look at him," Nick said, tipping his head in Tristan's direction as our family said their goodbyes to the Elders. "He can't wait to get those pasty hands of his all over you. Notice how Dadcula's giving him the evil eye?" he whispered in my ear. "Yeah, he knows *exactly* what Tristan is thinking about."

I elbowed Nick hard, observing my father with strangled breath. His jaw clenched and his veins pulsated beneath nearly translucent skin. "Knock it off, Nick, and you know how much I hate it when you call Razvan *Dadcula*."

He rubbed his arm and laughed. "Oh, shit," he sputtered soon after. "You really have lover boy worked up. Look," he said, wrenching my head in Tristan's direction.

"Oh, no," I muttered, the brilliant red glow surrounding Tristan intensifying. I'd seen this happen before but always behind closed doors.

"I hope somebody's prepared you for what's coming," Nick whispered past a menacing grin. "Because you're one of us now, he won't go easy on you." I scrunched my nose and wiggled out of his reach. It seemed nothing would ever separate my brother from all things immature.

Razvan cupped his fingers in our direction. Before Nick grabbed my hand and propelled me dizzyingly toward the Elders, he said, "I love you, Celeste. Call me selfish, but I'm glad things turned out the way they did. Now I don't have to worry about planning your funeral someday or hiding from those crazy fuckers because I refused to let you die." He handed me off to our father and then vaporized within a flaming orb.

Razvan's eyes followed Nick. He shook his head, a suggestion of a smile playing around his mouth, and I sensed a melding of machismo and embarrassment. "We shall see you soon," he said, when finally turning his attention to me. He pecked me on the cheek, in a manner befitting a king. "Safe travels, dearest daughter."

Bianca pulled me close, a radiant smile stretching ear to ear. "I have given Fane strict instructions he put Raina to bed hours before sunrise," she said with a mischievous wink. "Farewell, my darling. We're off to New Jersey."

I watched her drift higher, then higher still, and I stood there, unable to tear my eyes away, in awe of her butterfly-like grace, her ascent like a well-choreographed dance. A bloody tear slid down my cheek. I hadn't realized how much I had missed her. How she had sacrificed so much for Nick and me.

Tristan swept the tear away with the back of his hand. "What is this? Now is the time for celebration, my love. A time to truly begin our life together."

Matilda swooped before us, an angry breeze with a tumultuous air. "Are you quite done, Tristan of Tomisovara? Because the time has come for Celestine to bid her farewells." She turned to me, lips straining against a smile. "I wish you the best of luck. Godspeed and out you go, Celeste of the Family Torok."

Elizabeth approached me first. *Were those tears I saw in her eyes?* "Until we meet again, my dear, Celestine. Do not fear what lies ahead," she said. "Regardless of the distance between us, one of us shall always assist you in your endeavors, when appropriate."

Leonardo kissed me squarely on the mouth, his breath a mix of eucalyptus and sauerkraut. "I have entertained that very notion since you arrived." He licked his lips and seemed to study the ceiling. "Though I must say, it was rather anticlimactic. Much ado about nothing," he said with a wink.

"Do take care," Socrates told me. "I warrant we shall see one another again—and sooner than I would like."

I stared at the floor, gnawing my lip. "I'll miss you all," I sputtered, the words surprising me most of all. "Thank you for believing in me."

"If I may," Nostradamus began as he wedged himself between Tristan and me, "I should like to accompany my protégée home."

Tristan begrudgingly took a step back. Nostradamus laced his arm through mine, and we soared into the night's sky.

CHAPTER TWELVE

ostradamus released me, and I followed him, in awe of his rap-tor-like grace, my attention often diverted to the palace we'd left behind. Startled by our sudden appearance overhead, a dinosaur ducked just as I soared over the final mountaintop. Newly formed clouds ambled across a crescent moon and permitted a meager sliver of moonlight. Despite my preternatural vision, I couldn't distinguish much of anything above or below and increased my speed so as not to lose sight of Nostrada-mus.

Ominous dark clouds multiplied as we continued our journey, carrying with them the threat of rain. They parted once we neared the Missouri River. As we flew across, the wind intensified, creating anemic waves, crests shim-mering in the moonlight like haphazardly strewn garland. The wind at our backs propelled us along but made navigating cell towers and tall buildings hazardous.

From the air I spotted the wrought iron railing surrounding the wid-ow's walk atop the old Victorian mansion that had not only staked a claim on the historical registry but also my heart. As we swooped lower, I saw that Raina's light burned in her window and smoke billowed from the brick chimney despite the warm evening. Red and pink rose pedals smothered the old wraparound porch floor, and my favorite Righteous Brothers song, "Unchained Melody," rattled the windows in the foyer. I swallowed past a distasteful mingling of anticipation and apprehension. *Will time alone with Tristan be different now?*

Nostradamus dove then climbed and circled the apartment building next door, its parking lot practically adjoining the mansion's old carriage house.

What is he waiting for?

A bickering couple raised their voices, and I realized Nostradamus was waiting for them to take their argument inside. We rode the air current, and, in a continuous loop, we circled the house. I had never seen the house from that vantage point, and I noted several shingles in need of repair, plugged gutters, rotted soffit boards, and peeling paint.

After the couple huffed off in separate directions, I drifted down, my feet contacting the ground just as Nostradamus brushed several stray leaves from his velvet tunic.

"After you, mademoiselle," he said, tipping his head toward the side of the house.

I puffed my cheeks as I studied the stone and wood exterior. "Why don't we just use the door?"

He wagged his finger. "Practice makes perfect. Might I suggest the upper floor?" he said, and I followed his gaze to the second story, comprised entirely of disintegrating cedar planks.

Imperceptible molecules. Mind over matter. Imperceptible molecules. Mind over matter. Remembering an old but sturdy bookcase lined the entire wall on the inside, I chose a spot near the corner. I imagined my body nothing more than a big glob of pliable putty, the stone and wood an accommodating sieve. I then imagined myself in the middle of the bedroom I had previously designated a sitting room/library. I took a deep breath, closed my eyes, and then smacked into the siding—like a bird unaware of a glass partition—and ricocheted off the house. "Heavens," Nostradamus said and helped me to my feet. "To hear Leonardo tell it, you claimed victory when last attempting teleportation." A shadow blanketed the moonlight overhead, drawing our attention to the roof, where Leonardo sat twiddling his thumbs, legs swinging like a restless child's, *bonk-bonk-bonking* against the eave.

"May I render assistance?" he asked.

Nostradamus folded his arms and looked down his nose. "Please do, for it seems you either exaggerated her success or chose to knowingly share a falsehood."

"You are wrong on both counts," Leonardo said. "I merely awakened her ability. Allow me to demonstrate."

Deep inside my head, I felt the familiar tickle, as if tiny combs raked specific portions of my brain.

"Try again, dear girl," Leonardo whispered.

Random thoughts faded into nothingness, Leonardo's suggestion commanding my psyche. Following a minor jolt, I appeared on the other side and found Tristan waiting there, wearing a salacious grin and not much else. I tossed him a cashmere throw I'd scooped from the back of a chair, jerked my chin toward a shoulder, and wondered how he had arrived ahead of us.

"Leonardo and Nostradamus are just outside," I whispered.

"Accompanying you here was not enough?" he said past a set jaw and blazing eyes. "They intend to join us?"

"I haven't told Nostradamus goodbye."

Nostradamus materialized alongside me and offered Tristan a curt nod.

"Very well, I shall leave you to it," Tristan said, a slight edge to his voice. With that, he vanished.

I threw my arms around Nostradamus. "Had it not been for you, I don't know how I would have managed," I told him, the words hardly worthy of all he had done for me.

"It was my pleasure, mademoiselle." He drew me closer, then whispered in my ear, "You will change the world a little at a time, Celeste. Of this, I am certain."

And, as a tear slipped from my eye, he faded within a celestial mist.

"Celeste," Tristan whispered, filling the room with lust and paralyzing expectation. I turned, expecting to find him there, but didn't see him. I murmured his name, the final consonant still on my lips when he appeared, crossing the room in a blink's time, and pulled me into his arms. He kissed me urgently, forcefully, so differently from the times before, and I knew everything Nick had said was true.

CHAPTER THIRTEEN

O ur lips still connected, he swept me up and took me to our bed, where rows of candles lent a consecrated ambiance. The flames seemed to flicker at his command, creating images on an adjacent wall of lovers in various throes of passion.

He pulled off my jeans, slowly and methodically, his lips sucking, kissing the soft flesh inside my thighs, the backs of my knees. My head spun with desire, and I reached for him while I murmured his name. Grabbing my ankles, he spread my legs wide; his lips roamed once again as warm determined fingers disappeared inside me. On the brink of ecstasy, I snapped my eyes open when he stopped, and I bolted upright, trembling in delirious anticipation as he began removing my blouse. He tossed it aside and his fingers strolled under the straps then along the top of my bra, finally snaking their way underneath.

I quivered, wet and ready, and whispered his name. "Tristan," I repeated, loudly, pleadingly, desperately, and he raised his head. Devious honey-gold irises haloed his crimson pupils. A mischievous smile corrupted sensual lips. Elongated, glimmering canine teeth shredded my bra and then his tongue—hot, wet, and feathery soft—bathed my nipples in euphoria. I shook violently, shredding his back, relishing his bloody flesh beneath my fingernails. He rocked backward, righting himself in one fluid motion. He stripped off his pants, a smile affecting every glorious inch of his face when my hungry eyes moved over him, and I ran my tongue over piercing fangs. Then he stood over me, straddling me, tormenting me. He flipped me onto my stomach, tugged my knees toward him, and thrust himself inside as I screamed his name. On the precipice of orgasm once again, I clung to him when he shifted position and rolled me on top of him. He gripped my shoulders and guided me into a seated position, then cupped my breasts, fervent fingers looping my nipples. Grinding, writhing, our bodies in unison, we climaxed simultaneously, Tristan howling while I sank my teeth into his neck. I began to convulse as an ungodly energy surged through my body. I absorbed his power and with it came a clarity, a complete understanding of everything within the universe.

A moan swelled in my throat and with it escaped a gush of all the amorous things left unspoken. Taking my face in his hands, his eyes whispering *I love you*, he drove his fangs into my jugular, and we began again.

Hours later, Tristan collapsed onto his back and combed his fingers through drenched hair. He sighed blissfully, then cradled me in his arms. I stroked his chest, and he kissed the tip of my nose, then cocked his head toward a window drizzling condensation.

"It can't be morning already," I groaned. "Can't we just lie here?"

"It's not safe, Celeste," he said, nuzzling my ear.

"But you slept in my bed before—"

"Indeed, I did, my love. At my own peril. But now, I have you to worry about."

"But the blinds are closed, the curtains drawn. No one's going to come in here and open them."

He arched a brow. "Of this, you can't be certain." He was right. I thought of the time the maintenance crew barged into my former apartment unannounced as I was climbing out of the bathtub.

"Daylight has become your enemy. You must always remember to cover yourself from the light of day. Promise me," he said, lifting my chin.

"But I remember you, Nick too, often—"

"Greeted the sun? Yes, but never for more than an hour, two at most, and never without concealing every inch, head to toe. Come, I have a surprise." He swept me into his arms and glided across the hall, where he unlocked the utility closet and swept the door to the wall.

In addition to a broom shedding bristles, a neglected Dyson vacuum, and a mop that had yet to meet water, the room hid a gleaming coffin large enough to accommodate two. Following a prolonged kiss, he laid me inside and settled in beside me. He moved his arm overhead, and I scooched closer. Snug up against him, I stroked his cheek and ran my fingers over his lips.

"It's so good to have you home, Celeste," he said through a yawn, bringing my hand to his lips.

"It's good to be home. I'm looking forward to a long lazy night, just you, me, and Raina."

His chest heaved and he expelled a long sigh. "I depart come sunset."

"No," I said, propping onto an elbow. "Can't it wait?"

"Our foe has rallied, and the Omniscients demand our attendance, Celeste. What would you have me do?"

I was formulating more questions when his breathing slowed; soft nonsensical murmurs escaped his lips, long dark eyelashes erratically fluttering. I swept a stray strand of hair farther from his eyelid and considered discovering the answers to my questions by stealing a peek inside that complicated head of his. Met with hundreds of voices speaking at once and vivid chaotic images—most involving strategic plans or ghoulish battle scenes—I terminated the connection by filling my head with random trivial thoughts.

Then he murmured her name.

Intruding upon his private thoughts once again, my breath caught when I saw his wife, Alexandra. Although her complexion was fairer, her eyes more green than blue, her features a bit more prominent, the resemblance between us was undeniable. Involved in a bitter argument with a merchant who'd swindled her out of a silver sixpence, she flung long golden waves over a defiant shoulder while jeering bystanders garbed in ruffled linen shirts overlaid with doublets jockeyed their pints of ale outside an English pub.

She set down a bucket of coal and raised a fist, her other wrapped tightly around a parcel of bound wheat. Tristan abandoned a conversation with several sixteenth-century English noblemen and swung a leg over a gleaming black horse. The stallion pounded hooves against compacted earth, dust settling on the horse's gilded armor-plated chest piece. Tristan dismounted in a fluid slide, served her a rakish grin, and bowed arrogantly.

"Milady, may I be of assistance?"

"Indeed, my good sir. This lubberwort has trifled with the wrong sort. I shan't be a willing participant to his thievery."

The scene faded, and Tristan's thoughts shifted to a lowland lush meadow bursting with deep purple columbine, tall pink foxglove serenaded by energetic bees, ice-blue forget-me-nots, and lemon-yellow daffodils. From his horse, he collected a cloak bearing the king's crest. He tossed it among a grouping of red poppies, took her in his arms, and laid her down. Her long hair spread about her, backdrop worthy.

He undressed her tenderly, and I swallowed past a lump when his hands, his lips, began to explore her body, slowly, painstakingly. I felt a flush of resentment, prickly sensations building from my scalp to my toes. How different he had always been with me until tonight! Foreplay had always been practically nonexistent, an unnecessary extravagance. Was it because he had loved her more?

He moaned suddenly and turned away from me, and his thoughts once again became erratic. He flipped back over, a radiant smile stretching his lips. I dipped in again and found him and Alexandra on a beach, her arm slipped around his waist.

She smiled up at him as he tossed a baby into the air, seagulls swooping and squawking in the background, and then the memory vanished, as though a candle abruptly extinguished.

I jumped when he cried out beside me, his fangs erupting past taut lips. I shook him gently and his torturous wail ebbed to a strangled moan. Another memory had surfaced: Tristan, head in hands, surrounded by mass graves and hushed condolences. The body collectors wheeled a death cart, wooden wheels creaking and squalling, toward the plague pit reserved for victims of the Black Death. Black pustules dotted Alexandra's pallid flesh, her arm escaping a waxed cloth confinement. Tears swamping his face, Tristan howled a grief-stricken scream and lunged for the cart. Longtime friends, Ariel and Paulo, tackled then restrained him, long after a wall of fire consumed the bodies of his wife and child.

Bloody tears ran down his cheeks, soaking the pillow we shared. I whispered his name, and his eyes fluttered open. "Baby, I love you so much," I said. "I'll never leave you."

He smiled, turned into me, and pulled me close. "And I love you. Sleep now, my love."

I woke to Fane's disturbing grin as he pinched open the coffin lid. "Rise and shine, my slumbering properly deflowered flower. For a rapturous rendezvous, though riotous it may have been, is no excuse for laziness."

I ignored him and discovered Tristan gone without as much as a goodbye. A toxic mingling of anger and sadness reddened my cheeks, and I wanted to wrestle the lid closed before Fane noticed.

The lid snapped shut and he yelped. He forced it open and began hopping on one foot and then the other. "Now look what you've done, you insolent hussy. Thanks to you, I've chipped a nail."

"Maybe you'll remember that the next time you come in here uninvited. How can you wear those ridiculous things anyway? They don't even look real."

"Humph. I shan't entertain the slightest offense, given the criticism comes from someone with about as much fashion sense as a common beggar. And to think, finding myself with rapturous spare time on my hands since Bianca's return, I chose to spread my renowned good cheer with the likes of you."

I pushed him out of the way, and then I tumbled from the coffin. "Don't do me any favors."

"I would have thought the aftereffect of such glorious ecstasy might have altered your usual sour mood."

"Don't you have anything better to do?"

He puffed his chest beneath a neon orange Nehru jacket and straightened the braided ropes canopying exaggerated shoulder pads. "Alas, no."

I shoved him out of the way, my intention to grab a bottle from the refrigerator, but he beat me to it, intercepting one in a grand flourish.

"Ah, 2019." He rolled his tongue across his palate. "Acceptable, I suppose, though aged blood too often compromises the bubbly undercurrent. Allow me," he said and poured me a glass.

Wearing an obnoxious grin, he watched me sip from the glass. I rolled my eyes while I continued to drink, still dehydrated from the night before. He quickly became bored and began fumbling with the large colorful buttons scattered disproportionately over his jacket.

"I have missed you," he said, without making eye contact. "You are the salt to my pepper, the logic to my illogic, the yin to my yang."

I set the glass aside, crossed my arms, and squinted with suspicion. "What do you want, Fane?"

He gasped and clutched his chest, then dropped his head and slouched his shoulders. "I expose my innermost feelings, and that is your response? I *have* missed you . . . terribly."

I scuffed my feet back and forth over the Italian-tile flooring. "I'm sorry, okay? I didn't realize you were serious. You seldom are."

"And?" he said, raising his head just enough for me to see his eyes.

"All right. I missed you, too. *And* thank you for taking care of Raina."

"How she missed you! 'When is Mummy coming home? What do you suppose Mummy is doing at this very minute? Is she thinking of me?' Quite redundant, it was. I can tell you, with all certainty, that I shall never own a parrot."

I picked up the glass and hid a grin. "Fane, she's just a kid. And from what Bianca told me, I think she's equally taken with *you*."

His eyes suddenly shone with excitement. "I dare say she is most intuitive, particularly as it involves that dreadful game hide-and-seek. Most often, she only requires a night, two at most, to find me."

"Oh my God. *A night or two?* She's five years old, Fane."

He crinkled his nose, and I knew an argument was forming. "Five, you say? To forfeit discussion, allow me only to remind you that the young lass has had over two hundred years to cultivate her cunning and resourceful skills, skills which she too often displays at that dreadful school."

I felt what little color I had drain from my face. Maybe Bianca hadn't told me everything. "What skills exactly?"

"Perhaps I have overstepped."

"Oh no. You are not going to shut that annoying trap of yours now. Spill it."

"As you wish, but before I say a word more, do show some mercy, dear girl."

"Keep talking, Fane."

"She may have taken a shortcut, as it were, to the schoolyard on occasion."

"What kind of shortcut?"

"Why travel down two flights of slippery stairs when one can simply fly out the window? Such a preposterous notion."

"What else?" I asked, horrified at the possibilities. Because I knew Fane habitually saved the worst news for last, I felt my anxiety escalating.

"Certainly you have heard her speak of Blain Beaumont?"

"Yes, the bully. What about him?" I asked past a lump.

"That is not how she refers to him, now is it?" Fane asked, beneath raised eyebrows.

"No, she calls him Blain the Meddlesome—"

"Vermin. Quite right, Mummy Dearest. At her wit's end one particular afternoon, what do you suppose became of prickly little Master Beaumont before she chose to grant him a few hours of repose within her desk?"

A hand flew over my mouth. "Oh my God. What did she turn him into?"

"A bloated rodent, what else?" Fane threw back his head and laughed. "Not only was Raina spared an afternoon of vicious maltreatment but her contentious school chum endured hours of passionate interrogation when prompted for an explanation for his absence, to which he, of course, could provide none."

"Is that it?"

"To offer supplementary accounts would prove redundant."

"So you're saying this is commonplace?" I asked between gritted teeth.

"Who in heaven's name could blame her for acting out?" Fane asked, rushing to my side. "Those hideous schoolmarms chastise her with every breath." In very Fane-like fashion, he imitated the teachers. "'Eat something other than meat, Raina. Did your mother even take time to cook that? You are getting blood all over the cafeteria floor, Raina.' Pick. Pick. Pick. Add Blain the Vermin to the mix and, I dare say, I considered keeping her home. And I would have, had she not thrown a fit the likes of, well, me."

I felt a migraine coming on and refilled the glass. "When you say you *witnessed*, did anyone witness you witnessing?" Suddenly any supernatural stunt Raina may have performed seemed much less damaging in comparison.

He laughed, and I caught a glimpse of diamond tongue studs. "A trade secret, I regret to say, you inquisitive fiend."

"So you're saying you made yourself invisible."

"Precisely, my perceptive chum," he said, a pyramid of bracelets jingling as he wiggled his wrists. "The Hidden Cloak, though most challenging— and not so unlike teleportation—definitely has its advantages."

"Will you teach me sometime?"

He rolled his eyes and collapsed into a chair. "What were you doing with the Elders all this time? Enjoying the sights, while I endured the never-ending ramblings of that precocious child?"

I folded my arms hard across my chest. "Will you or won't you, Fane?"

He sighed and looked away. "I cannot. There, I have disclosed my short-comings, which you shall revel in till time eternal, to be quite sure."

"Why can't you?"

"Because *I* was neither granted the Power of Persuasion nor the power of telepathy, my obtuse friend, both of which would greatly benefit such instruction."

CHAPTER FOURTEEN

I insisted Fane treat himself to a night on the town, which was a much greater reward for me. Raina was due to return home any minute, and I readied a cozy little nook off the living room, adding a few more books to her stack of ones most cherished, afterward tidying up boxes upon boxes of intermediate puzzles previously strewn about the floor.

An hour passed and when she and Bianca hadn't arrived, I decided to collect a dusty bookcase from an otherwise empty bedroom. The door creaked open on rusty ornate hinges. Once inside, I ran my fingers over the hand-painted, flocked Victorian wallpaper, the floral pattern somewhat faded and worn but one of the reasons I had fallen in love with the house.

Rather than drag the bookcase down the long flight of stairs, I imagined it in the corner of the little nook. When I arrived downstairs, I found it there. Arranging the books alphabetically, I tucked them inside, then stepped back to admire my handiwork. Discovering one out of sequence, I plucked it from its spot and a photograph taken of me fluttered toward the floor. Swiping a piece of lint from the backside, I realized it was a fiber from Raina's favorite blanket. I visualized her clutching the photo as she reclined in her tiny coffin, lined with astrological images, surrounded by militia sentries comprised of various stuffed animals. I sighed and felt my heart drop. That was the last photograph she'd ever have of me, and I would never have one of her.

Bianca's cheery greeting echoed throughout the house, and I returned the photograph to the book. I glided toward the grand entry hall, and Raina whirled around. Instantly, she took a quick step back and hid her face within Bianca's billowing skirts.

Bianca looked at me, a valley forming between her brows. "Whatever is the matter, my pet?" she asked Raina.

"She is one of *them* now," Raina whimpered.

Bianca covered a laugh. "I assure you, she is not, my precious. Come now, out where your mummy can see you."

Raina shook her head and refused to look at me.

"You have a glow. And your eyes look a bit depraved, darling," Bianca informed me.

Confused, I tossed my arms in the air.

"The S-E-X," she mouthed. "It seems to have had a lingering effect." She coaxed Raina from the folds of her skirts and knelt so they were eye level. "Mummy has come a long way. Do you know why?"

Raina shook her head, peering at me through her tiny fingers.

"Because she has missed you terribly. So much that she could not stay away another minute."

"It's true," I said, dropping to my knees and opening my arms wide. "Would you like me to tell you about all the different animals I saw while I was away?"

She nodded, her eyes shiny with anticipation. Then she ran to me, wrapping her arms tightly around my neck, her short legs around my waist.

"Please say you shan't ever leave me again," she whispered in my ear, her soft breath falling in harried, staccato bursts.

Later that night, after hearing all about the magical creatures within the Hollow Earth, Raina yawned and slipped from my lap. Teetering toward the nook, she plopped down and began repositioning the miniature furnishings within her dollhouse. Humming the seventeenth-century ballad "Bessy Bell and Mary Gray," she looked from me to Bianca until she was satisfied she had our undivided attention.

"I think not returning to school is in Raina's best interest," Bianca said in a hushed tone. "The headmistress, the lot of them, really, have expressed further suspicion. This places the Realm in a most precarious position. I simply do not see any other recourse."

Raina would be heartbroken, but I agreed. I didn't see an alternative. "But I have to work—"

"You *prefer* to work," she corrected. "Two decidedly different inferences." She clasped my hand and emitted a feeble laugh. "Oh, I do not fault you. Rearing a child—even one as exceptional as Raina—is often insufferable."

I squeezed her hand. "Why do I feel so guilty?" *She's not even mine.*

"Tut, tut. She shall see you every day, and she absolutely adores Fane."

"So, you've already told him?"

She nodded, the corners of her lips twisting in a maniacal grin. "I suppose you can imagine the drama."

I didn't care to. Fane was exhausting. "Is Tristan with Dad and Nick?" *He left without saying goodbye.*

"The entire coalition has relegated its attention to the Far East, the threat being what it is."

I knew the threat was the Harvesters. "What's the attraction?"

She sighed, releasing her angst in a prolonged breath. "Internment camps have always provided access to easy prey, a multitude of victims long ago defeated." She laughed suddenly, the sound so sinister Raina glanced again in our direction. "With any luck, the Harvesters have already killed those responsible for such a horrid injustice. And if they haven't, well, we shan't lift a finger to save their wretched lives, I can assure you."

"Why can't you combine the potion with a vaccine and destroy the Harvesters like we've done before?"

"It *was* most effective, 'tis true." She twittered a laugh. "Imagine their surprise when, after gorging themselves on tainted blood, those gluttonous vampires found themselves robbed of immortality. For one thing, there simply was not sufficient time to prepare and distribute the vaccine in this instance. I do so hate to rush off, Celestine," she said, her gaze flicking from me to Raina.

A surge of apprehension came over me. "So soon?"

"Darling, you know very well that my place in times of peril is at your father's side."

"When do you think you'll return?"

Her eyes glazed over, her skin shone yellow, then polished pewter, and I knew she was observing the ongoing battle in Asia. Rather than answer, she suddenly appeared beside Raina and brushed her lips over her forehead. "Do be a good girl and watch over Mummy. Grandmamma shall return at the first opportunity."

After Bianca left, Raina and I worked every puzzle, our combined preternatural abilities making easy work of even the most challenging ones. After we'd stacked the last box neatly on the bottom shelf of the reclaimed bookcase, Raina sighed, and I saw a lifetime of disappointment reflected in her beautiful brown eyes.

She would never know a lover, never have a career, never bear children. Her waking hours must seem like one tedious loop. Attending the Academy Montessori was a bright light in her otherwise dreary existence, and I was the one appointed to tell her she would never return. The words on the tip of my tongue, I stalled.

"What's wrong, Mummy?"

I feigned a smile and gathered her to me. "I was just thinking how much I've missed you."

"Will you tell me of the dinosaurs again? P-l-lease."

"Oh, not again." I teased as I rolled my eyes and wiggled her onto my lap.

A few minutes before dawn, I fell asleep with Tristan on my mind and Raina snoring softly beside me. An hour before sunset, she moaned, afterward crying out while she kicked and screamed.

I tried to shake her awake. "Raina, you're having a nightmare," I cooed, dodging her flailing limbs and tiny white fangs. Pinning her down with one arm, I managed to open the coffin lid, then lift her out. Her eyes snapped open, pupils dilated and quickly transitioning from orange to black. I held her close, walking the room as I rocked her. "Shush, baby, everything's all right."

"Mummy, I saw the Bad Ones again," she said and buried her head in my chest.

I knew she meant the Harvesters. I could easily imagine the horrifying things she had experienced during the vampires' siege of the ship. "It was only a dream, Raina. Sometimes it helps to talk about it. Do you want to do that?"

She raised her head, wide eyes returning to normal as she searched the room. "They flew through the fog," she said, the fangs corrupting her pronunciation of some of the words. "And I-I saw their wicked teeth. Then I saw their eyes of red, Mummy. And I was so scared!" Whimpering, she gripped my nightshirt with both hands.

"*What* is going on in here?" Fane said, wafting through the door. "How can I be expected to acquire my beauty sleep amid all this hullabaloo? I thought perhaps the circus was in town and Raina was hosting a few rowdy elephants and a gaggle of hyenas." He pretended to search in the coffin, under it, and then the closets and dresser drawers. "I give up. Where, oh where, are you hiding those boisterous ingrates, Raina?"

Raina giggled and shook her head, glossy ringlets falling about her face. "No elephants, silly. No hyenas."

"No hyenas? Are you quite sure? Because I am certain I heard a wretched screeching sound, but perhaps it was only your mummy singing your favorite lullaby."

I scrunched my face, offering a sarcastic smile. "You're hilarious, Fane."

He dropped to his knees and buried his head in Raina's lap. "Dearest Raina, *please* tell me there are, at the very least, lions, tigers, and bears."

"No, Fane. Not a one," Raina said, patting his head, her eyes glowing with anticipation.

"Well, that is most disappointing, as I simply adore a circus," Fane said, popping upright. He paced the floor, scratching his chin. "Hmm, I have an idea. There must be a circus to be found somewhere in this tepid town, and, Raina, you and I shall find it."

"I think Raina needs to get some sleep. And I think she's seen more than her share of clowns, lately. Don't you, Fane?"

Fane landed a smirk, then said, "I think not."

Raina gasped, then pattered applause, as his feet tripled in size within colorful clunky boots, his face snow-white beneath a bulbous red nose.

CHAPTER FIFTEEN

I bristled when Fane appeared in my bedroom the following evening. I
yanked up my trousers, jerked the zipper closed, and covered my naked
breasts with both hands.

"Aren't you supposed to be watching Raina?"

His answer came in the form of a yawn, his gaze rolling over my body.

"Most perplexing. How one can consume merely liquid, yet gain considerable weight is beyond my comprehension. I dare say it looks as though
you have swallowed a rather significant object. Perhaps, unknowingly, you
partook of a bed pillow during a fitful sleep."

I felt the heat rise, a slow burn rippling through my body. I pointed to
the door. "Out, Fane."

"No need to worry about me. I am perfectly comfortable where I sit."

Nostradamus's words replayed in my head: *To think it, is to bring it to
fruition.* I envisioned Fane pinned to a wall just outside and smothered a
triumphant laugh when a whoosh of air slammed the door. Unfortunately,
I'd done something wrong because I turned to find Fane still seated in the
chair and grinning like an idiot.

"It seems your little plot has failed miserably. Get rid of me, will you? That's gratitude for you. And to think I left the boudoir of a rather comely young lad to do your bidding. Is there no end to my charitable and selfless deeds?"

Buttoning my blouse, I showed him my back. "Didn't anyone ever teach you about boundaries?" I asked through clenched teeth.

He pressed a palm my way. "I suppose my remark was a bit incendiary. For that, you have my heartfelt apology. After all, who among us appreciates attention drawn to our disgusting shortcomings?"

"You call that an apology?"

He smiled past jagged teeth and batted a pair of false eyelashes. "Alas, 'tis the most I can offer."

"I'm late," I said, more to myself than him, turning in circles as I searched the room for my car keys.

Fane whistled. "Looking for these?"

"Damn it, Fane." I snatched the keys away, the keyring slicing his finger and filling the air with the decadent scent of fresh blood.

He glared at me as he slurped blood from the wound. "You are positively wicked," he said past a pout. "By the by, when, precisely, do you intend to advise that precious child she shall no longer attend that veritable prison? She was most upset that no one bothered to awaken her at the proper time."

I ran my fingers through my hair and cursed when a fingernail snagged a stubborn tangle. "Oh crap. I totally forgot." *How could I have forgotten something so important?*

"I surmised as much. Which is why I took the initiative."

"Thank you, Fane. How did she take it?" I glanced at my watch. "And please give me the short version."

"Better than one might expect . . . once I vowed to introduce her to many enchanting adventures."

Only partially listening, I turned in circles while quietly ticking off every item I needed to remember. Racing across the room, I grabbed my shield from the nightstand and my gun from the safe. "Okay, I've got to run. Promise me, Fane: No more hide-and-seek."

⁓ ⁓ ⁓

Clocking in at ten minutes until ten p.m., I slammed the locker door closed on a bulletproof vest, various toiletries, and a photograph of Nick taken in happier times, which led me to contemplate the remedy for my upcoming photo ID and the reason a vampire's image couldn't be captured on film. Maybe it was time to consider an alternate vocation.

Until then, I planned to put away as many dangerous criminals as inhumanly possible.

Turning the corner to the detectives' bullpen, I found an attractive brunette seated at my desk. Biceps bulged beneath her oxford shirt and her thighs resembled tree trunks. She looked as if she substituted steroids for food. She leaned left, then right, and cracked her neck and the sound permeated the room. I suddenly had a craving for walnuts and earplugs. I cleared my throat to get her attention.

She spun the chair around, her eyes darting to the detective shield clipped on my belt. "What do you need?"

Her aggressive tone reinforced my steroid theory. "I'm Detective Crenshaw. You're sitting in my chair."

She trilled her lips and gathered a few folders and personal items. What she didn't stuff into pockets, she secured under one arm. "Sorry, Goldilocks, I was told you wouldn't be back for a few more days. I'm Detective Reed, by the way," she said without extending her hand.

"I haven't seen you around. You must be new."

She delivered a snappy nod, her eyes scanning the department. "Transferred from Chicago. Captain Burke told me to use your desk until mine arrives." She ratcheted upright, threaded a thumb through a belt loop, and threw her shoulders back. "There must have been a breakdown in communication."

I resisted a scowl and managed a blank stare. "Looks like we'll be sharing a desk. Grab a chair from the canteen while I make room."

She returned to find me scooping a photo of Nick and me and one of our biological parents into the top drawer. I tossed an autographed Royals baseball in the second drawer alongside a Kansas City Chiefs paperweight.

She brought me a cup of coffee, a kind of peace offering I assumed. "Thanks," I said, producing my blood-filled thermos, "but I always bring my own."

She shrugged. "The coffee's that bad here?"

"Worse. Some say it can eat the lacquer off the desks."

"Good to know," she said, retracing her steps to the canteen with a Styrofoam cup in each hand.

"How long have you been a detective?" I asked when she returned, mostly as a gesture of goodwill. Small talk was not my forte.

She positioned her chair opposite mine, the chrome feet scraping the floor and marring the yellowed linoleum.

"Three years."

"Why'd you leave Chicago, if you don't mind me asking?"

She served me a hard stare and appeared to debate her answer. "I prefer not to air my dirty laundry."

"I get that." *I had enough to fill every washing machine in the city.* Something about her was off. I attempted to access her thoughts and failed. Unable to read her mind, I was left to rely on the techniques I'd picked up as a detective; I held her gaze, kept quiet, and waited for her to elaborate.

"Let's just say I left Chicago PD because I needed a change and leave it at that."

I thought about my own uprooting, leaving New Jersey and returning to my birthplace after Nick's stubborn streak cost him his mortality and me my life as I knew it. Maybe all the shit I'd been through lately was altering my perspective. Still . . .

"Fine by me," I said and surrendered both palms. "Change is rough, but it can be a good thing." I nearly choked on the lie.

"We'll see," she said looking down flared nostrils. "Burke tells me you transferred from days?"

I nodded. "I've got a foster kid. I need to be home during the day."

"When do you sleep?" Her question seemed forced, expected. Her blank eyes and clenched jaw confirmed she really didn't give a shit. But it was more than that; it seemed like she was assessing me, worried I might already know something about her past that she didn't want known.

What that something was, I couldn't begin to guess. "Every chance I get," I said without missing a beat. "You got kids?" I asked, turning the tables, putting her in the hot seat once again.

She shook her head. "Never found the time or a worthy sperm donor. How'd you end up with a foster kid?"

Ah, now she'd served the ball back in my court. She knew how to play this game. "An incident last year left her an orphan." I shrugged to make my detachment more convincing. "She got attached to me, so I thought I'd step in until DFS could find her a good home." *Last year? Hardly. The incident nearly two-hundred years ago left her an orphan.*

She crossed her arms and sneered. "Oh, you're one of those. I bet you have a houseful of mangy stray dogs and cats, too."

My attempt at diplomacy was nearing an end. Reed definitely rubbed me the wrong way. "Nope, just the kid," I volleyed back (*and a very gay and very annoying vampire*). I had a feeling her superiors may have suggested a job change and not only celebrated her leaving but also declared that day an official fucking holiday.

"You working the gang-related homicides? Because if you are, I'm gonna be right up-front. I do things my way. If given the choice, I prefer to work alone."

I tipped my head toward the captain's office. "I haven't been assigned anything yet. And, believe me, Detective, I hear you loud and clear. I had you pegged for a lone wolf right out of the gate."

"It's nothing personal, Crenshaw. I just find it's easier to concentrate, particularly when I'm dealing with six gangbanger-related homicides and escalating turf wars. I don't need a bunch of mommy-drama, nor do I have time to look at a collection of *adorable* photos."

Determined not to be the first to break a dead stare, I gave in but only because Burke signaled me from his office. I was grateful for any excuse to get away but surprised to find him there after six p.m. I tipped my head in his direction. "Well, looks like we'll know whether you're flying solo soon enough. Keep your fingers crossed, Detective," I said, offering her a sarcastic smile.

I stepped through his door and pretended not to notice the golf bag tucked away beside a file cabinet every bit as dull and rusty as the man who rarely used either. Recently undergoing a half-assed renovation, the room reeked of enamel paint, of a chemical composition so strong the K9 Unit might very well mistake Burke's office for a meth lab. An eleven-by-fourteen-inch photo of him hung crookedly on the wall behind his desk, squeezed alongside various articles boasting his achievements over the years.

He glanced up, his eyes sweeping over me briefly then returning to a sportsman magazine. "Welcome back, Detective."

"Thank you, Captain. I'm surprised to find you here at this time of night." I wanted to drill him about Reed, but Burke despised workplace melodrama as much as I did and, like me, he respected the right to privacy. Besides, he probably wouldn't know the answers to the kind of questions I wanted to ask.

Instead of offering me an explanation for his late night, he motioned for me to take a seat. He looked toward the door. When open, it provided an adequate view of anyone entering the squad room. He checked his watch and mumbled something I probably would have preferred not to hear anyway.

"Quaid should have been here by now," he said long moments later, still flipping through photographs of downed deer and glassy-eyed trout.

"Quaid?"

"That's right. He'll be working the graveyard shift from now on." He studied me for a moment. "You look different, Crenshaw. A bit green around the gills."

"That flu really hit me hard, sir," I lied, "but I'm feeling much better."

"Glad to hear it." *Rustle, flip. Rustle, flip.* "So your partner hasn't been in touch?"

I shook my head. Quaid had never been a part of my personal life, and I preferred to keep it that way.

"I guess you won't be surprised to learn Quaid had no choice." He grunted a chuckle. "Unless you consider resigning after a thirty-year tenure an option."

I wondered what had happened in the short time I'd been away, but, just like the questions I had about Reed, I wasn't about to ask.

Burke pointed a short stubby finger at my face. "Keep him away from the media. If the press can't be avoided, you take the lead. So why the transfer, Crenshaw? I'm sure it's in your file, but why not save me the aggravation?"

"Personal obligations, Captain." *And a sudden opposition to daylight.* Hoodies weren't exactly considered appropriate law enforcement attire.

He waved any further explanation away. "Good enough," he said nodding as he unwrapped two pieces of Juicy Fruit gum and crammed them both in his mouth. "Finally giving up the cancer sticks. It's pure hell."

The captain's communication skills paralleled an antiquated telephone system, pretty much consisting of two longs and a short. He referenced his watch again, an angry flush further eroding his sunbaked features, which brought to mind a cranky sea captain. His posture seemed to relax when I saw Quaid's reflection appear in the smudged photo frame behind the desk. Quaid plopped down in the chair next to mine and gave me a quizzical glance but didn't offer a greeting to either Burke or me.

The captain scowled. "You're late."

Quaid shrugged. "I'm here, which is more than I intended an hour ago."

"Actions have consequences, Detective."

Quaid smiled thinly and leaned back in the chair, satisfied when the front legs no longer contacted the new faux-wood vinyl flooring. "Something I'm sure the voters are beginning to realize, now that that buffoon has completely fucked up this city."

Burke folded his arms across a barrel chest and took a measured breath, breathing in, then out, in wheezy spurts. "Every television station and every newspaper are now well aware there's no love lost between you and Mayor Sullivan. You have a gripe about police funding or the DA's policy, take it to your union rep, not the goddamn press. Like it or not, we answer to the mayor, Quaid. Keep those type of remarks under your hat or else. If I hear you've come within ten feet of a member of the press or the mayor, you're fired. Do we understand each other?"

Quaid propelled himself forward, a homicidal glint in his eyes, and the front legs of the chair clacked against the floor. "Aye, aye, Captain."

Burke swept a hand down his face, then cupped both armpits. "From here on out, the only on-call detectives are the two of you and Detective Reed out there. Ramirez, Chastain, Donahue, and Franklin will assist only when necessary. That includes weekends. Keep working the sex trafficking ring you've been assigned," he said to Quaid. "*Only* conduct interviews during the day that can't be handled otherwise. Crenshaw will assist on every one of them. Think of her as a glorified babysitter. Just don't expect any overtime."

Quaid smacked the desk. "That's bullshit."

"That's karma. The same goes for you, Crenshaw—no overtime. It's not in the budget. Now, get the hell out of my office."

CHAPTER SIXTEEN

———

"Well, aren't you just full of surprises," Quaid said behind me as I headed toward my desk. "Just couldn't stand the thought of working with anyone else?"

"Whatever you want to believe, Quaid."

"Did you happen to catch me on Channel 5?" he asked, ignoring Detective Reed and smooshing his generous backside on the corner of my desk.

"Regretfully, no."

He laughed, unveiling several capped and discolored teeth. "Goddamn idiot mayor. He thinks he can cut this department off at the knees and still expect results."

"Maybe the pandemic shrank the budget more than we realize, and he had no choice."

"Oh, you're correct about that. It's a budget issue, all right, but it has nothing to do with the pandemic. Get your head out of the sand, Crenshaw. Empty prison cells are money in the city's pocket. With that guy," he said, jerking a thumb toward the mayor's portrait sullying the wall, "it's all about the bottom line. He doesn't give two shits about the incarcerated. Mark my words. Before you know it, they'll be handing out flower bouquets instead of citations."

I blew out a bellyful of frustration. "Above my pay grade, Quaid. Fill me in on the STR."

He shuffled toward his desk and returned with a stack of folders. "STR? Well la-di-da. That's what's wrong with your generation. Three damn words are too much effort."

"Fine. Fill me in on the sex trafficking ring."

"See? That wasn't so hard." He waited for me to agree. I didn't. Instead, I cupped my fingers, motioning for him to get on with it. "Most of the vics are under twenty-five, some as young as fourteen. We believe the perps kidnapped most of them from shopping malls or large retail chains."

"How many?" I asked.

"Twenty-four."

I whistled low. "Anything from surveillance footage?"

"The few images we have don't reveal much. These guys are pros. They know where the cameras are and choose those vics just out of range."

"Opportunists then?"

Quaid nodded, returned to his desk, and leaned back in his chair, fisting split vinyl armrests. "I'm thinking they probably work in groups of three, four at most: a scout, a lookout, and the muscle."

I shook my head. "I'm thinking two men. Three or four would be too conspicuous."

"Two, four. What the hell difference does it make?"

"Is the FBI involved?"

Quaid emitted a disingenuous laugh. "With that dick for a mayor? He's shot down the recommendation, using the excuse that, so far, we can't prove an interstate crime was committed."

"Are there any locations where more than one woman has gone missing?"

Quaid thumbed through a folder, and I resisted the urge to break his hands. For as long as I'd worked with him, he refused to enter information into the database, preferring instead to do everything longhand, requiring precious time spent riffling through wilted folders.

"Yeah, here it is. Budget Bizarre, off Interstate 435 at the Sixty-Third Street exit. Meghan Whitlow and Rona Gonzales were both reported missing after failing to return from the store."

"Okay," I said, tapping a pen against my front teeth. "What time of day?"

More riffling tested my limited patience.

"Ms. Whitlow allegedly visited the store around three in the afternoon, Ms. Gonzales sometime after work, most likely between the hours of six p.m. and eight p.m." Quaid dropped the folder on the edge of my desk.

I leaned forward in my chair and the springs squeaked disproval. "How far apart did the abductions take place? Was it days? Weeks?"

Quaid tipped his head toward the folder. "Something wrong with your eyes, Crenshaw? Or do you just like hearing the sound of my voice?"

"What I like is legible handwriting, Quaid. What I prefer is accessing reports from my computer."

He wagged his head while rolling his eyes. "There you go again, Crenshaw. Sheer laziness. Three words are too many, writing reports longhand is *just too grueling*," he said mocking me, his lips ballooning into an infantile pout.

"It's important, Quaid. A little thing we call MO. Remember that?"

"Relax, Crenshaw, I'm just bustin' your balls." Quaid perused the report, his head moving comically as his eyes tracked every line.

He suddenly gripped the back of his neck. "Holy shit. You might be onto something." He rounded my desk, a shoddily manicured fingernail pinpointing the appropriate information. "Both went missing on a Wednesday, exactly one week apart."

"Two women . . . tell me security has been heightened."

Quaid shrugged. "We've requested additional patrol."

"And?"

He cocked his head to one side. "Come on, Crenshaw. You already know the answer to that. The department's budget doesn't allow for those kind of extravagances," he said past a smirk. "Not when there's rows of flowers to be planted along every major boulevard and bogus touristy commercials to be made."

"Okay, Quaid. Put a damper on the negative crap. It's exhausting. What about the store? Surely a successful conglomerate can afford to add security detail."

Quaid arched an eyebrow. "Seriously, Crenshaw? Large corporations only care about their bottom line. And should a bunch of suits even consider it, by the time additional expenditure gets approval, we'll have found the missing women. With any luck."

I rolled my eyes then fixed a hard stare. "Who else is working the case?"

He jerked his chin toward Detective Reed. "Most of the detectives are focused on the escalating homicides."

It was my turn to arch a brow.

"Oh, don't look so surprised, Crenshaw. Compared to a bullet-riddled body splayed across Main Street, a missing woman is a lot easier to ignore."

I laughed sinisterly. "But it's not just one missing woman."

"Yeah? Tell that to the mayor."

Mindful of the late hour, I put in a call to Detective Regina Ramirez and Detective Lucy Chastain anyway, two veteran detectives who'd assisted Quaid and me on several missing persons cases in the past. Regina answered on the second ring.

Following a brief update, we discussed the logistics of an undercover sting; she and Lucy alternating Wednesday morning and afternoons, briefly patronizing the store before returning to an unmarked vehicle parked just outside camera range.

I intended to cover Wednesday night. I thanked her and ended the call, then accessed Lucy's number on speed dial.

"Celeste, what's this I hear about you working nights? Please tell me it's just a rumor."

"I'm afraid not. I'll tell you all about it someday." *I could tell you stories that would make your ears bleed.*

Like Regina, Lucy was all in, anxious to see the offenders behind bars. I ended the call, sidestepping her luncheon invitation, and returned the handset to the cradle. Quaid's mind was elsewhere. Deciding to follow Elizabeth's advice, *practice makes perfect,* I maneuvered through his jungled maze of extraneous thoughts and plucked out those relevant without breaking a sweat. Just as I figured, he was mentally packing beef jerky, assorted donuts, potato chips, and bottles of soda into his rundown Ford Escape, in preparation for the six-to-seven-hour sting. To be fair, I didn't really need the power of telepathy. I'd worked with him long enough to know how his annoying mind worked.

"Listen, Quaid. I've decided it might be best if I handled the sting on my own. If they're as savvy as you say, they'll spot you a mile away."

"Have it your way. In the meantime, I'll reach out to the other precincts and suggest stepping up patrol at the other locations."

I bounced around the idea for a few minutes. "Yeah . . . I'm rethinking that. Patrol cars cruising the stores is too risky. That will only put those guys on alert, maybe sabotage the sting operations."

Quaid narrowed his eyes. "What am I supposed to do? Sit here and twiddle my thumbs? This is *my* operation, in case you've forgotten."

"Look, Quaid. This isn't a pissing contest. What's with you? The Detective Quaid I know is interested in one thing and one thing only: solving the case."

"You're right," he said, scrubbing his head, eyes roving over the clock on the wall. "I'm pissed off and dead on my feet, Crenshaw. I'm usually in bed by this time of night. Thirty years I gave this department, and this is what I get . . . the damn graveyard shift."

I was grateful that Captain Burke had left the station—Reed following behind a short time later (without any kind of explanation, goodbye, or a kiss my ass)—before Quaid fell asleep at his desk. I spent the rest of the night deciphering his crude chicken scratches, entering only the relevant facts into the database. It didn't take a profiler to realize the abductors had a type: young, petite, dark-headed, and, according to family members, "outgoing, kind, and extremely trusting." Other than the preference for only dark-haired victims, the other parameters were not surprising. Predators always went after the meek and gullible.

I opened a new document and keyed in all the suspected abduction locations, scattered throughout the metropolis. I placed a call to outlying sheriff offices and smaller policed townships. By three a.m., it became clear my nighttime resources were limited. I gave up the prospect of contacting small town police personnel by phone and instead composed a blanket email, alerting the various sheriffs and police chiefs to the situation. A few hours later, I'd successfully sent twelve emails with a plea the recipients contact me personally with any relevant information.

I scoured the internet after that, my attention focused on small-town online newspapers, specifically reports of missing females. After getting a hit on a woman abducted from a bowling alley parking lot in Clinton, Missouri, I uncapped my thermos tucked within a coolie bag I'd stashed inside a locked drawer and swallowed a mouthful of tepid blood. I continued to surf the net despite the pinkish hues hanging low in a vivid blue sky, just outside the long row of windows. My fingers danced over the keys and my thumb spun the mouse wheel as I scrolled through article after article. Concentrating my efforts on towns south of Kansas City, I came across another article from Warsaw, Missouri, chronicling the disappearance of a fifteen-year-old girl allegedly abducted from Warsaw's local Walmart. Further investigation into the limited disclosures identified two essential qualifiers: both young women went missing on a Wednesday afternoon, both victims described as having dark hair.

A strand of muted sunlight encroached the dingy windows, and I jerked the coolie bag and an emergency hoodie from the drawer and scooped up my purse and jacket. I saw no reason to send Burke an email to advise him of my plans. From what I knew about him, he'd given up the notion of driving crime from the city long ago and preferred instead to skate a straight and leisurely path all the way to retirement. I shook Quaid awake before shrugging into the hoodie, afterward exiting the building. I recoiled when a ray of sunlight scorched my face, cinched the hood tighter, and sprinted for the car.

CHAPTER SEVENTEEN

~~~

O nce I arrived home, I discovered Fane in a fetal position beneath
Raina's coffin. I tossed a blanket over him, then inched her coffer
open, grinding my teeth when the hinges squeaked. Cradling the
photograph of me that I'd seen earlier, she slept peacefully, the suggestion
of a smile on her lips. I chewed the insides of my cheeks while I resisted an
urge to wake her.

Late that afternoon, I awoke to find Fane in the living room, thumbing
through a *Vogue* magazine while offering vulgar commentary.

"Where's Raina?" I said, looking past him toward her nook. When he
still hadn't answered, I asked him again.

"Well, is that not a fine *How You Do?* as they say in Missouri."

I blew out a long breath and considered strangling him. "They don't say
that."

"I beg to differ. I will have you know—"

"Fane. Where. Is. Raina?"

His nose saluted the cobwebbed ceiling I'd been meaning to take a
broom to. "In her sleep chamber, where else might she be? After our day's

adventure, the wee one was practically in a stupor and fell asleep in my arms as I read her favorite tale." He released a high-pitched groan. "If I am subjected to one more ghastly reading of that trope-filled *Alice in Wonderland,* I shall slit my own throat. Whoever thought it a grand idea for young children to idolize obviously demented Alice suffers similar mental decline."

"It's a classic, Fane."

"Ha. The same could be said of dinosaur excrement, but do you see me devouring it?"

He yawned, stretching lanky arms over his head. "You scarcely made it home before the witching hour. Which reminds me, I have something for you."

He drifted toward the entry hall table, where he rifled through a red velvet purse embellished with silk embroidery and ivory tassels. When he couldn't find what he was looking for, he dumped the entire contents on the table, to include several bottles of perfume, a couple jars of moisturizer, false eyelashes, an array of lipsticks, necklaces, earrings, and a few items that resembled things that might be found in a fifteenth-century torture chamber.

"Egad. I was quite certain I had lost this little gem. I have searched for it the world over—and I mean that quite literally," he said, fondling what the terribly adventurous might consider a sex toy. "Oh, if this priceless instrument could talk, the stories it would tell."

Thank God it can't.

"Voilà!" he shouted and produced a corked nineteenth-century medicine bottle.

"What is that?"

"A clever concoction of rice bran extract, cocoa butter, jasmine, volcanic ash, and red petroleum."

"You shouldn't have, and I mean every word."

"Humph," he said, uncorked the bottle, and waved it under my nose.

"I hope it's not perfume because it smells disgusting."

"No, my inane pet. It is a tried-and-true remedy that slows the effects of the sun."

"God, that's awful," I said, crinkling my nose. I crammed the cork back inside the bottle.

"I must say, your lack of etiquette often perturbs me. I find the benefits of this revolutionary elixir outweigh the rather odiferous component. I once spent a week on the sands of Sri Lanka with nary a solar burn."

"Thanks? That was very thoughtful?"

"Pfft. I shall add disingenuous to your social attributes."

"As delightful as this has been, Fane, I have a lot to do. I'll see you tonight."

"And deprive you of a titillating blow-by-blow account of today's glorious outing? I should think not. How would Raina feel to learn her *mummy's* interest in her wee mundane life is something akin to evacuating one's bowels?"

I collapsed on the sofa. "I'm all ears."

He giggled and I twisted his nipple ring. He alone had always found the size of my ears a source of amusement.

"Ow! Unhand me, you contemptuous shrew!" He leaped beside me, knees bent as he balanced precariously on the tips of exaggeratedly pointed patent leather shoes, a long, braided hair extension whipping the bridge of my nose. "Oh, wherever shall I begin?"

"Please, Fane, I'm begging you. Just a brief recap."

"Righty, oh," he said with a flippant salute. "We began our little pilgrimage at the Nelson-Atkins Museum of Art. I regret to say the security guards there so lack a friendly demeanor and, as you know, I do love a man in uniform."

I covered my face in my hands. "Oh, dear God."

"Do compose yourself, Negative Nellie, for the occasion was most uneventful."

"So why are we discussing it?" I said through clenched teeth.

"Did I say uneventful? Perhaps I spoke too soon." He scooted closer, practically upon me. "It would seem a pompous artist—I believe it was Renoir—had the audacity to capture our poor little castaway's mother, or an impeccable likeness by all accounts, with canvas and brush."

"Oh, no. Poor Raina. How did she react?"

"How did she react? Why with alternating fits of rage and uncontrollable tears. She was inconsolable. So much so, those fabulous men in uniform abandoned their posts and advanced upon us, as if blowflies to a pungent carcass. I attempted to ward them off with a girlish shriek, but they persisted, manhandling me in a most stimulating manner."

His eyes rolled back as he shuddered, and I shoved him backward.

"And *then?*"

"Abracadabra. We took to the air, you silly imp."

I thought about those misfortunate and very confused security guards, unable to validate their unfathomable story because even the most high-tech surveillance equipment wouldn't have captured either Raina's or Fane's image. "Poor baby. How is she now?"

"As right as rain. Nothing cures malaise quite like soaring over the Kauffman Stadium aboard the Goodyear Blimp, the crowd below shrilling unbridled delight as those tantalizing ballplayers manage yet another homerun."

"Aboard? Never mind, I'd rather not know. And then you came home?"

"That was certainly our intention." Fane's tone rose a couple of octaves and experience dictated that I brace myself. "In my defense, the wee tyke is particularly fond of ice cream."

"And?"

Fane distanced himself and perched on the opposite end of the sofa. "She has become most independent, would you not agree?"

"You're stalling. Cut to the chase."

"At Bianca's insistence, I encourage that very independence whenever the situation arises. That said, I may have given her my blessing when she maintained that she, and she alone, should prepare her noxious little dessert at a quaint little place known as the Dairy Queen."

I clenched my fists but managed to keep my hands to myself. "What happened?"

"The entire affair would have proceeded without incident, mind you, had the persnickety little devil simply acted with resolve. As it were, she vigorously debated whether to cover the horrid mess in rainbow sprinkles or a generous glop of cookie dough. Revolting, I dare say. My stomach persists its wretched churning as we speak."

"Damn it, Fane. What *incident*?"

"The police may have responded to something they refer to as a 10-88."

"Shoplifting."

"Bravo. Most astute. Although upon their arrival, there may have been talk about a 10-64."

"Oh God. A crime in progress." I raked my face with all ten fingernails.

"That's the one."

"Fane shall read me this one later," Raina said, gripping Lewis Carroll's fantasy novel by its spine and setting it aside. "He so enjoys Alice's many adventures."

I muffled a laugh behind the sock puppets Raina had tugged over my hands an hour before. "Oh, I'm certain he does." I'd debated a discussion surrounding her visit to Dairy Queen. Because I was afraid it might jog her memory of Renoir's painting, I decided against it. Besides, I was confident Fane had learned a valuable lesson and would never again place her in a similar situation. "He should be here soon. What have you two got planned?"

She shrugged, her tiny shoulders contacting her ears. "He always surprises me."

"Surprises are fun. But when you're not at home, you mustn't forget that not everyone around you can do all the cool stuff you can do."

"Like dancing on air?"

"Yep, like dancing on air, growing your teeth, making toys come to you—"

She looked up at me and her lower lip quivered. "No matter how much I try, I cannot make my toys obey."

"Oh? Well, that's what these are for," I said, tickling her legs. "Anyway, when we can do things others can't, it sometimes makes them feel bad about themselves and we don't want that, do we?"

She shook her head hard and fluffy brown ringlets fell across her nose.

"So we mustn't fly or grow our teeth anywhere but right here at home."

She began to cry.

"What's wrong?"

"However will Fane and I go on magnificent adventures if we mustn't fly?"

I hadn't thought of that. Parenting was hard enough. Raising a perpetually five-year-old vampire required flexibility and a lot more patience than I'd ever anticipated.

"You know what? You're right. So, let's agree that when we fly, we make absolutely certain those who can't fly don't see us fly. What do you think?"

She bobbed her head up and down and jumped into my arms.

CHAPTER EIGHTEEN

he police scanner squawked a message when I was halfway to the station. An armed robbery was in progress, and I had just passed the location. I radioed in my intent to handle the call and spun the car around.

The convenience store within view, I killed the headlamps and parked the 2020 Dodge Charger in a deserted parking lot next door. The store was situated just off the interstate and I considered the robbers were most likely pros; location was everything, but no more so than when committing a crime that required a speedy getaway. I scanned the area for the lookout. Not seeing a car, I assumed it was stowed behind the building.

I switched off the car interior light and eased the car door open. I didn't intend to make my entrance in the usual manner. But was I capable of teleporting through the building without Leonardo or one of the others to guide me? The Hidden Cloak would have been my first choice, but I didn't have the slightest idea how to harness that particular power, and, from what I'd been told, attaining invisibility required even more skill and endless patience. I closed my eyes and filled my lungs with fetid night air. Then I focused my thoughts on penetrating the brick exterior. Soon after, I chipped my front teeth on a row of bricks and blackened both eyes.

Behind me, I heard Nick's infectious laugh. "What the hell are you doing?"

I whirled around, intermittently massaging my aching mouth. "I might ask you the same thing," I said through clenched teeth. "And keep your voice down. There's an armed robbery in progress."

"Yeah? We'd better get in there then, don't you think?"

I grabbed his shirtsleeve. "There's no *we*, Nick. If the suspect sees anyone come in, he might start shooting and kill everyone inside."

"So, what's your plan? Auger through the side of the building using your teeth?"

I blew frustration out of my nose. "It's called teleportation. I just haven't quite perfected the technique yet."

"No shit. Well, you know what I say. Who needs all the bells and whistles when the basic model gets the job done," he said past a grin. He whipped the door open before I could stop him and zipped inside, so quickly that even my vampiric eyes caught only a fleeting glimpse of the movement. Panicked, I zoomed after him without realizing I'd breached the glass door without opening it.

"What the fuck was that?" the suspect asked, and I assumed he wasn't talking to himself. A second assailant popped into view from behind the counter, jabbing an unimpressive .22-caliber barrel in various directions, eyes widening despite the skintight ski mask. The first guy must have sensed our presence and opened fire. A 12-gauge shell shattered a glass liquor case behind me, and I plucked a few shiny shards from one shoulder blade and dropped to the floor. Hugging the shelves housing assorted snacks and sundry items, I duck-walked in his direction. *Where the hell is Nick?*

A gusty breeze swirled my hair about my shoulders and quickened the ceiling fan overhead. A blink later, the gunman flew backward through the glass beer cooler. Nick hovered over the bleeding and motionless body, his fangs on full display, then confiscated the sawed-off shotgun.

"Get. Out. Of. Here!" I mouthed to Nick, then sailed behind the rack of magazines near the checkout counter. "This is Detective Crenshaw of the Kansas City Police Department. Drop your weapon on the counter and come out, hands where I can see them!" I told the second assailant.

"Fuck you, Pig. I got a hostage. Come any closer and he's dead."

Shit! Would I be able to zip over the counter and subdue the shooter before he could fire his weapon? Or should I call for backup and a hostage negotiator once I was certain Nick had done as I asked?

"Blessed Mother of God," Socrates said, materializing a section at a time. "Just when I had a malevolent horde of Harvesters within my grasp, I was alerted to your pathetic peril. Dear girl, you needn't physically contact the fiend to render him incapable. Think of his wrists," he said, grabbing mine. "Then, in your mind's eye, simply snap the bones in two."

I shivered when he implanted the instruction and wondered if I would ever get used to the unsettling sensation, an itch inside my head I couldn't scratch.

The perp behind the counter produced a bloodcurdling howl. Socrates grinned and folded his arms across a linen shirt soaked with black goo. From previous experience, I knew that goo represented Harvester blood. "Now that the situation is under control, I shall bid you au revoir until the next calamity arises."

"Wait. How do I explain . . ." I said, my question trailing off when I realized Socrates was gone. My eyes flew to the storeroom. For a brief moment, I wished I hadn't insisted Nick leave.

From behind the counter, the hostage ratcheted to a standing position, hands held high above his head, and he looked around the store, as if he expected to see someone besides me.

No matter what he *thought* he may have heard, I knew neither Nick nor Socrates could be captured on any security footage. And neither could I. Which presented a problem.

"He's unconscious," he said, jerking his head over a shoulder. "I didn't touch him. I didn't do anything . . ."

I managed a weak smile and signaled for him to come around the counter. "It's safe. You can come out now. Where do you keep the security cameras?"

"There aren't any," he said, hanging his head. "Look, I know that's really dumb, especially in this neighborhood. But I just never found the time or the extra money, you know?"

"Well, the important thing is we caught these guys," I said as I collected the 12-gauge and checked the first assailant for a pulse. I felt my gums tingle when I saw all that blood, when I smelled that sweet, irresistible scent, so I tugged an N95 mask from my hip pocket and secured it over my nose and mouth. Feeling the perp's weak pulse, I radioed dispatch. "This is Detective Crenshaw, Shield Number 1599, requesting an ambulance and backup at the 10-65 location." I ended the transmission and told the storeowner, "I'm going to cuff these guys. Then I'm going to check behind the building, make sure they don't have another accomplice waiting back there."

The storeowner's jaw dropped. "You're going to just leave me here with them?"

"You know how to use one of these?" I asked, pressing the shotgun his way. His skin turned ashen, but he nodded. "Good. But don't shoot anyone unless they give you no other choice." I clinked my lone set of cuffs on the first suspect. The second guy was still unconscious, and I snagged a coil of baling wire from a display and hogtied him.

I pinched the delivery door open and squeezed through. The lookout waited inside a battered seventies Chevy. His head bobbed up and down, and I assumed he wouldn't hear my commands over the music flowing through his earbuds, so I tapped on the window.

Complying with my gesture, he ripped out the earbuds. "Out of the car. Hands where I can see them," I said robotically.

I wondered if the kid still had his baby teeth. His skin oozed naivety from every greasy pore. He opened the door a creak at a time and fainted as he spilled out. With no way to restrain him long-term, I tugged him upright, wrapped an arm around his waist, and sailed toward my vehicle, where I deposited him in the trunk, then moved the car just outside the store entrance.

Back inside, the owner eagerly handed over the shotgun, and I told him to take a break while I waited for the ammo and backup. The suspect lying just outside the cooler floated in and out of consciousness, and I tried to organize my thoughts, come up with a plausible explanation for his injuries and those of his accomplice. An idea occurred to me, and I grabbed a plastic jug of motor oil from a shelf opposite the cooler and poured a generous amount on the floor directly beneath the automobile parts display, tugged the perp's boots off, pressed the soles into the oil, pushed the shoes toward the cooler, then put them back on his feet. That part done, I returned the container to the shelf, flipped it on its side, and replaced the cap, making sure to leave it partially unscrewed. I was formulating a plan for the other guy's injuries when backup rolled up and four cops stormed the building.

"The situation's contained," I said, tipping my head toward their guns, drawn and leveled. "You can put those away."

"Nice work, Detective," one officer said, the others standing over the perpetrators and snickering among themselves while they discussed my restraining technique.

I tipped my head toward the parking lot. "The getaway driver is in the trunk of the Dodge parked out front."

He grinned. "You run out of wire, Detective?"

"Nope, just like to change things up."

A chorus of muted laughter reset my nerves.

"Anyone else here?"

I nodded toward the storeroom. "Yeah, the store manager is catching his breath in there. Tall guy. Red hair."

"If you'll open the trunk, we'll take it from here, Detective." He bounced two fingers off his forehead and offered me a smile. "Well done."

The ambulance whined to a stop outside, and an unmarked Crown Vic saddled up alongside. I reeled in a scowl when Detective Todd Franklin emerged, straightening his tie and hitching pristinely pressed trousers over narrow hips. Franklin was the squad's lead detective, the kind of guy who would stop at nothing and step on anyone to further his career.

I met him at the door. "Slow night?" I asked, distracted when the EMTs swept past with suspect two on a gurney. Franklin ignored me. "We've got this, Detective. I'm sure you have more important things to do."

"I didn't realize I needed an invitation, Crenshaw," he said, hands on his hips. "Did you fire your weapon?" he asked while studying the blood surrounding the cooler.

"No. Be careful," I said when he strolled that direction.

He whirled to face me. "I'm very familiar with crime scene protocol, Detective."

"I'm not worried you may contaminate the scene," I said. "There's oil on the floor over there."

"So that's what happened here?" he asked, a smirk corrupting his chiseled, clean-shaven face. "The suspect slipped and flew face-first into the glass?"

"He saw me come in and, my guess, he made a run for the storeroom where he intended to take cover."

"Fucking karma," Franklin said. "You gotta love it."

"Excuse me, Detectives," an EMT interrupted. "Anyone else injured? If not, we need to take off. We've got a guy with serious lacs over most of his body and another with several broken bones."

"Broken bones?" Franklin said, whipping his head in my direction.

CHAPTER NINETEEN

C onvinced I needed to master teleportation, I left the parking lot and drove one-half mile, before shutting off the engine. The area was secluded, tucked between groves of trees, and moonlight kissed a lush soybean field to the north. Recalling Socrates's advice, *Teleportation, at its essence, is merely emitting one's psychic field while commanding the molecules to separate, thus allowing movement through solid objects,* I applied his instruction. Which resulted in nothing more than an uncomfortable bout of indigestion and the beginnings of a migraine.

I tried several more times over the course of thirty minutes, stiffening when a cool sensation coursed through my body, followed by a feeling of weightlessness. I visualized myself beneath the tallest oak and, a blink later, I was no longer in the car, but instead surrounded by the grove, my feet rooted in a swamp of wet leaves, and I covered a triumphant scream.

Then I got greedy and decided to attempt the Hidden Cloak. I imagined the molecules I'd successfully separated imperceptibly small. Suddenly unable to see my feet, I fought to cull my elation-turned-panic, while my subconscious taunted me, daring me to complete the process. But what if I was successful and then couldn't reverse the spell? The possibility prompted a full-scale anxiety attack, and I aborted the plan entirely.

I shook one foot, then the other, afterwards stomping them both. Nothing happened. Forced to consider my limited options, I debated the hiking boots I kept in the car. But was the shaft tall enough to disguise my invisible ankles?

My panic reached a critical level, and I decided to summon the Elders. I was deliberating whether it best to inconvenience Socrates or Elizabeth, when my toes sluggishly materialized, then my feet, and finally both ankles. I blew out a long breath and dropped to my knees. Convinced I now had the ability to successfully teleport at will, as well as become invisible, I decided I'd had more than enough of supernatural stunts for one night.

Back at the station, I found Detective Reed seated at my desk. I glanced around the squad room. All the desks sat empty, most of the detectives allotted to dayshift, and I wondered why Burke hadn't assigned her to one of those desks. I resisted the urge to stomp in there and ask him.

Maybe our initial meeting wasn't the status quo. She was probably reeling from her move to a new city, a new department, stressed out over her caseload. Maybe, at the very least, she deserved the benefit of the doubt. I decided to give diplomacy another shot. "How's it going?" I asked, tucking the coolie bag in the bottom drawer.

She grunted something I couldn't quite decipher.

"I go by Celeste around here," I said, amiably enough. "Any luck on the homicides?"

She sighed and dropped the folder she was eyeballing hard against the desk before fixing those stern green eyes on me. "Christina," she said, jabbing her breastbone with the end of a pen. "A couple of the families have offered a reward, and we're following up on several tips."

"Good luck. Sometimes they pan out."

"So I've heard," she said mockingly, still squinting.

Her eyes scanned the dismal room, pond-scum-green paint and improper lighting not doing it any favors. "God, this place is depressing."

"Yep, you're right about that."

"When was the last time these walls were painted?"

"Probably the same year Eisenhower laid his hand on a Bible."

A grin suddenly appeared on her lips, revealing a slightly discolored, overlapping front tooth, but it died just as quickly. Quaid returned, eavesdropping, and eagerly joined the conversation.

"That damn paint has more lead in it than a tank of Exxon premium." He checked his watch. "You're late, Crenshaw. If you ladies are done with your chitchat, I've got some things we need to discuss," he said to me.

Reed snagged her jacket from the back of the chair. "See you around," she deadpanned and, without so much as a look back, left the room.

I waited until she was out of sight. "What things?" I hoped those *things* didn't pertain to the armed robbery and the strange circumstances surrounding the gunmen's injuries.

"I reached out to the Butler, Missouri, chief of police, Micah Tanner, and he shared some information on an abduction that took place outside the local and now defunct skating rink. He didn't give me a lot of details, but he did provide a link to a related newspaper article in the *Butler Weekly Times*, along with a photograph of the victim."

I perused the article, Quaid breathing down my neck. Britney Clark was eighteen years old at the time of her abduction, five-feet-two-inches tall, weighing approximately one-hundred-fifteen pounds. She had blue eyes and dark-brown hair. The detective appointed the case was apparently working the theory that someone who knew Britney was responsible for her disappearance.

I scrolled through facsimiles of two interviews Tanner sent Quaid, jotting down notes when appropriate, to include a contact number for Jennifer Wilson, Britney's closest friend. A comment from the second interviewee, Wanda Miller, Britney's employer at a local pizza joint, stood out. It involved "two suspicious men," approximately thirty years old, who had been hanging around the pizza joint the day before. Not surprisingly, she hadn't thought to get the license plate number and couldn't be sure of the make or model of the car in which they'd arrived. When asked why she hadn't summoned the police, she said, "This is a small town. I didn't want everybody to think I was paranoid."

Frustrated, my thoughts ran to Tristan and our last night together. Which only made my frustration worse. I pushed away from my desk, jerked the coolie bag from the drawer, and told Quaid, "Gotta visit the girls' room." Seated inside a stall, I relished the sip from the thermos, the blood reinvigorating my body and my ability to focus. When I returned to my desk, Quaid was gone, and I noticed the blinking light on my desk phone, indicating a missed call. I listened to the message twice and accessed Emma Harris's file from the Missing Persons folder before returning the call.

"Hello, I'd like to speak to Marcy Harris," I greeted the person on the other end.

"Speaking."

"Ms. Harris, this is Detective Crenshaw of the Kansas City Police Department. I apologize for the late hour."

"You must be busy," she said, her tone implying that was no excuse for not returning her call sooner.

"I was assigned your daughter's case only yesterday."

"So I've heard. I certainly hope you intend to do more than that other detective."

I couldn't be sure if she was talking about Quaid and thought it best not to ask.

"Does my daughter's disappearance have anything to do with the others I've heard about on the news? Can you tell me that much?"

Her voice cracked, and I sucked in a breath. "That's certainly a possibility." At this point, I had little more to offer, but I chose to give her hope. "We've received some additional information that may provide a lead on one of the missing girls. I'll keep you updated on any new developments and, please, don't hesitate to call if you have questions."

She ended the call with an incoherent string of words, and I assumed she'd lost all composure.

Quaid lumbered back in a short time later, zipping his fly. "What's with you, Crenshaw? You're like a jack-in-the-box tonight. I hear Franklin inserted himself into your armed robbery. Is that what's bothering you?"

My heart began to race, but I shrugged. "Why would it?"

"He was floating the idea of a police brutality investigation, but Burke shut him down. Apparently, the ER doc attributed your suspect's wrist fractures to brittle bones from his methamphetamine habit, rather than unnecessary force."

I rolled my eyes and attempted to temper the rage seeking an outlet. "Let's just get back to work. Anything else I should know pertaining to the abductions?"

Before he could answer, Captain Burke's door flew open. "Quaid, Crenshaw, in my office." He was already nestled in his leather chair when I came through the door, Quaid lagging behind, taking his own sweet time. "I just got off the phone with Drexel, Missouri, Sheriff Wayne Davis," he said, once referencing his notes. "They've had a similar abduction down there, and he thought it might be a good idea for our departments to collaborate.

"Witness description of the victim abducted outside a Dollar Spree Store was vague, the abductee's age reportedly within an eighteen-to-late-twenties age group with no other defining information. This witness described the kidnapper's car as being a dark-green, late-model SUV with blacked-out windows and a mostly shredded temporary tag affixed to the rear window."

"That's a pretty detailed description," I said, more to myself. "Who's the witness?" I got the sense whoever it was had a lot more to offer.

Burke puffed his cheeks. Rumor had it he frequented the bar at the corner before turning toward home most nights. He seemed in a hurry to get there. "Mamie Martin. Here's her contact information," he said, jotting down a phone number and sliding it across his desk. "Follow up with Davis with any information pertaining to our MPs that might prove helpful."

Back at my desk, I scoured the internet for online news services covering Bates County, Missouri, and came across a stingy article, "The

Disappearance of Drexel's Jane Doe," more an afterthought than a public plea for information. "Quaid, check this out," I said, scooting my chair off to one side so he could read the screen.

Soon after, he raked a hand through thinning hair. "Why don't you give that Minnie Martin a call?"

"It's Mamie. Don't you think it's too late? She might be in bed."

"So you wake her up. What's she gonna do? Hang up?"

I made the call and a seventyish-sounding woman with an unpleasant attitude greeted me from the other end.

"Who in hell is callin' me at this time of night?" she barked. "It had better be important."

I identified myself and told her the reason for the call.

"That poor girl," she said, setting most of her irritation on a back burner. "I don't suppose you're callin' to tell me you found the fools who done that?"

"I'm afraid we haven't, Ms. Martin. I was hoping there might be other things you've remembered about that day."

"It's Mrs. Martin. Give me a minute to think, will ya? You woke me from a sound sleep."

I waited through the silence, punctuated by rattling papers. I assumed she'd taken notes.

"There were five of them."

"The men who kidnapped her?"

"Of course. Who else would I be talking about?"

Five men? That revelation was like a punch to the gut. Every piece of intel we had, thus far, suggested only two kidnappers were involved in the sex-trafficking ring. I had a sinking suspicion there was no connection between the sex traffickers and the five men Mrs. Martin witnessed kidnap the girl outside the Dollar Spree Store.

"Did you notice anything in particular about any one of them?"

"They were unkempt, shaved heads the lot of 'em. Their clothes were wrinkled and filthy, and they looked like they hadn't acquainted themselves with soap and water for months."

"How old would you say the men were?"

She chuckled past a smoker's cough. "Listen, doll, when you get to be my age, everybody looks young."

"If you had to guess—"

"I never been a bettin' sort, but I'd throw a dollar at three of 'em bein' no more than thirty years old."

"What about the others?"

"Younger, I'd say."

"Any idea who the girl was?" I asked.

"This is strictly rumor, so don't hold me to it; a few folks are of the notion that girl was none other than Elsie Hanover."

I scribbled her name on a notepad. "Was Elsie a local girl?"

"Up until two years ago when she lit outa here like a demon set her tail afire."

"Then why would those *folks* think it was Elsie, Mrs. Martin?"

"I suppose I'm to blame for that. Now, don't go and get the wrong impression—I've never been one to participate in a gabfest, but if the girl I seen get pushed in that car weren't Elsie Hanover, she was the spittin' image of her."

"What makes you so sure?"

"That scribbling on her shoulder, for starters."

"She had a tattoo of some sort?" I asked and pitched forward in my chair. Quaid grew restless, pacing a path in front of my desk, so I put the call on speaker.

"Some kind of symbols I could never make heads nor tails of."

"Can you give me a description of the girl?"

"Her hair was dark, too dark, like the color come out of a box."

"Height? Weight?"

"Them men towered over her, and I expect they was no taller than six foot. Judging from the way one SOB slung her inside that car, like she was nothin' but a feather, I'd put her at a hundred pounds at most."

"Where were you when this was taking place?"

"Just outside the building, waitin' on the OATS Bus."

"So you were on a bus?"

"Clean the wax outa your ears. How could I be on a bus that ain't even arrived?"

"Okay, now I understand." Apparently, Mrs. Martin had been awaiting the arrival of an Older Adult Transportation System vehicle. "A few more questions, Mrs. Martin, and I'll let you get back to bed. Did the men say anything?"

"Not one word."

"Did the girl seem to know them?"

"No, ma'am. I don't believe she did. Any girl who would spend so much as a minute with those nasty, vile creatures ain't right in the head."

"Thank you, Mrs. Martin. You've been a tremendous help. Please call me if you think of anything else."

"I don't waste my money on them fancy carry 'round phones, so I didn't get your number."

I gave her the number and my extension. I had a feeling I would be talking to her again. I disconnected, not surprised to find Quaid winging both nostrils.

"She's a gabber, I'll give her that," he said with a shake of his head. "She's also got a real shitty attitude."

"I don't disagree, but she's also given us the best lead we have."

After dragging a fresh whiteboard from a small storage room across the hall from Burke's office, I scavenged through a drawer filled with pens until I found a marker that hadn't lain dormant since the Vietnam War while Quaid looked on, fisting a steaming cup of coffee.

Beginning with the recent facts I'd learned, I chronicled any pertinent information Mamie Martin had shared regarding Drexel's missing Jane Doe and the intel Chief Tanner had provided on the Britney Clark abduction.

Then I returned to my computer and began the time-consuming task of compiling all the key points the other detectives had collected on the remaining twenty-four victims. Three hours later, with Quaid fighting sleep and giving the occasional critique, I printed the Word document I'd created and began transferring the data from it onto the board, separating one case from another with a crudely drawn vertical line. By six a.m., Quaid had refilled his cup three times, my fingertips were black, the marker completely dried up, and every inch of the whiteboard was covered. I took a step back and studied my achievement, feeling both victorious and a little overwhelmed.

Pinpointing possible similarities was still difficult, even though I'd attempted a conscientious congruency. Riffling through my drawer again, I rescued a red marker from several dust bunnies nesting at the very back, then circled each abduction location. My OCD in overdrive, I went in search of a green marker to highlight the time of day the kidnappings took place while Quaid propped his chin in his palm and whistled "Here Comes Santa Claus."

"Festive, Crenshaw," he said through a yawn. "Ever hear of a ruler?"

I didn't appreciate his comment regarding the imperfect lines I'd drawn and felt a slow flush building. "Maybe if you'd done something other than sit on your ass, the lines may have been straight."

"Your attitude and all those messy lines remind me of my ex-wife. She once took up embroidery. Every damn stitch was catawampus."

I wondered which ex-wife but didn't have the energy to ask.

He stretched his arms overhead after referencing his watch. "We're off the clock, Crenshaw. Until tonight," he said, throwing on his suit jacket as he ambled toward the door.

Detective Reed rounded the corner and careened into him, Quaid's enormity propelling her backward. Stunned initially, she quickly recovered and appeared to wait for an apology that never came.

"I thought you'd be gone by now," she said past a sniff, her eyes rolling over my computer.

"I was just on my way out."

Fane was waiting for me as daybreak chased me through the front door. Disappointed that there was no sign of Raina, I sighed, my purse slipping from a slumped shoulder.

"Is she asleep?"

He nodded past a yawn.

"What have you two got planned for today?"

"Inasmuch as that tyke abhors that dreadful sunscreen—whoever could blame her—and the allure of fancying myself the caped crusader with Raina my trusty sidekick has worn off for us both, I decided to relegate our adventures to more hospitable hours."

I laughed, easily imagining the two of them decked out in the matching superhero costumes I'd found in Raina's closet, Fane's intention to protect their skin from daylight. "So, you're saying that from now on you plan to wreak havoc only at night?"

He snickered. "My, you are an astute vixen, are you not? It occurred to me that it is not as if we require an unlocked gateway or gregarious attendants in order to enjoy the museums, the art galleries, or the thrilling amusement park rides for that matter."

I puffed my cheeks at the thought of numerous alarms going off throughout the city in the dead of night and shared my concern.

"Pfft," Fane said, flicking a wrist weighed down by a pyramid of colorful bracelets, "this ain't my first ro-day-o, as they say in Missouri."

"They say ro-dee-o, Fane. Ro-day-o is a street in Beverly Hills."

"Well, heehaw, I believe I have made my point."

I sniffed my contempt, and I got a more pungent whiff of his overpowering perfume.

"We returned from our little adventure scarcely an hour ago," he said, clicking his heels together.

"Where did this *little adventure* of yours take place?"

"In a quaint little town they call Saint Joseph."

My brows furrowed. "What's in Saint Joseph?"

"An array of activities. The lunatic asylum to name but one."

I calmed a shudder. "The Glore Psychiatric Museum that's supposedly haunted?"

"Yes, indeedy. Raina and I had a grand time scaring the ghosts. Turnabout is fair play, don't you think?"

It could have been far worse. At least if they'd set off any alarms there, it would only serve to elevate public intrigue. "You said to name just one. Where else did you go?"

"Nearly colliding with a whimsical billboard, how could we possibly resist the invitation to the Jesse James Museum? I do so love Greek revival structures."

"And notorious outlaws, apparently."

Fane batted his eyelashes and once again clicked his heels together. My gaze flew to a pair of western boots I'd never seen him wear before.

"Do *not* tell me—"

"As you wish," he said, bending over and scraping off what looked like a dried splatter of *very* old blood from one instep. After sniffing the rust-colored powdery specks trapped beneath one fingernail, he sucked it clean. Instantly, his body convulsed, and his pupils dilated as if he'd just taken a hallucinogenic drug.

I grabbed hold of his shoulders and shook him. When that didn't produce results, I slapped him hard across the face.

Fane screamed, bolted from the sofa and cowered in a corner, his eyes flitting around the room. "Is he gone?"

"Who?"

"That treacherous scallywag Bob, that's who."

Anyone who'd spent any time at all in Missouri, or knew anything of the history surrounding Jesse James, was aware Robert "Bob" Ford, a former accomplice of Jesse's, shot him in the back of the head while the two men shared dinner at Jesse's home.

"Will you relax, Fane? He was never here."

I wasn't surprised Fane had experienced psychometry, a telepathic transmission in layman's terms, after ingesting Jesse's blood. I *was* surprised that he didn't immediately suffer a slew of impressions—images, sounds, smells or, particularly, emotions—after pulling on the boots the outlaw was wearing at the time of his death.

"Are you certain?" Fane asked in a high-pitched whimper.

"Oh, for God's sake," I said through clenched teeth. "Yes, I'm certain, and it serves you right. You are going to return those boots before the museum reopens."

He crept from the corner, occasionally looking behind him. The floor creaked and he squealed, landing beside me in a cowardly swoosh. "Is that, or is that not, proof positive that your prior declaration was most erroneous?" he said in a falsetto. "It *would* seem the late Mr. Ford chose to accompany me home."

I arched a brow. "I never said it was Bob in the room." He shrieked again and clung to me like a frightened child. I pried his fingers loose. "I meant what I said. You are going to return those boots, and you're going to do it now."

"I shan't argue," he said, struggling to remove them. "I must say, for a man with such an immense legacy, Jesse's feet were inordinately small."

I helped him remove the boots, afterward noticing a curious pierced earring. "What is that?"

"Must I return it? Legend has it *this* is the very tiepin the rambunctious devil wore when gunned down."

I glanced about the room, feigning a shiver. "I suppose, if you're willing to take that chance. Is that blood I see on the tip?"

Fane screamed, dancing around the room as he ripped the pin from his ear.

CHAPTER TWENTY

ane and Raina were already gone when I tumbled from the coffin. I
hadn't slept well, which was unfortunate; the undercover operation
began tonight, and I needed to be on my game. I pushed thoughts
of Tristan away, the same thoughts that had prevented me from getting a
good night's sleep. I missed him and if rarely seeing him is what the future
held, something would need to change.

I texted Regina Ramirez to see if she remembered to stash the dark wig
I'd need for the sting in my desk drawer. Gentlemen may prefer blondes, but
these predators were no gentlemen.

I remembered, she responded immediately. *It's under your desk in a brown
paper bag. Walked around the store for a couple of hours today. No luck. Nothing
suspicious outside either.*

I thanked her, then dug through my closet for a short denim skirt I
hadn't worn since high school and hoped it would still fit. I tossed it on a
chair and went in search of the sluttiest shoes I could find. Unburying a pair
of Jimmy Choo black stilettos with rhinestone overlays littered across the
heel, I grimaced. Bianca had bought them for me for my high school prom,

and my feet hurt just looking at them. Failing to find a blouse risqué enough to attract attention, I wished I'd consulted Fane. Risqué was his trademark. Whipping open my lingerie drawer, I considered various alternatives and decided on a red camisole overlaid with black floral lace. Envisioning myself in the entire ensemble, I cringed and rescued a trench coat from the back of the closet. There was no way in hell I could possibly endure Quaid's bulging eyes or abusive commentary.

I headed for the bathroom and unstuck a vanity drawer seldom opened, its contents mostly cosmetics. I applied some foundation with a light touch, powdered my cheeks with a rosy blush, swept my eyelids with a soft blue shadow, and curled my lashes mercilessly before applying two coats of mascara. Because I couldn't see my reflection, I hoped I didn't look hideous and nearly forgot to apply lipstick.

The precinct door swept open, and I hurried past Detectives Donahue and Franklin, but not before Franklin took the opportunity to look me over and mumble something I wished I hadn't heard. I drilled my eyeballs into the back of his head as he swaggered toward the parking lot.

"What's your rush, Crenshaw?" Donahue said, lingering behind. "Long time, no see."

He was a big, gator-necked man, long on smiles and short on succinctness. Much like his lovable ancestors, he had a passion for Irish whiskey and racy limericks, both obsessions often overlapping his on-duty hours. At any other time, I might have enjoyed our accidental encounter, but tonight I had my head wrapped around entrapping dangerous men.

"Sorry, gotta go; I've got a date. Let's catch up sometime."

"A date, huh?" he said, spirited green eyes snaking over my trench coat. "Who's the lucky guy?"

"Guys," I said, tossing my hair and flashing him a toothy smile.

He grabbed his chest and stumbled backward. "Whoa. *Guys* is it?"

I shook my head and rolled my eyes. "It's a sting, Donahue."

He laughed and bumped my elbow. "I'm just messin' with you. Ramirez told me all about the undercover op. You want someone to watch your back?"

"Nah, piece of cake. Thanks, anyway."

"Sure thing. Hey, don't be a stranger, Celeste. Good luck," he said, more as an afterthought, as he raced after Franklin.

I found Quaid sipping a Diet Coke while studying the Missing Persons Board. I hoped another victim hadn't been added. Although the men had abducted Meghan Whitlow midafternoon from Budget Bizarre off Sixty-Third and Rona Gonzales had met her fate in the evening, serial offenders often varied their modus operandi in order to prevent capture. Regardless, I had a hunch the kidnappers would return to the location that had served them well but vary the time of day. With any luck, they'd decided to stick to Wednesdays.

"If you need me, give me a call on my cell. I'll be working the stakeout," I reminded him.

"Is that why you've got that bag of hair under your desk? I thought it was a wet rat and almost stomped it to death."

"I think the bigger question here is why you were under my desk going through my things."

He shrugged. "I thought it might be food."

I planted a hand against a hip. "If it was food, Quaid, that *food* doesn't belong to you."

He shrugged off the rebuke. "Where you headed, exactly?"

"Budget Bizarre on Sixty-Third, just off I-435."

"Bring me back a bucket of Popeye's chicken. I'll pay you later."

"No can do."

"Fine," he said, shoving sausage fingers into a pocket and pulling out a wad of wrinkled bills. "Keep the change."

"I'm not getting your chicken, Quaid."

"I'll just ride along and get it myself."

"The hell you will. Low profile, Quaid. That zoot suit of yours screams plainclothes cop."

"Have it your way, Crenshaw. But we both know you're going to miss me." He waved a hand over his shoulder as he made his way toward the canteen.

I parked in the back corner of the parking lot. The stingy beams thrown off the dim security lamps proved accommodating, and I settled in, sinking comfortably against the soft leather seat. A dark sedan circled the lot twenty minutes later and my preternatural vision identified two males, late-twenties, both wearing caps slung low. I had my hand on the door handle when the car came to rest just outside the crosswalk. One man leaped out and opened the trunk. He stepped inside the store, disappearing beyond the automatic doors. He returned a few minutes later accompanied by a woman in her sixties pushing a full cart. Unless they'd brought their mother along for the nefarious act, the only thing of which these two might be guilty was sponging off of dear old mom.

After the three left, I moved the car to a well-lit area, turned on the interior light so I'd be seen, fluffed the wig, and reapplied lipstick. The Glock, stowed away in a thigh holster, was chafing my skin and I repositioned it. Removing the trench coat in the cramped front seat required a contortionist's skill, and I dislocated a shoulder in the process. I popped it back into place, not surprised that the intense pain prompted protruding fangs. I flicked off the interior light and waited for my teeth to recede. Then I sauntered toward the entrance, swinging my hips and clip-clopping the stilettos against the pavement. Chuckling to myself, I assumed I looked less like a runway model and more like an old nag entering the Kentucky Derby.

Once inside, I walked every aisle in the store, twice. Afraid someone might alert store security, I returned to the toy section and selected a book, a puzzle, and a gothic doll for Raina.

Passing the women's clothing section, I attracted a clique of mean girls who followed me around the store making snide remarks. They brought back more than one unpleasant memory of high school, igniting a slow burn as I suffered the recollections. I managed to ignore them until a spitball hit me in the back of the head. I spun to face them and resisted the urge to pluck the shield from my bra. I decided it wasn't worth blowing my cover.

"Don't you ladies have anything better to do?"

"Don't you?" one said, afterward blowing an impressive bubble with the enormous wad of gum ballooning a cheek.

I turned around and kept walking, spitballs pummeling my ass like rubber bullets. They had great aim, even better salivary glands. Because they'd drawn so much attention to me by that point, I felt any kidnapper worth his salt would move on to easier prey. I produced my shield and shoved it under Bubble's nose. "Move the fuck along."

Her mouth fell open and she backed away, mumbling an apology. The rest of her entourage ran for the exit, and she bolted after them.

I was nearly to the checkout lanes when a cold blast swept through me. My heart began to race, every exposed vein throbbing against skin transitioning to a luminous green. A woman shrieked, and I closed my lips over angry erupting fangs and dropped Raina's gifts on the floor. A throng of terrified customers darted out of my way, one woman blessing herself, another pulling her child behind her, as I dashed toward the exit. Once outside, my head swiveled in the direction of the highway, my sense of smell responding eagerly to the scent of fresh blood.

CHAPTER TWENTY-ONE

T wo, maybe three, people followed me outside, happy to keep their distance. Inside, those less courageous peered from the glassed entry. Those who were shorter either elbowed their way past the taller shoppers gathered at the doors or leaped into the air in order to see over them, reminding me some of the whack-a-mole game I played with Nick as a child.

An occasional breeze intensified the metallic odor and wafted the scent over the parking lot. Well-defined images of the brutality taking place less than a couple of miles away came with it. What a burden Bianca's psychic ability must have seemed to her all those years!

With plans to take to the air, I glanced over my shoulder. The shoppers inside and the ones who had come out hadn't dispersed, and I realized a clandestine departure was out of the question. I tore off the Jimmy Choos and bolted toward the car. The Glock rubbed against the soft flesh on the inside of my thigh as I ran, slowing me down. Reaching between my legs, I yanked it from the holster and tucked it in my waistband. The tires spun against the asphalt and created a black smoke barrier as I steered the Dodge out of the lot. Time mattered, but thinking about the carnage that awaited, and remembering my near failure at Gettysburg, a part of me was in no hurry to get there.

I heard the rat-a-tat-tat of bullets fired in rapid succession as I swung into Funky Moves' crowded parking lot, the weapon undeniably an AK-47. Running the Dodge onto the curb nearest the main entrance, I began the exhausting execution of the Hidden Cloak. Sweat swamped my brow, seeping into and stinging my eyes.

My clenched jaw ached, and I realized I had chipped another damn tooth. I spat out the fragments and heard them ping against the window, but I couldn't see them. Nor could I see my forearms. I wanted to keep trying, encouraged by my progress so far, but more shots spilled into the parking lot. Time was running out. I had to come up with an alternate plan!

Elizabeth appeared in the passenger seat and studied me. Past a dramatic sigh, she said, "I assumed the plan was to disarm the criminal, not oneself."

Under different circumstances, I might have found the double entendre amusing. "I'm really in no mood for lame jokes."

"Just what exactly was it you were trying to accomplish?"

"I thought it might be best if I were invisible."

"Well, aside from the majority of your upper appendages, I regret to advise that you have failed miserably."

I exhaled through flared nostrils. "I'm well aware of that. Look, are you going to help me or not? Because I need to get in there."

"Then I suppose there is no time for protracted explanation," she said, fishing around inside my head, after which an electrical surge coursed through every vein, every muscle, and every cell, the sensation like electrocution, and I could no longer see my feet, my hands, or my torso.

"When you wish to reverse the incantation, simply imagine yourself visible once again and it shall be. Godspeed, my child," she said, tipping her head toward the building, burgeoning fangs swallowing up her lower lip as she sniffed the air like a four-legged predator. "Restraint will undoubtedly prove arduous."

I wished Nick were there to keep me in check. "Can't you stay? I'm not sure I understand how to reverse it." *Or if I can resist sinking my fangs into some unsuspecting innocent.*

"How many times must we say it, Celestine? The Powers of the Ancients now reside within you. All that is required is your belief."

"Wait! What am I supposed to do if something goes wrong?" I asked, but she was already gone, evaporating within a pungent sulfuric fog. Panic set in, but I couldn't think about the worst possible scenario now. I had to get inside the nightclub. Besides, if I failed to restore visibility, hadn't the Elders promised they would always assist me whenever I needed them?

I bolted from the car, looking over my shoulder and hoping to find Elizabeth near, then charged the main entrance and collided with a woman rushing the door. She lost her balance, and I grabbed her arm to break her fall. Wearing a quizzical expression, she patted down the air in front of her, like a mime trolling for handouts on a busy street corner. Making a wide arc, I managed to squeeze past her and nearly tripped over the dead bouncer, blood seeping from vertical bullet holes dotting his T-shirt.

Bullet holes pockmarked the stark cement walls in a random pattern. Men and women stampeded the entrance, most of the men leaving chivalry on the dance floor or a barstool. Some screamed. Others appeared dazed, wide-eyed and pale despite the strobing rosy hues thrown off the spinning disco ball. A rotund man in his forties bulldozed his way ahead of the others, knocking down one woman and nearly trampling another. I sent him a telepathic command, surprised when he complied with my suggestion, and he assisted the first woman to her feet, then carried the other to safety.

The gunfire had stopped, making it difficult to pinpoint the shooter's location. The musicians had abandoned the stage and their instruments. Riddled with bullets, the purple metallic drum, previously bearing the band's name and logo, now looked more like a colander. Near the back of the club, frightened patrons resembled mummies, motionless and deathly white, and plastered their sweaty palms over their mouths to muffle screams as they hid behind tables, upended to serve as makeshift shields. Blood-spattered bodies littered the dance floor, several couples still intertwined in a final tender embrace.

So. Much. Blood.

Unlike the battle of Gettysburg, the dead and wounded lay in an enclosed environment, with no wind or fresh air to dilute the overpowering, exhilarating scent. My body shook with a mild quiver that progressed into a teeth-chattering tremor. My biceps, triceps, pectoral, hamstring, and calf muscles bulged, vibrating with superhuman strength, daring me to act on my desire. Razor-sharp incisors engulfed my lower lip, and I nearly gave in.

But then I saw him. Huddled behind a column as he reloaded, long slippery hair slung behind narrow Quasimodo-like shoulders, a sinister smile revealing the deranged inner workings of a born killer. He blinked and I was on top of him. The column obscured him from the others, and I wanted him to see me. I concentrated with the kind of intensity that bursts blood vessels, but nothing happened. I tried again, this time envisioning an opaque shroud, then the dismantling of that shroud, one section at a time. My hands appeared, then my arms, and then the remainder of my body, like water washing over mud to reveal everything beneath. I saw my eyes, red-framed golden orbs, reflected in his. I smelled his fear, rancid and feral, not unlike Vykoka's when Bianca surrounded his pack of werewolves and destroyed him. Inching my face closer, I clacked my teeth, and the little color that remained left his face. His eyebrows nearly met his scalp, and within one eye a blood vessel burst, the subconjunctival hemorrhage so dramatic the white sclera turned completely red. A soundless scream revealed his discolored teeth and a wad of tobacco. I could hear the thumping of his heart, felt it pumping wildly as it fed the bloody river coursing through his veins.

The music resumed—"Ghost" by Justin Bieber—while the disco ball began another revolution, flinging a kaleidoscope of color on the walls, and I drew my Glock and rammed the barrel against the shooter's head. I stroked the trigger, my eyes wandering over the carnage he had caused. God, how I wanted to end his miserable life. He squirmed beneath me, desperate to escape, and I dug my knees into his groin. A line of blue burst through the door, guns drawn, and swept the club in tactical formation. I disarmed the killer, then whacked his head with the butt of my gun and knocked him unconscious.

"This is Detective Crenshaw, KCPD speaking," I called out. "Don't shoot. I've got the suspect in custody." Then I stepped out from behind the column and laid down my weapon and the assault rifle.

"Let's see some ID," one of the officers said. "Slow and easy."

"The suspect is over there, behind the column," I offered, jerking my head toward a shoulder. "I could use a set of cuffs."

He nodded to another cop, who sprinted toward the column.

I plucked my shield from my cleavage and yanked off the wig. "I was working undercover, just up the road, when I heard the shots."

"You said you heard the shots?" he asked while retrieving my weapon and handing it back to me. "From up the road?"

"That's right. From the Budget Bizarre parking lot," I replied, hitching a thumb in that direction.

His brows furrowed, and I knew he was busy doing calculations. "That's a couple of miles away."

I shrugged. "Not quite. And I'm sure you're aware how the sound of gunfire carries."

He eyed me with suspicion. "Yeah, but through a concrete building?"

The medical examiner had already been summoned, and I decided to wait outside for the ME's van. The vacated patrol cars flashed red and blue lights and served as a convenient beacon. A squadron of ambulances shrilled in the distance, emergency lights illuminating the nearby highway and announcing their impending arrival.

Two forensics investigators hopped out of their van as four media wagons rolled up and officers worked to cordon off the area. Directing a brief but firm reminder that the media stay behind the yellow banner, I returned to my car and shrugged into the trench coat. Soon after, the ME arrived, and I met her near the entrance.

Claudia "Juice" Romano ducked under the yellow police tape as effortlessly as an overweight woman nearing the age of fifty could. She served me a curt nod and hesitated just outside the door. Between gloved fingers, she gripped a straw protruding from a juice box and slurped the last few drops before fishing a surgical mask from a pocket.

"Nice to see you, Detective. How bad is it?"

"Bad enough."

"Is the shooter alive?"

"Unfortunately."

Stern eyes cut my direction, but I sensed a smile lingered beneath her surgical mask. "Give Gloria Hall a call, will you? My assistant is out with COVID-like symptoms, and I'm assuming by *bad enough*, I'm going to need all the help I can get." She pushed a latex covered palm toward me. "As far as COVID goes, I'm certain I wasn't exposed, and I'm fully vaccinated."

A lethal mortal virus is the least of my concerns.

I hadn't talked to Gloria Hall in some time. She'd given up her full-time ME position two years ago, preferring an on-call status, which allowed her more free time to enjoy her favorite pastimes: cooking, soap operas, and making her husband miserable.

I punched in her number, finding it necessary to reprimand a particularly assertive reporter from the *Kansas City Star* as I waited for her to pick up.

"Hell-O." Gloria answered on the second ring. I distanced the phone from my ear when she began to yell. "Stanley! Turn down the GD TV! I'm on the phone."

I gave her a play-by-play, and she assured me she'd show within a half hour. I was about to go inside to inform Claudia and to assist with the witness statements when I heard Larson Lindley, a detective from a neighboring precinct, call my name. I turned as he breached the crime scene tape. Behind him, the convoy of ambulances swung into the lot.

"I thought that was you," he said, his eyes snaking over the parted trench coat and coming to rest on my cleavage. He hitched a thumb toward the building. "Business or pleasure?"

I thought about the goose egg and the blue balls I'd given the shooter and smiled. "Both."

A valley formed between his brows as he considered another question. Instead of asking one, he tipped his head to several cops and four detectives I recognized from his precinct, who were busy detaining and questioning the people who'd managed to escape the building.

"I was just headed in to interview some of the witnesses," I said as several EMTs threaded a path with their gurneys.

He plucked a pristine notebook from an inner jacket pocket. "I'll give you a hand. Nice outfit, by the way."

Gloria's stature complemented her big personality, so when a large form blocked the entryway, I knew she'd arrived.

"Hidey ho," she boomed, and I noticed Claudia cringe. She stepped out of the way, allowing the arresting officers room to escort the shooter outside. "That little pipsqueak is responsible for all of this?" she asked of no one in particular.

Claudia sighed. "They come in all shapes and sizes. Thanks for coming, Gloria."

"Where's Detective Crenshaw?" I heard Police Chief Patterson ask.

I hadn't seen him arrive and assumed he'd entered through the rear exit in order to avoid the press. I didn't have any more questions for the witness I was interviewing, other than a second contact number, and granted her permission to leave.

"There you are," he said as I made my way across the dance floor, a slow flush warming my body as I endured his long, sweeping gaze.

"I was working a sex trafficking case," I offered as explanation.

He nodded past a scowl. "I hear you were first on the scene?"

"Yes," I said and left it at that.

"What was the perp's state of mind when you arrived?"

"Uh . . . homicidal."

Patterson had always rubbed me the wrong way. He was sexist, rude, and impatient, and I was in no mood to placate him.

"Try to keep up, Detective," he said snarling. "We've identified the shooter as Andrew Thompson. Did Thompson appear to be hallucinating? Was he cognitively impaired?"

I felt my eyes narrow. "He had the presence of mind to load a 75-round magazine, Chief, so I think it's fair to say he wasn't cognitively impaired. I also think, by his actions, his mental instability is obvious."

"Oh, you do, do you? I'm trying to get ahead of an insanity plea, Crenshaw. According to that piece of shit, a *vampire* sat on his nuts, confiscated his weapon, then hit him in the head."

I forced a chuckle. "That's pretty bizarre, Chief. He's either hallucinating or . . ."

"He plans on pleading insanity to spare himself death row. Get onboard, Detective. I want every loophole at his disposal closed and cemented over. And what's this I hear about a transfer to nights?" Before I could respond, Patterson said, "The DA's going to want to talk to you first thing in the morning. So, I suggest you go home and catch a couple of hours sleep. You're going to need it."

From the experiences I'd had with District Attorney Mitch Sullivan, the chief wasn't exaggerating. Sullivan was a pretentious little man with his eye on a congressional seat. Apparently, a lack of humility was inherent; those behind the scenes equally detested his brother the mayor, often utilizing similar vulgar terms whether referencing one man or the other.

"It will all be in my report, Chief. I don't see how a face-to-face is going—"

"Maybe I didn't make myself clear, Detective," he interrupted. "Come morning, you *will* be in the DA's office, first thing."

I was more worried about impending daylight than missing a few hours of sleep, but because it seemed there was no way I could avoid it, I said, "If it's all the same to you, Chief, I'd like to finish up here."

He grumbled his acceptance, and I returned to the witnesses.

"Glad to see you're in one piece," someone spoke behind me an hour later.

"I'll be with you in just a minute," I said to the next witness, then turned to give Quaid my utmost attention. "What are you doing here?"

"I was in the neighborhood. I heard it was you who took the son of a bitch down."

I nodded. "So you were in the neighborhood, huh?"

"I would have been here sooner, but while I was on the way I got a call on a possible abduction. Looks like you were right about the abductors sticking to Wednesdays."

Shit! If I could have only remained, another victim wouldn't have been grabbed. I raked tense fingers through tangled honey-colored strands. "Tell me we have a lead this time."

He sucked his teeth and hitched his off-the-rack pants toward his rib-cage.

"This one got us some intel. She took off toward the loading docks, and they caught up with her there. . ."

"Where there's no shortage of security cameras."

He winked. "That's right. We're running the abductor's image through FRT now. The camera also caught one of the driver. It's grainy, but we both know they've worked with a lot less."

Facial recognition technology had helped us solve a number of cases over the last five years, so I was, guardedly, hopeful.

"Were either one of them baldheaded?"

"Your guess is as good as mine. They both wore hats."

"Do we have an ID on the vic?" I thought it pointless this early in the investigation, but I asked anyway. I resisted a volley of toe taps as he leafed through his notes.

"Kayleigh Mateo. She had just clocked out and was leaving the store."

"So she worked there?"

"When she wasn't busy doing other things."

I threw my weight behind one hip and blew out my frustration. "Cut the cryptic crap, Quaid. What other things?"

"Simmer down, Crenshaw. I'll get to it."

"Now would be nice."

"I wondered why she ran toward the loading dock, so I browsed through some pretty mind-numbing footage. Twenty minutes before her shift ended, Ms. Mateo was helping a delivery driver unload something other than inventory."

"They were having sex?"

He nodded. "That would be my guess. They disappeared behind the truck—out of range, but the camera caught the driver rounding the truck, approximately ten minutes later, zipping his pants. Ms. Mateo appeared, buttoning her blouse, a few seconds after that."

"So when she ran toward the loading docks, she probably assumed the driver was still there—"

Quaid nodded. "And thought he could help her."

Thinking aloud, I said, "It's possible they'd been watching her, knew she worked Wednesdays, and knew what time she'd leave the building."

"Sounds like a plausible theory. Want me to give you a hand?" Quaid asked and tipped his head toward the remaining twenty-some nightclub witnesses.

"I'd appreciate that." Even though we had the shooter and his weapon in custody—and I had caught him in the act—protocol dictated a thorough report. Regardless, I found it difficult to mask my resentment; I had a feeling we'd soon see a dramatic increase in abductions, and I was anxious to return to the cases I'd been assigned.

CHAPTER TWENTY-TWO

I t was after seven a.m. when I returned to the station, the trench coat draped over my head and partially blocking my vision. I pulled a duffel bag from the trunk and thought this a prime example for keeping an extra set of clothes in the car. Inside the locker room, I changed into a pair of generic trousers and a matching blazer, scrubbed any trace of makeup from my face, slathered on Fane's ghastly sunscreen, and hoped my fangs wouldn't decide to make an appearance if Sullivan pissed me off. He usually did. I glanced at my reflection in the floor-length mirror and plucked a few pieces of lint from the blazer. Because the mirror reflected only my clothing, I blotted my face free of any possible residual sunscreen with a moist paper towel.

Once parked outside the Jackson County Courthouse, I sat in my car with a hoodie snugged around my head. The granite memorial occupied the building's focal point and glistened in the early light. Thanks to Bianca, I carried with me a simulated memory of all the carnage that took place on that very spot, nearly thirty years ago. I had intended to avoid the marker, more specifically the names engraved alphabetically with detached precision, but instead I left the car and kneeled before it, my fingers trembling as they tracked my parents' names. The epitaph offered no explanation, the city electing not to memorialize the explosion itself. Law enforcement blissfully unaware of the Harvesters' presence that day, any information pertaining to the murderous vampires' siege following the explosion would always remain a painful secret.

Shoulders slumped, I inched my way toward the entrance, taking cover whenever I could within the shade provided by competing rows of redbud, crabapple, and Bradford pear trees. Once inside, I took a long breath and narrowed my eyes, determined I would not allow the DA to bully me into submission. I heard Sullivan's rant as I neared his office, every angry word reverberating off the staggered marble columns in the lobby.

I saw him through the windowed door, face purpled by his customary rage, sausage fingers gripping a monogrammed pen mercilessly. He noticed me and cupped his fingers. When I didn't respond fast enough, he whistled as if I were something that wore a collar and tags. I ran my tongue over my teeth and took a deep breath before stepping inside.

"Chief Patterson said you wanted to see me."

He checked his watch, beady eyes looking past a smug smirk. "You're late, Detective."

"Don't you have my statement?"

"Is that what you call *this*?" he said and tossed a document across his desk.

I studied it briefly. "It looks accurate," I said past a squint. "I don't know what else you could possibly need from me."

"I *need* a death penalty conviction. The defendant's lawyer is busy scheming an insanity plea as we speak."

I looked away, so he couldn't see me roll my eyes. Of course, the shooter was nuts. "With all due respect, sir, what kind of rational person shoots fifty-six people?"

He leaped to his feet and pounded his desk. "Goddamn it, Detective! I intend to see this defendant strapped to a table and executed. The good people of this city won't settle for anything less."

I knew the desire of the city's *good people* was the last thing on Sullivan's mind. Their votes to secure his seat in the US House of Representatives, though, was an entirely different matter.

He lowered his voice and attempted to woo me with his charm, something about as alien to him as adequate oral hygiene. "Tense situations have a way of eroding vital information, Detective. I think if you give it some time, you may recall more important details."

Pressing my spine to the chair, I latched my arms across my chest. "Just what exactly do you expect me to testify to?"

Veins surfaced across his forehead and reminded me of a long-legged spider spinning a web. "I don't think I like your tone or your implication."

"Mr. District Attorney, if you're suggesting that I fabricate certain details to suit your narrative, we have a problem."

"You seem to be the one here with the problem, Detective. Who would know better than a seasoned detective that anything less than a death sentence opens the door to early parole or an appeal? I want this goddamn animal off the streets for good," he said, jabbing the desktop repeatedly.

I lurched forward and slapped a palm on the desk. "What do you want me to say? He enjoyed a candy bar or played a videogame between reloads? Maybe called his mother or a friend to say he'd be late getting home? I don't see how the addition of such mundane details might serve to circumvent an insanity plea."

"Let's stop the dance, Detective. I'm concerned about this story he's telling. I want that story discredited. The jury needs to hear your perception of his state of mind, a lucid conversation with you that disqualifies the ridiculous account the defense plans to sell the jury."

"There was no conversation."

"Goddamn it," he said, fisting the pen, which began leaking ink. "You expect me to believe you simply approached him and he surrendered his weapon?"

"The details are in my report."

Sullivan snatched the document from his desk and began to read. "I approached the suspect and disarmed him."

I threw my palms in the air. "That's what happened. I took him by surprise. He didn't see me coming because his attention was on the weapon. He had the barrel pointed at the ground, so I saw an opportunity and took advantage of it."

"And you expect me to believe that there were no words exchanged?"

"We fought over the weapon. He continued to struggle, so I rendered him unconscious to contain the threat."

"Why didn't you shoot to kill, Detective? That lunatic had already murdered two dozen innocent people and wounded thirty-two others! For God's sake, you were within your rights!"

Don't think I wasn't tempted. "I follow my training. He wasn't an active threat at the time."

"Oh, is that right?" Sullivan said, leaning across the desk. "Well, Detective, if the jury buys his story, he's certainly an active threat now."

"From what I heard, it's quite a story. Something about a vampire?" I forced a laugh, but it fell flat. "I feel confident twelve everyday citizens will find his testimony difficult to swallow. Give them some credit."

"You'd better hope so, Detective," he said, leaning back in his chair and interlacing his fingers. "Otherwise, the mayor just might strip you of your shield, and you'll spend your days issuing citations for parking violations."

I pinched my flared nostrils closed. "If there's nothing else, Mr. District Attorney, it's been a long night, and I'd like to try to get some sleep."

───

I threw myself behind the steering wheel and headed for home, reflecting on my conversation with the DA. It *was* possible a jury would find the killer insane and that a judge would then remand him to a low-security psychiatric facility. What would happen if he managed to escape? Had I put potential lives at risk by not pulling the trigger? I felt sure Matilda and the other

Omniscients—and the Elders, for that matter—would have disapproved of how I handled the situation. The only law they believed in was the law of averages, and it was almost a given that the mass murderer would strike again if given the chance. But I had plans for Andrew Thompson II. If he ever walked the streets of Kansas City again, I'd be there to welcome him back.

Back home and greeted by dead silence, I tossed my keys on the table, my eyes wandering to Raina's nook. I never would have guessed that just the sight of her could take my mind off all the ugly things I witnessed while away from her. I squeezed into a tiny chair, reserved for me only, and closed my eyes, summoning time spent there in that whimsical, happy room with Raina and Tristan.

Raina appeared around the time warmth spread from my toes to my eyes and I nearly drifted off to sleep. My heart skipped at the sight of her, and I opened my arms.

"Hey, sleepyhead. Why aren't you asleep?"

Rubbing her eyes, she folded herself in my lap and whimpered, "I had a dreadful dream."

"Oh, no! Another one? I'm sorry to hear that," I said and nestled her close. "But remember what I said? Sometimes, it helps to talk about it."

"Fane says I mustn't ever share my very scariest dreams with you. He says if I do, you shall worry and worry and worry."

"Hmm. What if I promise not to worry?"

Her big brown eyes studied mine. "If I do tell you, must we tell Fane?"

"I think, just this one time, it can be our little secret."

"I do so love secrets!"

"I know you do," I said, rocking and tickling her until she squealed. "Now, what was this nightmare about?"

Her lower lip began to quiver. "I simply can't say the words aloud," she sobbed.

"Aw, Raina. It was only a bad dream, baby."

She shook her head and between sobs, she said, "The Bad Ones made Tristan b-l-eeeeed."

By the Bad Ones, I knew she'd dreamt of the Harvesters again. Although I felt sure it was just a dream, probably brought on by a flurry of crazy things Fane had involved her in earlier, I swallowed past a lump.

"Oh goodness, that doesn't sound possible." I gnawed my lip while I scratched my head and tried to think what best to say next. "Um, I've forgotten; what is it the Realm calls Tristan? Is it puppy dog?" Raina giggled and leaned back so she could watch my exaggerated expressions. "No, that can't be right. I know—scaredy-cat."

Raina shook her head. "Nooooo, not scaredy-cat. We call Tristan the Supreme Warrior."

"That's it. Now I remember. Do you know why we call him that?"

"Why?"

"Because he is the Realm's greatest and most feared warrior. I am told that sometimes when Tristan appears, the Bad Ones take one look at him and fly away."

"*They* are the scaredy-cats."

"Yes, they are," I said and kissed her forehead. "So no more worrying about Tristan."

She narrowed her eyes and puffed her lower lip. "The Bad Ones better fly away, or Tristan shall get them."

"That's right, Raina. They had better fly away if they know what's good for them." I looked away so she couldn't see my eyes. Fane was right; I was worried. After consoling Raina and swaddling her within the coffin, I failed to console myself and attempted contact with Bianca.

CHAPTER TWENTY-THREE

I heard Bianca whisper my name, jolting me from sleep. Raina slept peacefully beside me, and I grimaced when the coffin's hinges squeaked as I pressed the lid open.

Worry lines tracked her forehead as she assisted me out. "What is it, darling?" she said, and I brought my finger to my lips. Anticipating more squeaking, I grinded my teeth while lowering the lid, then escorted her into the hallway.

I swept my bangs from an eye and observed her sheepishly. The fear I'd experienced earlier seemed a bit overdramatic now. Her sword hung at her side, the blade noticeably dull in places and discolored by things I preferred not to think about.

"I shouldn't have bothered you, Mom. I'm sure it's nothing."

"Nonsense. I have never known you to raise the alarm unless the situation warranted it. Now, tell me, what is it that frightens you so?"

"It's Raina. You know how she sometimes has those . . . premonitions?"

"Indeed, I do. The child is most intuitive."

"Well, she had a night terror that woke her from a sound sleep."

The beginnings of a grin died on her lips. "Children often have those, you know. Whatever was it about?"

"The Harvesters attacking Tristan."

A frown corrupted her beautiful face. "And what would you have me say to such an obvious possibility?"

"Wow! Really? Well, definitely not that," I said, turning away from her, fraught once again with the level of fear that flipped my stomach.

"Forgive my bluntness, Celeste," she said, sweeping a hand through my hair. "This evening's battle was most harrowing. However, rest assured Tristan remains unscathed."

"All I could think of was the time Nick and I were on the Cape May-Lewes ferry and Tristan came to our rescue when the Harvesters attacked—"

"And he was nearly destroyed. Yes, I remember it well." Bianca sighed.

"Then you must realize why I had to know nothing's happened to him."

She squeezed my hand and pulled me close. "Iubirea mea, you cannot possibly think I would fail to alert you should such a cataclysmic event occur?"

"No. I mean, of course, I know you would."

She raised my chin, the tip of her long fingernail pricking my skin. "Then let us put an end to this nonsense."

"When will he, when will all of you, come home?"

"We shall drop in as often as the situation allows, but, in truth, I anticipate a protracted battle." She emitted a long sigh. "Once we drive those abominations from one continent, they happily invade another, amassing more recruits with each passing day."

"Then, why can't I help? The Realm is outnumbered. It seems to me—"

"You are not ready, my darling," she interrupted. I was ready to protest, to remind her I assisted the Realm in taking down the Harvesters last year after they'd breached the preschool and abducted all those children when she pressed a finger to my lips. "While it is true your assistance was invaluable, our enemy now outnumbers us four to one. The enemy with whom you fought were new in the blood, Celeste, their powers rather pedestrian when compared to those possessed by the fiends we battle this day."

"Yes, I know. And like I said, that's all the more reason I should be there with you, Mom."

A sly smile played across her lips, and I knew she was aware of the things I'd left unsaid. "Yes, Celeste, but the powers Nostradamus gave you, though most impressive—unarguably superior to all within the Realm—are presently uncultivated."

Even though I'd been successful in reversing the Hidden Cloak, I knew she was right. "Okay, but what about the potion? I know Torok Laboratories has stepped up production on the COVID vaccine, internationally. We're slipping in the potion, right?"

She looked away, wringing her hands. "I'm afraid that is presently not a viable option."

"I understand the time constraint, but if the lab is stepping things up anyway . . ."

She blew out a long breath. "I didn't wish to alarm you, but we absolutely cannot. The Realm's stockpiles have dwindled, Celeste. And should our supply become tainted, should every blood donor receive the vaccine that includes the potion, well, I don't imagine I have to tell you of the repercussions."

I shook from my head visions of the Realm, to include my parents, Nick, Tristan, and me, feeding on the innocent, once left with no other recourse. "But isn't there a way to identify those who have received the potion and those who have not?"

She threw her arms around me and kissed my forehead. "Despite painstaking diligence, mistakes happen, Celeste. Mistakes we cannot afford. That and time is presently a luxury. I really must go, my darling. The battle awaits."

With that, she was gone, her lavender and tuberose scent lingering in the air. She'd done nothing to minimize my fear. Instead, with this new revelation, she'd only compounded it.

I discovered Fane sleeping soundly beneath my bed, the duvet he'd tugged from the bed shrouding his body. A sudden shift in his position revealed unusually long eyelashes, which fluttered every now and then, and a smile as tender as it was rare. He looked every bit a sleeping angel, the fiendish side of him lying dormant while he dreamed of clever ways to upend my life. I thought to wake him, to tell him Tristan was safe and that he should let Raina know if they woke before me, but then remembered my promise to her.

Seated at the small desk beneath one of Tristan's favorite paintings— Rembrandt's *The Return of the Prodigal Son*, I drew a crude picture of Tristan. Beneath it, I wrote:

Dear Raina,
The Supreme Warrior sends his love.

I crept back inside the coffin and tucked it in her tiny fist.

That evening, I delayed my return to the station so that I could spend as much time with Raina as possible. We talked about Bianca's visit, more specifically about Tristan.

Despite my doing everything conceivable to convince her that he was fine, she clung to me most of the evening. For one fleeting moment, I considered quitting my job.

I was at my wit's end when Tristan materialized before us. My eyes rolled over his sinewy muscles, glossy dark hair, and the bloody sword he'd attempted to hide from us, slung low behind one hip. I saw the urgency in his eyes, and I knew he already had one foot out the door.

"Tell me the reason behind all this commotion," he said, scooping Raina from my lap. "For, as you can see, I am in one piece, am I not? I still have my fingers," he said, tickling her until she couldn't draw a breath, "and my nose," he said, grinning, after which he sniffed her exaggeratedly from head to toe as though he were a dog tracking a scent.

Raina's giggles subsided, and she wrapped her arms tightly around his neck. "I was horribly frightened, Tristan. I thought I shan't ever see you again."

"Yet, here I am," he said, winking at me.

"Won't you stay, Tristan? Please say you will," she said, a tiny hand reaching up to brush his cheek.

"You know I cannot, Raina," he said, kissing the top of her head while pulling me close. "But I shall count the minutes, no, every single second, until I see you again."

She shook her head and tightened her grip.

"Raina," I whispered, "the sooner the battle is won, the sooner Tristan can return. So, give him a kiss for good luck, and I'll give him one, too."

She pulled away and looked into my eyes. "Yes, then he shall be doubly lucky." She smashed her lips against his cheek and wiggled her head. "Time for your kiss, Mummy."

Tristan leaned down and our lips met and smoldered, sizzling flickers enhancing the pure joy behind Raina's dark eyes.

"Adieu, my loves," he said and then he was gone.

"No! No! Tristan, come back," Raina called into the night.

Fane came to the rescue with candle in hand and shut off the lights.

He responded to my confused expression. "Prepare to be amazed, for it is said that I, and I alone, am the master of shadow puppetry."

"Fane, are there no limits to your talents?" I gushed sarcastically.

He narrowed his eyes and smirked. "Raina, wish Mummy a wonderful eve as the Adventures of Magical Creatures will soon begin."

"Can't she stay?" Raina blubbered, swiping bloody tears from her eyes.

"I'm afraid not. You see, Morgawr is quite shy, and he shan't stay long unless Mummy departs. Consider this but a tantalizing preview," he said and faced the wall, the candle at his back, arms contorted and flapping, hands booked together and opening then closing, casting a shadow on the wall that resembled a winged sea monster.

Raina squealed her delight, hopping on one foot then the other "We bid you good eve, Mummy. Please go now," she called over her shoulder.

Fane looked from me to the door and flicked his wrist.

"Thank you," I mouthed.

Quaid was already in the bullpen when I arrived, his feet propped up on his desk as he skimmed a report. "No luck with FRT. No DMV matches either and no hits through Clearview."

"Shit," I said, shoving my chair into the desk. "I find it hard to believe those men have never had a felony conviction or a driver's license."

"Reminds me of a slew of armed robbery cases I solved in the nineties," Quaid began. I resisted an eye roll and prepared for one of his mind-numbing trips down memory lane. "Stephen Tiller. When I frisked him, I found a New York, a California, a Montana, and a Missouri driver's license, not one of them bearing a close resemblance. He'd worn a different disguise in each photograph. Criminals are smart."

"We'll see about that."

He clacked his pen against the desk and grinned. "That's what I like about you, Crenshaw; you're ballsy. By the way, some woman called, said she couldn't remember your extension. She wants a call back."

"What woman?"

He reached across his desk, groaning when the edge compressed his plump belly. He squinted as he attempted to decipher his own handwriting. "Mannie Martin."

"Quaid! It's *Mamie* Martin. The same woman I talked to before. You were sitting right here."

He shrugged and passed me the note, which included her phone number.

I glanced at the schoolhouse clock above the doorway, grimacing when it verified that I'd spent twenty minutes on a useless conversation with Quaid. I punched in Mamie's number and resisted gnawing my fingernails while I waited for her to pick up.

"It's you again," she greeted past a snort. "And if you're thinkin' I know that on account-a I got caller ID now, you're dead wrong. Who else calls an old woman in the dead of night? It sure as hell ain't some lover boy."

"I'm sorry, Ms. Martin," I said and glared at Quaid. "I just got your message."

"It's missus, like I told ya before. I hope your snoopin' skills are better than that memory of yours."

I cleared my throat, along with the blistering remark on the tip of my tongue. "What can I help you with?"

She laughed, her laugh sounding more like a death rattle. "What can *you* help *me* with? I'm the one handin' out the favors here, girly."

"Yes, ma'am, and I appreciate any information you can give me. Did you remember something else?"

"Indeedy-do. That one feller that threw that girl in the car—like she weren't nothin' but a sack of taters—had one of 'em tattoos on the back of his shaved head. Looked like someone had carved it into his thick skull with a dull needle and then asked a kinygardener to color it up."

My ears perked up. "Can you describe it?"

"At first, I didn't know what to think of it. But later when I was sitting there drinkin' my afternoon Miller Lite, waitin' on Judge Judy's television program, it come to me. It looked to be an upside-down crucifix. Like one of 'em devil worshipers I seen on a PBS documentary."

"That information will undoubtedly prove beneficial, Mrs. Martin. Thank you—"

"I ain't done yet. That same piece of horse dung had a scar, too. On one of his cheeks. Coulda been his left one. I don't remember, so I can't be sure."

CHAPTER TWENTY-FOUR

I didn't share the information with Quaid, and it was also something I felt we should keep from the press. With that in mind, I was relieved he had ventured off toward the canteen prior to that part of the conversation. He was about as good at keeping secrets as Edward Snowden.

A bit of a control freak, I studied the board to make sure Quaid had entered everything we knew about the most recent abduction—Kayleigh Mateo from the Budget Bizarre.

I had returned to my desk to grab a red and a green marker when Quaid's desk phone and mine rang, simultaneously.

I ended the *Officer Down* call nearly as quickly as it began and shouted for Quaid to grab his bulletproof vest. He held the door while I jerked my Kevlar vest from my locker, a bead of perspiration on his upper lip, and we charged toward his unmarked car, a black Dodge Challenger hugging a curb, emergency lights visible within the grill. The tires gripped the pavement, despite Quaid's heavy foot, and he completed an impressive U-turn, which rocked me toward him, then away.

"What's the 10-20?" he shouted as he activated the LED stick lights.

"Fifty-ninth and Lincoln Avenue. Bully's Bar and Grill. The gunmen have two officers pinned down in the parking lot."

"Who got hit?"

I shook my head. "Dispatch didn't say."

We parked at the corner and duck-walked the rest of the way, bullets pinging off the mangled chain-link fence constructed years ago to protect a building that was no longer there. We drew closer and I saw Officer Kennedy Baker taking cover behind the squad car, sweat glistening off her dark cropped hair, Officer Bradley Lewis squatting alongside her. Kennedy spotted us and huffed a sigh of relief, then signaled toward an open second-floor window. I'd known Bully's owner, Cicely Jones, for years and assumed she still called the upper floor of the building her residence. Because it was common knowledge that Cicely could handle a shotgun and a fillet knife with equal proficiency, I was surprised to find that element of trouble on her doorstep.

Three patrol cars skidded to a stop nearer the corner, a line of blue closing ranks around a vehicle that had smashed into a traffic light pole. A few minutes passed and all but two of the officers abandoned their quarry and crept in our direction.

"Cover me," I told Quaid and dashed toward the main entrance. Hugging the building, I stole a peek inside, finding it difficult to see much beyond the metal bars covering the glass door. The spirited jazz music, which usually spilled its way into the street, was absent, the colorfully tiled dance floor empty. More bullets rat-a-tat-tatted sheet-metaled automobiles, projectiles finding their way through windshields, from the sound of it. I crept around the side of the building—my intention to teleport inside and take the perpetrators by surprise—and rocketed toward the second floor, positioning myself just outside Cicely's second-floor apartment. Bracing myself, I imagined the exterior nothing but a flimsy curtain. A short time later, with nothing to show for my third attempt but a bruised shoulder, I discovered Nick behind me, hovering near a sycamore tree, like a surveillance drone.

"Here we go again. Who are you trying to impress, Celeste?" He shook his head in disbelief. "You always had to do everything the hard way. Work smarter, not harder, I always say." He grabbed my arm and whizzed us both behind the building where an outside door led directly into Cicely's apartment.

"What are you doing here?" I whispered once we stood in the living room. "I would have made it inside, one way or another."

"Woulda, coulda, shoulda. You're welcome."

"You should be with Mom and Dad. And Tristan," I said through a snarl.

"Chill, Celeste. Now," he said, scrubbing his palms, "let's show these assholes who's boss. I see four guys with guns." He stretched his neck to get a better view of what lay beyond the living room. "One guarding the stairway, one nursing a bitchin' bullet hole, and two jerkoffs raining some impressive lead and brass on those cops below. I'll take the fucker at the top of the stairs."

"Nick, get back here," I hissed, but he'd become a blur of black. The stair guy flew past on his way to the bottom, Nick following overhead wearing a disturbing grin. The men firing on the police hadn't heard the commotion, and I smothered a sigh of relief.

"One down," Nick mimed, shapeshifted into a raven with a five-foot wingspan, and zipped toward the gunmen targeting the police officers in the parking lot.

I sailed toward the guy with the bullet hole spurting blood, thankful he had surrendered to unconsciousness. Despite plugging my nose and looking away from all that blood, I remembered how sweet Nostradamus's blood had tasted, the euphoria I had experienced, and I felt my fangs prick my lower lip.

"Don't do it, Celeste!" Nick said, tackling me and sending me backward. The shooters heard that, and a volley of bullets flew past. Nick transitioned back to Nick, but tripled in size. He soared toward the men, creating a transient tornadic whirlwind, the velocity upsetting knickknacks arranged with meticulous detail on floating walnut shelves. The propulsion upon impact sent the men flying through the open patio door, one landing on a patrol car parked below, the other—spread-eagle—in the middle of the parking lot. I cuffed the injured perp.

Nick was nowhere in sight, and I wondered how in the hell I was going to explain everything.

Twirling in a circle, I fisted a clump of hair at the back of my head. "Suspects are disarmed," I said meekly into my radio.

Tactical boots pummeled the outside stairs leading to the second floor. Quaid was the first one through the door.

"What the hell happened up here?"

Before I could come up with anything plausible, Officer Lewis approached.

"Detectives, it looks like the gunshot victims in the car on the corner were involved in a shootout with these guys."

I now understood why three patrol cars had swarmed the car that had careened into the light pole. That it wasn't just a case of a drunk driver losing control of his vehicle, but rather a rival gang member incapacitated due to a gunshot wound.

Quaid curled a lip. "Another goddamn drive-by."

"One of the officers on scene said the dead guys on the corner are members of the KC Crusaders," Lewis added.

"So our prisoners came in to take cover?" I asked Lewis. "Or were they customers headed out the door?"

"According to the owner, she asked them to leave following a heated argument over a pool table in the back. The gunfire began as soon as they went outside."

"So they were ambushed?" Quaid asked, scrubbing the crevices eroding his forehead.

Lewis puffed his chest while sucking in a beer belly. "It looks that way. Seconds later, they barricaded themselves inside. We think the officer who was shot was patrolling this end of the grid, heard the shots and responded immediately—"

"And the men in the passing car shot him," I finished for him.

"Yup, that appears to be the situation. He managed to make it inside before he went down," Lewis said, twisting his lips and hooking his thumbs in his belt loops, rekindling memories of Barney Fife from *Mayberry R.F.D.*

"Where's the officer now?" I asked.

"He's still downstairs. The ME isn't finished with him."

Quaid and I rushed the stairs, Quaid huffing and puffing by the time we reached the bottom. The ME had already finished her exam and was zipping up the body bag.

Our eyes met, and Medical Examiner Claudia Romano tipped her head. "Detectives, we meet again."

Quaid grumbled a greeting and unconsciously cracked his knuckles. I wondered how many officer shootings he had witnessed throughout his career.

"He didn't have a chance. Bullet to the head." She unzipped the bag and drew our attention to the bullet hole drilled through the officer's skull. "The two of you delivering the death notification?" she asked as she zippered the bag and wrenched off her gloves.

I deferred the answer to Quaid, who looked as if he'd just seen a ghost.

He sniffed and blew out a long exhale. "I've known Carl—Officer Schmidt—for years, so it only seems right. What a waste," he said, more to himself. He turned away and removed a wrinkled yellowed handkerchief from a breast pocket, then blotted both eyes.

Cicely crept up behind me and laid a hand on my shoulder. "He didn't die alone. We comforted him as best we could," she said, tipping her head toward a throng of men and women respectfully keeping their distance as they waited for Detectives Donahue and Franklin to take their statements. "I don't think he suffered."

I squeezed her hand. "We appreciate that." Fighting through various emotions, I set them aside. Even had I wanted to grant Officer Schmidt immortality, not only was it much too late but there were witnesses.

"You don't come around much anymore," Cicely said past sad eyes.

I smiled and gave her the short version. "I've been busy. But I'll try to do that."

I found Quaid outside, fishing a pack of Winston cigarettes from an inside jacket pocket. The death of his friend had hit him hard, and, thankfully, I didn't anticipate any questions about what had transpired before he arrived in Cicely's apartment.

"I thought you quit," I said quietly.

He toed the ground. "I did. And now, I've restarted. You know how it is: an addict looks for any excuse."

"Hey, why don't I handle the notification?" I asked softly.

He wagged his head. "Carl and I went through the Academy together. I was the best man at his wedding." He laughed suddenly. "Believe it or not, he and his wife Glenda chose me as their kid's godfather."

I wanted him to keep thinking about happier times. "So they only had the one?"

He laughed again. "No, they had three; the other two came along a few years later. I guess Carl and Glenda had come to know me better by then and either decided the other two kids would be better off on their own or they gave that honor to someone else."

"Aw, Dennis, I don't believe that." It seemed odd but necessary to address him by his first name.

He studied me through bloodshot eyes. "Yeah, you do." He snuffed out his cigarette and referenced his watch, his eyes turning to a lone media van, just arriving on the scene. "Fucking vultures. I'd better let Glenda know before she hears it on the news."

"I'll come with you," I said, rounding the vehicle.

"Nah, this could take a while. You mind hitching a ride back with Officers Baker and Lewis?"

"No problem and I get it. You'd rather be alone."

"Crenshaw, I've been alone most of my life."

CHAPTER TWENTY-FIVE

etective Reed launched her personal car, a pristinely restored
1970 Ford Mustang, over the crumbling concrete and brought it
to an abrupt stop, the engine emitting one final growl before she
switched off the ignition.

"Busy night," she said. "I came as soon as I could."

I fed her the details, particularly those pertaining to the possible involvement of a gang, and awaited her input.

She shifted her weight and parked one hand against a hip. "There's a
lot of chatter on the street about a drug war between the KC Crusaders and
their rivals, the Main Street Ghosts. In fact, I had just given up on an all-night
stakeout near the Ghosts' headquarters, when a call came in about a possible
home invasion two blocks east. Like I said, I came as soon as I could."

"This can't leak to the press. I don't want to tip off the perps." I waited
for the words to sink in. "Do you have any intel on a street gang embracing
a satanic cult affiliation?"

Her expression surprised me and was difficult to read. She seemed angry? Or was that surprise I saw on her face?

"It's unusual," she stammered past a squint. "What does that have to do with what happened here?"

I shook my head. "It doesn't have anything to do with it. I received some unusual eye-witness testimony to a kidnapping case, and I wanted your opinion."

"What kind of testimony?"

"An atypical tattoo—an inverted cross."

Reed's lips twitched sarcastically. "And you think your guy is not only a gang member but has, what, a satanic fetish?" She emitted a guttural laugh. "It could have been a depiction of the Cross of Saint Peter—the Petrine cross."

I shrugged. "I suppose that's possible. But we're talking about five abductors. So, you can see why I thought a gang may have been involved."

"I think you're barking up the wrong tree. Gangs don't usually participate in serial abductions. Rape, sure, but once they're finished with their victims, they usually release them, unharmed."

Unharmed! I chewed the inside of both cheeks and wondered how much time, if any, she'd spent with victims of rape. "Well, you know what they say: There's a first time for everything."

Reed shortened the distance between us. "Do me a favor, Crenshaw: don't stir the hornet's nest on a speculative assumption. I'm this close," she said, pinching her fingers, "to a massive weapons and fentanyl bust."

I wagged my head and pressed my palms her way. "You got it, Detective." *Unless I happen upon some damn compelling evidence.*

"And in return, *if* I spot a banger with a similar tattoo, I'll let you know."

My instincts convinced me she wouldn't tell me shit until after she'd made her arrests. Reed wasn't only a lone wolf, she was a glory hound—proficient in accumulating collars and marking her territory. "You do that."

"How's the officer?" she said, tipping her head toward the bar.

"He didn't make it."

Her eyes scanned the perimeter and then widened, like a terrifying thought had just occurred to her. "I don't see your partner. It wasn't him, I hope."

"No, but he'd known the murdered officer and for some time. He insisted he be the one to tell his wife."

She nodded, her gaze flying to her shoes. "Shit, that's never easy."

Officer Kennedy Baker swept past, hand in midwave as she headed for her patrol car, Officer Lewis trailing behind. "Officers, I'm going to need a lift back to the station," I called after them.

Baker nodded her acknowledgement.

"Be careful out there, Detective," Reed told me passively, then squared her shoulders. "And remember what I said about not stirring the hive."

All the way back to the station, the things Reed had said, and her attitude in general, continued to rub me the wrong way, and I was counting the minutes until end of shift. My shoulders slumped when I found Captain Burke waiting near my desk when I slunk into the Detectives' Den.

He looked as if he'd left the house without so much as a glance in the mirror. His hair stood on end, reminding me of an agitated rooster in the midst of a cockfight. A circular red glob, midway between the collar and hem of a misbuttoned shirt, suggested he had a fetish for ketchup and a loathing for drycleaners.

"This won't take long, Detective," he began. "Chief Patterson expects me to release a statement to the press, and I could use some firsthand intel," he said, motioning for me to follow him into his office.

"I'll do what I can," I said, still trying to come up with any explanation that didn't include an overzealous vampire brother.

"Real shame about Officer Schmidt," he said, wagging his head. "He was a damn fine cop." He motioned for me to take a seat while he perched inches away on the edge of his desk.

"Go, Detective," he said rolling his hand. "Tell me everything you can, aside from the identification of the shooters. I've already been briefed on names, gang affiliations, et cetera."

"Okay," I said after clearing my throat. "I went around to the back of the building and took the staircase to the second floor. Once inside, I had to disable an assailant—the guy guarding the interior stairway to the lower level. We had a brief altercation, which led to him falling down the stairs. He hit his head on the door and lost consciousness. I disarmed and cuffed him."

Burke nodded along. "Then what happened?"

"I saw a second gunman crouched down in the corner across the room, bleeding from, I assumed, a gunshot wound. I cuffed him then attempted to provide assistance."

"Did the bullet come from your gun?"

"No, sir."

"Where was his weapon at the time?"

"Beside him. He wasn't a threat by that point."

"What about the men in the parking lot?"

"I have no idea, Captain. It was too dark in the apartment. I heard some sort of struggle, but I never saw anything."

Burke scratched his chin until I thought it might bleed. "Is it possible there was someone else in the apartment?"

Oh, it was possible all right. "I suppose it's possible. Like I said, it was dark."

He scrubbed the back of his head and puffed his cheeks. "Both men found inside weren't fatally injured, as I'm sure you know, Crenshaw. But because the two scraped off the parking lot are currently playing footsie in the morgue, Internal Affairs may have a few questions. Make yourself available, Detective." He tipped his head and fixed a hard stare. "Any reason you need to get your union rep involved?"

Not unless someone witnessed my out-of-control brother toss two gang members through an opening as if they were Frisbees. "I can't think of a single one, sir."

"Looks like that's it then." He slapped his thighs and launched off his desk. "Oh, one more thing."

I knew what Burke was about to say. Thompson's arraignment sat on the docket, scheduled for the following day, and I assumed Burke wanted to make sure I'd be there, my presence to bolster the prosecution's argument against bail if necessary. The court had its fair share of lenient judges, but I seriously doubted any one of them would grant bail to an alleged mass murderer.

"The nightclub shooter—Thompson. He's got the best lawyer money can buy, and I need you in that courthouse tomorrow. If this guy makes bail, I'll never hear the end of it. So, let's pull out all the stops. Whatever it takes, Crenshaw. He comes from a wealthy family with the means to extradite him to a foreign country. Make damn good and sure the judge is aware. And his father owns a private jet, which increases the flight risk. Eleven a.m., sharp. No excuses. Go home and get some sleep."

I couldn't imagine the DA failing to make those talking points, but I kept my opinion to myself. "Who's presiding?"

He crinkled his nose and searched his pockets for an antacid, and I knew it had to be Judge Raymond "Boys-will-be-Boys" Lemont.

"Just be there, Detective."

CHAPTER TWENTY-SIX

I removed my Glock, cell phone, car keys, and shield, placed them in the tray along with my purse and hoodie, then set the tray on the conveyer belt. After I passed through the metal detector without a hitch, I remembered Lemont's stance on weapons in his courtroom and asked security to secure my handgun until my return. They presented me with a semi-legible receipt, to which I raised both eyebrows.

I stepped inside the courtroom and Sullivan's head immediately swiveled ninety degrees. Maybe those who swore the DA had eyes in the back of his head were onto something.

Wearing a smirk and a seventy-dollar suit, he settled into a wooden chair rumored to have once endured the weight of Maurice Morton Milligan, a prosecutor renowned for his successful 1939 prosecution of Kansas City political boss Tom Pendergast. Indicted on income tax evasion, Pendergast served fifteen months in a federal prison while Milligan enjoyed a brief celebrity status.

Lemont took his time entering the courtroom. I imagined him snickering behind the door to his chambers, relishing the bailiff's announcement of his name as though he came from royal lineage and was about to address his subjects.

"The Honorable Raymond Stuart Lemont presiding," the bailiff repeated loudly.

Lemont appeared in the doorway, pausing there as if he expected a round of applause.

"All rise," the bailiff instructed the court. He waited for Lemont to settle into a chair more like a throne, a smug smile playing out on Lemont's face as he looked down on the court from his elevated perch. "Be seated," the bailiff told the court, then took six precise steps backward, where he remained, legs splayed, arms crossed.

Just as Sullivan feared, Thompson pled not guilty and his lawyer requested bail. Lemont raised his chin arrogantly and appeared to deliberate. I prepared to voice my objection and repeat every one of Burke's arguments.

"Not today, Counselor," Lemont eventually said, giving the bench two dramatic whacks with his gavel.

Sullivan turned, a suggestion of a smile aimed my way. I didn't acknowledge it and, instead, slipped from the courtroom.

Later that night, I dragged myself into the station. Raina had awakened around four p.m., about the time I'd crawled in beside her in the coffin I shared with Tristan and closed the lid. I hadn't heard a peep from Internal Affairs, but the possibility hung over me like a soggy umbrella.

I noticed Quaid's absence immediately, despite the fact that upon my desk sat a vase filled with yellow roses, white baby's breath, pastel daylilies, foxglove, and coreopsis. I tugged the card from the plastic floral pick and read the inscription.

The community thanks you.
Captain Burke

My heart swelled as raw emotion bubbled to the surface. Any acknowl-edgement from Burke was extremely rare, so the gesture took me by sur-prise. I blinked away a threatening tear and opened my emails. I discovered one from Quaid, the content so troubling I gave him a call. When he didn't pick up, I grabbed my purse and headed toward his house, a ramshackle bungalow pinched between a post office deserted long ago and a board-ed-up Craftsman-style house.

After banging on the door for nearly ten minutes without a response, I peered in the dingy windows, shades partially drawn over most of them. Spotting him slumped in a green vinyl recliner, I wrestled the window ajar, but the gap was too small to squeeze through. I envisioned myself standing alongside his chair and materialized a few feet short of that. He was pale, sweaty, and possibly comatose. With trembling fingers, I discovered a pulse. I shook him, and when he didn't respond I slapped him hard. His eyes flicked open, and he grabbed my wrist.

"What the hell, Crenshaw?"

"That's what I'd like to know, Dennis." Beside him lay a loaded Heckler and Koch handgun and an empty bottle of oxycodone lay on the tray table alongside his chair.

He babbled incoherently, and I lurched sideways just as he vomited pill fragments. He floated in and out of consciousness while I cleaned him up, and I debated whether to call 911.

"Talk to me, Dennis, or I'm calling the Bus."

"Go away."

"No, I won't go away. Did you try to kill yourself?"

"Why the hell do you care? Why does anyone care?" Self-pity—Quaid was definitely on his way back.

"Because you're my partner. And it's more than that, you idiot. I'm here because I *do* care. You don't want to die, Dennis. If you did, you wouldn't have sent that email."

He puffed his lips and a particle of dried vomit fluttered onto his chest. "I didn't expect you to find it until after."

"I'm not buying it. I think it was a cry for help, you stubborn ass."

He shrugged and struggled to sit upright. "Great bedside manner, Crenshaw."

"Is this about Officer Schmidt?"

"Lucky son of a bitch is in a better place."

I huffed my irritation and then got in his face. "I doubt his wife and kids think he's so lucky."

He waved me off. "Just go. Don't worry. I'm out of pills. Take the gun if it will make you feel better."

I shoved my arms hard across my chest. "As if you don't have another one hidden around here somewhere."

"Sorry, Crenshaw. I didn't realize I was a criminal and you were the fucking ATF."

"I won't leave you like this, Dennis. You need to talk to someone, somebody a lot more equipped than I am."

"Like who? A shrink?"

I nodded. "You wouldn't be the first. The stigma is long gone. Back to the 1970s, where it's keeping your godawful wardrobe company."

He laughed until a coughing jag stopped him. Then he squeezed my hand. "You're right. I never intended to kill myself," he admitted a few moments later. "I just wanted to get away from it all, just for a little while."

"I get that, Dennis, I really do. But I don't think you should be by yourself right now. Is there someone I can call?"

He shook his head, his eyes focused on his hands, folded in his lap. "My wife left me ten years ago, come Christmas. My daughter doesn't talk to me and my son . . . never made it home from Iraq."

"I'm sorry," I managed past a long swallow. We hadn't been partners for that long, but how did I *not* know this?

"Go on, now. Really, I'll be fine."

"I'm not leaving. But I will give you two options. Either I stay with you through the night and you check yourself into Hope Memorial in the morning, or we head that way now."

"I'm not checking myself into a goddamn psychiatric hospital. I may as well kiss my career goodbye."

"That's ridiculous. You just lost an old friend to a violent crime. I can't begin to imagine the effect that must have had on you. But I know it isn't the first time it's happened to someone in the department, and, unfortunately, it won't be the last. Believe me; no one is going to think less of you for asking for a little help."

He looked away, seemingly focused on an enormous cobweb spanning the width of ratty draperies.

"Okay. Just let me pack a few things."

I stayed with Quaid during the check-in process. I left him only then because his doctor told me I couldn't stay. I promised to check on him at shift's end and pretended not to notice when his eyes threatened tears.

Back at the station, I slung my purse over the back of my chair and accessed my emails. One, marked interoffice, contained information about a GoFundMe page someone had started for the Schmidt Family. I clicked on the link and made a one-hundred-dollar donation. I closed the page and, after giving it some thought, I accessed the link again and made a two-hundred-dollar donation in Quaid's name.

Yawning, I sagged into my chair and jumped when my desk phone rang. "Detective Crenshaw."

"Yeah, Detective, this is Detective Keith O'Leary with the Belton Police Department."

"What can I do for you?" I said, straightening my spine.

"I got your email surrounding the recent abductions. Just before Christmas 2020, a couple of deer hunters came upon the body of a nineteen-year-old Raymore woman—"

"Sorry for the interruption, Detective O'Leary, but why would the Belton Police Department have an interest in a Raymore crime?"

"Her body was found within our jurisdiction. Her name was Callie Sutherland, and she was abducted from a Raymore grocery store, reputedly by five men."

Five men. A chill ravaged my spine. I remembered the case, more specifically Callie Sutherland's description. Her blond hair and the fact the abductors murdered her and burned the body were definitely disqualifiers. But, like I'd told Reed, there's a first time for everything.

"I don't think there's any connection to the cases I'm currently investigating," I told him, and I heard him sigh.

"Care to elaborate as to why, Detective Crenshaw?"

"Although the men who took our vics also seem to have a fetish for younger women, those targets are brunettes, every one of them."

His disappointment was palpable. "I see."

"Was there any security footage from the store?"

"The images were blurry, at best," he told me. "I'd be happy to send you the MPEG file."

"I'd appreciate that. And, in return, I'll send you the assailants' images we obtained from the store security camera following our latest abduction."

"I'd appreciate that, Detective."

"Were there any witnesses to Callie's abduction?" I asked.

"One rather evasive witness, but she did sit down with our department's sketch artist. I could include a copy of the sketches with the MPEG if you think it might help."

"It couldn't hurt. I think we both can agree we need to put these guys away and the sooner, the better."

After we'd swapped email addresses, we had no sooner ended the conversation than the attachments appeared in my inbox. And even though I couldn't wait to get a look at them, I kept my word and sent O'Leary the MPEG file containing the camera footage first. His immediate reply consisted of a thumbs-up emoji.

An initial glance at the drawings was disappointing. The men depicted didn't look anything like the men in our video. But on closer inspection, it became clear that one of them, the one with the facial scar, irrefutably matched Mamie Martin's description of the man who'd thrown Elsie "Jane Doe" Hanover into a waiting vehicle.

CHAPTER TWENTY-SEVEN

I made space for Callie Sutherland's name on the whiteboard. Under it, I listed the location where the deer hunters had found her body— O'Leary was detailed enough to include that, too—and the possible connection to the Elsie Hanover case. I then drew intersecting lines, which visually connected the two victims.

When I returned to my desk, I saw O'Leary had followed up. This time his email included a subject line that read: *Well, that was anticlimactic.*

Not surprisingly, that was the sum of his correspondence. I got the sense O'Leary was profoundly efficient, probably because he was every bit as concise. In my experience, the two traits effectively worked hand-in-hand.

Through that one single line, I felt the weight of his disappointment and, following several debate-filled minutes, I picked up the phone. "I was going to hold off until I knew more," I said after a brief reintroduction, "but it's possible the same men who killed Callie were involved in an abduction in Drexel, Missouri. So, thank you again, Detective. Your information may prove invaluable."

"No kidding?" he said, and I pictured him on the edge of his seat. "What makes you think they're connected?"

I told him about my conversations with Mamie, more specifically the description of the man with the scar and tattoo.

"I won't lie to you, Detective; the possibility of a satanic cult's involvement raises the hair on the back of my neck. We've had our share of cattle mutilations, but this would make it appear they've escalated their rituals."

I heard him swallow past a lump, and I drummed a pen against the desk. "And you never made any arrests in the cattle mutilations?"

"We rounded up a few suspects, but ironclad alibis ruled them out."

I wished him luck and promised to keep him updated.

I left the station shortly before my shift ended and swung by Hope Memorial. Losing an argument with the charge nurse over HIPPA's rules and regulations, I had turned to leave when the doctor who had admitted Quaid overheard the conversation and took me aside.

"We're going to keep him a couple of days, just long enough to complete a more in-depth evaluation. If that goes well, and I believe it will, I'm going to recommend some time off, regular therapy sessions, and a short-term trial of antidepressants."

Good luck with that. "I know it's early, but can I see him?"

He shook his head. "I'm afraid not. We find it's best for our patients to undergo a kind of disconnect from anything or anyone who might trigger a relapse until we've equipped them with the skillset necessary to cope with those triggers."

"Will you tell him I was here?"

"Of course, Detective . . .?"

"Crenshaw. I don't suppose I can get an update later on today?"

He dipped his head and pinched his eyes closed, which suggested my request was much more than an inconvenience. "Call the hospital later this evening. Here's my personal extension," he said and handed me a card.

When I arrived home, I found Fane waiting on the sofa. His crossed legs pumped the air and his chest heaved up then down between drawn-out theatrical sighs, his traditional way of communicating impatience. Feeling a lot like Pavlov's dog, Fane's demeanor the unconditional stimulus, I automatically glanced at my watch.

"What *is* your problem? I'm home early."

He vanished without a word, leaving behind a whiff of Chanel Number 5 and a feather barrette.

<hr>

Hours later, a half-hour before the sun disappeared entirely below the horizon, Raina and I greeted a breezy evening and set out toward a park, a few blocks down the street, our plan to test-drive a kite Fane had "procured" for her. After unfurling the Mylar material that, of course, resembled a bat, and successfully spreading it out—despite Raina's insistence she help—I instructed her on proper technique. Her tiny hand grasping the control line, I watched her run at full speed across the park, her bright eyes brighter still as the kite lifted higher and seesawed through the air.

The park was crowded with many children and their parents enjoying the final remnants of a perfect day. Kites filled the air, blanketing the sky with all shapes, sizes, and colors. Toddlers played in sandboxes, squealing as fingers and toes explored the fine, granular texture. Exhausted parents surrendered to their preschoolers' pleas, many of them panting while they pushed swings toward puffy clouds.

The breeze picked up, and out of the corner of my eye I saw Raina lose her grip, and the kite sailed away over the treetops. Anticipating her next move, I shouted her name, but her feet had already left the ground. Her tiny body grew smaller and smaller until she appeared nothing but a miniscule dot in the sky. A crowd thronged, unified in a horrified whispered cluster, fingers following the nearly indiscernible speck that was Raina. A grandmotherly type tugged her cell phone from a gingham dress pocket; I assumed she intended to call for help and I panicked. Suddenly, conversations ended mid-sentence, park-goers stood stock-still, while traffic came to an abrupt halt, a deathly silence permeating a square mile of cityscape. Soon after, Bianca appeared from within a rose-colored shroud.

"Darling, children are impetuous, particularly that one. Might I suggest you relegate such adventures under the cloak of dark?" she said, shrinking farther into her velvet cape.

"Mom, save the lecture, okay?" I said, my gaze following hers as we watched Raina soar higher. Rocketing skyward past treetops, unmanned kites, and a flock of confused nightingales, I went after Raina. Battling a strong headwind and unable to direct her course, she tumbled head over heels, grasping the air as if it were something tangible that could slow her momentum. I swooped up behind her and cradled her in my arms. Desperate to return to the crowd so Bianca could reverse the incantation, I made our descent faster than I would have liked, and the harsh landing sent shockwaves throughout our bodies.

Bianca delivered a blank stare and folded her arms across her cape, the hem to her customary gray flannel battle dress peeking from beneath, and secured a renegade strand of long red hair within the coiled knot at the nape of her neck.

I inverted one hand, keeping the other on Raina's shoulder. "Well, Mom. What are you waiting for?"

"Oh, no, Celeste. This is your mess, and you shall clean it up."

I scanned the crowded park, over swings halted in mid-swing and children's exhilarated expressions frozen in time. My anxiety was nearing a fever pitch, and it was all I could do not to dance from one foot to the other. "I can't, at least not as quickly as you could. Come on, Mom. Fix this!"

"I will not. While I've always been grateful you were a cautionary child, so unlike Nicholas, I took pride in the fact you were never a coward, Celeste. You can do this. You *will* do this."

"How?"

Bianca puffed her cheeks. "Imagine a clock, then simply turn back the hands of time."

"How many minutes? Do I need to be exact because—"

She shook her head. "The clock is merely a focal representation. Your lack of confidence is complicating the matter, dooming you to failure, Celeste. Do you recall the time Nicholas learned to ride a bicycle?"

I threw my arms sideways, the majority of my attention on the statue-like mortals around us. "Yes. What about it?"

"You refused to even sit on yours. You were so afraid of failing."

I blew out my frustration. "What's your point, Mom?"

"Nicholas sped away a short time after, clanging that wretched bell attached to the handlebars, and when he didn't return right away, you set your fear aside without so much as a second thought, boarded yours, and off you went."

I fixed my eyes on hers, knowing I would find all the self-assurance I needed there. Instead of a clock, I envisioned a bank of clouds rolling across the sky and persuaded them backward. Soon after, conversations restarted in midsentence. Children's laughter once again filled the park. And before I could thank her, Bianca blew Raina and me a kiss and faded away.

Raina's brows crinkled as she studied my face. "Mummy, your eyes are a curious yellow." She covered my eyes with her hands and whispered, "We mustn't let them see."

~~~

By nine o'clock, I was pacing the floor. Where was Fane? I couldn't very well take Raina with me to the station. I blew out my frustration; I had no choice but to call dispatch and inform the department I was taking a sick day. The call connected and I ended it when Fane's aura arrived, fogging the room with a chartreuse glow and the faint but nauseating scent of decaying honeysuckle. His body followed a split-second later. He was the only member of the Realm to claim this strange phenomenon and the rationale behind it remained a mystery. I wondered if it had something to do with his perpetual hyperactive state.

"You know I have to get to work! Where have you been?"

Dressed in a gauzy Victorian gown, so thin it revealed the lacy bustier beneath, he threw himself on the sofa, sprawling across it seductively as if he were the nineteenth-century socialite Lillie Langtry and the couch was the bed belonging to her lover, Edward—the Prince of Wales. Fane smiled wickedly. "He was always Eddie to me." He batted his eyelashes and expelled a melancholy sigh. "Try as I might, I could not resist seeing the battle with my own eyes. Little compares to our winsome warriors with their unmatched brute strength and cunning superiority on titillating display."

"So that's where you've been?"

"Indeed."

"Dressed like that?"

He lifted his skirt, exposing his thighs, a broadsword with a gilded copper hilt, and a few other things I'd rather not have seen. "How else would I conceal my trusty saber?" His eyes were bloodshot but glinted gold and he popped upright. "Would you like to hear all about my rousing escapade?"

"Yeah, give me a second," I said as my cell phone blasted Jeff Buckley's rendition of *Hallelujah.*

I ended the call and grabbed my gear, slamming the door on Fane's quizzical expression. According to Regina Ramirez, the two men responsible for the Budget Bizarre abduction were now in police custody.

CHAPTER TWENTY-EIGHT

B y the time I arrived at the station, the interrogations were under-
way, Detective Ramirez grilling one suspect, Detective Chastain
questioning the other. I observed Ramirez's strategy in a room
across the hall that contained the digital recording equipment, a camera
inside the interrogation room feeding the equipment both high-definition
video and audio. Detectives Donahue and Franklin watched Chastain's interrogation of the second suspect play live from an adjacent room. From
Ramirez's approach, it quickly became clear that she and Chastain had chosen the textbook tactic of pitting one suspect against the other. It was a big
gamble and could go one of two ways: either the perps took the bait and
turned on each other, or they lawyered up.

"The deal's off the table when the clock strikes ten, Cinderella," Ramirez
said, sweeping the case file from the table, which contained photographs of
the missing women and, most likely, two dozen or more blank pages. Leading the suspect to believe we had a lot more information than we actually did
was another textbook strategy. "Enjoy your Coke, Mr. Grady. There's no room
service at Fort Leavenworth," she added and intentionally slammed the door.

I met her in the hall.

"I hope Lucy's having some luck," she said, whacking her thigh with the folder.

I shrugged. "Donahue and Franklin are monitoring the interrogation. I wanted to see *you* in action. Nice job in there. He looks as if he's ready to crap his pants."

She grinned and popped the lid on an Orange Crush soda. "Hang tight a minute while I snag an officer to keep an eye on my detainee, then we can join the guys."

Lucy Chastain was young, petite, and extraordinarily attractive. Regina Ramirez stood five-feet-ten-inches tall in stocking feet and tipped the scales at two hundred forty pounds. She waxed a stubborn mustache, but only for special occasions, and her hair stylist had long ago accepted the fact that only death could part Regina with her Farrah-Fawcett hairstyle.

While Regina always chose the art of intimidation, Lucy relied on a damsel-in-distress approach. Both were equally effective, Lucy's tactic no more so than at that moment; the four of us exchanged high-fives as we watched the accused confess.

Lucy opened the door, presenting a wide grin and the confession—the holy grail of procedural documents.

"I could use a few unfriendly faces in there. He shut down completely when I pressed him for the details."

Three of us followed Chastain back into the room. Franklin led, which was just fine by me—I had cameras to avoid. Ramirez stayed behind; her detainee was in for a long night. I leaned against the wall—out of camera range—and allowed Franklin to run the show.

"Hello, Mr. Moore, I'm Detective Franklin. Mind if I call you Billy?"

Moore shrugged, but I saw his jaw flinch and heard the chain linking the handcuffs jingle as he scratched his nose.

"This is how this works, Billy. You give us *all* the information we're going to need so we can locate the women, and we'll see that the judge takes that into consideration."

"Fuck that, man. That wasn't the deal." He tapped his index finger repeatedly against the tabletop, the cuffs clanking against the edge. "She told me I'd do no more than five years if I confessed," he said, jerking his head toward Chastain. "She didn't say shit about anything else."

Detective Franklin leaned on the table, resting the brunt of his weight on his hands, before wrenching his head sideways and giving Chastain a look that could kill. I'd been on the receiving end of that predatory stare and didn't envy her. Apparently, Lucy had offered the suspect the plea deal before Franklin and Donahue arrived in the observation room.

"Oh, she did?" Franklin asked, still glaring at Lucy.

"That's right," Billy said, squaring his jaw. "And I want that shit in writing!"

"Just so I understand the situation, Detective Chastain didn't have you sign a plea agreement before you signed the confession?"

I watched the color drain from Billy's face as Franklin's words sank in.

"She fuckin' *said* it, man! All I had to do was confess, and I wouldn't be lookin' at twenty years."

Franklin clucked his tongue and leaned across the table. "Well, see, Billy, a verbal agreement doesn't amount to diddly-squat when it comes to the law. I'll tell you what I'm going to do. If you'll tell us where those women are and who else was involved, besides your scumbag buddy in the next room, Detective Chastain will get you those forms and you'll be looking at no more than *ten* years behind bars."

Lucy made a run for the door.

"Screw that! I'm not telling you shit. I rat those guys out, I'm as good as dead."

Franklin shrugged smugly. "You think about it, Billy. For your sake, I hope you reach the right conclusion before your buddy does or the deal's off."

Franklin slipped up beside me. "Get in there and see how Ramirez is doing. I'm not about to let this asshole off easy."

Ramirez was waiting out in the hall when I left the room.

She cradled a second but unopened Orange Crush with one hand and held a wrestler's grip on a thick strand of red licorice with the other.

"The little weasel lawyered up," she advised me in between chews. "He's a lot more afraid of the people he's working for than he is jail time, or us. How's it going in there?"

"Lucy cut a deal before she got all the information and Franklin's not happy about it."

"Let me guess. He was hoping I was having some luck, so he could renege." She shook her head. "Damn alpha males. Maybe if he'd play nice, we could get those women home safe. Not everything has to be a pissing contest."

"How did we catch these guys, anyway? Not another abduction, I hope."

Ramirez's exaggerated smile revealed a half-chewed glob of licorice. "An ex-girlfriend gave up Moore. She not only told us where we could find him but also implicated Cecil Grady in the abductions. You know what they say—hell hath no fury like a woman scorned. I swear to God I think we've solved twenty-five percent of our cases courtesy of pissed-off exes."

Donahue's head appeared in the doorway. When he saw Ramirez, he stepped into the hall. After learning of her detainee's refusal to talk, he offered to take a crack at him.

Ramirez popped the lid on the soda and chugged half the can. "Knock yourself out. Step lightly because, like I told Celeste, he's requested legal representation and the suit's on his way."

Donahue grinned and surrendered both palms. "I just want to make sure he understands his options."

Lucy rounded the corner with the appropriate documents and pulled Donahue aside before he could disappear inside the room that held Grady. Following a hushed conversation, he escorted her back inside the interrogation room Franklin occupied.

Ramirez raised both eyebrows. "I wonder what all that was about?"

"Lucy probably felt like she needed a bodyguard and not because of Billy Moore." It was obvious Franklin intimidated her, and she wanted

Donahue alongside her in the room. "Mind if I give your guy a try?" I asked, hitching a thumb over my shoulder. "I'm sure you could use a break."

"Be my guest," she said and tossed me the folder.

I waited outside the room and watched her return to the Detectives' Bullpen. Before stepping inside, mostly out of habit, I glanced at the video monitor located above the door and connected to a CCTV camera inside the room.

Nostradamus materialized beside me, snippets of body parts at a time, raking tense fingers through his thick beard. "That contraption could present a problem," he said, tipping his head to the camera.

My mind on getting the suspect to talk, I had forgotten about the questions that would inevitably arise surrounding my absent image. "What should I do?"

"Render them useless, of course."

"You're saying I should disconnect the cameras?"

"Do you have a more viable suggestion?"

I shook my head.

"Harness your telepathic ability, Celestine. Envision the contraptions useless and it shall be so."

I scratched my head. "That's it?" I said past a hollow laugh. "Come on, I'm going to need a little more guidance."

"Consider the appropriate technique and simply focus your efforts on the outcome."

"Right. All I have to do is think it and it happens. All of you keep telling me that, but it can't possibly be that simple."

"Why not? Why do you persistently doubt yourself? We are all exercising the utmost patience, Celestine. However, the time has come for you to utilize your capabilities without benefit from us." Within a poof of iridescent mist, he evaporated.

In my mind, I disconnected the cable attached to the camera. Perhaps with a bit too much enthusiasm because the cable twisted, snapping the air in a serpentine motion before coming to rest. I closed the door behind me, and Cecil Grady greeted me with homicidal eyes and a blatant disregard for authority.

The epoxied cement floor gleamed, and the soundproof solid core masonry blocked walls didn't. There were two high-definition IP cameras in the room. I parked my chair directly across from his and out of the primary camera's view. The other, mounted on the wall on one side of the room, I attempted to disable telekinetically. The cable started to sag, then melted. Which wasn't the strategy I had in mind, but the end result was the same. Grady was so focused on saving his ass that he didn't seem to notice.

Pulling a form from the folder, I tossed it on the table between us. "I'm Detective Crenshaw. I understand Detective Ramirez has read you your Miranda rights and that you have requested counsel. I wanted to make absolutely sure you understand that once your attorney arrives, *no one* in this department can do anything to help you."

He lunged at me, baring most of his teeth. "Bitch, I *said* I want a lawyer."

I shrugged off the disrespect. I'd been called worse, but I'd long grown tired of guilty repeat offenders and their total disregard for innocent victims. I'd already dipped inside his head and knew he was guilty of this particular crime and so many others for which he'd never been held accountable. I thought about Marcy Harris and the other mothers, at their wit's end as they endured sleepless nights, wondering if their daughters were alive or dead. I was willing to set aside my principles, the fundamental honesty I'd cut my teeth on, if that meant Cecil Grady didn't get to walk away from this one. "Oh, that's too bad, Mr. Grady. I've read your rap sheet. Convicted of a felony before you turned eighteen . . . your mother must have been so proud."

He flared his nostrils, and a charging bull came to mind. "Leave my mother out of this or I swear—"

"You're really in no position to make threats, Mr. Grady." I clucked my tongue and rattled off the remainder of his more serious convictions. "Yeah, the judge isn't going to go easy on you this time around, regardless of the unfortunate obstacles life has thrown your way. You can count on that. And, with your friend, Billy, in there this close," I said, pinching my fingers, "to spilling his guts, there won't be any leniency offers coming your way. But," I said, gathering the folder, "we all make our own decisions in life. Let's hope you've made the right one for once. I'll show your attorney in when he arrives."

Grady leaned back in his chair and laughed. "If you've read my rap sheet, cop, you know I'm wise to your fuckin' mind games. My lawyer will convince the jury that whatever Billy says is conjecture, his word against mine. And I'm. Not. Talkin.'"

I glimpsed into his memories and plucked one I now knew would work in my favor. "That's too bad." I leaned across the table and whispered, "But should you choose not to honor your mother's last wish, I suppose that's your call."

He shifted uncomfortably in his chair, raw emotion evident in his eyes. "I don't know what you're talking about. Where's my fuckin' lawyer?"

I ignored the question. "Oh, I think you know. I mean, how could you possibly forget something as important as a promise to your mother? You know, the one in which you swore you'd never *ever* commit another crime following your last arrest."

He put all of his weight behind the table between us, but the bolts securing it to the floor didn't budge. "Shut your goddamn mouth about my mother!"

I disregarded his demand. I needed—wanted—him to suffer the emotional hell he'd caused so many women, particularly his own mother. "But you sure didn't keep that promise, did you, Cecil? Come on, it wasn't even that long ago," I said, slapping the table with both palms. "Wasn't it, what, just three months ago that your poor sick mother managed to walk several blocks to the bus station on a *very* hot summer day, where she caught the first of three separate buses, just so she could visit you in prison. I can't help but think that long exhausting walk, combined with the emotional despair she must have felt, accelerated her fatal heart condition."

"How did you know about that?" he asked between clenched teeth, fists balled and resembling small boulders.

"It's not important. The important thing is, if you ever really cared about your sweet, sweet mother, that you turn your life around. Today. She sees you, you know, and wonders whatever happened to that chubby little freckled-face boy who once picked her dandelions."

He dropped his head. His shoulders shook harder as the minutes passed, while his tears plopped one after the other onto the Formica table-top. "How do you know that?" he whimpered, without raising his head and I knew I'd reached the tiny shred of humanity he had left.

With Grady's confession—the names of the kingpins and the location of the women—recorded and handwritten, I stepped outside the room and texted Franklin to let him know, afterward nearly colliding with a hag-gard-appearing man outfitted in a wrinkled suit and a coffee-stained tie.

"Where's my client?" he barked.

I flipped through the folder and handed him the Miranda waiver Grady had signed. "There must have been some confusion. I'm sorry you wasted your time."

I slipped back inside, anxious to collect Grady and steer him toward booking. I hadn't had the opportunity to repair the damaged cable and thought it best to distance myself as quickly as possible.

Ramirez met me in the hall once I'd deposited Grady. "You got him to talk?"

"I did," I said, waving the confession overhead.

"How?" she asked, catching up and strolling alongside.

"Let's just say he had a change of heart."

Ramirez fist-bumped my shoulder. From behind, I heard Franklin cele-brate my victory. Soon after, he charged past, dragging Moore by his collar.

Donahue caught up just as the sergeant placed Moore in the holding cell with Grady. "The captain's going to meet us at the stash house, along with every available uniform and SWAT. Let's get this party started," he said, rubbing his palms together.

CHAPTER TWENTY-NINE

"If all twenty-four women are inside, we have to assume there's probably at least six men, more likely twelve, guarding them. This is going to get real ugly, real fast." Ramirez said what I was thinking. Donahue drove us and skirted every red light, nearly colliding with one vehicle at an intersection. Franklin offered criticism from the passenger seat, deserved or otherwise, and whenever he saw fit. Chastain sat between Regina and me in the backseat and checked her weapon a third time. I knew for a fact the only time she'd ever fired a gun was on the firing range and, according to department gossip, her low score had prompted the department to insist she spend additional hours at the range.

Captain Burke, Chief Patterson, and the five of us converged on the house, simultaneously—a nondescript four-story and the largest of the renovations in the failed Roosevelt Park Restoration Project. Vehicles lined the street, and judging from the license plates, few belonged to locals.

SWAT had already surrounded the house, the exterior so dimly lit their silhouettes were barely discernible. Of course, they'd taken the time to study the structure's schematics and five team members were stacked a stair apart on an outside staircase leading to the third floor. Fortunately, it seemed the majority of the houses along the street stood vacant.

Burke signaled us over. "We're assuming from the out-of-state tags we're going to encounter a lot of johns. Regardless of your personal opinion," he began, his gaze stalling as it met Ramirez's, "try not to shoot any."

Chief Patterson emitted his trademark grunt, and I assumed he agreed. He gave the order to the team commander, Mack "Buzz" Redman, who deployed his squad in a choreographed, seamless manner. Knowing every man and woman on the team was well versed in crisis entries, I felt confident none of the abductees would find themselves victims of friendly fire. One SWAT member stood off to the side, obviously awaiting instruction. On his commander's signal, he nodded his understanding and charged past the others, breaching the front door with a battering ram. Ten members of the Special Weapons and Tactic team swarmed the interior, and the sound of gunfire immediately blasted the quiet neighborhood, the flashes off the high-caliber discharges seen from the sidewalk.

Burke waved us through. Franklin eagerly took the lead. A bullet whizzed past Donahue's head, grazing his ear, and Chastain instinctively dropped to the ground. Ramirez helped her to her feet, and Chastain, appearing shell-shocked and embarrassed, filed in behind her. Donahue appeared more pissed than injured and rushed the house with renewed purpose.

"I'll take the rear, Captain," I said and sprinted in that direction before he could stop me. I entered onto an enclosed back porch, now serving as a catchall. The smell of decaying garbage stung my nostrils and a rat the size of a Chihuahua scurried across my instep. I inched the interior door open and crept inside. On the floor above, women screamed amid the sound of feet in motion. Bullet holes decorated the ceiling, glimpses of the second floor visible here and there as plaster rained onto the ground floor like fairy dust.

But because of my preternatural vision, I had no need for portholes. Directly above me lay a safe room, completely encased in lead. Within it, a dozen women cowered in a corner, five captors—armed with semiautomatic weapons—looming over them. I recognized Britney Clark and Emma Harris as two of the women. A SWAT squadron loitered within a walk-in closet, designed to disguise the safe room just beyond it, and debated their options: wait the kidnappers out or take Patterson's suggestion and call in the explosive team to blow the door. Either way placed the women in a much more precarious position.

After a few minutes of contentious debate, Chief Patterson relegated the decision to Buzz, who opted to penetrate the door by way of a plasma cutter. That would require even more time, time that could cost the women their lives.

I'd already toyed with the idea of attempting Mora Temporis, then teleporting through the lead exterior but, as difficult as stone was to penetrate, I was convinced I'd fail. Which left me with only one option.

I glided upstairs, following the stairway that led from the kitchen. Rounding the landing leading to another flight of stairs, I encountered a thug so big he made The Rock look like Pee-wee Herman. Slack-jawed and frozen in place, he studied me with wild eyes as I hovered near the ceiling. He took several steps backward and raised his weapon. I growled a laugh and exposed my fangs. He fired a succession of frantic bullets, which I dodged and weaved until I grew tired of it and metamorphosed into an enormous steel-plated cockroach, my inspiration an intrusion of creepy crawlers scuttling along the baseboards and mapping a route from the kitchen to the upstairs.

His next round pinged off my antennae, the ricocheted bullet wobbling through the air, carrying with it a high-pitched whine. Whizzing in the opposite direction, it punched the shooter between the eyes. He never knew what hit him.

I reached the second landing, and I heard the SWAT officers' subdued voices from a bedroom down the hall; although the safe room was soundproof, they must have realized the kidnappers had the capability to monitor the bedroom and every square inch of the house, thanks to a sophisticated surveillance system within it.

Chief Patterson stood before a camera located within a clock on the wall and attempted negotiations, his typically stern modulation exchanged for something sounding almost human. While he waited for the men inside to take the bait—a promise that if they released the hostages his men would stand down and vacate the premises—I focused my attention on Mora Temporis. The blades on the ceiling fan ceased revolutions, the background music, courtesy of an outdated Muzak system, ended midchord, while the clock on the wall suspended time. But only for sixty seconds. *What in God's name am I doing wrong?*

"Oh, for pity's sake," Matilda suddenly said beside me. "Can you not walk and chew gum at the same time? Think of it as a throttle rather than a switch. One can't simply set the wheels in motion and take one's foot off the gas and expect to arrive at the destination."

"What does that even mean?" I asked through clenched teeth.

"Simply put, retain the command whilst engaging in your secondary agenda. Try again, Celestine. When you wish time to resume, simply command it, and it shall be."

The process reminded me of the time Nick taught me to drive a car with a standard transmission. *"Clutch, gas—simultaneously,"* he'd screamed when the car began rolling backward down an embankment. "Clutch. Gas. Clutch, gas," I murmured, triumphant when I slipped past motionless law enforcement officers stationed outside the safe room, most of them tall and well built, all equipped with lethal weapons and a fixed intimidating stare. One officer was in the middle of sending a text—elbows cocked to the side, biceps flexed, fingers and thumbs poised over the keyboard. Another officer stood frozen, lips in midsentence as he cupped the ear of an immobilized comrade to his right. At odds with the squad commander over his decision, Patterson had been pointing an accusatory finger at Buzz when time stopped and the digit hung in the air, his stationary scowl further corrupting hostile features.

The door's exterior was stainless steel. But I assumed, as with the room, within it lay a lead core that might take me considerable time to penetrate.

I had anticipated a high-tech combination lock, not a retinal scanner, and I returned to the kidnapper bleeding out at the top of the stairs. After wrenching out one of his eyes, I tore back down the hall and plastered the squishy eyeball against the small screen. A squiggly infrared light came to life and thirty seconds later, gears and sprockets began to whine, and the door swung open. I rushed in, collected the captors' weapons, and secured the firearms in a room across the hall. I returned to the safe room and remembered to fry the surveillance equipment. Concentrating on the wall clock just outside, I instructed the minute hand to reflect an earlier point in time—exactly seven and a half minutes—and ended the spell.

Patterson finished his salacious remark just as Buzz and the others noticed the open door and a flurry of activity within the safe room. While the kidnappers inside attempted to make sense of the situation and searched frantically for their missing weapons, SWAT stormed the interior and took them into custody. Ramirez, Chastain, and I comforted the quivering women and questioned them regarding the whereabouts of the others. We learned that the remaining victims *were* somewhere on the premises, several often secured in the attic and a few—personally selected to service the kingpins—were always kept in a high-security wing on the third floor. Getting no argument from Chastain, we agreed she would remain with the women until the EMTs arrived, while Ramirez and I searched for the other abductees.

I tipped my head toward the third-floor stairway. "The attic or the suite?"

"The suite," Ramirez responded through clenched teeth. "Maybe we'll get lucky and corner those prick ringleaders in there."

"Hold up," Detective Franklin said from behind. "Donahue and I will go in first," he said, puffing his chest. "You two can provide backup *if* we need it."

Ramirez curled a lip. "Screw that, and your boys' club."

She flung the door to the wall and revealed three women, two suffering a near-comatose state, undoubtedly from a heroin injection, the third somewhat more coherent and doing her best to protect the others. She indicated someone else was present by way of an almost indiscernible nod, her eyes darting toward a closet on the opposite side of the room from which a torrent of gunfire immediately ensued, bullets pocking the wooden door that soon resembled a block of Swiss cheese. I flung myself inside and across the room while Ramirez backed out the door, nearly knocking Franklin and Donahue down the stairs. The door swung closed, and the woodwork encasing the windows sailed across the room and became an effective barricade, which prevented Franklin, Ramirez, and Donahue from entering the room. A three-headed gargantuan dragon emerged from a sulfuric haze and spewed fire, setting the closet ablaze. Screams sounded from inside the inferno and the closet door flew open as the men within attempted escape.

"It is me—Leonardo—to the rescue," the dragon whispered in my ear. "Well, what are you waiting for? Extinguish the flames, dear girl, while I acquaint myself with those despicable menaces."

My eyes scanned the room for a fire extinguisher as the flames grew higher. Out of the corner of my eye, I saw the more capable woman persuade the other two under the bed. Donahue, Franklin, and Ramirez tried but failed to breach the door.

"Make it rain, Celestine!" Leonardo called over a reptilian shoulder once he'd successfully incinerated the suspects and, following a raucous inhalation, blew their remains back inside the closet. "Oh, for God's sake," he said and stomped scaly webbed feet in my direction. "Must I do everything?" A leather whip among the torture devices became an anaconda, then a fire hose gushing water. Once the fire was out, the smell of searing flesh permeated the room, and Leonardo looked at the ceiling. "There are more damsels in distress, you know. Perhaps, I shall stay the course," he said but disappeared instead.

"Don't go! How am I supposed to explain—"

Elizabeth appeared, rolling her eyes. "If it isn't just like da Vinci to make a mess and charge the women with cleaning it up."

"What the hell am I supposed to do now?"

"I suggest we begin with those agitated creatures beyond the barricade."

"What do I tell them?"

"Oh, use your imagination, Celeste. You are a very clever girl, after all." I opened my mouth with plans to disagree, and Elizabeth met my intent with a prolonged sigh. "Who is to say how those imbeciles managed to set the room ablaze?"

"Uh, I don't know. Maybe the fire marshal."

"Pfft. As I am in no mood to argue the point, I think we can both agree this *fire marshal* of yours won't conclude a fire-breathing dragon the origin."

"What about the witnesses?" I whispered and gestured toward the bed.

"Humph. Hysterical females have often relayed unsubstantiated claims."

"Then what about the door? How am I supposed to explain why the door was barricaded?"

Elizabeth waved her hand and the woodwork soared across the room and clacked into place. My concern regarding further inquisition from Franklin, Donahue, and Ramirez on the tip of my tongue, Elizabeth slapped a cold finger against my lips. "Their last memory is of the door swinging shut. Now, if you will excuse me, a leisurely bath awaits—one I can only hope will rid my glorious body of the stench of charred wood and entrails."

Franklin threw his weight behind a shoulder and was the first to burst through the door. "Why'd you close the . . ." he began, and I followed his gaze to the scorched ceiling, then the charred walls, and finally the mounds of ash within the closet.

"What the hell?" Ramirez asked as she, too, surveyed the aftermath.

Donahue eventually looked at the ceiling. "Thank God for sprinkler systems."

If only.

Franklin scratched his head, then stuffed his hands into pockets. "Why would they start a fire? It doesn't make sense."

I shrugged. "An accident? A distraction maybe? A ruse to get us to back off? Who knows?"

"They were in the closet, weren't they? Maybe one struck a freakin' match so he could see to reload and caught a bunch of clothes on fire. What difference does it make now?" Ramirez interjected. "The perps are dead and the . . . Where are the women?"

Following a great deal of persuasion, all three women snaked from beneath the bed and out into the open. The drug-induced stupor prevented two of the women from offering much. The third eyed me cautiously but kept her mouth shut except to inform us that there were more hostages in the attic.

Ramirez bumped my elbow, her face contorted with a disturbing grin. "Come on, it's time to rescue the toys in the attic."

Franklin snapped his fingers like a preschool teacher demanding undivided attention. He radioed Captain Burke and brought him up to speed. "The lower levels have been secured and ambulances are waiting outside," Burke responded.

"Ramirez, you and Crenshaw take the women out. Donahue and I will check out the attic," Franklin ordered once he'd ended his communication with Burke.

Ramirez plastered her hands on her hips and took a defensive stance. "Who the hell do you think you're talking to?"

Franklin was about to say something when Donahue threw his palms in the air. "Play nice, kids. I'll escort the women."

Franklin pushed past Ramirez when she was halfway up the narrow staircase. Even in the dark, I could see her bared teeth. When his reckless, heavy footsteps caused the stairs to creak, she hissed her favorite obscenity. Discovering the attic door locked, he slipped a knife from an ankle strap, inserted it into the keyway, and began to rock the blade back and forth.

Ramirez breathed down his neck. "What's with the cloak and dagger shit?" she whispered. "Get out of the way."

"What do you think you're going to do?" Franklin asked.

"I plan to kick down the damn door! It's not as if they don't know we're here. Thanks to your gigantic Herman Munster feet."

The tumbler clicked, and Franklin grinned over his shoulder. He turned the knob, but something was blocking the door. The room stank of bodily fluids, decaying food, and marijuana. He put his shoulder into it and managed to shimmy it partially open. A bullet whizzed through the air, and he ducked and lost his footing. Ramirez broke his fall.

"They're blocking the door with a piece of damn furniture," Franklin whispered.

"Amateurs," Ramirez mumbled. "Police!" she called over Franklin's shoulder. "Surrender your weapons and come out."

"They sure as hell know we're here now," Franklin said through gnashed teeth as he prevented Ramirez from muscling her way past him.

"Take a look outside. KCPD and SWAT have the house surrounded," I shouted through the door.

"Yeah?" said a voice from inside. "And we've got hostages."

My eyes penetrated the two-inch plaster as if it were a dirty windshield. There were six captors and fifteen hostages—six more victims than we'd anticipated. Not one of the persons inhabiting the room appeared a day over twenty and not one of them was Elsie "Jane Doe" Hanover. The girls were quiet, some sleeping, others bordering on a drug-induced stupor. The abductors' arsenal included two Walther PPQ M2s, two Smith & Wesson 380s, and two low-caliber Berettas that looked like they'd been rescued from a junk pile.

Franklin disappeared down the stairs, but I heard him radio SWAT, give our location, and request backup—to include a couple of snipers—outside on the widow's walk abutting the room.

"I'm going in," Ramirez said, turning to face me. "Are you with me or not?"

Following a heave and a grunt, we managed to push the door ajar enough to squeeze through. Soon after, footsteps pitter-pattered across the roof overhead, and I knew the team was formulating a plan to propel from the roof onto the wrought-iron railing just outside.

"Now, where's the fun in that?" Leonardo whispered in my ear, and the attic walls contracted, then expanded, as he sucked the oxygen from the room. Antiquated insulation fluttered from the wooden truss supporting the roof and rained down like miniscule snowflakes.

"How are they supposed to breathe? You're going to kill them all!" I screamed as bodies slumped to the floor, one after another, the larger of the mortals falling first.

"Nonsense. However, you may have a point should you refuse to act posthaste. A few minutes at most, if memory serves." Da Vinci peered overhead as the footsteps pattered to a halt. "Oh, this seems a trifle straightforward, indeed. What you need, dear girl, is a challenge. Oh me, what to do, what to do? I know. Let us begin by dispensing with that pesky railing," he said, and I watched wide-eyed as the wrought iron creaked and groaned, the hinges loosening before giving way altogether, and the entire structure plummeted, landing with a high-pitched *thwack!* on the driveway below.

"Why did you do that? Are you fucking insane?"

"I find your question may require protracted debate, and we simply haven't the time. I suggest you turn your attention to the matter at hand."

I spun a tight circle. "Shit! I don't know what to do. I guess I could handcuff those guys and confiscate their weapons, but how am I going to explain how I singlehandedly managed that?"

"One minute," Leonardo said, counting down. "Might I suggest the power of persuasion?"

"Okay, okay," I sputtered, tugging the hair at my temples sideways. "I'll do it, and then I'll somehow convince Ramirez and Franklin that they assisted. Right?"

"Thirty seconds. I do believe that big fella—Franklin, is it?—is turning a bit blue."

I rocketed around the room, gathering all the weapons. Then I set out to handcuff the suspects. Coming up three sets of handcuffs short, I improvised, grabbing several strips of zip ties I spotted on a table.

"Two seconds," Leonardo said, buffing a nail with a file comprised of fish scales.

"I can't! I'm not sure—"

"Focus, Celestine! I will not assist."

I squeezed my eyes shut and concentrated on Ramirez and Franklin, burying the explanation deep, the sensation disgustingly similar to stuffing a turkey. Satisfied, Leonardo waved his hands with a grand and annoying flourish, which restored oxygen to the room, then he evaporated.

Franklin was the first to gasp a breath. "Well, that was easy," he said, puffing his chest. "Apparently, my reputation preceded me."

I glanced around the room, noting no one—whether hostage, suspect, or detective—appeared the least bit confused or suspicious, and I blew out a long and deserved breath.

Once the paramedics arrived, Ramirez and I assisted the women who could walk outside. I had just returned outside with the remaining two hostages when Captain Burke approached.

"Good work in there, all of you," he said.

"We think there's another suspect inside, Alexander Wright. We ran the plates on a Porsche parked inside the garage, and it's registered to his alias—Jason Newcomb."

"Have we ID'd the six shooters from the upper floor?" I asked.

He nodded. "If Cecil Grady was telling the truth, we got all the key players. Except for Wright."

"I thought he fled the country." *In which case, he would have left the Porsche behind.*

"So did the Feds. Apparently, he's been hiding in plain sight." He hitched a thumb over one shoulder. "One of his hired guns has already cut a deal. He's singing like a goddamn canary. If he's in there, and his man swears he is, I don't plan to leave without him. Every available officer is occupied—"

"I'll take another look around."

"Watch your back, Crenshaw. I don't have to tell you what we're up against."

Wright had more than one alias. He had been on the FBI's Most Wanted List for the past decade. His rap sheet included a laundry list of felonies to include gun smuggling; human trafficking; heroin, cocaine, and fentanyl distribution; and murder. I'd seen photographs of what Wright had done to his third and fourth wives. If he was inside, I had plans for him.

Tapping into my preternatural vision, I explored every inch of every room through lath and heavy plaster. I found him hiding in the basement, pinched behind a rusty boiler that hadn't been in use since the late sixties.

My lips stretched into a maniacal grin, and I shapeshifted into the exact image of his third wife just as she'd been found, blood still oozing from the fifty stab wounds he'd inflicted. I whispered his name as I hovered over the boiler. He looked up, his eyes like cocktail coasters, his lips parted in a frozen scream. He fumbled but eventually managed to tug a .45-caliber Heckler & Koch handgun from a custom-made holster. The gun shook as he took aim, and he dropped it altogether when my arm elongated and I grabbed him by the throat and suspended him overhead.

"Do you miss me, Alex?" I said and gradually transitioned into his fourth wife, whom he'd bludgeoned to death. An ax handle protruded from the side of my head, just as one had jutted from hers when she arrived in the morgue. I replicated her flesh, the way it hung from shattered cheekbones, and the bruised tissue surrounding her eyes, and even her nose, which the coroner had described as "a smooshed mound of red clay."

"Do you still think I'm beautiful?" I growled through a gap where teeth had once been.

His heart beat frantically, and his pulse knocked against his neck. His skin was no longer pink but an insipid shade of gray. His feet pedaled the air madly in a desperate attempt to escape. Morphing back into my true form, I drew back my lips to accommodate expanding fangs and smiled when his heart stopped.

Now completely surrounded by hostile apparitions, I considered my next move. The house was host to women and men who had died violently, heinous acts perpetrated upon them before they drew a final breath. I'd seen their ghosts the moment I stepped inside the house. Some roamed the halls with heads in hands. Some searched for missing appendages. All searched for revenge. And I planned to release them from purgatory.

Shoulder to shoulder, the grotesque entities crept closer, filling the basement and advancing upon me like zombies in a trite video game. Sparks flew from my fingertips and the apparitions stopped midstride.

I zipped from the basement and searched the house. Once satisfied everyone inside had gotten out—including Burke—I returned to the basement, drained the dilapidated boiler, and wrenched open the valves. Then I drifted outside.

When I approached the car, I found Franklin sitting stone-faced behind the wheel. Donahue was sprawled across the passenger seat and massaging his temples. Ramirez and Chastain were leaning against the hood, both drawing hard on unfiltered cigarettes.

"Crenshaw," Burke barked as I neared the car. "Any luck?"

"Negative, Captain. No sign of him."

Burke scratched his head before raking a hand through what was left of his hair. "Why would the informant lie about that?"

I shrugged. "Maybe Wright slipped out when he saw an opportunity."

Aggravation flushed his cheeks, and he threw his arms in the air. "You want to tell me how that's even vaguely possible? All the exits were covered—every window, every door, every goddamn mousehole!"

"I wish I knew, Captain. I want him behind bars as much as anyone."

He opened his mouth to say something else when a huge explosion rocked the neighborhood.

CHAPTER THIRTY

The house was dark and blissfully quiet when I returned home. I tossed my keys and watched them sail through the air, then group together in an organized row before tumbling soundlessly onto the entry hall table. Levitating myself a foot off the floor with plans to clandestinely climb into my coffin for a few hours of undisturbed sleep, I discovered Fane poised inside, ankles and wrists crossed like a forsaken cherub, a dramatic yawn revealing a tongue stud that looked suspiciously like an emerald-and-diamond earring I'd received as a graduation present.

"Well, thank the stars I have been bequeathed time eternal. I cannot begin to count the precious minutes I have wasted awaiting your return."

"Look, Fane. I'm sorry I had to leave so suddenly, but—"

"Spare me the tedious details."

I trumpeted my lips.

I was exhausted, the only thing on my mind sinking into my coffin and staying there for as long as possible. "Why not spare me *yours*? I'm tired, Fane. It's been a long day."

"You don't have the slightest interest in your beloved's prickly battle?"

"He seemed fine when he came to visit Raina. I assume if he weren't I would have heard."

He shot out of the coffin, his body prone and supported by nothing but air, a palm cupping his chin as he taunted me with a wicked smile. "Oh, dear. A mere assumption is enough for you, is it? It would seem the honeymoon is over indeed. Nary six full moons have illuminated the amorous bed of our young lovers, yet one appears passionately indifferent." He clucked his tongue. "Poor misguided Tristan. It would seem a charlatan bitterly awaits his homecoming."

"Oh, shut up, Fane."

"Um, *shut up, Fane.* You are every bit as predictable as you are heartless."

I tugged him toward the floor, ripping the hem of his Victorian gown in the process.

He shrieked a decibel I was certain would wake Raina. "Now look what you've done. It is not as if one can replace a gown worn by the infamous Frieda von Richthofen at the local Macy's."

"Frieda who?" I waved away his response. "Never mind. I really don't care. Is Tristan all right, or isn't he? I don't have the time or energy for your annoying games."

He turned a somersault in midair and cradled his cheek in the crook of one shoulder. "Well, if you insist on dragging it out of me. Ah, the glistening biceps, determined brow, and chiseled chin of our beloved warrior, the infamous Tristan of Tomisovara. 'Tis true, he could set a corpse's heart to fluttering." He paused, pumping his crossed legs for effect. "Smite, smite, smite! The Harvesters fell one after another as if shoddy structures in a developing country following a devastating quake. Allow me a demonstration."

Before I could resist, Fane propelled me inside the Circle. Swords flew in all directions, the decapitated heads of Harvesters following after. Fire-breathing dragons, I suspected Nick and Paulo, spewed flames, shriveling and crisping the disjointed heads beyond recognition. Bianca shapeshifted from an imposing multiheaded octopus wielding eight razor-sharp tentacles, into a nightmarish twenty-foot reptile with foot-long talons and an exoskeleton comprised of spiky shards extending in all directions. Crushing a throng of Harvesters on the run, she relied on Razvan—a goliath gladiator with flashing red eyes and swooping mechanical blades for arms—to destroy the few Harvesters who managed to escape. The smell of smoke, seared flesh, and determination filled the air; the black blood of the Harvesters layered the ground and trees, saturating every member of the Realm with a putrid, gooey coating. Tristan stood victorious alongside the others, spectacular muscles pulsating as though yearning for more conflict, stingy moonlight highlighting well-defined cheekbones, glossy dark hair, and sultry eyes.

I escaped from the Circle feeling stimulated, breathless, and inadequate, despite the supernatural phenomena I'd performed earlier.

"Fa-a-ne, don't *ever* do that again!"

"Tsk. It served you right, you know," Fane said past painted lips. "Had you not deprived me of much-needed slumber, I might have had the energy to participate in a strictly verbal elucidation. And do not threaten me, my overly confident compatriot. Do not dismiss my genteel nature as one of meekness."

I showed him both palms. "Okay, I'm sorry." I skimmed his shimmering translucent forearm with reluctant fingers. "I do appreciate everything you do, Fane. I know caring for Raina isn't something you . . . expected. But she adores you, and I'm, well, somewhat fond of you myself."

"Humph," he said, plastering his padded bustier with lean forearms. "*Somewhat*, is it?"

I laughed and embraced him, his skin silky and somehow colder than my own. "Don't push it, buddy." I sniffed the air. "Wait! Is that my perfume I smell?"

"Someone may as well put it to good use. Ta-ta," he said and vaporized.

Later that evening, after promising to take Raina to an evening event at the Kansas City Zoo that upcoming weekend, I kissed her goodbye. I smiled as I passed the window and saw her inside with Fane, both their heads bent and touching as they attempted a new puzzle. With Tristan perpetually off hunting ruthless vampires, what would my life have been like without her? And what would I do without Fane's assistance? Reflecting on Bianca's warning, I sighed as I threw myself behind the wheel, forcing the image of the beautiful child Tristan and I would never have the opportunity to create from my mind. *Were* the Harvesters the result of forbidden reproduction? Was that why Bianca remained adamant vampiric offspring were born without souls?

I shook my head hard once I arrived at the station, the drive there lost to thoughts of adorable toddlers tottering throughout the house Tristan, Raina, and I shared. Was Tristan enough for me? Was immortality a paltry tradeoff for a life, no matter how short, filled with memories of cooing babies, first birthdays, first steps, first words, high school graduations, grandchildren . . . all the heart swelling moments of motherhood?

CHAPTER THIRTY-ONE

I had just slid the strap to my shoulder bag over the back of my chair when Burke summoned me into his office.

"Good job on the sex trafficking case, Detective. I thought you'd like to know that forensics discovered bone fragments and several teeth while sifting through the debris from the boiler explosion. They've identified the remains as belonging to Alexander Wright."

I feigned surprise. "No kidding? Huh, I combed every inch of that house."

"Don't beat yourself up, Crenshaw. Rats are masterminds when it comes to hidden tunnels. Anyway, according to the informant, all high-ranking individuals in the organization are now either dead or in police custody. That's not to say we don't intend to keep our ears to the ground. Ramirez and Chastain have contacted the parents of the six girls who weren't on our radar or your impressive little whiteboard out there. Take that thing down before you clock out. Anyway, another mystery solved by our department. They all resided in Kansas. All runaways. I think it's safe to say they'll be sticking close to home from now on."

I couldn't imagine the level of anxiety the parents must have suffered. "Let's hope so."

"That's not why I called you in here. I just received a requisition order from IT for a CCTV camera and one of the IP cameras in Interrogation Room 1. The IP camera apparently short-circuited. We're lucky it didn't burn the whole place down. But, this is where it gets interesting. The IT guys tell me the CCTV camera appeared to have been intentionally disconnected. I don't suppose you'd know anything about that?"

"No, sir." I had to throw him off my scent and wished I could accomplish that without throwing Ramirez under the bus, but I had few options. "Who was the last person the camera recorded going through the door?"

"Ramirez. I've already talked to her. The camera also recorded her leaving the room. According to the report, *you* obtained the suspect's confession; the audio from the second camera confirms that. Which means, and correct me if I'm wrong, you were the last one through the door."

I considered various scenarios, and a whirlwind of options came to mind. "Come to think of it," I said, "you're right about Ramirez. But I wasn't the last. I distinctly remember seeing some suit enter *after* I left the room. I guess I just assumed it was someone from the DA's office or a detective from another shift I had yet to meet. You might want to watch the footage again."

Burke winged both nostrils. "I'll do that," he said and accessed the file on his hard drive while I gritted my teeth and inserted the image inside Burke's psyche that I needed him to see.

"Well, I'll be damned," he said moments later, then mumbled an anemic apology. "I don't recognize that guy. Never seen him before. You can bet I plan to get to the bottom of this."

"I have no doubt, Captain. Are we done here?"

Burke gnawed his lip and studied me, his steely gaze meant to unnerve me. "Not quite. While we're on the subject of unexplainable circumstances, we received an anonymous tip, which solves the mystery surrounding the two men who fell to their deaths in the parking lot at Bully's Bar and Grill."

"No kidding?" I asked past a lump in my throat.

"It seems a member of the KC Crusaders has claimed the bragging rights. Apparently, he stayed behind that night to even the score."

I attempted to disguise a giddy exhale. The lucky breaks just kept coming. That wouldn't be the first time a gang's new recruit wrongfully confessed. I could easily recite a handful who had risked jail time to ingratiate themselves with a particular gang. And, this time, I couldn't be more grateful.

"Well, I guess that explains that."

"Does it?" he asked, pitching forward. "I'd like to know how it was you weren't aware of this guy's presence?"

I shrugged past a tremble. "It was dark. So dark that I couldn't see my hand in front of my face. And remember, I'd found myself thrust into a situation which required me to fight for my life, Captain. All without sufficient backup." I forced a laugh. "I'm human after all, not some kind of superhero."

He grunted his response, then said, "There's something else we need to discuss."

I nearly choked on the apprehension.

"We're spread thin, as you know. With Quaid out for God-knows-how-long and a couple of detectives on vacation, we need to fill spots whenever the situation calls for it. I want you working the unsolved homicide cases until I say otherwise. Which reminds me," he said, sorting through papers spread across his desk, "a few minutes ago, I intercepted a call from the sheriff in Drexel . . ." he paused and referenced his notes. "Wayne Davis is his name. Here's his number," he said and passed me the sticky note. "The Jane Doe who was missing . . . they just discovered her body."

─ ─ ─

Back at my desk, I gave Davis a call, and he answered on the first ring and instructed me to meet him at his office. When I arrived, a harried-appearing man with bloodshot gray eyes and a silver goatee raised his head. The placard on his desk confirmed his identity.

"Sheriff Davis, I'm Detective Crenshaw."

He reached across the desk and extended his hand. "Thanks for coming, Detective."

"Where was the body discovered?" I asked.

"In an abandoned farmhouse about ten miles northwest. As I told you on the phone, I thought it best to meet here. Some of these places aren't even on the map. I'll grab my keys and you can follow me."

Once inside a white Dodge Challenger, he started the ignition and gravel swirled below the baritone rumble thrown off dual chrome exhaust. He waited for me to maneuver my car behind his, and a cloud of dust concealed his taillights as he sped away, our bright headlamps illuminating the upper leaves of majestic cornstalks aligned in row after row of perfect symmetry as we traveled down the road.

The body was nude, mutilated, appeared exsanguinated, and had been there for a while. Insects had deposited eggs inside several gaping wounds, vermin had piecemealed flesh from bone in a random chaotic pattern, and bird droppings surrounded the body and competed with the chalk outline drawn by the investigators. The air stank of decay and the old, mostly windowless, house sagged beneath our weight. I noticed Sheriff Davis was content to guard the door.

After informing forensics of my intention, I rolled the body onto the opposite side. The shoulder tattoo Mamie Martin had described was intact and remained clearly defined despite the red-blue-purple discoloration of the skin surrounding it, a result of livor mortis.

Outside, the Cass County ME's van squealed to a halt, gravel dust blanketing the thigh-high grass in a gritty silver haze. The medical examiner swung one leg over the rotted threshold and clambered inside. Joy Trumbull was middle-aged, athletic in appearance, her words moderately friendly, her expression quite the opposite.

After tugging on latex gloves and pinching a surgical mask in place, she crouched to examine the body. The forensics team immediately gathered varying sizes of evidence bags they'd collected and stepped away. I stood close enough to Trumbull to appreciate her meticulous examination but far enough so as not to cast a shadow on the victim. Following a cursory inspection, she applied considerable pressure and managed to wrench the corpse's legs back together again.

"Well, people, if this isn't a case of déjà vu, I'll buy the beers."

A glance around the room convinced me the forensic team agreed.

I inched forward and waited until she'd discarded her gloves and removed her mask. I extended my hand and introduced myself. "You said déjà vu. Are you referring to the Callie Sutherland case?"

She nodded and signaled the team to load the body into the van. "That's right. You're outside your jurisdiction, Detective. Mind if I ask why?"

"We've recently closed an investigation into a sex-trafficking ring. Initially, I thought maybe the men responsible might have been involved in the Sutherland killing, but—"

Before I could offer Mamie's testimony surrounding the men with the tattoos, she shook her head and interrupted.

"Kidnappers don't sample their wares, Detective . . . at least not until their handlers give them permission. Nor do they take things too far and destroy the merchandise. The men responsible for this crime and the murder of Callie Sutherland are vicious predators, not dimwitted muscle carrying out orders."

"I agree but, with all due respect, how can you be sure the two cases are connected? Callie's body was burned nearly beyond recognition and discarded in a field."

She raised an eyebrow and hinted at a smile. "Someone's been doing their homework." She looked away briefly, her eyes settling on a weeping willow tree just outside the lone worm-eaten window frame. "But the corpse was not burned beyond recognition, Detective. And, as with this young woman's body, those animals left their calling cards."

Why had Detective O'Leary omitted that information? "Which are—?"

"The inverted cross on the inside of her upper thigh, for one," she said with a nod toward the victim's torso. "Crudely carved. Premortem, I'm willing to bet. Like I said, animals."

"And the others?"

"The puncture wounds just below the ear," she said, pointing to the body. "I suspect inflicted with some sort of hook scraper like those used in soldering. And the thirteen knife wounds—no more, no less—strategically placed to make each one count."

The investigators dismantled then loaded high intensity LED lamps into their vehicle as I said goodbye to the medical examiner and thanked Sheriff Davis, promising to keep him updated. I slipped behind the wheel, a wave of nausea prompting me to inhale shallow breaths before successfully completing a U-turn, tires slipping on muddy vegetation. At a stop sign just over the rise, I pulled over suddenly, thick gravel crunching beneath the overinflated tires. I flung the door open and raced around the car, my feet sliding when contacting the soft shoulder. I vomited between dry heaves. Just when I thought I was finished, the retching began again. A terrifying explanation occurred to me as I thought about that single night with Tristan upon my return. I sputtered a laugh and quickly dismissed the ridiculous possibility that had popped into my head.

CHAPTER THIRTY-TWO

I had never vomited after visiting a crime scene. I certainly had never vomited a liter of blood that resembled bubbly orange soda, from mixing with gastric acid. Maybe my thermos had gotten too warm. I convinced myself the blood was the culprit and made a mental note to pack icepacks around the thermos in the future.

Headlights drew closer, and I tore the passenger door open and crawled inside. Circumventing the console, I fought another surge of nausea, threw the car into drive, and punched the accelerator. The temptation to ignore the stop sign altogether passed, and I brought the car to a transitory stop. The headlights—I assumed belonging to the sheriff—lit up the rear window, further illuminating my pale blond hair and the ashen fingers gripping the steering wheel. I turned left and continued down another country road plagued with potholes and deep and wide crevices—the result of heavy farm machinery—and hit the brakes more than once to avoid small game pursued by either a red fox or a mange-ravished coyote.

My stomach churned, threatening a spewing encore as I left behind the headlights tailing me and turned onto Interstate 49. Ten miles down the highway, I had to pull over again. Three more times before I passed the first exit to Grandview, Missouri. Dispatch alerted me to a one-eight-seven—a reported homicide—midtown. Activating the lights and siren, I stomped the accelerator and took the off-ramp, veering onto northbound US Route 71.

Boarded-up windows testified to the city's blight. The car screeched to a stop at a busy intersection as I attempted to avoid a homeless man pushing a lopsided shopping cart. Once I'd assisted him across the intersection, I dove back inside the vehicle, minutes later curbing it between a dark alleyway and a crumbling driveway attached to the midtown property. The house was dark, the only movement a flap of screen mesh fluttering its objection to the gentle breeze that intermittently rattled the screen door. I was nearly to the porch when Reed's Mustang rumbled to a stop behind the Dodge.

"Have you called the ME?" she asked, detouring around broken glass, a discarded refrigerator, a rusty bicycle, and several abandoned toys as she approached.

"I haven't found a body yet."

I watched her stalk the perimeter. She stayed low to the ground—minimizing her silhouette, gun hand braced by the other, while employing cat-like movements that required precision, experience, and muscle.

"Over here," she called soon after entering a backyard sentried by wire fencing usually relegated to a chicken coop.

Dispatch hadn't offered any details to include the body's location on the property. Reed was intuitive, impressive, and annoying.

Standing over the body, I said past a burp, "This doesn't appear to have been a drive-by." After slipping on a pair of gloves, I checked for a pulse.

Reed shrugged. "Maybe the vic lived here."

"Maybe. But it looks as though he was running away from the house when someone shot him in the back. If he lived here and someone was giving chase, why wouldn't he seek safety inside? There's no sign of lividity, so he hasn't been dead long."

She shrugged and delivered an apathetic stare. "Too bad dead men tell no tales. But if they did," she said smirking, "I guess we'd be out of a job." She showed me her back and radioed a request for the ME and forensics. The radio squawked a shots fired announcement a few minutes later, the address just a couple of blocks east.

She clipped her radio back on her belt after stating her intent to respond. "You got this?"

Before I could formulate a response, she sprinted toward her car and left the scene.

ME Romano arrived ahead of the team from the forensic department, sporting a floral scarf that failed to obscure meticulously arranged rows of hair rollers. In the dim light cast by a neighboring house, her face glowed beneath layers of night cream. Silk pajamas peeked beneath a utilitarian robe, which suggested "Juice" Romano had not detoured from her bed en route to the crime scene and that she had a soft side. Two forensic officers slugged alongside moments later, one rubbing sleep from her eyes, the other failing to pump his slumped shoulders.

After commandeering a pair of sterile tweezers from her kit, Romano lifted the victim's plaid shirttail and honed her flashlight on his lower back. "You see this?" she asked me. "If I'm not mistaken, that's a 9mm bullet wedged between his lower vertebrae, fired by someone with a whole lot of hate for our victim. Someone who wanted to incapacitate him and watch him suffer. Second one this month. Don't quote me—my memory isn't what it used to be—but I think the first victim's name was Barstow, if that means anything to you. And to confirm a connection with our other victim," she began, while gripping the corpse's nondescript black ball cap, "let's see what's hiding under here."

Slipping the cap from his head, Romano revealed a bald head and an upside-down-crucifix tattoo.

The ME responded to my prolonged gasp with a quizzical expression, the oily sediment accentuating the well-earned frown lines spanning her broad forehead.

"He have any identification?" I asked.

"Why? Do you recognize him?"

I shook my head. "No, but the tattoo corresponds with witness testimony pertaining to the kidnapping and subsequent murder of a Drexel woman." *And possibly a Belton teenager.*

Romano slipped a gloved hand into the victim's back pocket and tugged a wallet free. She nodded at one of the investigators who in turn maneuvered a bright lamp, illuminating the driver's license. "Jacob Cahill. Born December 9, 1990. Looks like his cell phone is missing, too," she said, gesturing toward an empty pouch.

It was possible he had lost the phone while running, ditched the phone earlier, or the killer had taken it from him. "How about a receipt for the phone? Maybe there's one in his wallet."

She dug through his wallet. Coming up empty, she searched all his pockets. Tugging a scrap of paper from a coin pocket, she said, "This could be it, but because of heat transfer from the body, it's mostly illegible. I'll ask forensics to work their magic. If they're successful, they'll give you a call."

I cocked my head in the direction of the house. "He live here?"

"Nope. But if I thought he was involved in your Drexel homicide, I'd secure a warrant to search the property anyway. No one has come out, so I think it's safe to say the house is either vacant or whoever lives here isn't at home."

Thanks to my preternatural vision, I'd already scanned every nook and cranny. The only inhabitant was a scrawny old calico cat that appeared to be abandoned and on its ninth life. I intended to make Animal Control aware before my shift ended. I inched a notepad from a blazer pocket. "Can I have his address? I think I'll start there."

"You're the detective. If it's current, up until tonight he called 4545 Gladstone Avenue home."

CHAPTER THIRTY-THREE

〜〜〜

Missouri law requiring a search warrant for a homicide victim's dwelling remained a contentious argument, one in which I had no desire to participate, so I contacted Judge Brinkman. Steering the Dodge toward Mission Hills, an upscale neighborhood within the Country Club District just south of the Plaza, I passed several mansions architected by Frank Lloyd Wright.

Arriving at my destination, my gaze swept over a long, winding driveway every bit as clean and shiny as a Tiffany porcelain platter . . . and I decided to park on the street. When I knocked on the door, he welcomed me as he might an enlarging hemorrhoid. The motion lights sentineling his house greeted me with equal ferocity.

Snugging the belt to a smoky-brown bathrobe and eyeing me as if I were a Girl Scout peddling last year's chocolate mint cookies, he said, "This couldn't wait until morning, Detective?"

"As I explained to you on the phone, Judge, there's reason to believe the homicide victim played a role in the murder of two women. If he was involved, it's possible I'll find incriminating evidence on the premises."

Brinkman blinked long. "You seem to have me at a disadvantage, Detective, because I don't remember that part of the conversation. It *is* the middle of the night for God's sake."

"I'm sorry, sir, but I'm sure you can understand the urgency."

He pressed the warrant into my waiting hands. "*Please* confirm the address. I'm certain you're a delightful young woman, but I'd rather not see you again, particularly in the dead of night."

Dying evergreen bushes, losing the battle to stack upon stack of bagworms, hid the majority of Cahill's midcentury tract house. Lopsided wood shutters hung on for dear life like a mountain climber who'd lost his footing. I sidestepped a gaping crevice that spanned the concrete porch from the steps to the front door. Nearby, a Nike shoebox duct-taped to the vinyl siding served as a mailbox. The front door being locked, I had to trudge around back. The knob twisted freely on the backdoor but didn't allow entry. Following a brief inspection, I noticed that the top of the door sagged crookedly, humid conditions and decades of neglect contributing to swelling and rot. I squeezed my eyes shut with the intention to teleport inside, when a neighboring porchlight flashed a warning and I reconsidered.

I shouldered the door and the wood creaked and groaned, parts of it splintering before breaking contact with the frame. I crept inside and eased the door closed.

Inside, a welcoming party of cockroaches led me from the kitchen into the living area, scurrying in various directions like store customers granted a five-minute free-for-all. A stained couch lay upended. Beyond it lay a shattered window, obscured from the street by unrestrained vegetation. The smell of sewer gas permeated the house, despite the reluctant breeze trickling through the broken window. My eyes watered as I sucked in a deep breath and held it while wrenching open the front door to allow more ventilation.

Slatted wooden crates had become makeshift tables. Someone had wired a bottle of Michelob beer with an electrical cord and socket, and it served as the room's meagre light source. Down a dark narrow hallway, I encountered soggy carpeting and the first of two bedrooms, which lay empty: no furnishings, window coverings, or closet doors. In the second room, a waterbed oozed water, a result of malicious punctures. Drawers fitted along the frame spilled clothing and assorted articles: coins, drug paraphernalia, empty cigarette packages, and soda cans. Early editions of *Playboy* and *Hustler* magazines littered the drenched carpet, some of the pages beginning to curl and bloat. A poster depicting Heath Ledger as the Joker failed to enhance the decor, the villain's smile intensified by a black light mounted above.

Someone had tossed the place, searched it from top to bottom. What were they looking for? Drugs? Cash? Evidence that might incriminate them in the Jane Doe and Callie Sutherland murders? And why would someone slash the bed? No one in their right mind would choose a waterbed to stash items they didn't want found, unless those items were encased in a waterproof container. I discounted that theory immediately; the only orifice was a valve, which was much too small to slip a container through, and it would have prevented Cahill easy access even if he'd managed.

I backtracked down the gloomy hallway and headed for the kitchen. Stopping outside the bathroom door, I stuck my head in. My eyes darted to the toilet and sink. I couldn't decide which was dirtier. A toilet plunger had long ago surrendered and lay on the floor of the dirt-ringed bathtub. I decided to have a look inside the medicine cabinet and discovered a bottle of aspirin, an unopened container of deodorant gathering cobwebs, and a sample tube of toothpaste still in the box. A peek inside the tiny linen closet revealed chips off various soap cakes, discolored wash cloths and towels, and a small door near the baseboard, which allowed access to the plumbing. I pried it open and from deep within, crammed between leaky pipes, I rescued a pair of women's panties. Pinching the lingerie between my fingers, I glided toward the kitchen and searched for a plastic baggie. Finding only one remaining at the bottom of a crumpled box, I secured the panties inside and tucked the bag in my jacket pocket.

I tossed the box back under the sink where I'd found it. The floor creaked under my feet, and it suddenly occurred to me that the rug in front of the sink was the only throw rug throughout the house. I flipped it aside and discovered a section of linoleum that appeared new. The composition and pattern were the same—inexpensive vinyl, manufactured to resemble stone pavers. Cahill had replaced it recently. I grabbed a utility knife I'd seen during my search for the baggy and removed it. Cahill had also replaced a section of subfloor just beneath. Rather than take time to look for a screwdriver to remove the dozen or so wood screws, I focused on the outcome, and watched as the screws turned counterclockwise simultaneously and, once freed, clinked against the floor. I popped one side loose, then the other, and tipped the plywood toward the cabinet.

"What have you got hidden down there, Cahill?" I said aloud and lowered myself into the hole.

It was pitch black under the house, but I could see everything clearly, from the mice scurrying back and forth to the papery snakeskins attached to the foundation and the raw sewage seeping from the house. My eyes fell on a Rubbermaid tub in the corner, the lid showered with rodent droppings. Duck-walking over to it, I pinched the lid open. Stacked inside were baggies crammed with twenty-dollar bills. I shoved the bundles off to the side, thinking it possible he'd stashed the murder weapon with the cash. At the bottom of the tub, I found two bags of a powdery substance, I suspected heroin, and another bag filled with opioids. When I didn't find anything else, I snapped the lid back on to protect the contents from the rodents. Sucking in my stomach, I wiggled back through the opening and laid the sections of plywood and linoleum back in their original positions.

My stomach rumbled from the rotten egg odor. I dashed to the front door and secured it, then sprinted out the back and phoned dispatch and requested a forensic team. The neighboring back porch light still glowed caution, and a set of eyes peered through white, heavily starched eyelet curtains. I hopped the chain link fence perceptively dividing Cahill's property, which resembled a warzone in comparison. Walking the perfectly symmetrical cobblestone pathway, I passed a garden shed that looked more like an inviting guesthouse and knocked on the back door to the main house painted an eye-pleasing green.

I saw the resident's silhouette through the door, the top portion glassed. She held a cell phone in one hand, a baseball bat in the other.

"Who are you and what do you want?"

"I'm Detective Crenshaw. I'd like to ask you a few questions about your neighbor." When I got no response, I plastered my identification against the glass.

A series of deadbolts clinked and clacked before the door sprang open.

"Sorry to bother you, ma'am. Someone broke into Mr. Cahill's house tonight. Did you happen to see anyone suspicious lurking around?"

The older woman shook her head, glasses on a leash around her neck tinkling against a large gold-plated crucifix.

"Are you sure? Because it seems as though you keep a close eye on the neighborhood."

She gnawed her lip and flushed embarrassment.

I smiled my detective smile. "And that's a good thing, a neighborly thing, Mrs. . . . ?"

"Ludlow. I suppose it could have happened while I was at church. Tonight was bingo night."

"Can you tell me about anyone who may have visited Mr. Cahill over the past few months? Women? Men?"

"Every now and again, a man would show up on his doorstep. Sometimes the same man, other times a different one. Always late at night and always arriving with their head lamps off."

"Why do you suppose they had the lights off?"

She arched a brow. "My guess is they were up to no good. The two of them would exchange no more than a few words and things I couldn't identify in the dark."

"Like what? Drugs? Money?"

She shrugged. "Like I said, I couldn't see because it was dark. If the porch light was on, Cahill would turn it off."

"Is there anything you can tell me about the men who stopped by? Any distinguishing clothing? Age, height, weight? Tattoos?"

She curled her lip. "I've seen *his* tattoo," she said, nodding toward Cahill's residence. "And every night I pray he'll be evicted from that house."

"I understand. What about the other men, Mrs. Ludlow? Any other information that might help identify them?"

She shook her head. "I wish I could be of more help, but it was too—"

"Dark. Right, I understand. But you said sometimes it was a different man, and I'm wondering how you knew it was a different man?"

"The cars were different, so I guess I just assumed the men driving them were different, too."

My stomach rumbled again, and I decided to speed things up. I dipped inside her head and waded past recipes, an extensive QVC wish list, and tomorrow's to-do list. When I didn't find anything relevant, I decided to wrap things up.

"Mrs. Ludlow, I should tell you that Mr. Cahill was murdered earlier this evening."

Her eyes flew to his house.

"At a separate location," I added quickly.

"Oh dear."

"Because it's my job to find those responsible, are you absolutely sure there's nothing else you can tell me about the men who came to his house?"

She wagged her head and took a step back. "I'm sorry, I can't help you. Other than a masculine physique, I can't offer any details."

"Is it possible any of those men had a similar tattoo?"

Her brow crinkled as a forefinger river-danced over her upper lip. "Come to think of it, just like Mr. Cahill, not a one of them had a hair on his head, so I suppose it's possible . . . you know, the reason they shaved their heads. I could tell that much because of the streetlights," she added quickly.

I glanced over my shoulder, tipping my head toward the darkened house on the other side of Cahill's property. "Who lives there?"

"The Crowders, Jeremiah and Minerva. If they'd seen or heard anything untoward, they would have called the police."

"Thank you, Mrs. Ludlow. I appreciate your time. The crime scene investigators are on their way, so don't be alarmed should you see people coming and going." I tugged a card from my breast pocket. "If you happen to remember anything else, anything that struck you out of the ordinary, please give me a call."

Twenty minutes later, I greeted the forensic team. "I need you to put a rush on these," I said and dug the baggie from my pocket. "And pay particular attention to the waterlogged bedroom." I hitched a thumb over my shoulder. "You can't miss it. There's also a tub of cash and illegal drugs under the floor directly in front of the kitchen sink. The board's loose, so watch your step."

While I waited for them to collect evidence and retrieve the cash, I paid a visit to Jeremiah and Minerva Crowder. Metal bars covered every window, and a welcome mat suggested hypocrisy. Stumps, once ornamental bushes, lay abandoned and surrounded the attractive two-story colonial. I rang the bell, but it went unanswered. Back at Cahill's residence, I found the crime scene investigators applying luminol to a second set of crusty bedsheets I'd seen piled in a corner. I assumed they were testing for both blood and semen. A rival lover would certainly explain the property destruction, particularly the slashing of the mattress. *Maybe even the panties.* That same level of rage would also explain why someone would shoot Jacob Cahill in the back. But I hoped I was on the right track about my discovery linking Cahill to Callie Sutherland and Elsie Hanover.

An investigator turned and acknowledged my presence, the same CSI I'd seen at the Cahill murder site. "We didn't find any fingerprints, other than the victim's. It appears someone recently laundered the sheets ripped from the bed. Luminol testing didn't reveal any blood or semen on either set. We'll take them back to the lab and retest just to be sure."

CHAPTER THIRTY-FOUR

It was nearly five a.m. when I returned to the station. I sat in the parking lot, debating a sip from the bottle within the coolie bag. I opened the bottle and sniffed the contents. The smell wasn't anything out of the ordinary—metallic yet sweet, but something had made me sick, and I didn't intend to take any chances. Twirling revolutions in my chair, a coping mechanism I hadn't been able to overcome, I felt disappointment weighing heavily on my shoulders. I felt sure forensics would have uncovered evidence that would prove at least one of the rapes and murders had occurred at Cahill's residence.

With plans to check my email and call it a night, I opened an email marked *Urgent*, forwarded from Detective Franklin with a request I respond, the original sender Liberty, Missouri, Chief of Police Bernard Stapleton. I rolled my eyes and raked both hands through my hair; it was no secret that Franklin avoided any communication requiring much more than a yes or no response.

It was also no secret that he considered the other detectives, including me, little more than his personal gofers.

The email detailed the murder of Celine Dover, twenty-two, a college student at William Jewell College in Liberty. A farmer had discovered her remains a month ago within a soybean field northwest of Liberty, near the Kearney, Missouri border. The ME estimated her time of death a few days prior to discovery. There were no witnesses and the killer succeeded in leaving no evidence behind—the exception being a scrawled inverted crucifix on the inside of the victim's thigh, the same mark ME Joy Trumbull had recently brought to my attention.

After careful consideration, I shared the Jane Doe discovery with Chief Stapleton, with the insistence that the carved inverted crucifix—the singular piece of evidence linking the victims—remain confidential until further notice. I hit send before opening an image he'd attached of the victim. That simple inclusion convinced me of Stapleton's compassion for the victim, his resolve to find her killer, and that he felt certain by humanizing the victim his determination would prove infectious to the KCPD. He was right; staring back at me was a beautiful young woman with brown hair, seafoam green eyes, and a toothy smile—dazzling despite slightly overlapping front teeth.

⌁ ⌁ ⌁

Candlelight illuminated the window shade within Raina's bedroom when I arrived home. I crept inside with plans to retrieve a chilled bottle of blood from the fridge before either she or Fane realized I was there. After verifying a lot number different from the bottle inside my coolie bag, I unscrewed the top and sipped cautiously. Convinced I hadn't suffered any ill effect from the small quantity, I tucked the bottle away in the fridge and sauntered toward Raina's bedroom, her melodic giggling filling the house with everything wonderful. I watched them from the doorway. Their backs to me, Fane acknowledged my presence with an ear suddenly perked in my direction. Raina instantly popped upright, her usual smile, which always greeted me, replaced with a concerned frown.

"Who is that with you, Mummy?"

"It's just me, Raina," I said, inching toward her.

She backed away, shaking her head, and clung to Fane.

"Raina, what's wrong?" When she didn't answer, I looked to Fane and tried to make sense of his expression. Was it shock? Disappointment? Fear?

"I hear the beat of your heart and that of another," she said, pointing a tiny accusatory finger. She began to cry. "Please, Mummy. Why won't you tell me?"

I opened my mouth, desperate to form a response. "Baby, I don't know what you mean. Fane, what's going on?"

Crimson flashes sparked across his retinae. By Raina's side one moment, mine the next, Fane propped an ear against my pelvis. "A grave misfortune inhabits your womb," he whispered.

I pushed him away, and he toppled over. "That isn't funny, Fane."

"If only I were playing a cruel trick," he said, and his horrified gaze convinced me he wasn't.

"Oh, God. I can't be pregnant," I said, more to myself. *How could I have been so careless?* "But it was just the one night," I whispered to Fane, who served me a justified smirk.

"Careless, indeed. I, for one, find our distinguished warrior's virility not the least bit surprising," he said with a concerned expression. "Do not fault yourself, dear friend. For I doubt a chastity belt, your modern-day voodoo, or a cork for that matter, could have staved off his potent seed. Go, seek your mother's counsel," he whispered urgently. "I shall do my best to distract Raina. Until the matter is resolved, your absence is most advantageous . . . for her sake. Be gone," he said, pushing me toward the door. "I shall communicate your excuse."

I backed from the room, lightheaded, reeling from Fane's pronouncement and his atypical gruffness. I experienced the familiar twinge deep inside my head, like a feather tickling my brain. Bianca must have sensed something wrong and attempted to access my thoughts. I immediately thought about nothing but the homicide cases. I knew what she would recommend.

I knew what the Realm would demand I do.

After packing a duffel bag and grabbing a dusty sleeping bag from a closet shelf, I wrenched the rickety doors open and lugged everything inside the carriage house.

Discovering a heap of rags in a corner and a stapler on a workbench that hadn't been in use for decades, I covered the windows with the rags and stapled them in place.

My back against the door, I sank to the concrete floor, my fingers tracing the letters—the initials of bygone residents—immortalized in the cement decades ago. Zippered within the sleeping bag soon after, I struggled to keep my mind off the life growing within me and eventually fell asleep with Tristan foremost on my mind.

When I woke, just after sunset, I slipped from the carriage house and stole one long look toward the house, then I threw myself behind the wheel and steered the car toward the station. The sky clear, stars twinkled overhead. One in particular blinked randomly, as if confirming it knew my secret and passionately disproved.

Detective Franklin raised his head when I slung myself through the doorway. Six feet and two inches of hard lean muscle pitched his small office chair forward, rusty springs and worn leather creaking in response.

"You look like shit," he offered pointedly.

"Nice to see you, too."

He bolted upright, his bulky silhouette reflected in the window, and dropped a folder on my desk, the velocity so fierce it parted my bangs. "I spent most of the day and evening compiling this crap. Inside, you'll find information that may shed some light on your killer. Once you make the arrest, I expect the majority of the credit."

I threw myself into my chair and leaned into the split-vinyl headrest. "What kind of information?"

He tapped the manila folder and narrowed his eyes. "You expect me to read it to you, too? Where's your commitment, Crenshaw? Sometimes, in order to solve a case—"

"Don't patronize me, Detective."

"And don't interrupt me, *Detective*. It pisses me off. Serial killers, and that's the angle you're working, don't hit the floor running one morning because they've decided to go out and savagely rape and murder women. The murders aren't random. Those particular offenders plan every detail. And they have an uncanny sense of the walls closing in, and they get the hell out of Dodge. I contacted some of my law enforcement buddies in both Arkansas and Oklahoma. I'm surprised, and more than a little disappointed, that you didn't think to expand your search. That would have been my first move."

I resisted a harsher retort but not the shit-eating grin. "I guess that's why you're the Lead Dick, Detective."

He bent at the waist, his nose within an inch of mine. "And don't you forget it. I'm headed out. A look inside," he said, indicating the folder, "chronicles similar murders within a tristate area. Bon appetite and you're fuckin' welcome."

I sneered at the back of his head, which competed with an intricate spider web draped across the header as he swaggered out the door. I plied the contents from the envelope and spread them across my desk. The mug-shots caught my attention first, and I separated them into groups of ten. Franklin had meticulously attached the arrest records and other pertinent information, a kind of criminal bio. I was midway through the second stack of mugshots when a chronicle of the convict's distinguishing marks caught my attention—a crescent-moon birthmark on his right forearm, a two-inch scar on his left cheek, and a Petrine cross tattoo extending from the top of his head to the base of his skull. David Lee Snyder, twenty-nine, had spent half his life sneering at prison guards and pissing in a stainless-steel toilet. His rap sheet read like an instructional booklet on How to Fuck Up Your Life. Early on in his criminal career, he'd had to answer for multiple acts of vandalism and animal cruelty, specifically cattle mutilation. A year later, at the ripe old age of seventeen, Snyder escaped a conviction charge on two counts of criminal stalking, both women suddenly developing a case of amnesia when the time came for them to testify against him. Arrested and convicted multiple times for possession of various quantities of methamphetamines (a local gang member the suspected trafficker), the amount, not surprisingly, escalated with each arrest. Following his last apprehension, Snyder failed to evade a conviction. Because the aggravated assault occurred during a narcotic transaction and the arresting officers discovered Snyder's twelve-inch Bowie knife, a federal judge extended him an invitation to Fort Leavenworth Prison. Handed down a sentence of ten years, Snyder served twelve, awarded two additional years for bad behavior after beating a fellow inmate to a bloody pulp.

Twisting the ends of my hair into a coiled mess, I forwent a deep dive into NCIC, mainly because I knew the National Crime Information Center had always been Franklin's go-to information gathering source. Instead, I ran Snyder's name through CHRI, hoping I'd be rewarded with a list of known associates. Hitting a dead-end, I exited the Criminal History Record Information site and decided to share what little information I had with O'Leary.

He answered on the first ring. I opened the conversation with the very real possibility that one of Callie Sutherland's killers lay naked and stone cold on a slab in the Jackson County Morgue. The connection was bad due to an unexpected thunderstorm—the lights flickered on and off, golf-ball-size hailstones pummeled and pocked the metal roof, but I thought O'Leary had requested the killer's name. I saw no reason not to share the information. His response crackled in my ear—words reduced to random syllables—following a blinding flash of pitchforked lightning. An alarming pop punctuated the perpetual hiss emanating through my earpiece, and I nearly dropped the phone. The line went dead, leaving me little choice but to wait out the storm.

An opaque wall of rain obscured everything outside the row of aged wood-framed windows, thick coats of paint failing to disguise widening weather cracks and years of structural neglect. The lights blinked off, on, then off again, and my eyes adjusted to the claustrophobic darkness instantly. The generator hummed, vibrating the building, and the lights glimmered lazily, gradually dappling the room in a despondent glow. Outside traffic lights slept, while powerlines shook in an epileptic-like frenzy. Rain swamped the squalid street as though it were a sinner afforded baptism, the oil slick beneath sheets of rainfall shimmering like glistening cellophane.

My desk phone trilled an annoying *b-r-ring*, and I raced from the window to answer it.

"The weather any better there?" O'Leary greeted.

"The rain's really coming down."

"The weather bureau just canceled the tornado warning for Cass County, but, sorry to say, they extended the one in your neck of the woods."

The wind picked up, howling over my reply, and neighborhood debris swirled over the road. A spidery oak limb groaned then cracked and hurtled toward the window. I ducked under the desk instinctively as the impact fissured the glass and buckled the gutters.

"Detective Crenshaw?" O'Leary shouted.

"Still here," I said, both eyes opened wide and locked on the storm.

"Maybe you should take cover."

I choked on a laugh. "Here? That's a fool's errand . . . no basement. I'll be fine. I didn't catch your response before the line went dead earlier."

"And I didn't catch the name of the guy on the slab."

"Jacob Cahill."

He produced an anguished sigh. "Doesn't sound familiar."

"What about David Snyder?"

"Snyder . . . Snyder . . . David." I could hear him snapping his fingers in an attempt to jog his memory. "Can't help you there, either."

"There's another reason for my call. A colleague has recently provided me considerable information on convicts bearing similar tattoos. I haven't had a chance to go through everything yet, but if there's anything I think might be of help, I'll make sure it reaches your desk."

"I appreciate that. The APB I issued remains in effect, and I don't know a detective or a beat cop who hasn't committed the forensic sketches to memory."

In my experience, the momentum behind an all-points bulletin was always short-lived. And renderings from a sketch artist tended to fade away much more quickly than a photograph. But because the Belton PD was a much smaller organization, the community more closely knit, it was possible the killers remained on every cop's radar twenty-four seven.

While the storm raged north to other counties, I spent the next few hours leafing through the information acquired from Franklin. My head pounded and my eyes felt like two marbles in a sandpit. I paid particular attention to the notations regarding physical disparities, as none of the headshots captured the suspects from behind. It eventually became clear that the majority of the criminals Franklin had amassed in the file remained housed within the walls of one penitentiary or another and, therefore, couldn't be guilty of either the Sutherland or the Jane Doe murder. I resisted a compulsion to shoot Franklin an email and thank him for wasting my time. Had he omitted the files on those behind bars, I could have wrapped up the process hours earlier. To compound my frustration, I also didn't uncover any obvious connection between David Snyder and Jacob Cahill.

Guilt needled its way in as my gaze darted to Burke's vacant office. Now that those involved in the sex trafficking racket were behind bars, my assignment was the unsolved gang-related homicides, not the Sutherland and Hanover cases. Regardless, I planned to shadow David Snyder at every opportunity. I searched the file for his last known address and entered the information into my cell phone. With my thoughts once again straying to Tristan and our unborn child, I needed a distraction and decided to focus my attention on the unsolved homicides Burke had assigned me.

CHAPTER THIRTY-FIVE

⌐⌐⌐

I went back to the station four hours before my next shift began. It was becoming more and more difficult to keep the truth from Bianca. I often felt her rooting around inside my head even when I slept. I met Ramirez at the door.

"Burke's been a raging prick. I hope to God we make an arrest soon." She waved a hand overhead on her way out the door. "See you when I see you."

Burke *was* riding the detective squad hard. Undoubtedly, the majority of his impatience was due to impassioned threats from the mayor. Instead of reading the concise reports other detectives had entered into the KCPD database, I poured over the initial case files related to the recent gang-related homicides. Maybe Quaid's old-school approach wasn't so ridiculous after all, because from a deep dive into the first victim's extensive criminal history, I learned that he was a Grim Gladiators gang member and a known drug trafficker. His products of choice—methamphetamines and cocaine laced with fentanyl. The Jackson County Sheriff discovered his body while attempting to serve an arrest warrant. According to the report, there was no sign of forcible entry or illegal drugs found on the premises, which suggested the victim knew the killer, whose motive may have been to rob him of large quantities of narcotics and cash. The crime scene photos revealed a seventy-two-inch TV equipped with a Bose Smart Soundbar and a bronze silk sofa manufactured by Benetti's Italia, a high-end Italian designer. All within a dilapidated house begging for demolition. My eyes flew over the coroner's report, which was far more in-depth. I covered an audible gasp and fell back in the chair. Unlike the detective's brief summary, which listed the cause of death as "fatal stab wounds," the coroner's report stated the killer had inflicted thirteen wounds—the same number of wounds inflicted upon our Jane Doe and Callie Sutherland.

Energized, I plucked another folder from the stack. That of a Dark Knight gang member, known to his associates as Gunner because he not only trafficked in methamphetamines but also illegal weapons. He'd suffered multiple arrests over a nine-year period and was out on bond for his latest when a passerby alerted 911 to his bloodied corpse slumped over the steering wheel of a supped-up '74 Pontiac Firebird. Cause of death—thirteen stab wounds.

Jerking another folder free and thumbing through the pile of documents until I found the coroner's report, I learned our third gang member's cause of death was identical. The same applied to the fourth, fifth, and the sixth dead gang members. All were known drug dealers, yet the evidence log didn't cite confiscation of illegal drugs or large amounts of cash.

I dropped my head in my hands and massaged my temples. Elated but confused over the cause of death connection I'd found between the gang-related homicides and those of Callie Sutherland and Jane Doe, I slipped the documents from the final folder, dwarfish in comparison to the others, which seemed to take about as much time to absorb as a Tolstoy novel. Clive Barstow's mugshot commanded my attention, more specifically his bald head. Squinting at his profile shot, I hissed disappointment. Like Snyder's headshot, it was impossible to get an adequate view of the back of Barstow's skull. Skimming on to the coroner's report and finding the cause of death a

9mm gunshot wound that shattered the entire section between the thoracic vertebrae and the sacrum, I wondered if this was the first of the two victims Romano had mentioned. I also wondered about a connection between those responsible for the lethal gunshot wounds and those responsible for the fatal knife wounds. Maybe the gangs had discovered Cahill, Snyder, and Barstow had robbed then murdered their members and were out for retribution. I tossed the folders aside and decided to re-interview the witnesses to Gunner's murder.

I found Liza McCuskey strung out in an alley between a strip joint and a pawnshop. The report listed her as twenty-two, but she looked every bit of forty-five. The color of her hair reminded me of chili peppers and hung limp against bruised and bony shoulders. Her face wasn't a ray of sunshine; it forecasted Noah's flood. I flashed my shield, which convinced the john pressing her against a building to take off. She was hesitant to talk until I showed her a crisp twenty-dollar bill. She reached for it, feigning goodwill the way addicts always do.

"Not so fast, Liza. You tell me what you know about Gunner's murder and there's more where that came from."

She shook her head, so hard her entire body shook with it, then she wrenched her head sideways and puked. A man wearing a T-shirt advertising the club swaggered from the strip club's rear entrance, whistling as he unzipped his pants and peed a steady stream. I assumed he was the bartender.

"When you're done there," I called out, "bring her a club soda—room temperature, no ice."

He wagged his penis, then zipped up. "I don't know if you noticed, princess, but we don't do curb service."

"You do tonight. Make it fast and the KCPD might even throw you a tip."

He scurried back inside, and I hoped he planned to return.

Liza hitched her short skirt back down over skeletal hips, losing her balance twice. Her fishnet stockings were ripped here, torn there, and could have snagged a small shark. If she had worn panties when she came into the alley, she didn't have them on now.

I pointed to her hand. "What happened there?" It looked like a defensive wound to me. "Did that happen recently?" She hid her hand behind her back. "Maybe around the time somebody stabbed Gunner to death?"

"Like I told those other cops, I got nothing to say."

"I think you were there, Liza. Witnesses saw you with Gunner an hour before a passerby discovered his body. And that knife wound on your hand isn't just a coincidence."

She turned her back and faced the building. The bartender crashed through the rear door.

Wearing a scowl and a snippet of actual barbed wire for a nose ring, he pressed a plastic cup in my direction, then exchanged the club soda for a ten-dollar bill and took off.

I bumped Liza with my elbow. "Here, drink this."

She gulped the entire glass, and I fought the urge to get her something to eat. She belched then swiped a grimy hand across her mouth and headed toward the street.

"Have it your way," I called after her. "Just don't say I didn't warn you when the next cop you meet arrests you for murder."

She stopped dead and whipped around to face me. "I didn't kill him."

"But if you know who did and you don't come forward, you're considered an accessory after the fact. Which means prison time, Liza. That's one hell of a way to get clean."

She began to tremble, so violently her knees buckled, and I could hear her teeth chatter. "I talk, I'm dead. That motherfucker is crazy."

"Then tell me off the record: No written statement. No subpoena to testify."

Her dull eyes brightened. "I still get the money?"

"That depends on the information. I want a name."

"I don't know his name. You gotta believe me," she whined like a kid advised of bedtime.

"I don't believe you, Liza. But let's start with a description." I'd made two attempts to make sense of the jumbled thoughts inside her head. Reading her mind was a lot like wading through the waste in Chernobyl.

"I didn't see him real good, okay?"

"But you were in the car?"

She nodded and looked away.

"Then help me understand; if you were in the car, why didn't you see him?"

"Because I had my face buried in Gunner's balls."

"You were performing oral sex?"

She sniggered. "Yeah, if that's what you want to call it. I give him a blow-job, he gives me crank."

"And what happened when the killer began stabbing him?" She hid her face in her hands. "Come on, Liza. I'm trying to understand why you didn't see the person who opened the door, or leaned in the window, and stabbed Gunner to death?"

Tears began to stream down her face. "Blood was squirting everywhere, Gunner making this horrible gurgling sound, and I-I tried to get down, get on the floor. But then . . . the guy with the knife grabbed my hair and yanked me up, and all I could see was that knife. I pushed my hand toward him, you know, like when you tell somebody to stop."

"And that's when he stabbed you?"

"Yeah, that's when he stabbed me," she murmured.

"How did you get away?"

"A car pulled up across the street. A bunch of guys got out and he grabbed the drugs and the money Gunner had on him and ran. They weren't after him or anything, he just ran."

"Where did you run, Liza?"

"Into the bushes until the guys went inside a house and I knew for sure the guy with the knife was gone. Then I went home."

"Before you answer, remember everything you say is off the record. Most of all, you have to know that the killer didn't intend to leave any witnesses. He wants you dead, Liza. For all we know, he could be out there right now looking to finish the job. I'd like to find him before he has the opportunity to do that. So tell me his name."

"I told you. I don't know it."

Because she'd returned to working the streets, it was possible Liza didn't know the killer's name or he hers. But drug addiction was a powerful motivator. Maybe she was willing to risk her life for her next fix.

I dug around in my pocket and withdrew all the cash I had. "Then give me a description," I said, walking toward her and fanning various denominations. "You must have seen something."

"Okay, okay," she said, staring at the cash. "Gunner pushed me off him when the guy started stabbing him, you know, to try to fight him off. Before I made it down to the floor, I saw the back of the guy's head. He didn't have any hair, and he was white."

"What else?"

"He had a tattoo, but I couldn't see all of it because his jacket covered some of it and his neck was all scrunched up, you know, from leaning in the window."

"To the best of your knowledge, what did it look like?"

"It was fucking weird. It looked like an up and down line on the top part, a sideways line below that."

I handed over the money and gave her my card. "In case you remember anything else or decide to clean up your life."

CHAPTER THIRTY-SIX

I clocked in early the next evening, just after sunset. I tipped my head to Captain Burke in passing and hoped he'd keep walking. He stopped and looked at his watch.

"Your shift doesn't start for another four hours."

"I thought I'd interview more witnesses to the Gunner Rice homicide. This being a weeknight, I'll probably have more luck if I get an early start."

"From what I hear, Crenshaw, they haven't been very cooperative. I hope to hell you have more luck than the rest of them," he said, tipping his head toward the bullpen. "In case you don't follow the news, the media is scaring the hell out of the public with their serial killer headlines. Citizens on edge doesn't fare well for the department. Get me a suspect, Detective."

I debated whether to share the information Liza had provided. Because I still didn't have anything concrete, and she hadn't signed a formal statement, I decided to postpone that conversation.

"I'll do my best, Captain."

I rifled through the case files and jotted down three addresses. The first one directed me a block and a half from the crime scene. I killed the engine just outside a quaint little bungalow with steps leading to the house lined with pots filled with geraniums and variegated Vinca vine. I knocked on the storm door, and a vacuum cleaner hummed to a stop. A middle-aged woman answered the door; pink sponge rollers peeked out from a haphazardly tied purple bandana.

"Can I help you?"

I identified myself and told her I was looking for Grace Newbury.

"My daughter isn't here. She has band practice Tuesday and Thursday evenings." She jammed a fist against a hip. "What's this about?"

I decided to tread lightly. I had a feeling that if her daughter Grace had witnessed relevant information, it was because she was somewhere she wasn't supposed to be. "It's my understanding she may have some information that might prove beneficial."

"What kind of information? Did she see a car accident?"

"Something like that. I'm in a bit of a hurry, so if you could tell me where I might find her—"

"Rockhill High School. You'll find the band room around back. You can't miss it. Just follow the racket," she said and smiled a tight smile while easing the door closed.

I pulled around to the rear of the school, my headlights the only thing lighting up the rooms beyond the windows. The parking lot sat empty. Grace Newbury was somewhere other than band practice.

The second address took me to a vacant house. A dumpster decorated the lawn, evidence that the new owner was in the process of rehabbing the property. I arrived at the third address and wrenched open the gate to the chain link fence enclosing the front yard. A snarling Rottweiler charged from the side yard, and I implanted a suggestion just as it prepared to launch one hundred pounds of sinewy muscle into my face. It yelped and tunneled under a bush.

"Who's out there?" asked a woman armed with dark, callous eyes and a 12-gauge shotgun.

"Detective Crenshaw, KCPD. I'm here to talk to Nathan Brewer."

She stepped out onto the porch and craned her neck left, then right. I assumed she wondered why her watchdog wasn't watching. "Like I told those other cops, my son seen nothin'. He can't help you."

"Did they tell you there's a reward for any information leading to a conviction?"

She placed the shotgun against a post and plodded down concrete steps, no longer obscured in their entirety by green deteriorating outdoor carpet. She narrowed her eyes and cocked her head toward a shoulder. "What kinda reward?"

"A thousand dollars."

She shook her head. "You expect someone to put a target on their back for a measly thousand bucks? Not enough. Close the gate on your way out."

"If your son has information and doesn't come forward, that makes him an accessory to murder."

"Oh yeah?" she said, grinning a grin that could stop a clock. "Who do you think you're dealing with? Go peddle your bullshit somewhere else, Miss Cop, 'cause I ain't buyin'." She stomped back up the stairs, grabbed the gun, and slammed the door.

Deflated, I threw the car into gear and returned to the station. I needed a solid connection between the local gangs and the creeps with the tattoos. Although I'd asked Reed about the possibility, I hadn't run my suspicions by any of the other detectives. My stomach flip-flopped at the mere thought of contacting Franklin, and I dismissed the idea. Besides, if I knew him, he was busy cradling a bottle of whiskey or a voluptuous, desperate divorcée. I perused the pathetically short contact list stored on my cell phone, not surprised when I realized I hadn't added Donahue or remembered that he had been assigned to the Gang Task Force from 2015 to 2020. Seated in front of my computer, I scrolled through the precinct directory, sweaty fingers coming to rest on the wheel when my eyes froze on my biological father's thirty-year-old contact information.

Like an endless list of things in the department, updating the directory had taken a back seat to tasks more important, such as solving crimes and booking offenders. Assuming the desk sergeant had access to information more current, I popped from the chair, the rollers howling a clickety-clack sound as they skated over heavily waxed linoleum before the chair careened into a wall.

Rounding the corner, I discovered Sergeant Casey Simmons manning the front desk, sporting an irritated expression, a bruised forearm, and a pair of bifocals held together with an uneven strip of surgical tape and a whole lot of luck.

He looked up without raising his head and sighed. "What do you need, Detective?"

"I have a few questions for Detective Donahue and can't find his contact information." I tapped my foot while his arthritic fingers crawled over the keyboard. "Here we go. Donahue, Danny Ray." He scrawled Donahue's phone number on a Post-it note, then plastered it on the faded Formica countertop that separated us. "Anything else?" he asked, like there had better not be.

"This should do it," I said, waving the little green square over my shoulder as I turned away.

The call went to voicemail. Fighting a surge of annoyance, I left a message instructing him to call me. My desk phone rang, as if on cue, and I answered, expecting Donahue.

"Detective Crenshaw?"

"Speaking."

"Hi, this is Marcy Harris. You probably don't remember me."

"I do, Mrs. Harris."

"I should have called to thank you and the other detectives right away, but I—we—have been so focused on Emma after what she's been through. She can't sleep, and with the daily therapy sessions, there just never seems to be enough time for anything."

"I completely understand. It was nice of you to call."

"You saved our little girl," she managed through one hiccupped sob. "There just aren't enough words—"

"Yet, you've communicated them beautifully. I'm so glad things turned out the way they did. Please give my best to Emma, Mrs. Harris."

"Be safe, Detective," she whispered before ending the call.

The warm feeling of self-satisfaction quickly eroded as my gaze strayed to Quaid's desk. I had broken my promise and the sour taste of guilt coated my tongue. I grabbed my purse and plunged eight quarters into the near-empty candy machine. Armed with Quaid's favorite snack, two packages of Reese's Peanut Butter Cups, I sprinted outside.

CHAPTER THIRTY-SEVEN

I found Quaid yawning at an old *Andy Griffith Show* rerun as he sat slumped in a worn Queen Anne wingback chair upholstered in a paisley print. He heard me come into the common room and twisted around to face me.

"You're going to be late for your shift," he said, turning his attention back to Opie and Aunt Bee.

"I had a few things to wrap up, so I went in early. Thought I'd take a break and see how you're doing."

He shrugged and I pulled up a chair after setting the candy bars on a table, damaged by hot coffee cups over the years, within his reach. He unwrapped a package and emitted a soft moan as he chewed, savoring the chocolate.

"I used to enjoy fishing," he said with a nod toward the television. The scene had changed to Andy instructing Opie on how best to cast a line. "I caught a twenty-five-pound trout from Lake Taneycomo in 1998. That sucker nearly pulled my shoulder out of its socket. I heard some guy from Springfield won a ton of money last year when he snagged a forty pounder."

"Why'd you quit?"

"I lost my appetite, I guess. For both fish on a line and on a plate. Seemed barbaric to traumatize something just for the sport of it."

"There must be other things you enjoy, Dennis."

He tipped his head toward a shoulder and served me a tenuous grin. "You sound like my shrink." He massaged his knuckles, then wadded up the empty Reese's package and tossed it toward a trashcan. We watched it sail through the air, Quaid smiling when it landed inside. "Bowling. I've always enjoyed bowling. Believe it or not, I've won my share of trophies."

"I didn't know that."

"There's a tournament in Vegas this fall. I'm thinking about entering."

"That's great. I'm sure you've got some time built up; you should go, maybe take in the sights, catch a few shows, you know, really enjoy yourself."

"I'm not coming back."

I cocked my head, unsure as to his implication. "From Vegas?"

"To the department."

"I'm sorry to hear that," I said, scooting closer and covering his hand with mine. "I really am. But I'm sure you know what's best."

"I've got some money put away and a partial pension coming. I thought I might try to reconnect with my daughter."

"There's nothing more important than family," I said, a catch in my throat as I thought about my unborn child.

I left Quaid, both of us promising to keep in touch. I'd intended to tell him we'd rescued the missing girls and update him on the cases I was currently working. But it was clear Quaid needed to distance himself from all things savage.

<hr />

Donahue hadn't returned my call, but it occurred to me on the drive back to the station that Sergeant Simmons' illustrious career included a ten-year stint running the Gang Task Force. He raised his head, his right hand fisting a number two lead pencil, as I approached the desk. He tossed the cross-word puzzle off to one side, securing the compromised black-rimmed reading glasses and reminding me a little of George McFly in *Back to the Future*.

"Back so soon?" he barked, his eyes darting to Ramirez as she hopscotched her way up the stairs from the main entrance.

Ramirez swept alongside of me, not the least bit out of breath. "Hey, sorry to interrupt, but Detective Reed hasn't returned my call and dispatch doesn't have any record of her whereabouts. Can you tell me if she clocked in tonight?"

Simmons pitched an index finger in the air, then poked his keyboard like he was plugging a hole. "Nope, can't help you there."

"She probably overslept. The Fun Run ran late. I didn't get out of there until 1400. I couldn't even squeeze in a shower before my shift started." She graced me with an infectious grin. "Good thing you're downwind."

I twisted around and faced her. "The Fun Run?"

"Yeah, you know, a race. The proceeds go to the Battered Women Shelter."

Reed has a life outside of law enforcement? Good for her.

"She won, by the way. Somebody ought to swing by her place and wake her. I'd do it, but I'm late for my kid's ballet recital."

"I'll head over there," I volunteered.

Walking backward the way she had come, Ramirez said, "Appreciate it, Celeste. And please tell her I said thanks for sending my kid flowers." She flashed a wide grin. "It really made her day."

Before I could ask, Simmons jotted Reed's address on a Post-it note and slid it across the counter. He nodded toward the slip of paper. "I'm going to have to start charging you for those."

The address took me to Westport Manor Apartments, a red-bricked midtown complex resembling military barracks, located near a Civil War historical site where, in 1864, Major General Samuel R. Curtis and his troops defeated the Confederate Cavalry led by Major General Sterling Price. Reed's studio apartment was located on the first floor and the only one without a welcome mat. I rapped my knuckles against a door painted red and waited through a count of ten before knocking again. Pressing a preternatural ear to the door, I heard water railing against rusted pipes—a single plop ringing out once, contacting stainless steel—and the soft flutter of air conditioning escaping dusty vents. Baffled by another aquatic sound, I leaned into the door, searching the interior with a vampiric eye. An aquarium, the only furnishing other than a small old desk and a brown inexpensive IKEA sleeper sofa, took up the majority of the small room designated both living area and bedroom. Goldfish swam in mundane circles within their glassed confinement, two pressing bulbous eyes against the glass as though they were aware of my intrusion. Reed was asleep on the sofa bed, a tuft of dark hair peeking from beneath an army-green blanket, a pair of gray sweats and a Chicago Cubs T-shirt strewn across the bedding as if she'd pulled both off after climbing in.

I knocked again, this time shouting her name. Still no response. I focused my abilities on activating the smoke alarm. The shrill bleating awakened her, and she leaped from the bed, slurring a few profanities. I silenced the alarm telekinetically and knuckled the door.

"Christina, it's Celeste. I thought you might have overslept."

"Yeah, I guess I did," she shouted groggily. "I'll be in as soon as I get dressed."

—≈≈≈—

When I returned to the station, Sergeant Simmons wasn't at the front desk, so I retreated to the bullpen. I had just settled comfortably in my chair, my hand on the coolie bag, when he limped through the door. He shifted his weight, a grimace playing around his mouth, then used the doorframe for support.

"Any luck connecting with Reed?" he asked, mildly interested.

"Yeah. She overslept. She should be here soon. Hey, I have a question before you go."

He tipped his head to one side and puffed his lips. "Does it involve Post-it notes? Because I don't carry them with me."

I sputtered a feeble laugh. "Didn't you command the Gang Task Force for years?"

His expression implied he didn't appreciate the reminder. "That's right. Up until a hail of bullets shattered a kneecap and imploded a section of my lower spine. What about it?"

I lowered my eyes and hoped my expression conveyed some semblance of sympathy. "Do you remember any altercations with a gang exhibiting sacrilegious tattoos?"

A thumb and forefinger twisted his lips, and intense concentration deepened the crevices mapping his forehead. "Care to be a little more specific?"

"An upside-down crucifix."

"Sounds more like a cult to me. You think some cult is connected to the gang-related homicides?"

"That's what I'm trying to figure out."

Simmons shrugged. "Maybe you should be talking to DEA or ATF. These turf wars are fought for one of two reasons: drugs or weapons." He hobbled ninety degrees then took a step out the door.

CHAPTER THIRTY-EIGHT

The sun was peeping through a hazy blue horizon when I squeezed between the carriage doors. I wiggled inside the sleeping bag and zippered it. A gnawing sound alerted me to a mouse nibbling on the blood-soaked fibers, a result of the tears I'd shed earlier.

After unzipping the bag and depositing the creature on the carriage floor, I watched it scuttle beneath a rusty lawnmower, manufactured long before the invention of the gasoline engine. Finding it impossible not to think about Tristan and the baby, I counted to one-hundred, first in English, then Spanish, French, and finally Latin . . . the majority of the languages I didn't even realize I knew. Eventually, I grew sleepy, the competing heartbeat lulling me into a dream state.

Tristan awakened me, his nose nuzzling my ear first, soft warm lips exploring mine soon after. He slid in beside me, his hand reaching beneath my pajama top to grope a breast. My stomach churned and I bolted upright, lunging for the bucket I'd stored nearby.

"You are not well, my love?" he asked, bewildered, once I'd returned the bucket to the floor.

I shook my head. "Why are you here?" I asked, stalling. He patted the space beside him, but I remained on my feet.

The valley between his brows deepened. "I've missed you. Why are you in the carriage house? Why aren't you inside with Raina?"

"We need to talk."

"I can't stay long," he said, reaching for me. "Can't we—"

"No. It's important, Tristan." I searched his eyes. With no way to adequately prepare him for what I was about to say, I blurted it out. "I'm pregnant."

I took a step back, nearly tripping over the bucket, when an angry flush masked his beautiful eyes and a crimson mist hung heavy throughout the carriage house.

"Why are you telling *me* this, Celeste?"

A response caught in my throat. This wasn't the reaction I had expected. I knew how much he had missed his son and for centuries. And I'd convinced myself Tristan would be happy—thrilled—to welcome *our* child into the world. Clearly, I was wrong. "I know it comes as a surprise—it was quite a shock to me—but I thought you'd be happy. Think of it, Tristan, a baby, our baby, a sibling for Raina."

"No, Celeste," he said wagging his head. "I forbid it."

My mouth hung open, harsh words on the tip of my tongue, words I'd never, in a million years, thought I'd want to say to Tristan. "You *what*?"

"You will destroy it. The sooner the better," he said, zipping in front of me and blocking my path.

My legs crumpled and I sank to my knees. "You're talking about our baby, Tristan. How can you say something like that?"

Towering over me, his eyes wild, a snarl corrupting his beautiful face, he said, "I will not be responsible for unleashing a soulless perversity onto the world."

"And if I refuse?" I demanded, my anger palpable, the crimson mist heavier, more vivid somehow—the color of betrayal.

"If you refuse, Celeste, I promise you, I shall do it for you."

Speechless, I searched his eyes for an explanation, for the love I thought he had for me, the kind of love that was one of a kind, unconditional and enduring, and I found nothing but revulsion and indifference. "Tristan," I began, my arms reaching for him, my eyes begging he remember the extraordinary memories we had made together. "I-I think if you just take some time to think about—"

He rejected my touch, his finger poking my breastbone. "Get rid of it. Before someone discovers *your* mistake."

"*My* mistake? Tristan! Get back here, so we can discuss this," I screamed through the evaporating mist. My rage grew when he didn't return, all the things left unsaid to him escaping my mouth in a violent eruption, the timbre in my voice bursting every window. How could I have misjudged him? How could I have been such a fool? Everything I thought the future held, Tristan had obliterated in a few short moments. Even should he come to his senses and apologize, could I ever forgive his words or the animosity behind them? I cried myself to sleep once I'd decided Tristan would no longer be a part of my life.

Vibrations from my cell phone jerked me from a fitful sleep, alerting me to a missed call. I wrestled the phone from its cramped leather confinement and listened to a recording left by Cheyenne Foraker, a forensic expert who was new to the team. She'd managed to decipher the phone number assigned to Cahill's burner. Now I needed to provide Verizon a warrant so the carrier would release the phone records. Judge Brinkman wouldn't welcome another intrusion, and I wasn't looking forward to our interaction. I did claim an enormous victory when Cheyenne informed me the team was able to match Callie Sutherland's DNA to the panties I'd found in Cahill's house. I couldn't wait to tell O'Leary, but if I had to disturb Brinkman so soon, I thought it best to do that at a decent hour. Tristan entered my thoughts briefly, and I resented the sob lodged in my throat.

I snugged into a Kansas City Chiefs sweatshirt and tugged the hood over my forehead, securing it in place by jerking the drawstrings taut. I had an overwhelming urge to see Raina before work and headed toward the house. I drifted through the cheery yellow exterior and inched her casket open, careful not to wake her. I studied her peaceful expression for as long as I dared, then closed the lid. I had just entered my bedroom when Fane appeared in the doorway, his rushed momentum stirring up dust particles and segregated strands of his purple and black hair.

"I can hear it, you know. That forbidden entity growing within you. It would seem you have not as yet come to the proper conclusion."

"It's not an easy decision, Fane," I said, hating that my tone implied submission. I blinked hard, willing the tears away, and cursed myself when I once again thought about my conversation with Tristan.

"It is the *only* one."

"How can you be sure?" I shoved my hands behind my back when sparks flew from my fingertips. I needed him to maintain his loyalty. I felt sure Bianca would side with Tristan, abandon the battle, return to Kansas City, and badger me until I gave in. But this was *my* decision, one I didn't intend to make hastily, and I wanted to keep her in the dark as long as possible.

He cocked an eyebrow. "Would you have your own offspring join the ranks of our foe?"

I drifted closer, struggling to keep my fangs at bay. "Who's to say whatever plagues the Harvesters isn't more of an environmental consequence versus a congenital one? Has that *ever* occurred to any of you?" Even *I* didn't believe the words coming out of my mouth.

A golden aura bathed his face, and he leaned closer, his breath sweet yet musty like a beloved old book. "Are you willing to take that chance, dear friend?" he asked and faded away.

As much as I tried to deny it, regardless of the things he had said, I still loved Tristan. But I was no longer in love with him. Tossing several blood-soaked Kleenexes into the console, I slinked from the car when I arrived at the Brinkman residence. Summoned by a uniformed housekeeper, Judge

Thaddeus Maxwell Brinkman begrudgingly left a dinner table boasting fourth-generation, twenty-four-karat-gold candelabras; a silver platter brimming with assorted pastries; and a handcrafted dinner plate hosting succulent prime rib, garlic mashed potatoes, and a heap of seasoned green beans plucked from his own garden. Twitchy bushy eyebrows acknowledged my presence on his marbled stoop, but he didn't invite me inside.

"You again, Detective?"

I apologized for my unexpected arrival and explained the reason behind my urgent visit.

"Wait here," he snarled, partially closing the door. He returned moments later with a document containing his unique baroque signature. "Now, if there's nothing else, I'd like to finish my dinner. And, please, *don't* keep in touch."

With a bruised ego and the warrant in hand, I returned to the bullpen, scanned the document, and contacted Verizon's headquarters in New York City. Obtaining an email address to the appropriate department, I sent a cover letter and attached a facsimile of the warrant. After that, I decided to patrol gang-infested territories, hoping for a break in the case, and thought this best accomplished from a bird's-eye view.

I cringed, anticipating the excruciating effort usually required to make myself invisible. To my surprise, I succeeded on the first attempt. Skirting the treetops above Fifty-First Street and Hardesty, the unmistakable sound of lead striking sheet metal below caught my attention. Hovering directly over a ramshackle house, its roof more holes than shingles, I caught a glimpse of the gunman—a juvenile who fired bullets at traffic signs the way suburban kids lobbed baseballs at batters.

I swooped down, confiscating the gun as I glided past, and the momentum knocked him off-balance. Confused and frightened, he looked everywhere, his eyes wide but hawk-like. He dashed across the street and locked himself inside a weather-beaten house, the door displaying a No Soliciting sign that only an idiot would disregard.

This street relatively quiet, I decided to look farther east toward the most dangerous part of town. Bane Manor was a two-block area that even career criminals were eager to forfeit once the Manor Marauder Gang hustled its way in. Suspended in an oak tree, I turned my attention north when a barrage of bullets echoed down the littered and graffitied corridor. I flew in that direction, dodging whizzing projectiles.

Sirens screamed past moments later. Police cars screeched to a stop and formed a disjointed line. A SWAT wagon lumbered behind, taking up the rear and spewing choking exhaust. Gun-wielding males scattered, high on cocaine and latent testosterone, leaving trails of sweat, blood, and gunpowder behind.

I saw no reason to add to the line of blue and drifted over Prospect Avenue. My instincts took me south toward Eighty-Fifth Street, where gang members often gathered to exchange stolen property for cash, guns, or illicit drugs. Superior hearing alerted me to the sound of feet moving rapidly, muffled as they stomped tall grass and amplified once reconnecting with asphalt. Gravel pinged off an old train trestle, and I turned in that direction. A hooded figure crouched near a rusted metal column overlooking the Little Blue River. My stomach churned angrily as a laser beam danced across the tracks. The concealed runner uttered a gasp and froze. A precise red dot snaked across the wide steel beam before illuminating a sampling of his bald head. I traced the laser's origin just as the shot rang out and the runner fell from the trestle and splashed into the river below. His body surfaced soon after, facedown, the full moon spotlighting the crude tattoo on the back of his skull.

A car engine roared a quarter mile away. Tires reeled against hot, sticky pavement, afterward gaining purchase and righting a course toward Prospect Avenue. More interested in the victim than catching the killer, I hovered over the water. I levitated the body then inverted it. Soulless eyes stared back at me, more a consequence of life choices than death itself. A telltale scar marred the corpse's slack cheek, and I felt sure I'd found David Snyder.

The current picked up, waves lapping at the muddy banks and floating hypodermic needles and used condoms downriver. Because I was afraid the body might wash downstream, I telekinetically propelled it toward the shoreline. Snyder's ripped shirttail fluttered as his body glided above the water, revealing a leather belt, ornamented with bands of sterling silver and blue turquoise, and an empty scabbard that could have secured a twelve-inch knife. I searched the river, preternatural vision penetrating both the bed and every square inch of the bank.

Whooshing back toward the station, I dove inside the Dodge, the car fishtailing as I left the lot. I stomped the accelerator and the well-equipped engine responded with an indignant roar. Weaving in and out of cars filled with teenagers dangling limbs and their bottles of unsanctioned alcohol, I turned onto Eighty-Fifth Street and returned to the crime scene, sequestering the Dodge a half block away. A pack of wild dogs surrounded Snyder's body, fur bristled, tails erect, heads low to the ground. My fangs emerged over curled lips, and I soared toward the pack. Fire spewed from my fingertips and ignited rankled fur.

With a collective yelp, the pack scurried in various directions, the majority seeking concealment in the surrounding woods. I called dispatch and reported a one-eight-seven—a homicide. After reciting the coordinates, I waited for the ME's arrival.

Shifting anxiously from foot to foot, I approached Romano once she'd removed her gloves and had turned away from the body.

With her hands plastering her hips, she said, "Did you move the body?"

I pointed downstream. "The current didn't leave me much choice."

Her gaze raked over me, head to toe. "You're dry."

I shrugged. "That was nearly an hour ago."

A pronounced squint revealed her skepticism. "Another 9mm. No surprise. But this time, the killer set his sights higher. I guess he didn't plan on sticking around long enough to watch this one die, so he put one through his skull." She sighed. "No ID."

I know who he is.

I thanked her and slugged back inside the Dodge, returning to the crime scene once I felt sure Romano and her team had left the area. After camouflaging the car within a grove of trees a mile away, I made myself invisible and went in search of Snyder's missing knife. Scouring the path he had taken to the railroad trestle, I widened my aerial search to include a three-mile radius. With nothing to show for the time spent, I drifted toward the riverbank and cursed when thick mud slurped at my ankles, now visible since I'd reversed the Hidden Cloak.

Soon after, a red dot danced across the front of my jacket, and, for a moment, I completely disremembered my immortality. My law enforcement training took over, and I dove sideways, landing face first in six inches of gooey, foul-smelling mud, a bullet whizzing well over my head simultaneously. I heard exhaust rumble—the same sound I'd heard earlier that evening—and fade as the car headed toward the highway.

CHAPTER THIRTY-NINE

At the thought of disturbing Brinkman for a third time, my stomach was in knots, and I decided to wait until 5:30 a.m. to make the call. In the meantime, I placed a call to O'Leary and got his voicemail. I didn't want to give him the news on a recording and decided to try again later.

Brinkman agreed to provide me with a warrant to search Snyder's last known address, grumbled something inaudible, then abruptly disconnected. With any luck, I could make it to Brinkman's mansion in Mission Hills and get out of there before the sun came up.

When I arrived, he didn't greet me at the door. Instead, I found an envelope plastered to the storm door with my name scrawled across it in large angry uppercase letters.

Confident I'd find a link between Snyder, Cahill, and Barstow, I shrugged off Brinkman's insult as adrenaline coursed through my body. Convinced, more than ever, that those three men were involved in the women's murders, I fought the urge to grind my foot into the accelerator and steered the car toward Snyder's apartment.

When I curbed the Dodge near the manager's office within Happy Acres Apartments, I wondered why no one had sued the slumlord for false advertising. Not only did the building occupy less than a city block, but it was also sadder than an alcoholic at a juice bar. The sky intermittently spat abrasive pellets as menacing gray clouds competed with the complex's dismal exterior. I grabbed a KCPD ball cap from the back seat and ditched the hoodie. To his credit, the manager answered the door to his office/apartment in record time. He cracked the door ajar and the smell of cat urine wafted through the opening, the scent so strong it stung my nostrils. A sleeveless undershirt revealed the hair that covered his arms and shoulders, which was nearly as dense and unattractive as the shag carpeting inside the doorway.

I produced my shield, and he released the chain lock and swept the door to the wall.

"What can I do for you, Officer?"

"It's Detective and I have a warrant to search David Snyder's apartment. And you are?"

He grimaced and I had a feeling he knew Snyder well. "Lou. Lou Randall. Give me a minute, and I'll get the keys. He's behind on his rent, but I don't suppose you can do anything about that."

I shook my head. "You won't be getting any more rent from Mr. Snyder. He's been murdered."

The manager rolled his eyes. "No surprise there."

He unlocked the door and tailgated me as I stepped inside.

I whirled around and persuaded him to take a few steps back. "You can go now, Mr. Randall. I'll lock up when I'm finished."

"I'm not supposed to—"

"I'm a Kansas City Detective. If you're concerned I might take something, that legal document I showed you gives me permission to do just that."

"The door doesn't lock from the inside."

I held out my hand and wiggled my fingers. "Then give me the keys, and I'll drop them by your apartment before I leave."

I waited for him to shuffle toward his apartment. Once I'd stretched the latex gloves over my hands, I started in the bedroom, uprooting every drawer in the chest of drawers and bedside table, every article of clothing, even the mattress, which had more stains than an auto repair shop. Finding nothing of interest, I took a deep breath and entered the bathroom. Turquoise tiles had succumbed to missing grout and lay scattered here and there across the shower floor. An empty soap dish seesawed, one side clinging helplessly to one of the few tiles that remained intact. The medicine cabinet lay empty aside from the skeletal remains of indeterminate insects. I removed the lid from the toilet tank and looked inside. Then I moved on to the kitchen.

Examining a box of Cap'n Crunch, I first noticed the weight seemed off. I estimated the contents weighed several pounds rather than just under sixteen ounces as the box advertised. The top of the box looked suspicious, as though someone had opened it then reapplied adhesive. I ripped it open and dumped out stacks of bills bound with red rubber bands. I found a second box, then a third. I had a feeling forensics would soon recover Gunner's DNA.

I pulled open the refrigerator and a pungent odor persuaded me to take a step back. Rescuing a pair of tongs from the floor, I sifted through old takeout containers, produce that turned to jelly upon compression, and several packages containing pinkish-gray disks covered in green fur that may have been moldy lunchmeats. Grabbing it by the tongue, I tugged an orange juice container from the back of the refrigerator. I shook it, expecting it to slosh. When it didn't, I peeked inside and discovered a large quantity of illicit capsules and pills.

Stored inside the freezer were a mountain of Hungry Man dinners alongside several boxes of fish sticks. None of the boxes appeared corrupted—except one. Like the cereal box, Snyder had opened the package and resealed it. I shook the box, and it seemed empty. Using my fingernails, I separated the thick band of glue from the box, and from the otherwise empty container I plucked a woman's lace thong. Elsie Hanover immediately came to mind.

Lawn chairs substituted for traditional living room furniture faced a television mounted crookedly on the wall. Disappointed I hadn't found the murder weapon, I combed the apartment again. Finding nothing, I collected an empty trash bag from under the sink and stuffed the money and drugs inside. I returned the thong to the box and set it on top of the cash before securing the bag with a twist tie. I heaved the bag outside, locked the door, and pitched the evidence into my trunk. Randall was waiting outside, petting a cat and puffing on a cigarette.

"Did you find what you were looking for?"

"Not everything," I said and surrendered the key. *What did Snyder do with the murder weapon?*

CHAPTER FORTY

I returned to the station before heading home, grateful for the overcast morning, and berated myself when my mind wandered to Tristan. The more I thought about the things he had said and the way he had said them, the more I was determined he would never be a part of my life again. I resented the years I had wasted, the sacrifices I had made . . . my absolute devotion.

"Hey, Crenshaw. What have you got there?" Sergeant Nelson asked as I lugged Snyder's loot by the front desk.

"A bag of cash."

He arched a brow. "Looks heavy. Need some help?"

I tipped my head toward the Property room. "I'm almost there, but thanks." Once I submitted the evidence and filled out the proper form, remembering to remove the thong first, I headed for the crime lab.

I rapped my knuckles against the closed door before entering. I found Cheyenne Foraker bent over a microscope, and she glanced over her shoulder when I opened the door.

"Hey, thank you again for putting a rush on the Cahill evidence."

"No problem," she said, swiveling her chair to face me. "Something tells me you didn't come in here just to thank me again."

I laughed. "If you ever get burned out on forensics analysis, you would make a great detective."

She rolled her eyes but grinned. "What do you need?"

I waved the baggie. "I'm hoping you'll be able to match the DNA to another murder victim."

"I'll do my best. Let me guess. You need this yesterday."

I sighed and slumped my shoulders. "That would be great."

The landscaping crew had just begun mowing, trimming, and pruning at the apartment complex next door when I pulled in the driveway, creating a cacophony of sounds that echoed throughout the neighborhood: humming lawn tractors, whirling weed eaters, and buzzing hedge trimmers.

I went inside and zippered up the sleeping bag and jammed my hands over my ears. Unable to fall asleep, I wrestled my way out of the bag, tucked it under my arm, and headed for the house. Failing twice to infiltrate the basement's stone exterior, I jimmied open a window and crawled through, dragging the sleeping bag behind me.

I had just settled in when Fane appeared through a rainbow-colored fog.

"It seems a rather large rodent has once again accessed this repugnant dwelling."

"Look, Fane, I can't sleep with all that noise going on right next to the garage," I whispered.

"I thought we agreed that until you have made your decision, you are to keep your distance. Distance implies something other than mere feet."

"This isn't easy for me, Fane. And I miss Raina . . . I miss you."

"Tugging at my heartstrings, are we?" He looked away, but not before tears welled in his eyes. "I beg of you, Celeste. For days, the child refused to speak unless it were to whimper your name. It is only of late that I have persuaded her from her melancholy state."

"Why don't I just explain it to her?"

His eyes glowed orange, dimming to a pulsating sapphire blue. "And what would you tell her? That you have an infant growing within you, one you have yet to decide whether to grant life or death? Or perhaps you would rather share the possibility that that thing within your womb is quite conceivably evil incarnate?"

"You don't know that." I had never seen Fane so troubled or afraid.

"I should have alerted her, you know. Keeping your secret from Bianca could very well be the end of me." I went to him, and he brushed the back of his hand down my cheek. "Alas, dear friend, I fear we are both doomed."

"Just give me a little more time. Please. I promise that Bianca will never know you've known all along."

He nodded as tears once again flooded his eyes. "For centuries I have felt alone, Celeste. Save for the infrequent kind word, I have known little camaraderie or comfort. Until you. I simply cannot bear an eternity in which—" Overcome with emotion, he left me.

—⁓—⁓—

Jolted from a nightmare in which Tristan tore our child from my womb, I woke to the comforting sounds of chirping crickets and peeping tree frogs. The conversation with Fane continued to haunt me, and I successfully drifted through the stone exterior; maybe my success was due to leaving the sleeping bag behind. Back in the garage, I changed clothes hurriedly and, with one longing glance at the house, leaped into my car.

Franklin looked up as I cleared the doorway. "Well, if it isn't Detective Crenshaw. Phoned in any more anonymous tips lately?"

I knew he was referring to the caller who'd claimed responsibility for the deaths of the two men Nick had killed at Bully's. "Very funny. I wish I could take the credit. Maybe then Burke would appoint *me* Lead Detective."

"Only in your dreams, Crenshaw."

"I think the more important question is whether you've managed to ID the anonymous caller. Gangbangers or not, those men died, Franklin. So that makes the caller a murder suspect. And, correct me if I'm wrong, isn't rounding up murderers your area of expertise?" *Good luck rounding up Nick.*

Franklin smirked. "No surprise you can't take a joke, Crenshaw." He proceeded to bury his head in whatever he was working on. I slumped into my chair and resuscitated my computer, thwacking the enter key a few times before the monitor aimlessly exhibited signs of life.

"Somebody got up on the wrong side of the bed," he said, his sarcastic tone like a punch to the gut.

If only he knew.

"Consider yourself lucky that you've got Windows 7, Crenshaw. I remember when the department was crippled most of the time by DOS, a single-user, single-task operating system."

I gritted my teeth and hoped someone would summon him somewhere. "I don't know anything about computers. And I don't really give a shit. They either work or they don't."

"What's eating you, Crenshaw? You're usually not *this* unpleasant." When I didn't answer, he said, "Why are you here, anyway? Your shift doesn't start for another four hours."

I whipped my chair around. "What is this, a freaking inquisition?"

He showed me his palms. "Just taking an interest."

"Oh, really? Since when?"

"Since Burke assigned me as your partner."

I delivered a homicidal glare. My blood pressure hit Mount Everest levels and my scalp wept perspiration. "He did *what?*"

"You heard me. Thanks for that, by the way. Because of you, I have to rearrange my entire life and switch from day to night shift. Which is bullshit, since I'm the one with seniority. From the pissed-off look on your face, Crenshaw, I'd say you're about as excited over his decision as I was. This might brighten your day," he said, strolling over and tossing a folder on my desk. "The captain handed it off this morning. Ramirez, Chastain, and Reed have been chasing down leads all day."

"What is it?"

"A transcript of every phone call and text message from the burner belonging to Jacob Cahill. Looks like your warrant paid off."

"No shit," I whispered more to myself.

He sneered, predatory eyes crinkling at the corners. "I shit you not. I was able to track one of the numbers to a landline located at 2194 Genessee Street. That should really piss off Ramirez. Let's go check it out."

Franklin directed me to a nondescript taupe Taurus between a battered black Ford Escort and an even more pitiful looking sky-blue Chevrolet Spark; the only thing it ignited was my nausea.

"You're not waiting for me to hold your door, are you, Crenshaw?" Franklin asked, then tossed several empty food wrappers and bottled water containers into the backseat.

I glared at him. "No, I was trying to remember when I had my last tetanus shot."

"Gotta blend in, Detective." He started the anemic engine on the third attempt, the sound of the motor bringing to mind a Singer sewing machine.

Lurching around the final corner, the Ford shuddered to a stop. Franklin killed the engine, which expressed its gratitude by belching a cloud of oily exhaust.

"It's gotta be the third house, west side," Franklin said more to himself as the driver's door creaked open.

"The one with no windows or house numbers?"

"Is that sarcasm I hear, Crenshaw?" He tipped his head toward the numbered houses on either side. "Process of elimination."

"I thought maybe it was the odor that gave it away. Don't you smell that?"

Franklin sniffed the air, then drew his gun.

My eyes penetrated the mostly tarpaper exterior, the only material left to protect the structure from the elements. One body, a male's, lay just inside the entryway. Blood spattered the door. There was no one else in the house, but I couldn't tell Franklin how I knew that.

He tipped his head toward the backyard, sparse grass competing with heaps of trash. I took the cue, drew my gun, and breached the backdoor with a shoulder punch. Once inside, I drifted over linoleum poorly manufactured and hardly resembling marble. Leaving the kitchen, my feet hovered above multicolored carpeting that supported the 1970s vibe thrown off by wall decor comprised of Jimmy Hendrix, Janis Joplin, and Black Sabbath posters. My feet contacted tired and battle-scarred wood planks just as Franklin once again rocked the corpse farther from the door.

"The house is clear!" I yelled. "Come in through the back. You're destroying evidence."

"What evidence?" he said, gagging as he stomped toward the living room from the kitchen.

"That evidence," I said, motioning toward the body.

He reached into his trouser pocket and produced a jar of Vicks VapoRub. After dabbing a glob under his nose, he offered me some.

"No thanks."

"Lucky you. I take it you're scent deaf." He dry-heaved into a fist. "I'm about to lose my lunch."

"If you mean anosmic, no. My sense of smell is fully intact."

Franklin threw his hands in the air, wiggled his fingers, and shook his hips. "Woo, excuse me. I didn't know I was in the company of the fucking Scrabble champ."

"Just call it in, Franklin," I told him. "I'm going to have a look around upstairs."

I ignored him and continued my search of the house. Both bedrooms looked as though a bomb had gone off. Sidestepping a pile of clothing, an overturned mattress, and the contents of the closet, my eyes fell on what was left of an antique tobacco stand. The killer had slung it into a wall, shearing off two of the legs. The rich mahogany cabinet lay splintered, and a break in one side revealed the copper inlay. I remembered my father, Russ, had had one exactly like it, which he had inherited from his father and his father before him. I also remembered the cabinet had a false bottom in which my father faithfully stored his service revolver until Nick figured out how to open it.

Turning it onto its top and utilizing my preternatural vision, I saw the photograph hidden inside. Although the killer had taken the photograph with a Polaroid Instant Camera, the image was surprisingly sharp, and I easily recognized the nude body of Celine Dover lying in a soybean field. I couldn't put a name to the man standing over the body. But I knew I had seen him somewhere before.

I located the hidden screws—I'd remembered from my father's cabinet—and searched my pockets for a coin. Using a dime, I unscrewed three screws without issue. The head was stripped on the fourth and final screw, but I managed to force the bottom open, just enough to remove the photograph. I studied the male subject, and I felt certain the man in the photograph was Clive Barstow, the first of our homicide victims to take a bullet to the spine.

I set the photograph aside with plans to store it properly once the crime scene investigators arrived. A search of the other rooms proved futile: no women's lingerie, clothing, or jewelry, and no cash. Because criminals often duplicated their cronies' patterns, I searched the bathroom for cubbyholes. Finding none, I went back downstairs and traipsed outside, Franklin on my heels.

"The medical examiner's on her way. *What* are you looking for, Crenshaw?"

"Access to a crawlspace." I didn't intend to wiggle into another dark hole if I could help it.

"There is no crawlspace. The house has a full basement."

I shook my head. "I'm not seeing any windows."

"There aren't any, probably because the basement is only four feet below ground. I've already been down there, and there's nothing to see."

"If there's only a four-foot clearance—"

"Don't ask. Only one of the reasons I have a chiropractor on retainer. Care to hear the other reason?"

"Definitely not." With Franklin's womanizing reputation, it didn't take a lot of imagination.

"With the risk of offending you, I think I'll take a look around the basement myself."

"Knock yourself out," he said past a scowl.

Compared to Cahill's crawlspace, the basement was the Taj Mahal. But Franklin was right; the basement was empty. No washer or dryer, only an old rusty water heater emitting disturbing fumes, and a furnace that looked surprisingly modern. A rat scurried under the stairs, behind the furnace, and then scaled the rock wall. It suddenly occurred to me that in comparison to the square footage throughout the first and second floor, the basement was, maybe, two-thirds as large. Someone must have added an addition on the west side of the house, which meant that section *did* have a crawlspace. But why hadn't I found an exterior access? Amid scratching and clawing sounds, I heard muted squeaks coming from behind the furnace and decided to investigate. Easily squeezing between the wall and the ductwork, I encountered a discarded piece of sheet metal and scooted it off to one side. I discovered a dark recess, and, beyond it, the rat and her nest of babies snuggled under a heat duct within a crawlspace.

If *I* had no desire to wedge my body between the dirt floor and the joists supporting the west side of the house, I thought the corpse upstairs may have felt the same way, so I stuck my head through the opening and took a look around. To my left, an arm's length away, I saw an old Samsonite suitcase. It raked the sweet-smelling earth as I tugged it through the opening, and I turned my head to prevent the loosened particles access to my eyes, nose, and mouth. Snaking the case around the furnace, I set it on the floor and clicked the clasps open. Rooting through bundles of cash, at the bottom of the suitcase I discovered several bags of opioids. Satisfied, I clacked the clasps closed and carted the luggage upstairs, thumping the bottom against nearly every stair before I reached the top.

Franklin met me on the landing. "Where did you find that?"

"In the crawlspace," I said through clenched teeth.

"What crawlspace?" Before I could answer, he added, "It must be something heavy. You look like you're ready to bust a few blood vessels."

I'm ready to bust something. "Hey, do you mind?" I said, jerking my head to one side. "I'd like to get through the doorway, and you're blocking it."

"What the hell's in it? You did look, didn't you?" he asked as he followed me into the living room.

"Cash and illegal drugs."

"How much cash?"

I blew out a breath and pinched the area between my brows. "You really don't think I had time to count it, do you?"

"Take a wild guess."

I set the case down, stretched my back, and rested my right hand on my hip. "Tens of thousands, if those bundles are comprised of all twenties."

Franklin whistled. "No shit? So you think that stiff by the front door is a drug dealer?"

I shook my head. "I think he and four of his friends engaged in murdering drug dealers, afterward stealing their proceeds and their products. When they weren't too busy raping and killing young women."

Franklin's mouth dropped before he spread his fingers over his hips. He studied me for several minutes. I could almost see the wheels turning in his overinflated head, wondering how it was I just happened to know where I might find some pretty damn compelling evidence.

"Something bothering you, Detective?" I asked.

He shrugged and I noticed his jaw clench. "I consider myself pretty damn good at what I do, and I have the commendations to prove it. Yet, I didn't spot that crawlspace. If I was a betting man, I'd put my money on you knowing that crawlspace was there all along as well as what was in it."

"Right, Franklin. And I do, what, wait until you're with me to collect it? If I were up to something nefarious, why would I trade tens of thousands of dollars and drugs with a street value of even more for some lame commendation? Do you know how ridiculous that sounds?" He hid his hands in his pocket and seemed to weigh my words. I caught movement outside the front window. "Looks like the ME's here. I'll bring her in the back door. In the meantime, maybe you can give your paranoia a fucking rest," I said and sprinted outside. I waved hello just as the crime scene van screeched to a stop and tapped Romano's bumper.

"This is what happens when people don't get enough sleep," Romano yelled, poking an angry finger at the driver of the van before she exited her vehicle. "Why aren't we using the front door?" she asked me, her annoyance palpable as she followed behind me, knee-deep in the uncut grass.

"The body's blocking it."

She sniggered. "That sounds reasonable. Lead on, Detective."

After tugging her gloves in place, Romano rolled the body onto its side. "Is this what you're waiting for?" she asked, tipping her head toward the Petrine cross tattoo that shone brilliant against the victim's dusky skin.

I was already aware of its existence. I'd levitated the body a foot over my head while waiting for Franklin to come through the back door. Maybe it was all the pent-up anxiety over Tristan's reaction, maybe it was a subconscious obligation to protect my unborn child, or an obsession to make an imperfect world as perfect as possible before bringing another life into it. Whatever the reason, I had fully embraced my abilities and now had the confidence and wherewithal to execute them. "The tattoo certainly confirms our suspicions."

"Well, surprise, surprise," she said. "Another bullet to the spine. Guess our killer had some time on his hands." She nodded toward a chair directly across. "Make sure you go over that with a fine-toothed comb," she told a CSI. "It could be the shooter helped himself to a front row seat and we'll get lucky."

"Any ID?" Franklin and I asked simultaneously.

Romano inched a wallet from a blood-soaked denim pocket. "You're looking at Mason Muldoon, twenty-six. Looks like his driver's license has expired."

While she finished the cursory exam, I dashed upstairs to retrieve the photo, relinquishing it and the suitcase to an investigator when I came back down.

Once the ME signed off on the body, Franklin and I watched as they loaded it inside the coroner's van. He lit up a Marlboro and inhaled deeply, emitting an orgasmic-like moan. My eyes followed the van while I waited for him to finish his smoke, brake lights winking transiently when it approached the stop sign, taillights becoming nothing more than red streaks over damp pavement as it proceeded down Genessee Street.

Franklin snubbed out his cigarette, scratched a five o'clock shadow, and trudged toward the Taurus. I knew an apology wasn't coming, or much of anything else regarding his earlier suspicion. Chugging down Prospect Avenue, the Taurus backfired every time Franklin took his foot from the accelerator. He had just shoved an Aerosmith CD inside the player when my radio squawked a transmission:

"Home invasion. Westport Manor apartments. Proceed with caution; suspects reportedly armed."

CHAPTER FORTY-ONE

"That's where Detective Reed lives," I told Franklin.

"Detectives Franklin and Crenshaw responding. We're ten minutes out," he informed dispatch.

Ten minutes? The way the car was performing, I thought Franklin was absurdly optimistic. Sputtering and puking black clouds of smoke, the Ford lost its battle as we neared Thirty-Fourth Street, about ten blocks northeast of our destination. Franklin thumped the steering wheel, then popped the hood. A lock of hair danced across his forehead as he jiggled sparkplugs and beat the engine with a nightstick he'd collected from the backseat. Convinced of his mechanical ineptitude, I suggested a tow truck. He ignored me and jerked a dipstick from the engine. "Grab four quarts of oil from the trunk. The last person to fill the gas tank must have forgotten to top off Candi's oil pan."

Candi? "Four quarts? You can't be serious." I didn't know much about car maintenance, but I did know four quarts was more consistent with a complete oil change than a "top off." I suddenly had a hell of a lot of respect for Candi.

"Get a move on, Crenshaw," he demanded.

I handed off the oil and climbed back inside the car while Franklin murmured lovingly to Candi, his sweet nothings barely audible over the *glug-glug-glug* of oil bathing a grateful reservoir.

Back on the road, we were the first to arrive at the complex. Cries of anguish, interspersed with screams for help, directed us to an apartment situated directly across from the one Reed rented.

The door lay open and, with my hand on my holster, I stuck my head inside. "Is anyone else here?" I asked the woman cradling a gunshot victim.

She shook her head. "Please, help my niece!"

"Is this your apartment?" Franklin asked. When she nodded, he asked her name.

"Joanna Phillips," she managed between sobs.

The victim twitched involuntarily. Her eyes were vacant, but she attempted to say something, and, instead, gurgled past a mouthful of blood.

"And your niece? What's her name?" I asked and motioned for Franklin to secure the apartment.

"Lauren. Why are you just standing there? Why aren't you doing anything to help her?"

"All clear," Franklin said to me. "An ambulance is on the way, ma'am."

I saw the life leave the victim's eyes, and I looked at Franklin, who checked her pulse. A subtle shake of his head confirmed there was no need for an ambulance.

"Joanna, were you the one who called the police?" he asked, in a tone not unlike the one he'd used when speaking to Candi.

"Yes. What does that matter? You need to do something."

"Were you here when your niece was shot?" I asked, stooping beside her.

"No. I came home from work . . . and I . . . I found her like this."

"I'm so sorry, ma'am, but your niece was fatally wounded. She's gone."

"No, that can't be. She's so young. She's got her whole life ahead of her. You're wrong," she said, blinking past tears and clinging to the victim. "Lauren's gonna be just fine. You'll see."

"Joanna, you need to let go of her now, so we can do our job," I said softly.

"No," she said and tightened her grip on the victim. I attempted to un-tether Lauren and Joanna slapped my hands away. "I said no!" She swept Lauren's hair from her face. "We'll just wait right here until the ambulance comes," she whispered to the corpse.

"We need to give the paramedics room to attend to Lauren. You want them to be able to do their job, don't you?"

She nodded and released her grip hesitantly. Franklin and I eased the body to a prone position. I gestured toward three chairs bordering a com-pact kitchen island. "Why don't you sit over there while we wait for them? I'll sit with you." While she considered a response, Franklin helped her to her feet. "Can I get you a glass of water? Maybe there's someone you'd like me to call?"

She shook her head. "Lauren's all I got in this world," she murmured under her breath.

Franklin updated dispatch just as two units stormed the courtyard, guns drawn as they swept the darkened corridor. He called out, advising them of police presence and footsteps proceeded in our direction.

"It looks like the apartment across the way was hit, too," Officer Chase Winfrey said following a hushed conversation with Franklin. "We'll sweep it just to be sure whoever did this isn't hiding inside."

After the crime scene analysts finished collecting evidence and turned their attention to Reed's apartment, I allowed entry to two coworkers the victim's aunt—Joanna Phillips—had asked me to call. Detective Reed ar-rived and sidestepped the attendants pushing the gurney that carried the body toward the parking lot. I saw her through the open door and excused myself, promising Joanna that I'd return.

"You know the drill, Detective," Franklin said to Reed. "We'll need a list of everything that's missing. You probably also know I have a better chance at winning the lottery than you have at getting your shit back."

She toed off with him and narrowed her eyes. "I guess there's no urgen-cy then." Her eyes flew to a portable safe the thieves had tossed in a corner.

The door stood open with nothing inside. Her body tensed, jaw muscles flexing.

Winfrey reappeared in the doorway. "There was another break-in upstairs. Fortunately, no one was home."

"Any witnesses?" Reed asked.

Winfrey shook his head.

"Let's canvas the entire complex," I suggested.

"Already in progress, Detective. Most of the residents are probably asleep, but," Winfrey said past a shoulder shrug, "if we wait until a decent hour, some will have left for work."

Franklin overheard and turned his back to the crime scene investigators. "Yeah, a neighbor getting whacked can be real inconvenient. We'll lend a hand after the team is finished here."

Winfrey nodded and slipped past Franklin to advise KC-CSI where to go next.

"Have you ever seen the victim with any men you might remember?" I asked Reed.

"I've never even seen the victim or anyone who lives in that apartment. The only resident I've met lives on the second or third floor. I ran into him after he came down the stairs one night when I was leaving for work. He was in a hurry, so our conversation consisted of a head nod."

"The victim was a niece to the woman who lives there," I informed her. "She told us her niece only recently moved in."

"And you're wondering what the odds are a rash of burglaries occurs soon after?"

I shrugged. "It crossed my mind. I'll wake the manager and have a look at the security footage."

Reed laughed hollowly. "The manager doesn't live in this shithole. She calls home a swanky condo in Brentwood Village, another complex she manages."

CHAPTER FORTY-TWO

ranklin overheard and tossed me the car keys. "Be gentle with her. Candi doesn't like women. I'll hang around here and catch a ride back with Winfrey."

Chugging along, I finally arrived at Brentwood Village around five a.m. The complex was so large that locating the manager's office was a lot like navigating the hedge maze in Stephen King's *The Shining*. I knocked on Melody Eldringhoff's door and clumsy footsteps padded across dense carpeting inside. The door opened, revealing a scowling fifty-something woman.

I produced my shield and a hard stare. "I'm here about several robberies that have taken place at Westport Manor. It's my understanding that you're the building manager."

"I am. But unless there was damage to the building, I don't know what that has to do with me or the corporation I represent. The renters are responsible for their own insurance."

"There *was* damage. The burglars broke down two doors. They also shot and killed one of the residents. So, if you don't mind, I'd like to see the security footage."

A hand flew to her mouth. "That's horrible, but then, that neighborhood isn't what it used to be."

"Is that why you prefer to live here?"

Her eyes narrowed as she puffed her chest. "I'm a woman living alone, Detective. Can you blame me?"

My spine stiffened and I shifted my weight. "I'll wait outside while you change."

"We house the monitors in a maintenance building at the rear of the complex. I'll call the maintenance supervisor and ask that he meet you there."

Forensics must have given Franklin the all-clear because I found the maintenance supervisor, Tim Wallace, directing his cleanup crew inside Joanna Phillips's apartment.

"I'm Detective Crenshaw." My announcement startled him, and he whipped around, unsteady on his feet.

Sidestepping the wide ring of blood swamping the carpeting, he motioned for me to follow him outside. "Ms. Phillips is in her room, resting. Her friends asked that we try not to disturb her."

"Where are her friends now?"

He shrugged. "They left when we arrived but said they'd return before noon. Ms. Eldringhoff said you'd like a look at the security video?"

"I would. Do you keep them all or record over them?"

"They're kept for thirty days. After that, for cost reasons, we're instructed to reuse them."

The sun was peeking over the horizon, no longer an old friend bearing new and exciting possibilities but rather a demon of whom I should be leery.

"Would you happen to have another one of those?" I asked, motioning to his cap bearing the corporate logo. "I forgot my sunglasses."

"No problem. We keep them in the same place the video equipment is stored."

"How far away is that?"

"Just around the corner. Follow me."

I stuffed my bare hands in my pockets and scurried behind him, shrinking within his shadow.

Seated beside him, a Langston Properties cap pulled low on my forehead, I instructed him to rewind the footage. "Stop once you reach the 10 p.m. timestamp." Squinting, I leaned in. "Is this footage from the camera that monitors the northwest corridor? Because it doesn't look familiar."

"Yeah, the camera swivels. What we're seeing now is the south side. Give it a minute."

"So only a single camera monitors the entire front of the building?"

"I'm afraid so."

The angle changed and the windows bordering Reed's apartment came into view. I watched as one scene replaced another, the transition somewhat jerky. According to the timestamp, exactly two minutes separated surveillance of the south and north sides. Was two minutes enough to miss whatever had taken place outside the Phillipses' apartment?

A half hour passed, then forty-five minutes, and I offered to take the controls, so Wallace could return to his crew. Just as he got to his feet, two silhouettes appeared in the northwest corridor.

"Freeze it there," I said. The image was grainy, and I asked him if he could enlarge it.

"That will probably make it more distorted, but sure, I'll give it a try."

He was right.

I sighed. "Okay, minimize it, and let's see what happens next."

He let the recording play. One of the two figures standing directly outside Reed's apartment jimmied the lock and both figures disappeared inside. Eleven minutes later, a young woman entered the corridor from the parking lot and unlocked the Phillipses' apartment, just as the intruders exited Reed's apartment and took her by surprise. She turned to look at them, and her neighborly smile quickly disappeared. One of the men pushed her inside the Phillipses' apartment.

Seconds later, a flash lit up the window facing the corridor. I assumed it was the muzzle flash from the weapon used to kill her.

"Oh my God," Wallace muttered beneath a shaky palm.

I laid a hand on his shoulder. "You've been a big help, Mr. Wallace. I'll need to borrow the disk. Our tech department may be able to enhance it."

"I don't know," he said nervously. "I should ask Ms. Eldringhoff."

I felt my nostrils flare and forced eye contact. "I can get a warrant. In the meantime, two killers could leave the state."

He tossed his arms in the air. "What the hell. Jobs like this are a dime a dozen."

"Mind if I hang on to this?" I said, touching the brim of the cap. "I'll return it when I return the disk."

"Be my guest. How long do you—"

"I'll get the disk back to you just as soon as possible, Mr. Wallace. If your manager has a problem with that, have her contact me."

Before I headed home, I dropped both the disk and Candi by the station. I had intended to hang around while forensics manipulated the disk, but all the analysts were in the field. I thought of the baby again and immediately redirected my thoughts. I swallowed past a sob and the resentment I'd recently come to feel toward Bianca. I envied daughters who could tell their mothers anything.

CHAPTER FORTY-THREE

Franklin looked up from his desk when I entered the bullpen around nine p.m. and substituted a jut of his chin for a greeting. "I take it you came up empty on the surveillance cameras. Otherwise, I'm sure you would have let me know," he said accusingly.

"I just got here, Franklin," I said, slamming the desk drawer once I'd tucked the coolie bag inside. "But to answer your question—" my desk phone jingled, interrupting.

"Hey, Celeste. This is Cheyenne. I have some good news and some bad news. You seem like a glass-half-full kind of girl, so I'll give you the good news first."

I chuckled as I scooted toward the edge of my seat and drummed my fingers against the desk. "I appreciate that."

"The DNA on the thong *is* a match to Elsie Marie Hanover. We also recovered David Snyder's fingerprints and saliva on the waistband."

I dropped my head and blew out an anguished breath. "At least we know who killed her."

"Yes," she whispered. "There is some comfort in that."

"And the bad news?" I assumed it had something to do with enhancing the disk. I looked over my shoulder and found Franklin listening intently.

"No luck with the surveillance footage."

"Sorry, I didn't catch that," I said, and put the call on speaker. She repeated the information, and I thanked her before ending the call.

"What was the good news?" Franklin said, smoothing the remnants of a hangover from his brow.

"Forensics just confirmed my murder suspect," I told him. He started to say something else, and I interrupted. "Hang on. I need to make a conference call." Once I had Detective Keith O'Leary, Sheriff Wayne Davis, and Police Chief Bernard Stapleton on the line, I identified myself.

"Detective O'Leary, I also have Sheriff Wayne Davis of Drexel, Missouri, and Police Chief Bernard Stapleton of Liberty, Missouri, on the line." I cleared my throat after they'd processed the disclosure and mumbled their acknowledgement. "Gentlemen, we now have indisputable evidence that links one or more suspects to the murders of Callie Sutherland, Elsie Hanover, and Celine Dover."

It came as no surprise that O'Leary spoke first. "Are they in custody?"

"I'd be lying if I didn't say that I take great pleasure in telling you that they are currently taking up space in the morgue."

"How many? Five men were involved in Callie's murder," O'Leary reminded me, and I could easily visualize him snapping a few pencils in half.

"Four of the five men are dead. We're still looking for the fifth."

"Sheriff Davis speaking. I'm curious as to who they were and how they died."

"We've identified the men as Clive Barstow, Jacob Cahill, David Snyder, and Mason Muldoon. Sorry to say I can't take credit for their deaths. We've connected a large amount of stolen cash and illegal drugs to three of them. I'm awaiting forensic analysis, but it appears those men were also involved in several gang-related homicides."

Stapleton spoke next. "So they were robbing drug dealers?"

"It looks that way."

"And somebody connected to the drug dealers retaliated?"

"Seems like a plausible motive," I said. "I'll be sure to keep you all updated."

They all thanked me for the information, and I ended the call. My finger hovering over the last digit, I debated a call to Mamie Martin. Because she was largely responsible for the intel enabling me to identify our morgue suspects' involvement in three murders, I felt she deserved an update.

"It's your fifty cents," she greeted surly on the fourth ring. "Start talkin."

"Mrs. Martin, this is Detective Crenshaw—"

"Well, well, you don't say," she interrupted. "You're about as scarce these days as a dollar McDonald's hamburger. Spit it out quick, girly. *The Jerry Springer Show* is about to start."

"I wanted to let you know we've located the man with the scar and the tattoo. Because of your—"

She interrupted me again. "Other than seeing him behind bars, I couldn't give two shits. What about the girl?"

I cleared my throat and prepared to share the unfortunate news.

"That's what I thought. She's dead, isn't she?"

"I'm afraid so."

Following a long pause, she said, "You see that he don't walk away scot-free. You hear me?"

"Someone shot him. He's dead."

"Well, glory hallelujah. Is that it?"

"Yes, ma'am. Thank you again."

The Jerry Springer Show's intro blasted my eardrums and Mamie Martin disconnected without another word.

Franklin's expression conveyed his annoyance. He wasn't the kind of guy you kept waiting. "Bring me up to speed, Crenshaw. The DNA you collected from the stiff's—"

"Mason Muldoon," I interjected.

"Whatever," Franklin said, flicking his hand. "The DNA collected from Muldoon's was a match to one of your murder victims?"

"That's right."

"And those four other men you mentioned on the call—the ones involved in the murders—are now dead?"

I nodded along. "Yes, but I think there's still another one out there."

"Yeah, I caught that," he said, gesturing toward my phone. "What makes you so sure?"

"Witness testimony."

Franklin scrubbed his chin. "And you think those dead men are responsible for our unsolved gang-related murders and that's why they were killed?"

"I do. Retaliation is a fierce motivator."

Franklin whistled disbelief.

"Did you happen to finish the report on the Lauren Phillips homicide?" I asked, already aligning those facts pertinent, in my head, which I planned to include in the report.

"Yeah, and as a result, I didn't get out of here until almost noon. I'm running on empty, Crenshaw. Thanks again for the demotion."

Maybe there was hope for Franklin yet. Quaid usually left everything to me. "If I could change Burke's mind, believe me, I would," I followed with a sarcastic smile. "Did Lauren have any next of kin, other than Joanna Phillips?"

Franklin clicked a file on his computer and opened it. "Her dad's dead. She and her mother had a falling out, and she went to stay with her aunt—her father's sister—for a few days."

I clucked my tongue. "Horrible timing," I said more to myself. "Has someone contacted the mother?"

He tipped his head toward his shoulder, giving me the impression he thought the question so ridiculous it didn't deserve an answer. "Nothing was taken from the apartment. The video confirms her killers were inside just long enough to silence her?"

I nodded, just as Russ Nelson, the second-shift desk sergeant, poked his head through the doorway. "Some guy's up front. Says he's Detective Reed's brother. She here?"

"She doesn't come in until 10 p.m.," I informed him.

"That's what I thought. Hey, would one of you handle this?" he asked, jerking a thumb over a shoulder. "I'm swamped right now."

"Send him back," Franklin said before I could respond. Then he made a beeline for the bathroom.

A man in his late twenties appeared in the doorway soon after, wearing a hunter-green uniform—the name Dylan embroidered over a pocket—and a worried expression. Raking a hand through dark hair, he scanned the room, piercing hazel eyes coming to rest on me. I could see the resemblance.

I leaped upright and crossed the room to meet him. "I'm Detective Crenshaw. I understand you're looking for your sister?"

"Yeah, I went by her apartment again and she wasn't there. I've called her every day for a week, and she hasn't returned any of my calls."

I leaned against the doorframe and crossed my arms. "Is that unusual, Mr. Reed?"

"It isn't Reed. My sister's married . . . was."

"Sorry, I didn't know." *Your sister never bothered to share that information or the fact she had family living locally.*

"Please, call me Dylan. I probably shouldn't have mentioned her divorce. She's a very private person, so if you could keep that to yourself—"

I smiled. "Already forgotten."

"So have you seen Christina? I just want to be sure she's all right."

"I spoke with her yesterday. She could be sleeping. A lot of people who work third shift can't always fall asleep until late afternoon." I didn't think it was my place to tell Reed's brother about the break-in. I had no idea of the relationship between them. Her brother seemed sincerely concerned, but family dynamics were often very messy. I considered the possibility Reed had played it safe and decided to stay in a motel until we'd apprehended the perpetrators. But I couldn't imagine Reed running away from anything.

He wagged his head. "No. Her car wasn't in the lot."

I puffed my cheeks. "To be perfectly honest, I don't know your sister well. She hasn't been with the department very long, and, as you said, she's a very private person. I suppose it's possible . . . she's sleeping somewhere other than her apartment." I planted the suggestion that Reed had a lover and hoped it took root.

A transient flush reddened his cheeks. "That doesn't sound like her."

He was right. I couldn't imagine Christina involved in *any* kind of intimate relationship. But I had no other explanation as to why she'd avoid her own brother.

"When she comes in, I'll ask her to call you," I said. He didn't appear convinced. "Better yet, give me your number, and I'll phone you later this evening."

He plucked a pen and a business card from his shirt pocket. After jotting down his personal number, he handed me the card just as my desk phone rang. I slipped it into a pant pocket.

"Will you excuse me? I need to grab that," I said, jerking a thumb over my shoulder. "I'll be sure and give you a call later tonight."

The call had come in through extension 9999, a line reserved exclusively for crime tips. I identified myself and listened to a full minute of ragged breathing.

"This the TIPS hotline?" The caller finally spoke.

"Yes. What have you got?" I asked, plucking a form from my desk drawer before leaning back in my chair and tapping a pen against the padded armrest.

"Everything I tell you anonymous?"

"Yes. You have my word."

"If everything's anonymous, like you say, how am I gonna get paid?"

I puffed my cheeks. *What happened to all the good Samaritans? People happy to help their fellow man, not for money, just for the sake of doing the right thing?* "This call is associated with a specific form number. If your information assists us in solving a crime, a cash payment is dispersed to the person in receipt of that number."

"What if I don't feel safe showing my face at the police station?"

"You can send a proxy, someone you trust to accept the payment on your behalf."

"Okay. I think I know who killed that girl at Westport Manor last night."

"I'm going to need a lot more information," I said. "Let's start with names."

"Michael White."

"Anyone else?"

"Anthony Tiegs might have been with him. They usually hang together. He lives right down the street."

"Okay," I said. "Is that T-i-e-g-s?"

"You got me, lady. It's not like he writes me letters."

"What makes you think those two were involved?"

"Michael lives just across the street from the apartments. He's always casing the parking lot, you know, stealing stuff from unlocked cars."

"Michael have a gun?"

"Yeah, one he bought off of Anthony."

"What's Michael's address?"

"Shit, I don't know. It's the green house right across the street."

"What street?"

"Thirty-Ninth Street. I get my number now or what?"

I recited the number along with a warning: if the information didn't lead to an arrest, he wouldn't be paid.

I hung up, just as Franklin left the bathroom whistling an annoying tune. It may have been George Thorogood's "Bad to the Bone."

I waved a piece of paper through the air. "I just got a tip on the Phillips homicide."

"Well, what are you waiting for?" he said, rushing his desk and grabbing his jacket. "Get off your ass, Detective."

CHAPTER FORTY-FOUR

I was feeling particularly nauseous and not in the mood for Franklin's driving, which—on a good day—resulted in about as much G-force as an amusement park ride. "I'll drive," I told him as we neared the garage.

"Whatever you say. Don't ever let it be said I'm a chauvinist."

The verdict, to the contrary, had come in a long, long time ago.

"What are you doing?" he asked when I fisted the door handle attached to an unmarked black sedan. "Let's take the Taurus."

"I'd like to get there."

He rolled his eyes and said, "I'll check the oil, okay?"

I shook my head. "We responded to the Westport Manor call in that car. According to our tipster, the guy responsible for the murder lives right across the street. Don't you suppose he'll recognize the Taurus?"

"Well, shit, Crenshaw, that's an important piece of information. How about giving me all the details at once, instead of feeding me tidbits at a time?"

I winged my nostrils. "Okay, the suspect lives in a green house. The architectural style remains a mystery."

"Hilarious," he squeezed between clenched teeth, afterward slinging himself in the passenger seat while I sank into the deflated driver's seat and adjusted the position.

"Our alleged suspect's name is Michael White. His accomplice may be Anthony Tiegs. According to our informant, White does own a gun, which he bought from Tiegs. Apparently, White's main source of recreation is fleecing things of value from unlocked vehicles parked in the lot. It's possible he upped his game, deciding to rob the apartments instead."

"A real entrepreneur," I heard Franklin mumble. "Either one have a rap sheet?"

"I haven't had time to find out."

Franklin placed a call to the department and requested a background check. A minute into the conversation, he leaned across the front seat and asked me, "You get a home address?"

"No, the informant didn't know it. If I had to guess, I'd say 3935 Pennsylvania Boulevard."

"Yeah, I'll hold," said Franklin, resting an elbow on the console between us. His posture straightened and he whipped a pen from his shirt pocket, a notepad from the console. "Two counts of aggravated assault," he repeated. "Three counts of battery. Six counts of possession of stolen property." Feverishly taking notes, he paused, "What do you mean he didn't do any jail time?" Franklin continued to listen, his left hand balling into a fist. "The judge remanded him to Ramsden Detention Center every time?" He laughed cynically. "The one with the volleyball court and swimming pool? Un-fucking-believable." He put the call on speakerphone. "How old is the kid now?"

"He was sixteen at the time of his last arrest six years ago, so that makes him . . . twenty-two?" the voice on the other end said.

Franklin smirked and tucked a hand under the opposite armpit. "Well, that makes Michael White an adult now, in the eyes of the law, anyway. Looks like his days of doing easy time are behind him." He distanced the phone from his ear and leaned across the console. "Either that speedometer is on the fritz or you need to speed up, Crenshaw. The accelerator is the longer pedal on the right. It's what makes the car go."

I turned my head so quickly to sneer at him I nearly wrenched my neck.

"What about Anthony Tiegs?" he said into the phone.

"Got an address?" blasted through the speaker.

"According to our caller, he lives a few doors down from Michael White," I offered.

While we waited, Franklin drummed the console, repeating an annoying dysrhythmic beat, and I considered locking up the brakes or setting his fingers on fire.

"Yeah, okay, here we go. Anthony Tiegs, 3931 Pennsylvania Boulevard. He resides a few doors from White—at the time of his arrest, too. He narked on a small-time supplier after the prosecutor offered him a plea deal on a drug possession charge. Because he was only fifteen at the time, it was a small quantity of crack cocaine, and it was his first offense, he got his hand slapped and agreed to drop in on a parole officer every week for three months."

"How long ago was that?" Franklin asked our source.

"Five years ago."

"Which makes him twenty years old," Franklin said more to himself. I glanced in his direction and noticed a menacing smile that reached his ears. He thanked the officer on the other end and disconnected.

Taking Thirty-Ninth Street, I turned north when it intersected with Pennsylvania Avenue and curbed the sedan outside a 3800 address.

We left the vehicle and headed south. Franklin slung an arm around my waist, and I subconsciously recoiled, which only made him tighten his grip. "We're just a loving couple out for a stroll," he whispered in my ear. "But remember, it's all for show. I wouldn't want you to get your hopes up, Crenshaw."

"Who's the comedian now?" I said past gritted teeth. I tipped my head toward the green house on the corner. "Do we hit Tiegs's and White's houses simultaneously or do we focus on White?"

"I think White deserves our undivided attention. I'll make the introductions. You play nice around back."

I left Franklin on the front porch and crept around back. Crouched behind a rotted privacy fence, I heard a screen door slam. White skirted past me and ignored my command to halt. Rocketing over several piles of calcified dog manure, assorted eroding automobile parts, and the remnants of a toppled tree, my feet touched the ground directly in White's path and his eyes widened as he froze in place.

"Let's see some ID," I said, cupping my fingers.

"What are you, some kind of fuckin' ninja-cop?"

"Show me your ID," I said, fingering my holster.

"Why? I didn't do shit."

"Yeah? Then why were you running?"

"I thought you were a bill collector," he said smirking.

"We're looking for Michael White, and I think I just found him." I noticed he'd shifted his weight to the ball of his right foot. "Don't even think about running again, White. We both know you suck at it." His eyes flew to my Glock. "And going for my gun would be a huge mistake. Now get on the ground and put your hands behind your back."

He lunged for my weapon, and I backhanded him. Soaring through the air, hands and feet flailing, he landed with a thud on the backdoor stoop. I flipped him over and clinked the cuffs closed just as Franklin scaled a corroded, padlocked gate.

"Nice catch, Detective. Is your buddy, Tiegs, inside?" he asked White. When he didn't answer, Franklin prodded him with his foot. White didn't respond and he turned him onto his back. "He's unconscious. What the hell happened back here?"

I shrugged. "He went for my weapon, and I reacted. I know a little jujitsu. Sometimes it comes in handy." Franklin seemed more than a little skeptical, but his eyes were on the prize. "He's coming to, but I doubt he'll be cooperative. You stay with him. I'll have a look around," I said and swept around the side of the house, my eyes penetrating the clapboard siding. I spotted Tiegs hiding on the third floor behind a moldy shower curtain depicting nude cartoonish females. Aside from him, the house was empty. I drew in a deep breath, envisioned the desired outcome, and infiltrated two inches of stubborn stone.

Memorializing decades of dirty shoeprints, the disintegrating carpet gave way to blemished hardwood on the second-floor landing. From there, I listened to Tiegs's shallow breathing and the intermittent drip from a faucet at his back. I drifted up the last set of stairs and entered the bathroom, my gaze first settling on a sink caked brown with residue, then on a toilet that had long ago parted ways with both a seat and lid.

"Police," I called out while sliding a set of zip ties from a back pocket. I drew back the shower curtain and Tiegs pitched both hands in the air. "Anthony Tiegs, I'm taking you in for questioning regarding the murder of Lauren Phillips. Don't make me step in that hole from hell to get you."

CHAPTER FORTY-FIVE

W hite refused to talk and lawyered up. Tiegs, on the other hand, reverted to his old ways and sang like a love-struck canary. Franklin left the interrogation room whistling, confession in hand, intent on finalizing the plea before White's counsel could recommend a similar tactic.

"Per that agreement you just signed, I'll need a list and the whereabouts of the stolen items. Otherwise, you can consider our deal invalidated," I told Tiegs.

Tiegs clamped a sweaty hand over a greasy cowlick. "Shit, I don't know what we took. There was lots of stuff—some jewelry, some cash, a couple of laptops."

"Anything else?"

"A bottle of oxy," he said with some reluctance. "And a cell phone. I remember because I thought it was weird someone would leave cash lying around but keep a cheap cell phone in a safe."

"Where was the safe?"

"Behind the sofa. It was one of those sleeper ones, you know, with the springs."

"Was it in the apartment on the first floor?"

"Yeah, but not in the one Mike shot that girl. We didn't take nothin' from that apartment."

I cocked my head toward a shoulder and resisted sinking my fangs into his throat. "We'll make sure the judge gives you a medal. Where's the stolen property?" Rather than answer, he picked dirt from a callous between his fingers. "If White decides to punt first, it's game over for you."

He wiggled his spine straight and said, "In my basement behind a bunch of bricks."

"You're going to show me exactly where. And if it doesn't pan out, I'll make sure you share a cell with White, *after* I tell him how your testimony put him away."

───

Franklin drove, his eyes often snaking over the rearview mirror. I positioned myself sideways in the passenger seat—one arm slung over the seatback—and kept an eye trained on Tiegs, more a reflex from my training at the academy than a necessity. Once inside the house, I persuaded Tiegs down basement stairs slickened by mold and layers of debris, keeping a firm grip on his shirt collar.

"Are those the bricks?" Franklin asked past a sneer as he gestured toward three rows of bricks restacked unevenly beside a grimy water heater. "May as well be a neon sign, asshole."

Tiegs kept quiet as I secured the items within evidence bags, careful to store the electronics separately.

With White in lockup and Tiegs in holding—the plea agreement awaiting final approval—I handed off the stolen property to forensics.

"The phone belongs to Detective Reed," I told the investigator, "so if you could make it a priority, I'd appreciate it."

Her eyebrows knitted together. "She left her cell phone in her apartment? Personally, I'd sooner leave my cosmetic bag at home."

I shrugged. "I assume it's her personal phone. She probably doesn't need it when she's on duty."

"The department provides the detectives cell phones?"

I grinned. "Just another one of the perks. Let me know when you're finished with it."

"Will do." I started to walk away, and she called me back. "Oh, Detective. I'll need a signature . . . you know, chain of custody and all that."

"Oh, right. I know I've got a pen here somewhere," I said, patting down my pants. I tugged a ballpoint pen from my pocket, inadvertently dislodging Dylan's card I'd tucked away earlier. I watched it freefall toward the floor and caught it midway between, my eyes settling on the information below the company logo:

MIDTOWN SUPERIOR AUTO WORKS
Dylan Dover

CHAPTER FORTY-SIX

I made the connection immediately: Celine Dover. The young woman whose body a farmer had discovered in a soybean field northwest of Liberty near the Kearney, Missouri border. And now I knew why Reed had stashed the phone in a fireproof safe and that it had belonged to Jacob Cahill. I was also now convinced Reed had not only murdered Cahill but also Clive Barstow, Mason Muldoon, and David Snyder in retaliation for her sister's murder. And I now understood why the shooter at the railroad trestle had intentionally fired over my head.

I remembered Reed preferred to carry a Heckler & Koch handgun. I wasn't well-versed on that particular weapon, but I did know it didn't shoot 9mm ammo. Of course, most detectives owned a second gun, which they carried when off duty.

Reed was on duty the night White and Tiegs robbed her apartment. She hadn't stored her off-duty gun in the safe because she had plans to use it that night.

Four of the five men suspected of murdering three women were now dead. Was Reed out there now hunting the fifth man? I considered alerting

Ramirez or Donahue or Franklin but, deep down, didn't feel Reed deserved punishment for her crimes.

Sitting at Quaid's desk, which had recently been assigned to Reed, I wasn't surprised to find every drawer locked or that her computer was not only shut down but she'd also implemented password protection. Although I could see every item—from paperclips to pens and various notepads—within her desk, I was unable to adequately decipher every notation she'd made. I scrubbed my forehead, then leafed through the folders stacked neatly within a wooden tray on the corner of the desk. I scrutinized each individual case file related to the rash of inner-city homicides but didn't find anything I hadn't seen before. I blew out my frustration and slid the desk chair back in its original position.

Franklin smacked a hand down on my desk to get my attention, to which both my nostrils automatically inflated. "I'm making a Denny's run. You want anything?"

I squinted through an insincere smile. "No thanks."

He double-tapped the desktop and said, "Suit yourself, but don't forget I asked."

Sergeant Nelson had a phone in one hand and a radio in the other when I approached the tall desk he sentineled, the street side largely covered with images of missing persons and KCPD publicity posters. I waited until he'd finished the call and had sent his intended corresponding transmission over the airwaves.

"I'm headed over to Detective Reed's apartment. She could be on her way here. Give me a call if she shows up, would you?"

Nelson nodded and bounced two fingers off his forehead, his attention drawn once again to the clanging phone and his computer monitor.

I curbed the Dodge near the intersection of Linwood Boulevard and Prospect Avenue and waited for a convoy of firetrucks and ambulances to scream past, bright flashing lights constricting my pupils. Reed wasn't at home when I arrived outside her apartment. On a hunch, I broadened my search to include the blocks that separated Muldoon's residence from

Cahill's residence, Snyder's apartment complex approximately midway. Parking the car in a potholed lot attached to a deserted motel, I rocketed skyward, my hair streaming behind me as I glided over treetops. Soaring over Salem Heights—not so long ago taking the prize for Kansas City's Seediest Neighborhood, with a two-hundred-seventy-nine percent increase in violent crime—I spotted the pumpkin-orange roof of Reed's Mustang, tucked between an alleyway and two abandoned houses, and a convoy of unlicensed vehicles strung along the curb near the corner, a few graffitied with local gang symbols. Apparently, Reed wasn't the only one who had located our fifth suspect. Right place. Wrong time.

Projectiles whistled past—originating from the house—as I exited the car. The rival gang members responded immediately, the unmistakable rat-a-tat of automatic machine-gun fire reverberating off the house and all the surrounding houses, aligned in a unified row and constructed at a time when neighbors enjoyed rather than feared social interaction.

Another car rounded the corner, headlamps out, and squealed to a stop. Four men exited the vehicle and hopped the chain link fence. With the front of the house covered, I assumed they intended to snake their way in through the back door and surprise our fifth suspect. I caught a glimpse of Reed, pinned down halfway between the rear entrance to the house and an old shed. But I wasn't the only one aware of her presence.

"Reed, get out of there!" I yelled a blink before the gangsters trained guns of various calibers on both of us. Reed dashed toward the shed, nearly tore the door off its hinges, and tumbled inside. I had just clacked a fresh clip into my Glock and identified myself when a third bullet—fired from a sawed-off shotgun—struck my torso. The impact propelled me backward and I slammed against the ground. A sobering silence fell over the neighborhood; the only sounds were hushed voices and the scraping of neglected branches against gutters. Soon after, the whispers drew closer as soft-soled shoes crunched fallen leaves. I knew I was about to lose consciousness when my pores oozed sweat, a cold wave washed over me, and my ears began to ring. *Don't pass out!* On my back and out in the open, I scooted beneath an abandoned car. The lead pellets began to sizzle as bloody tissue closed over my wounds, and I covered a scream. Jagged incisors pierced my hand while superhuman strength expanded every muscle. Suddenly overcome with the desire to kill, I launched the car into the air, and the advancing footsteps stopped abruptly when sirens began to wail in the distance.

Crashing to the pavement, the car spun on its top in the middle of the street, as a lone male figure hurtled from the rear entrance of the house wielding a long-bladed knife. Reed tore out of the shed—a blur of Kevlar, handcuffs and dark hair in motion—and took pursuit. She caught up to him and the two scuffled as Reed struggled to disarm him. I didn't have a clear shot and zipped in their direction to assist her just as Reed sank to her knees and fired her weapon at our fleeing suspect. Her bullet met the target and he fell facedown in the dirt. The sirens drew closer, alerting the four shooters intent on killing the cult member, who had just fled the house. The clandestine posse made a run for it, toting AK-47s, AR-15s, and illegally manipulated shotguns inside the fleet of garish vehicles parked near the corner, and left behind the scent of gunpowder and burning rubber.

Rather than pursue them, I attempted to give Reed first aid. She clawed the gaping wound across her throat, tissue hacked, muscles exposed. Blood bubbled from her nose and when she tried to speak, her words gurgled.

"Don't try to talk, Christina. You don't have to confess to me." She tried to sit up, and I pressed her back down. "Look, I know what you've done, and I get it. The ambulance is on the way," I assured her, but I knew no one, other than me, could help her now.

She must have known she was about to die, because she shook her head, then tipped it toward the knife lying next to the man she had just shot in the back. "For. My. Sister," she said, manipulating her larynx, as blood spurted between words.

I could see the flashing lights from the emergency vehicles, and I knew I had to make a decision. My heartbeat accelerated and it was all I could hear. *Oh God. Can I do this? Does Christina Reed deserve immortality? Am I doing the right thing?* "Christina, you're dying," I said as I leaned over her, "but I can give you immortality. You just have to trust me." I waited until the last traces of life left her eyes, then I drew a deep breath and sank my fangs in.

Her eyes opened, wide and wild, her skin shrank then closed over the bite marks and the long, serrated slash across her throat that the suspect had inflicted. Her lips parted to accommodate long dagger-like incisors, and she emitted a primal growl, arched her back, and transferred all her weight to her lower extremities. She somersaulted backward and sprang onto her feet. I hissed a warning, my fangs once again obscuring my lower lip. She studied the preternatural glow in my eyes, then took a step back. The transformation was in the early stages, and I knew from experience that unmitigated pain would soon render her unconscious.

"They're coming," I said as the winged cacophony grew louder, and I watched her legs wobble while her eyes searched the night sky overhead. "Don't be afraid."

She opened her mouth to speak but, instead, passed out and crumpled to the ground. I picked up her gun, hurled it across several backyards, and heard it land on a nearby rooftop.

The Elders descended, wings sounding a final *whoosh* as webbed feet thudded the grassless yard. Nostradamus was the first to embrace me. "Do not torment yourself, my child. The correct decision is not one made either hastily or selfishly but one insufferable, nonetheless."

"Well done, Celeste," Elizabeth said, but her tone suggested uncertainty. She folded her wings and observed Christina through cold, beady eyes. "Matilda will be delighted."

Socrates grumbled something in Latin and didn't appear particularly pleased. Leonardo couldn't take his eyes off Christina.

I thought about the baby, the world in which we lived, and the unparalleled protection for the innocent I hoped Christina would soon provide.

Flashing red and blue lights and wailing sirens nearly upon us, the Elders formed a closed circle around Christina, then soared toward the Hollow Earth, the *chuff-chuff-chuff* sound from fluttering wings dissipating as a silhouette, not unlike the Rod of Asclepius, raced across the moon.

CHAPTER FORTY-SEVEN

I strolled midway between the front and back yards. "Over here," I called to the officers as they vaulted from their squad cars. I flashed my shield and identified myself when a rookie's twitchy fingers hovered over his holster.

"Officer involved shooting?" an older cop, Jimmy Flynn, asked.

I shook my head. "Gang retaliation," I lied without a glimmer of remorse or hesitation. I tipped my head toward the rookie. "Call it in."

"All these bullets for one guy?" Flynn asked as he followed me to the backyard and tiptoed around shell casings.

I shrugged. "I was late to the party."

Flynn whistled. "Holy shit, how many times was he hit?"

"Once that I'm aware of."

He shook his head in disbelief, then tipped it toward the road. "Any idea why that car is upside down and in the middle of the street?"

"I haven't a clue," I managed with a straight face. "It was there when I arrived. Call a tow truck and secure the scene, will you, Jimmy? I have to make a call."

Remembering my promise to Reed's brother, I jerked his card from my pocket and punched the number into my cell. He answered on the first ring. After fabricating a story about an undercover detail Christina had been assigned, I assured him she'd be in touch once the assignment ended. He seemed relieved, expressing his gratitude before ending the call.

Then I placed a call to Police Chief Bernard Stapleton, deciding he should be the one to inform Dylan that the men who had killed Celine, the woman I believed to be his younger sister, were dead. I didn't offer any details, but I hoped that someday Dylan would learn that it was his older sister, Christina, who had avenged Celine's death.

Romano rolled up twenty minutes later, just as the tow truck was wrenching the car in the road onto a trailer. She waited inside her Lincoln Town Car until the forensic team arrived. The man driving the Lincoln got out, opened the passenger door, and Romano stepped out after gathering the hem to a slinky evening gown.

"Fritz, would you get my kit from the trunk?" she asked the driver as her stiletto heels sank into the damp ground. She smiled after him as he trudged around to the back of the car. "Thanks, honey," she said when he returned with her bag.

She hiked up her gown and secured the modified length by wrapping Fritz's belt around her waist twice. Because he had the belt ready, I assumed this was something they'd done before. Then she swapped her heels for flats and tugged vinyl booties over those.

Following a sharp whistle, which caught Cheyenne Foraker's attention, Romano communicated something in sign language and Foraker ambled over, carrying a plastic jumpsuit. Romano wiggled into it, then spread open a hairnet, stretching it as she covered her head, mindful of her time-consuming coiffure.

Somewhat out of breath, she said, "What have you got, Detective?" Before I could respond, she threw a hand in the air. "Never mind. I just love a surprise."

Fritz chuckled and said, "We have four of them waiting for us at home."

The team had already set up the LED lights near the victim. The crime scene looked more like a movie set. Romano surveyed the perimeter surrounding the body. Satisfied, she stooped beside the dead man. "You found the body?" she asked me over a shoulder.

"Yes," I said without squirming.

"Interesting," she mumbled under her breath. "Too bad you didn't arrive sooner. He doesn't appear to have been dead long. I suppose you noticed the tattoo."

"I'm fairly confident he's the fifth of five men wanted for the rape and murder of three women . . . that we know of," I added, more to myself.

"So this is a vendetta?" Flynn spoke behind me.

I had to throw the cops off Reed's trail and keep them off. "Those five men were also responsible for robbing and executing drug dealers. So, yeah, I'd call it a vendetta." I tipped my head toward Cheyenne who had just bagged a twelve-inch knife lying next to the body. "And I bet the analysts will recover DNA from several of the victims on that knife." I doubted it. I'd reluctantly scrubbed it with bleach I'd commandeered from the house before the first responders arrived. Discovering Reed's blood might have proven difficult to explain. Besides, I suspected there was more than one knife involved, and we'd find it inside the house—if the killers hadn't disposed of the additional murder weapons. I leaned over Romano's shoulder. "Any ID?"

"That seems to be your catchphrase, Detective. Yes. Kyle Renner, born March 20, 1989."

"Did he live here?"

She held up a gloved hand. "I was getting to that. If his driver's license is accurate, yes, he lived here."

I pushed off the grass and got to my feet. "Flynn—"

"Secure the scene?" he finished with a wink.

I patted his shoulder. "I would appreciate that. With any luck, I'll be back with the search warrant within the hour."

As I rounded the house, I ran into Captain Burke. "Crenshaw, please tell me that body is connected to our unsolved homicides."

"I was waiting for all the forensic results before I updated you, but, yes, I think the five men responsible for not only the gang-related homicides but also the rape and murder of three young women are now dead."

"I'm told you signed several hundred thousand dollars and illicit drugs with an even higher street value into evidence."

"Yes, sir. I have a feeling we'll find more inside," I said, hitching my thumb toward the house. "I was just on my way to get a search warrant."

"Did the vic live here?"

I nodded. "He listed this address when he obtained his driver's license."

"Then screw the search warrant, Detective. I'll take full responsibility. The sooner we give the mayor something to chew on other than me, the better. Franklin's responding to a domestic hostage situation. Give Detective Reed a call and have her lend a hand."

I clicked my tongue. "Uh, I wish that were possible, Captain, but she's out with the flu. If it's the same strain I had, she probably won't be in for the rest of the week, if then."

Despite Captain Burke's assist, Flynn, a few other officers, and I managed to clear the house within an hour. Renner wasn't nearly as creative as his murder buddies. I found several bundles of cash and narcotics hidden within a false wall behind the washer and dryer and two other knives. He wasn't much of a handyman either; the section of paneling concealing the loot was mismatched and cut crookedly.

I waited for everyone to disband, then glided over rooftops, plucking Reed's 9mm handgun from one of them as I soared toward the alley where she had secluded her Mustang. Grinding the gears—I didn't have much experience with manual transmissions—the car shuddered and lurched as I headed toward Reed's apartment. Once I had parked it in her reserved spot, I floated over Thirty-Ninth Street, then over Broadway, dodging a Life Flight helicopter and an owl as I soared over Saint Luke's Hospital. My feet contacted the deserted motel's parking lot, where I collected my car and headed home.

EPILOGUE

I was dreaming I was hiding the baby from Tristan when I woke to the combined scent of lilac, lavender, and apprehension. Through the sleeping bag, I saw her shadow and the misty aura surrounding it. Unable to shield my every thought as I slept, I assumed Bianca was now aware of my secret. My hands trembled as I unzipped the bag. I was equally frightened and enraged. My skin prickled, heat rising within me, as I debated how best to handle her intrusion.

"It's my decision!" I blurted, my entire body unleashing angry orange sparks. "You have no right—" I stopped midsentence when her brows furrowed, and I noticed the blood staining the corners of her eyes and her cheeks.

"Celeste, I have come about Tristan," she said past an audible swallow. "Oh my darling."

I backed away, shaking my head, and knew I'd never see Tristan again. I dropped to my knees and buried my face in my hands because it was all a lie. No matter the things Tristan had said, no matter the look of disgust I remembered in his eyes, no matter how hard I tried to convince myself otherwise, I was still in love with him. My screams rattled the windows. I wanted to die and stay dead, to outrun that moment, to destroy whoever had taken him from me. Bianca reached for me, but I couldn't bear any form of intimacy. Accepting her comfort meant accepting the truth.

"Tristan!" I wailed into the night, my chest heaving amid hysterical sobbing. I saw his mesmerizing eyes, his contagious smile, smelled his animalistic scent that always evoked a sense of longing, felt his warm embrace, his spiritual kiss—all gone forever.

"Mom, I can't . . . How can I possibly survive this?" I blubbered when I'd finally caught my breath. "He was everything to me." She cocooned me in her arms and held me there long after my tears dried, salt-crusted scarlet-red patches matting my eyes and shriveling my cheeks.

"What happened?" I asked, abandoning the safety of her arms, when competing orange, purple, and pink bands of light complemented an ocean-blue horizon and trespassed a window, still uncertain if I could handle the truth.

"Must we speak of this now?" she said, trembling as she pulled me closer.

"Mom . . . I need to know."

Bianca pulled away, fingers gripping her cape. She looked away, tears swelling bloodshot golden eyes. "The battle was a success. We were in the midst of a celebration." She paused and gulped a deep breath. "Then *he* appeared and turned the Realm to stone. By that, I mean we could see. We could hear. But we were helpless to defend Tristan."

I shook my head in disbelief. "Who was *he* and how is that possible?" I had witnessed the Realm in battle. They were unconquerable, Tristan in particular.

She hesitated and her eyes burned red. "Cathàn of Brasov. His powers are limitless. I have never encountered anyone like him."

"Is he a Harvester?"

"No."

"Then why? Why would he . . . destroy Tristan?"

"His motive was revenge." She wrung her hands and stared at the ceiling. "Cathàn is Yesenia's son."

"Her son! What do you mean, *her son?*" She didn't respond; instead, she floated across the basement, as if she yearned to escape. "She conceived a child before she became immortal? And then, what, she *and* her kid received the Adaption?"

She stopped moving, a sudden gust of energy whipping her hair and her long cape into a frenzy. "No," she said, her back to me.

I clapped my cheeks, digging in my fingernails.

"I don't understand. Help me understand. Why Tristan? *He* wasn't the one who decapitated her."

She whirled to face me, and her eyes softened to a pale orange. "Yes, it is I who should have been the object of his rancor. But his motivation goes much deeper than the annihilation of his mother. His act was one of long-standing reprisal."

She reached for me, but I backed away.

"What are you talking about? Just tell me!"

"His revenge was directed at the father who had not only rejected him but demanded he be eliminated."

"What? Are you talking about Tristan?" I blasted, furling my hands into fists. "No. I don't believe it. He would have told me."

She reached for me again, and I backed farther into a corner. "Would he, Celeste? What would you have thought of him then? Yesenia disappeared for many years. Tristan should have known the reason, but when she returned, she convinced him she had destroyed the child."

I sank to the floor and buried my face in my hands. "I can't believe he never told me. I thought I knew him . . . I thought he loved me," I whimpered aloud.

"Do you not see? He did love you, darling, so much so that he could not risk losing you. That was the only reason he shielded his secret."

"No," I said punching my thighs. "He didn't love me. He loved Alexandra. I was only a pathetic substitute."

"I'm certain that isn't true."

I choked on a laugh. "Well, I'm certain you're wrong. I'm pregnant, Mom. And Tristan insisted I *get rid* of our baby. So, you'll have to forgive me if I don't share your opinion."

She dropped her head, and, for a long moment, she was speechless, something about as alien to Bianca as proper etiquette was to Nick.

"Oh my God. You *didn't* know about the baby." I found it impossible to believe I had somehow managed to keep it from her.

"Not until I arrived and felt his presence," she said, the pupils of her eyes emitting a color I had never seen before.

His? I was carrying a son! "I suppose you agree with Tristan," I said, cinching my arms across my chest.

Tears slipped from her eyes, dripping to the floor, red oil and water and mucus crackling upon impact. "I do not envy your decision, my sweet, sweet darling. Although I have never had a child of my own, I cannot imagine a life without you or Nicholas, and I would do anything within my power to protect either one of you. But, surely you can see, the recent turn of events gives me pause."

"So what are you saying? That I should destroy my baby because he may be like Yesenia's, some demonic entity?" She looked away and refused to answer the question. "That's what I thought. While I never expected that response from Tristan, I sure as hell *never* expected it from you!"

"If only I could provide a resolute answer, Celeste."

"What happens if I choose to keep it?"

She shook her head. "I cannot say. But promise me that you will give the matter careful consideration."

I had already made my decision.

"If Cathàn is as powerful as you say, how did you and Razvan—all of you—escape?"

"Quite simply. He allowed it."

"I find that hard to believe. Surely, he knows the Realm intends to retaliate."

Her eyes began to glow, a sparkling crimson halo illuminating green irises. "As *we* most certainly shall, once we convene with the Omniscients. In the meantime, I have arranged for Nick and Paulo to stay here with you."

"Why?" When she refused to answer, I attempted to retrieve her thoughts, without success. "There's something you're not telling me."

She glided over to me and took me in her arms, and I noticed she was trembling. "Cathàn intends to take you from us. He is determined we suffer unspeakable loss for all eternity."

"He intends to destroy me?"

She gripped my shoulders, her eyes penetrating mine. "God willing, we shan't allow that to happen, Celestine, but the circumstances call for the utmost vigilance, and I won't entertain any argument." She grasped my hand, squeezing it so hard that I winced. She placed her other hand on my stomach. "If you will not think of yourself, of Nick, Raina, me, or your father, consider the possible ramifications on the mortals should our assumption regarding this child come to be." Her kiss was cold, and she vanished amid a flash of blinding light.

I heard Raina scream seconds before she appeared in the basement. "Mummy, the Bad One . . . he has taken Tristan's head," she sputtered between sobs. "And now he shall come for yours."

ABOUT THE AUTHOR

S oon after thunderous applause rocked a packed auditorium, D. B. Woodling took her final curtain call and longed for the bright lights of Broadway. But her love of family prevailed, and she found satisfaction in the dimmer lights of Kansas City.

Launching her own production company, she portrayed every character imaginable—from Lady Macbeth to Shirley Temple. Eleven years passed and she relocated so far outside of the city that she had to find another outlet for her creativity and turned her attention to fiction writing. Five long years later, she published her first novel, *Shannon's Land* (since retitled *Retribution: A Lover's Tale*) as well as the sequel, *Shannon's Revenge: Broken Promises*, which was recognized for literary merit by the *Copperfield Review*. Having developed an appreciation for mystery and suspense writers like Michael Connelly and Karin Slaughter, she then switched gears and began writing the Detective Mike Malone Series. Once completing the third book, she wanted to attempt something decidedly different, and she reluctantly sent Mike on an indefinite hiatus. Swallowing past a golf-ball-sized lump, she created Celeste Crenshaw, the heroine in *The Immortal Twin*, where Celeste's story begins.

In 2016, following the death of her beloved Labrador Retriever, Woodling established Annie's Gift, a cause benefiting No-Kill Animal Shelters and select veterinarian clinics throughout the United States. She donates a large portion of her royalties to Annie's Gift.

ACKNOWLEDGMENTS

I knew writing this sequel would be every bit as challenging as a three-mile run. I just didn't expect that run to be down a pot-holed and slippery road amid a sweltering deluge. To my editor, Elana Gibson, you have my undying respect and gratitude. Thank you for pushing me to my creative limits, for making me realize that while the difference between acceptable and exceptional might be mind-numbing hard work, I have the capability and I have the drive.

Sue Arroyo, thank you for being a woman with a vision and the courage to follow her dream . . . congratulations on CamCat's third amazing year in the publishing world! To Maryann Appel, your concept of my world left me breathless. Thank you for a beautiful yet haunting cover, for your ability to reach into my soul and reveal the essence behind *The Immortal Detective*! To Laura Wooffitt, without you I'm destined to be just another in a long line of relatively unknown authors, irrespective of the book's merit. I look forward to absorbing, then implementing, all of your masterful marketing suggestions. To Meredith Lyons, thank you for your role in finding the perfect voice for Celeste. I can't wait to listen to the audiobook! Penni Askew, thank you for your laser-focused assistance in addressing those pesky copyediting issues. Helga Schier, I am always appreciative of your invaluable input, and your literary passion is an inspiration.

Finally, I want to thank my loyal readers. If not for you, those lonely hours spent attempting to find the perfect word or phrase, create memorable dialogue, twists and turns, and unforgettable characters would be meaningless. Thank you for joining me (and Celeste) on this second adventure. I'm looking forward to our next one.

If you like

D. B. Woodling's *The Immortal Detective,*

you will also like

Ash Bishop's *The Horoscope Writer.*

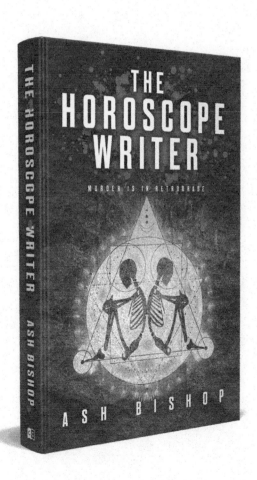

1

DETECTIVE LESLIE CONSORTE DIDN'T LIKE BEING WOKEN up in the middle of the night. In fact, he didn't like it enough to have turned off his cell phone and taken his home phone off the hook. The desk sergeant, a busybody named Roman Stevenson, had felt the situation warranted sending a unit by his house to pound on his door until he had dragged himself out from under warm sheets, grumbling, groaning, and belching out every cussword known to man, and a few based loosely on Latin roots: *crapepsia, shitalgia, cockpluribus*.

Stevenson hadn't been wrong. Leaning on his car door and surveying the damage, Leslie dreamed of the stacks of paperwork headed his way. A fifth-year cop named Lapeyre, dressed in uniformed blues, approached, picking through the crime scene, not so much to preserve evidence as to preserve his clothes. Lapeyre was a handsome kid, close-cropped black hair, dark skin, driven, focused, taller than Leslie by half a foot.

"It goes on for another three miles."

"This is a grisly thing here."

Leslie squinted his eyes, staring down the dilapidated Clairemont street. Clairemont was proof positive that racism was a baseless concept, or, put more simply, that white people could fuck up a community just as efficiently as any other race. It was a rotten little housing project of about fourteen hundred units: dirt lawns; peeling paint; ugly, unwashed cars and motor homes and non-working boats.

This street, Triana, was particularly bad because it was smeared with blood, muscle and bone. Someone had been dragged behind the bumper of a GMC truck. For about a mile.

"What are we looking at?"

"Dispatch got a call at 12:03. A neighbor reported hearing screaming, squealing tires, and then a grinding sound. Desk jockey logged it as a domestic dispute, though I think that's a bit of an under-classification."

"That's funny, Lapeyre. Any chance we can identify the victim?"

"It's unlikely. There's only about a third of the body left. It shook loose from the car down by the mesa."

Leslie crouched in the street, running his hand over the drying blood.

"Radley found fragments of a jawbone on the next block over. We might be able to get a dental match. I also managed to extricate a patch of hair from the fender of the murder car. I've bagged it for a DNA analysis. A SID team is prepping the car for impound on Derrick Drive. What do you want to do about this?"

"Let's knock on a door or two."

Leslie and Lapeyre walked up the nearest driveway, Leslie's suit looked like he carried it to work in a plastic bag. The top button was loose on the shirt, his tie hung low, the edges of the cuffs were frayed, and the collar was badly wrinkled. Leslie believed it was possible to machine wash and dry his dress shirts. The collar, it seemed to him, was the only part that didn't turn out so great. Before they reached the door, Leslie pulled Lapeyre to a stop.

"I forgot something," he said. He dug around in his pocket, finally drawing out a shiny, metallic object roughly the size of a billfold. He handed it to Lapeyre.

Lapeyre fumbled with it, trying to get it open with shaky hands. "Is this what I think it is?" he said.

"Congratulations, Detective. The captain passed word down to me as I was leaving work. I was going to tell you tomorrow, but I guess this is tomorrow."

Lapeyre didn't say anything else, but his eyes never left the badge. It reminded Leslie of his ex-wife's expression when he'd first popped open the engagement ring box. "It's a good moment, Lapeyre. You only make detective once, if you're lucky. Enjoy it." Leslie waited a moment while Lapeyre polished the badge on the front of his shirt. "Okay, let's solve this case, huh? After you, Inspector."

"Are you going to show me how to grill a witness?"

"I will show you the ways of the master."

The nearest house was a tiny three bedroom, one bathroom with a rotting fence and a weed-strewn yard. Leslie knocked on the door. They waited a few minutes. Lapeyre pulled out his badge to look at it again and Leslie told him to put it away. He knocked again, louder this time. No one answered. They moved to the next house, walking directly across the lawn. It was a small structure, probably close to seven hundred square feet. The roof was dilapidated, and a Trump flag waved above the faded painting of a bald eagle stretched across the garage, wings wide. They knocked and waited. No one answered.

On the third house, a blond woman in her fifties came to the door. She was wearing pajamas covered by a tattered robe. Her hair was unwashed and had a frizzy-fried texture Leslie always associated with the very poor and the chemically addicted. She smelled of recently smoked cigarettes.

"Yes?" the woman said. She was rubbing her eyes and blinking at them.

Leslie knew Lapeyre was waiting for him to speak but he didn't. After an awkward silence Lapeyre finally said, "Sorry we woke you."

"What do you need?" the woman asked; her voice held a slight edge.

"We were hoping you saw something tonight. There's been a crime. Outside your home, all up and down the street."

"That's terrible. I'm sorry I can't help you."

Leslie didn't like her, but he tried to remain professional. He leaned in and sniffed her.

"What the hell are you doing?" she said.

She smelled like very strong alcohol. Maybe 100 proof. "There was a brutal murder fifteen feet from your house," he said.

"I didn't see anything. I was sleeping."

"The murderer dragged his victim through the street. He tore the victim's body to pieces. His flesh is part of your asphalt now. It's part of your street."

"I don't know anything." The woman said, her shoulders shook in a quick jagged motion, but she got them under control again immediately.

"You watched it from the window."

"No."

"I don't know how much you saw, but it was enough to send you back to the kitchen. A decent person calls the police. Lets us get here in time to help, maybe. But you poured yourself a shot." Leslie sniffed again. "Several shots. Did it work? Did it make you forget the sounds?"

"Get out of my house!" the woman said angrily. "I'll call the cops."

Leslie idly waved his badge. "We're not in your house."

"I'll call my brother then. He'll kick your ass right out of here."

"Go ahead and call him. We'll wait," Leslie told her.

The poor, rugged blonde took a step back and pulled her phone from her pajama pocket. Then she lurched forward and struck Leslie with her phone-clinched fist. Lapeyre moved to interfere, but Leslie called him off with a curt head shake. With her other hand she clawed at him for a moment, like a sick bird, then she fell to her knees, crying.

"We need to know everything you can remember. The coloring, height, and weight of the victim. The same for the killer." His voice softened. "If you tell us everything you saw, it will help you forget. I promise."

The woman remained on the floor. Leslie pulled Lapeyre aside. "Get a statement," he said. "Be as gentle as possible."

"Yeah, right. Thanks," Lapeyre said.

"I'm going to go check out the murder car. Join me when you can." Leslie moved back out of the house without looking at the crumpled form of the woman on the floor, still sobbing. He walked slowly up the street to Derrick Drive.

He had been suffering from acute lower back pain for the last thirteen years. The cause had never been completely diagnosed but Leslie figured it to be a combination of too many nights chasing lowlifes down alleyways, too many hours behind desks perched on cheap chairs, his tendency to buy his own furniture and mattresses at thrift stores, and all the collective stresses of trying to keep a city safe from itself. The mileage of life. The pinching pain caused him to shuffle his feet when he walked, and he always appeared to be leaning slightly forward.

When he reached Derrick Drive, he followed the portable lights, flares, and flashbulbs to the murder car—which was, in fact, a murder truck. He pulled on a pair of rubber gloves and pointed his belt light at the truck's bumper. A SIDs guy, short for Scientific Investigation Division, was already swabbing at it with a Q-tip. Leslie didn't recognize him, but then as all the other departments felt the pinch of deep budget cuts, the SIDs were growing like weeds.

Leslie ran his light along the left side of the truck. He noted deep, jagged scratch marks in the faux chrome of the bumper, on the right fender, and just above the tailpipe. The SID was working over his shoulder on the taillight. Leslie told him, "It looks like the victim tried to keep up with the car long as he or she could. They must have been affixed to the bumper by something other than their arms. Make sure you run tests for trace elements of rope, tape, whatever the hell kind of epoxy could stick a person to a vehicle long enough to grind their bones to dust."

"Of course."

Leslie looked again at the long, snaking red swath as it disappeared down the street and around the corner. "No motive. Few witnesses. Not much left of the body. This must have made a hell of a racket, though. Make a visual record of the entire trail. Then call the fire department out to turn a hose on it. I don't want people waking up to find this on their street."

"You want to destroy the evidence?"

"No. Gather the evidence but do it quickly and get this massacre cleaned up."

"Are you sure, sir? Whitmire's going to be pissed if we compromise—"

"You SIDs guys are supposed to facilitate our investigation, not run it. Guy gets butchered in the street; it still belongs to homicide; right?"

"Yeah."

Leslie slid his hands into a rubber glove and gingerly felt around the back of the bumper. Something sticky transferred from the bumper to his index finger. He held it up to the light. It looked like candy from a toy store vending machine. He lifted it up for the pale man with the camera and the plastic baggies to see.

"Got an idea of what this is?" Leslie asked him. It wasn't quite the right texture to be brain or flesh.

The SIDs man shone a light on it, moving his face just inches from its quivering surface. Leslie turned his wrist to give him a better look, and it split, letting an inky mess free to run down onto his knuckles.

"Looks like sclera," the man said, taking it from Leslie gingerly and dropping it into one of his bags.

"I made detective because of my tenacity, not my brains."

"I'm pretty sure you found an eyeball, sir."

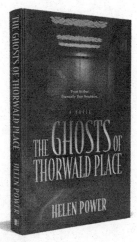

CamCat
Books